Nightshade kept me up all night! A tight plot, heartthrob heroes, and description so rich I could hear the jungle noise, feel the heat slide down my back. I'll be clearing out a shelf to make room for Ronie's books!
—Susan May Warren, RITA award-winning author of *Nothing but Trouble*

Valor, action, romance, heart—*Nightshade* is the perfect blend of everything I like best in a story. I can't recommend it enough!
—John B. Olson, author of *Powers*

Reading a Ronie Kendig novel is like watching a movie—a nail-biting, intense action movie. The words seem to jump off the page and leave you breathless as Colton (*Digitalis*) takes you from one heart-pounding scene to another. Novel Journey and I give it our highest recommendation.
—Ane Mulligan, editor of Novel Rocket

Balancing a story of high action and deep emotions isn't easy, but with *Digitalis*, author Ronie Kendig pulls it off with the casual grace of a truly talented storyteller. I don't know what kept me on the edge of my seat more, the fast-paced military intrigue or the powerful tugs on my heart. Doesn't matter: *This is one pulse-pounding adventure you don't want to miss.*
—Robert Liparulo, author of *Comes a Horseman, Germ,* and the Dreamhouse Kings series

Digitalis is a story of skill and purpose woven with love and spine-tingling danger. . .that will live long past the last page. None of us fully realizes the dedication of those who keep our world safe.
—DiAnn Mills, Christy Award–winning author of *Sworn to Protect*

An action-packed thrill ride from start to finish. If you liked CBS's long-running hit series *The Unit*, you're going to love Ronie Kendig's *Digitalis*. Enjoy the ride and the read. I only have one question— where do I sign up for *Nightshade*?

—Bob Hamer, veteran FBI undercover agent and the
author of *Enemies among Us*

Wolfsbane is a fast-paced, military suspense with just the right amount of romance to keep readers flipping pages. Ronie Kendig's smooth writing style, realistic scenes, and vivid characters blend beautifully for a must-read experience. A definite keeper!

—Robin Caroll,
author of *Deliver Us from Evil* and *In the Shadow of Evil*

Ronie Kendig serves up a mix of machine gun–fast action, touching romance, and more twists than a coil of detonator wire. Get a good grip on the edge of your seat before you start reading!

—Rick Acker,
author of *When the Devil Whistles* and *Dead Man's Rule*

Wolfsbane is rapid-fire fast-paced and will leave you breathless. An incredible story with intense characters who face timeless struggles. Another favorite for our shelf from Kendig!

—Kimberley and Kayla R. Woodhouse,
authors of *No Safe Haven* and *Race Against Time*

This type of thriller is hard to write, but if you can pull it off, you've got a potential blockbuster on your hands! Ronie Kendig had done just that. *Firethorn* has many moving parts that synchronize together with the beautiful precision of an expensive Rolex watch!

—Don Brown,
author of the Navy Justice and Pacific Rim series

Firethorn, the stunning conclusion to Ronie Kendig's adrenaline infused Discarded Heroes series packs all the expected emotional punch and accelerated action of a Kendig thriller, and then some! Her ability to tap into her characters' psyches and penchant for palpable heart-pumping action scenes are unparalleled in today's romantic suspense genre. I only wish there were more to come in this unmissable series.

—Rel Mollet, RelzReviewz

RONIE KENDIG

FIRETHORN

DISCARDED HEROES #4

BARBOUR
PUBLISHING

50503300277953

Other books by
Ronie Kendig

Nightshade (Discarded Heroes #1)
Digitalis (Discarded Heroes #2)
Wolfsbane (Discarded Heroes #3)

DEDICATION

To all American military heroes at home and abroad,
those who have gone before and those serving today—
THANK YOU!
Because of you, we are free!

ACKNOWLEDGMENTS

Special thanks to:

My Boots On Ground readers: You guys are amazing! Thank you for falling in love with this series as much as I did, for becoming so invested that you threatened me with bodily harm for not writing faster. Your belief in me and this series is awesome! Thank you!

The Barbour Fiction Team, especially Becky Germany, Mary Burns, Shalyn Sattler, Elizabeth Shrider, Laura Young, and Linda Hang—a hundred thousand thank-yous!

Andrew Kendall: For the amazing Nightshade insignia! You rock!

Agent-Man Steve Laube: If readers hate me after reading this book, it's your fault. Just sayin'. (Besides, you're the one who said, "It's always the agent's fault.")

Julee Schwarzburg: You are so tireless and encouraging, so challenging and supportive. Thank you not only for your editorial prowess but for being a sounding board when I questioned myself. You are a dream. May I keep you, please?

Candace Calvert and Richard L. Mabry, MD: Many thanks for your help with medical elements.

Cara C. Putman: Thanks for your legal help and for that spontaneous call so you could pray for me. You bless me!

To Michelle Stimpson, Michele Stephens, Terri Haynes, and Elizabeth Jackson: Thank you for your help to understand the African-American community on a deeper level, to open my mind to some things that just honestly never came to mind. I hope I have made Griffin and his family authentic. (All mistakes are mine!)

Knees On Ground prayer team: Your prayers have sustained, encouraged, and uplifted me. I pray God will bless you a hundredfold in return!

My arsenal of friends and crit partners: Lynn Dean, Lynne Gentry, Kellie Gilbert, Shannon McNear, Dineen Miller, Robin Miller, Sara Mills, Rel Mollet, John Olson, Jim Rubart, Camy Tang, Lori Twichell, Kimberley Woodhouse, and Rebecca Yauger.

NIGHTSHADE TEAM

Max "Frogman" Jacobs—former U.S. Navy SEAL, team leader

Canyon "Midas" Metcalfe—former Army Special Forces Group

Colton "Cowboy" Neeley—former U.S. Marine Corps Special Operations Command, sniper

Griffin "Legend" Riddell—former U.S. Marine Corps Special Operations Command

Marshall "the Kid" Vaughn—former U.S. Army Ranger

John "Squirt" Dighton—former U.S. Navy SEAL

Azzan "Aladdin" Yasir—former Mossad

General Olin Lambert, aka "The Old Man"—Chief of the Army, member of Joint Chiefs of Staff

GLOSSARY OF TERMS/ACRONYMS

ACUs—Army combat uniforms.

Beretta M93—Italian-made automatic handgun.

BUD/S—Basic Underwater Demolition/SEAL Training.

CamelBak—A portable hydration pack.

Fast-roping—The art of quickly descending from a hovering helicopter to the ground using a heavy rope.

Flash-bang—A nonlethal stun grenade that emits the extreme light and sound of an explosion.

Glock—A semiautomatic handgun.

HALO jump—High-opening low-altitude free-fall parachute insertion.

HK 9mm—Heckler & Koch semiautomatic handgun.

HK USP Compact—Heckler & Koch semiautomatic handgun.

IED—Improvised explosive device.

Klicks—Military jargon for *kilometers*.

M4—An assault rifle that is smaller and lighter than the M16.

M16—An assault rifle.

MARSOC—Marine Special Operations Command.

MI6—British Secret Intelligence Service.

MIA—Missing in action.

Mossad—Israeli Institute for Intelligence and Special Operations.

NVGs—Night vision goggles.

PTSD—Post-traumatic stress disorder.

RPG—Rocket-propelled grenade.

SATINT—Satellite intelligence.

Sitreps—Military jargon for *situation reports*.

Tango—Military slang for *target* or *enemy*.

VFA—Fictitious Venezuelan rebel army: *El Valor de Fuerzas Armadas de Bolivarian*.

RECON CREED

Realizing it is my choice and my choice alone to be a Reconnaissance Marine, I accept all challenges involved with this profession. Forever shall I strive to maintain the tremendous reputation of those who went before me.

Exceeding beyond the limitations set down by others shall be my goal. Sacrificing personal comforts and dedicating myself to the completion of the reconnaissance mission shall be my life. Physical fitness, mental attitude, and high ethics—The title of Recon Marine is my honor.

Conquering all obstacles, both large and small, I shall never quit. To quit, to surrender, to give up is to fail. To be a Recon Marine is to surpass failure; to overcome, to adapt and to do whatever it takes to complete the mission.

On the battlefield, as in all areas of life, I shall stand tall above the competition. Through professional pride, integrity, and teamwork, I shall be the example for all Marines to emulate.

Never shall I forget the principles I accepted to become a Recon Marine. Honor, Perseverance, Spirit, and Heart.

A Recon Marine can speak without saying a word and achieve what others can only imagine.

Swift, Silent, Deadly

THE INVITATION

W hat did he say?"

Gray haze snaked around the small jazz club. Dim light bathed the occupants in hues of red and blue, save the brightly lit stage where the blues band slunk through a song. Griffin Riddell lifted his bourbon glass and swirled the amber liquid. Sultry music drifted through the crowd and smoothed over his shoulders and mind.

"Look, I did not want to come to this smoke-filled hole, but I came so we could talk."

He took a sip. Lowered the glass. "I didn't ask you to come."

Her brown eyes flamed. "Ten days, Griffin. You came home ten days ago and have been pacing like a cougar, brooding like a grizzly. But you won't talk."

Another sip. He dumped the rest into his mouth and let it burn all the way down. Talk. She always wanted to talk. Why couldn't she just let a man be?

"What happened at the base? Why. . .what has got you so"—she pointed to him—"so like this?"

He leaned forward. "You said I should get out. Maybe it's time." That should be enough to get her off his back and out of his business. He poured more bourbon.

She snatched the bottle out of his hand and slammed it down on the table behind them. "Would you lay off that stuff! Your grandmother will whoop you down to the Mississippi if she whiffs liquor on you."

Irritation carved a long, hard line through his civility. "Treece, get out of my business."

"*Your* business?" Her wide nostrils flared. "I'm your wife. I would think it was *my* business too, our business." She planted her hands on her hips as she sat across from him. A lazy tendril of cigar smoke from a nearby table snaked toward her head.

Secretly, for one long minute, Griffin wished it was a noose. Right around her long, giraffe neck.

"We need to work through these things together," she said, her voice squeaking on his last nerve.

"Is that what you were thinking when you climbed into Darian Parshall's bed?"

She blinked those fake lashes and widened her eyes.

At her expression, he let loose a laugh. "Yeah. I know." Nothing like hearing from your brother-in-law that your wife found comfort in another man's arms while you're out doing your duty for God and country. The woman violated everything he stood for—*Semper Fi*. Griffin snatched the bottle, refilled his glass, and took a sip.

Her pride—and ample bosom—seemed to shrink before him.

That's right, woman. I know you been playing me. Just like everyone else. Including that pig-faced colonel who had done nothing but sit on Griffin's case since his unit returned from Afghanistan last month. That was fine. Griffin could handle pressure. Could handle a man not liking that another held more respect and admiration. And that—that was what ate the very fiber of Colonel Nichols's puffed-up, medal-heavy chest. When the colonel walked through the mess hall, the guys gave him the obligatory salute. But when they wanted advice, when they needed help, they came to Griffin.

"Fine." Treece grabbed her purse from the back of the chair. "You sit up in here in this stanky bar—"

"Club." He sliced a hand through the thick atmosphere. "It's a club."

"Same thang."

"No." The glass clunked as he slammed it down. "Club—a jazz club. The focus is music to relax the soul and mind." He pointed to the auto-graphed twenty-by-forty photo of soul legend Ray Charles hanging behind her. "You think he'd sit in a stanky bar?"

She rolled her eyes and neck. "Whatever, Griffin." She pushed to her feet.

"Ma'am, this Marine giving you a problem?"

That voice! Fingers tightening around the glass, Griffin tensed. *Don't react. Own this.* Right about now would be a good time to get some religion in him the way Madyar had warned him to. But he wasn't even sure God could tame the fury roiling in his gut right now.

"Uh. . ." Treece's brown eyes darted to Griffin. "No. . .my husband just isn't interested in my company."

"It seems he's not interested in his career either."

Wood groaned against wood as Griffin shoved to his feet. He towered over Colonel Nichols. "Sir." Why? Why would the man come up in here and start something after what happened a week ago? Wasn't it enough that he held a fist of control on Griffin's career? That he wrote him a bad eval and threatened to tank the last twelve-plus years of blood, sweat, and tears?

The colonel's denture-white teeth gleamed beneath a taunting grin. "Inebriated? And still in uniform?"

"No, sir." Had he really come straight to the club without changing? Right. . .the club manager had called in sick and needed the night off, so he asked Griffin to cover him. Being the good friend he was, he was there. Duds in the back room, but he'd forgotten them when Treece showed up, demanding his time.

And this is exactly what the colonel had been waiting for—a screwup. "Sir. I am sober. Enjoying a night with my wife."

Nichols's muddy eyes shifted to Treece. "Yes, a very beautiful wife. Must be hard to leave her alone here while you're deployed." The officer's stab hit right where the man intended.

Griffin fisted his hands.

Nichols noticed. Grinned more. "But I bet a man like you needs time away from the family."

Griffin's left eye twitched. *On the battlefield, as in all areas of life, I shall stand tall above the competition.* He reminded himself of the Recon Creed, of what he vowed to uphold. And that he'd have to answer to Madyar if anything happened here. Pops. . .his ticker wasn't so good.

There was more to think about than some knee-jerk reaction to a colonel who wanted to save face. He loosened his hands but remained straight and tall. He had to own this.

"Your record is flawless, Gunnery Sergeant Riddell."

He'd heard this speech when Nichols called him into his office.

"But your failure to report certain events leaves me questioning your integrity."

This was new. Tension flooded his muscles. "Sir. My field reports are complete and accurate."

"I'm talking about what you failed to report when you joined."

Heat swarmed Griffin's gut. *Oh Lord, no. . . .* No way he could have found out.

Nichols laughed. "You know what I'm talking about, don't you?"

"Griffin?" Treece's brown eyes flicked to his.

He gripped her arm. "Go home." He nudged her toward the door, his eyes still glued to his commanding officer. "Colonel Nichols, you come here knowing I'm enjoying this night with my wife, minding"— he clapped a hand over his chest—"my own business. I don't know what you're talking about or why you would do this, but—"

"Lying to an officer now?" The man looked down and shook his head. "Oh Gunny, I am disappointed."

Though he tried, Griffin groped for a tendril of sanity to stop him from fulfilling the fantasy of ripping the man's heart out. Heat infused his spine. Crawled up his neck. Throwing a punch, assaulting an officer—it'd end everything.

"I've had my eye on you. I knew you were too good to be true."

"You just had to go and get up in my business." The words were out before Griffin could stop and yanked the rest out in quick succession. "Why can't you just respect me, respect that I made a life and did my best, that I fought for my country?"

Nichols faced him, smile and amusement gone. "You really don't want to do this, Riddell. I filed a complaint."

Griffin's lips flattened. His chest drew up. "I did my job," he hissed. "I did it better than anyone on base, including you!"

Mouth curled, the colonel leaned in. "You lied. And now you're drunk and threatening an officer."

"Threatening?" Breathing became a chore. Aches wove through his jaw and head at his fiercely gritted teeth. "I'm Marine Special Operations. I do not threaten. I reconnoiter. I stalk." Adrenaline fed off the faltering expression on the colonel's face. Griffin dropped his tone a notch, and it came out in a growl. "I kill those in opposition to the success of my mission." It wasn't a threat. It was the way MARSOC conducted operations. But it felt good to see the man crawl.

Nichols took a step back. He gave a shaky, scared laugh. "You're just like your father."

Blood whooshed through Griffin's ears.

"I read the police reports. He strangled your mother with his bare hands, then bludgeoned her to death."

Demons unleashed. As if in slow motion, as if disembodied, Griffin's fist slammed into the colonel's face.

Crack!

Griffin blinked. Breathed. Blinked again.

Nichols, bent and cupping a hand under his spurting nose, sneered through the blood. "You're through, Riddell. I knew you were hiding something. Nobody—*nobody*—is that clean. I'm going to take you down. Make sure you—"

Treece reappeared. She got in the man's face, shaking her finger and head at him. "What did you think would happen, coming up in here, inciting a big black man with more muscle than you got hair? You did this on purpose!" Treece shrieked. "You came up in here taunting him and pushing—"

Nichols shoved her away.

Treece stumbled backward. She tried to catch herself. Her manicured nails slid along the glass-framed print. It slid off the wall. Landed with a resounding crash. She arched her back—lost her balance. Fell on the print. Glass shredded her arms and side. A screech knifed the dead-quiet club.

Griffin started for her, but out of the corner of his eye, he spotted Nichols darting out the door. He dove into the colonel. Tackled him across the threshold. The man squirmed and writhed. Nichols threw a punch.

Griffin caught the hand. Pushed it back, twisted, and pulled until he heard a crack. Nichols screamed. The man lifted a weapon from the side.

Training took over. With the heel of his hand, Griffin drove it hard and straight into the colonel's face. The man collapsed in a heap.

Fire lit through Griffin's back a split second after a familiar crack rent the air.

Everything went blank.

Pain unlike anything he had ever experienced punctured his mind and yanked him from the greedy claws of unconsciousness. Griffin groaned and blinked against a flickering light overhead. He squinted and scowled. *Where am I?*

He shifted and looked around, and in a rush, it came back to him. Sounds, smells, laughter, screams. "Oh no. . . ." Griffin slumped back against the bed and smoothed a hand over his face and shaved head.

"Welcome back to this side, Gunny."

Griffin started. A man stood in a black suit and tie, hands folded in front of him. White hair crowned a stoic face. "I know you?"

"It took two EMTs to revive that stubborn heart of yours."

The memory of his brain being fried like Madyar's Saturday morning eggs singed his mind. "That's what happens when two cops taze a man."

"They had reason. You're not exactly a small man."

Griffin fell silent. The sound—the sound of Colonel Nichols's nose being shoved into his cranium—haunted Griffin. "Is he dead?"

"I'm afraid so."

Griffin closed his eyes.

"His family wants you charged with murder."

Pinching the bridge of his nose made his head hurt more.

"But there were enough witnesses there who said you were merely defending yourself."

Griffin sized up the man. Military crew cut. Signet ring. What did the man want with a Marine? "I'm not Army."

"Point in fact, Mr. Riddell, you are not anything military. Pristine service to the United States Marine Corps. Thirteen years, in fact—a very unlucky number."

"What's unlucky is being under the command of Nichols."

Blue eyes held a hint of amusement. "A man nobody has to be concerned with anymore, thanks to you."

Guilt pushed Griffin's gaze away. "I didn't mean to kill him." Lame as lame came. But he hadn't. "He got in my business—personal business. Made a fool of me. Hurt my wife."

"Indeed." He came closer, hands tucked in his pockets. "Nichols illegally acquired a police report on the murder-suicide of Reginald and Grace Adams, your parents, then used that to bring down a Marine so respected and admired he was up for promotion to master sergeant. That made Nichols see red."

Griffin eyed the man.

"Your record is spotless—prior to a week ago. The men under your command say they'd follow you to hell and back."

"Oorah," Griffin mumbled, his brain caught on the fact this man checked him out.

"Tell me, what does serving your country mean to you now that your career is over?"

Wariness crowded out Griffin's relief. What kind of question was that? "What does it mean to me?" He drew in a ragged breath and let it out. " 'Never shall I forget the principles I accepted to become a Recon Marine. Honor, Perseverance, Spirit, and Heart.'"

Tiny lines crinkled against the man's weathered face as he grinned at the words from the Creed. He tossed a business card on the blanket. "When you can breathe without it feeling like fire, I want you to put together a team."

CHAPTER 1

The Shack
Four Years Later

"It's sad, really." Marshall "the Kid" Vaughn trudged away from the thumping rotors of the helo that had deposited them back at the Shack, his pack almost dragging on the ground. "Ya don't realize how much a person adds until he's gone."

"Legend's not gone." Max "Frogman" Jacobs hoisted his rucksack into a better group, his mind locked on Sydney and their two sons waiting for him at home. Poor woman had to be going out of her mind with two of his Mini-Me's running around.

"Yeah." John "Squirt" Dighton hit the light breaker, then waited for the six-man team to clear the door. "He's just temporarily detained."

Lights sizzled and popped to life. Groaning bounced off the grimy windows as he hauled the door closed, locked it, then started toward the showers.

The Kid grunted. "Forty-years-to-life temporary."

In the locker room, a depressive gloom hung over the team. They'd been on countless missions, hit just about every terrain and environment imaginable, but none had taken the toll the last couple had. And there was one reason—they were down a man. Griffin "Legend" Riddell. If Max could write the playbook, they wouldn't do another mission without the guy. But with the man in federal prison for murdering a congressman, it'd be a long wait.

It was quiet. Too quiet. Max looked around the Spartan room. Walls of lockers, most unused. A few benches. A giant once-white bin for dirty duds. And the team. Six men now. All very skilled. Good men. Even the one missing. Every man here knew Legend had been set up—he didn't murder that congressman. But nobody could prove it. The evidence was damning. Justice—*injustice* was more like it—came swiftly. Lambert, ever the puppeteer, couldn't pull the right strings to get Legend off.

"I'm heading up to visit him tomorrow. Anyone game?" Colton "Cowboy" Neeley slumped on a bench and ran a hand over his short dark hair. His blue eyes probed the group.

"Nah man. I've got a date," the Kid said.

Squirt beaned him with a towel. "What girl would go out with you, mate?"

The Kid snapped the terry cloth back at the former Navy SEAL. "Your sister."

Squirt froze. His jaw went slack. Then his eyes darkened.

Laughing, Canyon "Midas" Metcalfe rose to his feet from the corner. "You just proved his point by thinking your sister would actually go out with him."

Squirt swallowed, his face drained of color. "I introduced them at a New Year's party."

Midas laughed harder. "Your mistake, *mate*."

Shuffling closer, Squirt pointed a finger at the Kid. "I swear, you touch her, I'll shove a fistful of witchety grubs down your gullet."

"Give me credit, dude." The Kid raised his hands. "I'm a gentleman."

Max grunted. "Right." As he strode around the lockers to the shower well, he heard more threats and much more laughter from the Kid. Max shook his head. Would the Kid ever grow up, learn when to leave things alone?

As he tossed his oily, grimy duds on the bench, Max paused, thinking maybe he should send his report to Lambert now so he wouldn't have to mess with it tomorrow. The mission had been simple enough, a snatch-n-grab of an Iranian doctor. It'd been nice and clean, in and out. The report wouldn't take long. Then he could shower, bug out, and know he had the whole weekend with Syd and the boys.

Max jogged up the iron stairs, which creaked and groaned beneath his weight. Down the hall to the right. He punched in the code and entered the secure hub, the door hissing shut behind him. The most high-tech part of this dump of a warehouse.

Shouts drew his attention to the blinds. He jabbed two fingers between a couple and spread them to peek down into the main area. Squirt and the Kid raced into the bay and back the way they came. Squirt looked ready to kill. The Kid's face revealed his fear. Max shook his head again. Man, he wanted Griffin back. The guy seemed to bring balance to the team. Badly needed balance.

Max powered up the computer. Hand propped on the warped wood, he waited for the system to boot.

More shouts. Loud thuds.

He pinched the bridge of his nose. Would they never—?

Tat-a-tat! Tat-tat-a-tat!

Instinct drove Max to his knee at the sound of gunfire. He scrambled to the window. Through the slanted blinds, he peered down into the slab of cement. His brain wouldn't assemble what he saw. Gunmen. A dozen or more. Rushing into the Shack from the parking bay. Moving swiftly, as if. . .

They know the layout.

Max darted to the door and jerked it open. He sprinted down the hall toward the stairs. As his boot hit steel, he froze. A shadow emerged. Floated into the hall.

Too late.

Max jerked back. Pressed his spine against the wall.

By the showers, the Kid looked up. Max signaled to him. Then he made his best and loudest Nightshade whistle, hoping it would penetrate the building, give the men warning to take cover.

The Kid threw himself back into the locker room.

Men swarmed the corner. One looked to his left, one right. His weapon slowly rose as he traced the stairs with his M16.

Max leaped backward into the darkness of the office. He closed the door. As the lock clicked, darkness dropped like an anchor over the entire building. Behind him, a glow screamed his location. The monitor!

Max spun. Lunged across the desk. Stabbed the power button. And paused with his hand still near the monitor. If someone was coming after them. . .accessing this computer. . .

On his knees, Max yanked the cords free. With the box, he moved to the window and reassessed the parking bay. Another van with a half dozen men with AK-47s. They streamed into the warehouse.

Max's gut wound into a dozen knots. They were screwed.

Think! Hand on the door, he considered going back downstairs. But that would get him captured. Killed. Yet he'd rather be with his guys than running like a chicken.

No, not running. Considering options, gaining the advantage. Planning. The invasion force was armed to the teeth. They knew who they were coming after. They'd brought weapons. And those guys moved with precision. Swift, deadly precision.

Though Nightshade had a stellar ops record, perhaps they had finally met their match. Still. . .two to one? Nightshade had faced worse.

A large black Suburban screeched to a halt in the middle of the parking bay. Two men emerged, both wearing trench coats.

Max cursed his luck to be up here, away from his gear, his weapons. Up here without firepower. Thus, powerless.

Okay, enough. He was going down there. He eased the door open and slid across the hall. Bathed in darkness, he crouched at the edge of the landing, using the wall for cover. A dozen men so far, rushing here and there. Quick, quiet chatter between the men.

A smirk slid into Max's face. His team had taken cover, and these goons couldn't find them. If he could just get a weapon. . .

"Can't find them."

"They're here. I saw them go in," the man nearest the SUV shouted. "Find them! Lights!"

Light rushed through the building as headlamps from the vehicles stabbed the dusty, damp building. Max yanked back, out of sight. He needed to get down there, defend his men. His boot hit the landing.

Shouts erupted. A shot bounced off the steel rafters, taunting as it echoed through the Shack. Stilled, Max waited. More shouts. The sound of a scuffle. The half dozen men waiting by the SUV lifted their weapons to the ready.

The locker room door swung open. A man walked backward, his AK-47 aimed at a large form filling the doorway. Cowboy. Arms raised, dressed only in his jeans, he stalked forward. Someone shoved him from behind, which barely moved the big lug.

Spine pressed against the wood, Max peered down into the bay.

"You move one wrong muscle," the one in front of Cowboy growled, "and so help me God, I'll kill you."

"No you won't." Cowboy lowered his hands. "If you wanted me dead, I wouldn't be out here."

Ride 'em, Cowboy.

From the side entrance to the showers, three men dragged a shouting, cursing Kid into the bay. Max smirked that it took three tangos to wrangle the Kid.

Hand clenched, Max's mind went into overdrive. What could he do? *God. . .I need. . .something.* What could he pray for? Intercepting the team was impossible. Twelve, fifteen armed tangos against one unarmed man?

He latched on to the hope that they'd only found Cowboy and the Kid. No Midas, Squirt, or Aladdin. Good. Maybe they could regroup and—

A man flew through the bay door from the showers and landed with a thud a yard from the others. Midas flipped over, scissored his legs, and swept the thug off his feet. The Kid seized the confusion to attack the men guarding him. And impressively. With a hard right, he dropped the first and used that weapon to disable the second.

Cowboy took a step back and rammed his elbow into the gut of the nearest guard. The gunman bent forward—straight into Cowboy's meaty fist. The big guy pivoted, slapped the interior of the gunman's wrist, effectively seizing the weapon and flipping the muzzle around. He fired at the guy.

Crack!

In the split second it took for Max to realize the sonic boom that rent the air wasn't the report of Cowboy's .45 MEU but of a rifle, Max saw the man in the black trench coat drop to the ground. A circle spread out like a dark halo.

"Sniper!" someone shouted.

The dead guy had fallen backward. Most likely shot from the front. Which meant. . . Max's gaze rose to the rafters. With no light, it'd be the perfect hiding spot. But. . .who? Squirt? Aladdin?

Crack!

The man guarding Colton stumbled forward, then went to his knees before hitting the cement.

The man in the black trench coat nearest the SUV dropped. A pool of blood spilled out.

"There!" One guard swung and fired his fully automatic at the ceiling. Four others followed suit, firing at the bank of grimy windows on the southeast wall of the building. Aladdin!

Max followed their direction and watched. Waited, his breath caught at the back of his throat. Cracks and shattering glass blended with the staccato punches of the guns to create a wild cacophony of noise. Max tuned it out, praying whoever—Aladdin or Squirt—wouldn't be hit.

But then he saw it. A shift of a shadow. Like someone rolling. . .

The gunfire petered out as a body plummeted the eight feet to the ground. *Aladdin!*

The thud seemed to have supernatural powers as it pounded Max's chest and pushed him back. Away from the window but not far enough that he lost line of sight.

Silence dropped on the Shack.

"Where's Max Jacobs?"

As the question streaked through the warehouse, Max registered a red glow in the far corner. Even as he noticed it, he heard a beep. Another. His gaze darted to the source of the noise. Two men were walking the perimeter, their M16s dangling as they raised their arms and pressed something against the supports. Arms lowered and the men stepped back revealing gray bricks with wires.

Explosives.

Gotta stop this. Do something. His gaze collided with Cowboy's. The big lug gave an almost imperceptible shake of his head.

Max's nostrils flared as he wrestled with what to do.

"Where's Dighton?"

How do they know our names?

"Dead," someone answered.

Pulled back into the shadows, Max clenched his eyes and bit down on his tongue. Dighton was dead. What about Aladdin—had he survived the fall?

Sirens wailed in the distance.

"Load 'em up."

"What about Jacobs?"

"Outta time." The leader left as the gunmen dragged the team out of the building.

Stealthily, Max held on to the box and sprinted the length of the hall to the side of the Shack. In the conference room, he plunged toward the window. Craned his neck to peek out. Three vehicles—twin white vans and a black town car.

The guys were loaded into the van and one into the car.

The leader shifted, held something out, then it wavered.

Detonator.

Max spun around, searching for an out. Doors. Only one way down—the stairs. But they led to the bay, which would be engulfed.

Windows. Overlooked the dock. The canal. It was January. The water would be brutally cold. His split-second assessment told him no matter what route he took, it'd be deadly. Despite his training, if he didn't find shelter out of the water once he broke surface, he'd die an ice cube. If he stayed, he'd die a fireball.

Good thing SEALs are insulated against cold water.

Max vaulted toward the window, hurtling the computer through the window. The glass shattered as a violent force blasted through the air. It lifted him. Up. . .up. . . Flipped him. Searing pain sliced through his arm. Heat stroked his back and legs. Fire chased him out of the building. Into the night.

Boom!

Another wave slammed into him. Threw him backward. Toward the water.

Something punched his gut. Knocked the breath from his lungs.

Bright white lit the night. Blinded him. Then—almost instantaneously—black. Pure black. And he was falling. . . down. . .down. . . .

CHAPTER 2

Shanganagh Cemetery
Shankill, Dublin Ireland

Life and death had much in common with the clump of dirt in her hand: They were cold and hard. What difference did it make to be alive? Other than the fact one could sense the hurt, the pain that infected this world. On the other side—if one believed that sort of thing—you didn't care about those toiling through time. Pain was abandoned. Hardships forgotten. People loved a distant memory. Sorrow gone. Respite found.

You lucked out this time, Tina.

Squatting beside the mound of dirt, Kazi Faron rubbed the earthen material between her fingers. The pieces fell from her palm and were carried away by the wind. Just like life. Rubbed the wrong way, it vanished.

She stared down at the narrow angular box. A bitter wind swirled and nipped at her cheeks as she lingered, ignoring the shovel-wielding men huddled against the frigid weather, waiting to fill in the hole.

Waiting to fill the hole.

One that would never be filled.

Her breath puffed. Snowflakes danced and fluttered, a final peaceful adieu to the woman who would never draw another breath. Never feel the cold air. Never give another caustic laugh. Never. . .nothing.

Kazi closed her eyes and let out an agonizing breath. *It should have been me.* Molars clamped, she shoved down the torrent of emotions ready to regurgitate her fury. Her throat burned. Tears stung her eyes.

A blast of icy air whipped at her. Poking her, pointing out her guilt. White flakes, fat and plentiful, freezing her heart. Her soul.

A strange peace encompassed her, steeling her with purpose.

Another gust of wind, pushed up off the coast, whipped at the land on the other side of the tall hedgerow on the far end of the cemetery, hitting her. And with it came a laugh. Kazi blinked and looked around the rows of headstones, pulse hopscotching at the sound. "Tina?" The name was out before the idiocy of saying it registered.

The dead don't talk.

But memories lived forever. And Tina's laugh. . . Annoying and infectious, it'd rippled through the club on their first meeting, drawing Kazi to her. It'd been her luck to have to rout her accomplice from a steampunk club in the middle of London.

"And who are you to be tellin' me what I'd be doing? The Queen Mum?" The girl's shrill voice carried easily over the throbbing music. She leaned across a beefy man and grabbed a glass of white foam-topped black liquid and took a gulp.

"Shut up and move" had been the reply quickest on Kazi's tongue. But she thought better of it, spotting the bulge under the arm of the oaf. A weapon.

"Her first cousin, twice removed, then added again." Kazi had never taken cheek from anyone. She wouldn't from this wiry girl with nose and eyebrow piercings. But she needed her for the gig. Carrick had insisted on them pairing to finish the job. "Her paramour, Lord Carrick himself, says we need to talk."

Slowly as the girl's gaze roamed Kazi's conservative black jeans, black jacket, and cross-trainers, the smile and amusement drifted away on the thumping bass that vibrated the cement floor. Even amid the raucous noise of the nightlife, the sound of the girl's glass slamming against the table drew the gazes of those around them. She pushed to her feet, albeit wobbly.

Great, a drunk.

She swallowed—hard. Leaned into Kazi, tucking her chin. "Carrick?"

So, the girl understood. Maybe this would work.

Kazi nodded.

"Well." The girl smoothed down her bustier-styled top, her bosom heaving over the top, then adjusted her wildly absurd hat with a massive purple plume. "Can't keep the good lover waiting, can we?" A shaky smile lit her eyes.

"Oy!" The beefy guy grabbed the girl's shirt and yanked her down. "Who says you're leaving?"

In the space of one strobe-light flash, a knife glinted in the girl's hand as she pressed it to the man's neck. "I'm thinking it's me friend, Mr. Gerber, here that does."

The guy raised his hands and eyebrows as he leaned away from the blade.

On her feet, the girl jerked her head to the left. "Let's go, cousin." Without missing a beat, she plunged through the pulsating club.

Kazi followed. What sort of crazy had Carrick linked her to this time? Names meant nothing, Kazi knew that. Or at least she should. But when she'd heard Kristina Kelley, she'd expected someone a bit more. . .tame. The vitals told her Kelley was a Dubliner. And in the minutes Kazi had been in the club, it was obvious the girl was at home in the throngs, in the chaos. Kazi could relate. Here one could find anonymity. A twisted but comforting security. Nobody knew your identity. Nobody could—

Wait.

They were going the wrong way. Kazi glanced back over her shoulder, over the bobbing heads, past the chandelier sparkling with red, blue, and yellow lights, to the towering arched double-doors and the envious eyes of those still trying to gain entrance peeking in past the bouncers.

She looked back to Kelley—enveloped by the dancing crowd. Her purple plume waved a good twenty feet ahead of Kazi.

"Hey!" She shoved through the bodies, hurrying after the girl. Kazi cursed herself for letting this much distance grow. Each foot gave the girl precious minutes to find a place to lay in wait. She'd been led into a trap before. And this felt a lot like one. Out in the warm London air, Kazi stopped short. A dark alley met her. Lamplight to her right, maybe fifty feet. A hiss of a cat to her left. A trash bin. But no Kristina Kelley.

The gentle rustle of a tulle skirt behind her.

Kazi spun, saw the blur of movement, and threw herself up into the air. Pulled her arms into her chest, rolled her shoulders, twisting up and out of reach with an aerial. She landed, hands up, ready to fight as she crouched.

Wide eyes held hers. Then. . .laughter. Annoying, infectious laughter. "That was brilliant!" Kristina launched at her—

Kazi readied for a fight.

Arms wrapped around her.

She tensed.

The girl squeezed, then released. Stepped back, grinning like the Cheshire cat.

A hug?

"I know I'm going to like you. I'm Tina." The girl slapped Kazi's shoulder. "What's the gig?"

The clearing of a throat snapped Kazi from the past. A man in a wool coat and hat jerked his gaze from hers to the ground and coughed into his hand.

She grabbed a fistful of dirt and punched to her feet, gaze locked on the simple pine box. Kazi stood over the hole and extended her arm. "I'll make him pay, Tina." She let the earth slip from her fingers. She just needed one lucrative assignment to fund her retirement and revenge.

Thump. The sound of the dirt hitting the box pounded into her chest, riveting the resolution to her heart.

"For every. . ."

Thump–thump.

". . .single. . ."

Thump–thump. Thud.

". . .drop of blood."

Near the Shack

The burn radiated through every muscle in his chest as Max hovered fifteen feet below water. With a hand clamped over his right thigh, he focused not on the fire in his leg from the metal embedded there, or the fire in his chest from oxygen deprivation, but on the figures standing on the dock. Backlit by the raging inferno once called the Shack, the men were easily detectible in this murky water.

It'd been more than two minutes since he'd submerged. His best time in BUD/S was just shy of three. That was when he was in shape. He grimaced and trained his mind away from the throb in his skull that demanded he take a breath.

Finally, the figures faded.

Max eased himself to the surface, clinging to the wall of tires padding the cement wall. Though he wanted to haul in a deep breath, doing so could alert the tangos. Across the canal, his team was loaded into two vehicles. Four armed guards kept their weapons pointed at Cowboy and Midas as they carried a limp Aladdin between them.

Max flared his nostrils. *Gotta do something.* Max hustled up the tire wall and flopped onto the dock. He rolled, cringing as the metal chunk sticking out of his leg pressed against the ground. He stumbled to his feet and hobbled to an alcove that concealed a door.

Shouts and curses leaped into the night, snapping Max's attention to a sleek black limo where three men wrestled the Kid into the back.

Water dripping down his face, he appraised his leg. The steel went deep. If it hit an artery and he pulled it out, he was as good as dead. Spine pressed into the corner, he wished for Midas's quick healing touch.

Engines roared into the night. Once again, Max watched. Waited. He didn't want to expose his location. Watching as the vehicles vanished in the night with his men, Max fisted a hand and pressed it to his lips. Whoever had done this, whoever attacked them, killed Dighton—they'd pay. Max hated not being with the guys, but not being captured improved the chances of stopping whatever was happening.

But right now he had to get word to Lambert. To do that, he had to get out of here and find a phone. Mode of transportation?

My bike. Was it still stowed under the main bay? He'd always parked it there because it was a safe spot, tucked out of sight. Would it be that easy?

Probably not. But he'd be a fool not to check since he had no other way out of here.

First—he had to take care of the leg. He lowered himself to the ground, stretched out his leg, then tore off a stretch of his shirt. Once he wrapped the jagged piece with the shirt, he braced himself—and pulled.

"Augh!" Max clamped his mouth shut. Warmth gushed down his thigh. Teeth clenched, he snapped out the strip of shirt, dislodging the metal, and quickly wrapped the shirt around his leg to stem the bleeding. He pulled it tight, again groaning through the searing fire that lit up and down his body. A metallic flavor glanced over his tongue. Blowing out a breath through his mouth, he ignored the heat flush that swept his body and climbed to his feet.

Smoke and ash filled the sky, burning his eyes. That was nothing on what looking at the Shack did to him. Years of camaraderie. Missions. It wasn't the Hilton, but it was their five-star hotel after a mission. Nothing like coming home to familiar territory.

Now it was gone.

Since it'd take three times the energy to hobble around the pier to the burning Shack, Max opted to go to water. After all, he was a SEAL. At the edge of the pier, he considered the tires. And then his leg. No climbing. It'd be slow and messy.

Backward, he toed the edge—most of his balance on his left leg—and pinched his nostrils, the other arm crossed over his chest, and stepped off. He dropped. Water engulfed him. He launched toward the surface. Although he was sure the tangos were gone, he kept his movements fluid and quiet as he approached the dock nestled against the Shack's burning frame.

Heat intensified as did the smoke. In the distance, he heard the sirens. He hauled himself up over the edge and rolled, coming up and into a clumsy jog. Avoiding the flames that punched out of the broken windows and now-missing walls, Max made his way to the parking bay.

Dripping wet, he should be okay against the flames as long as he avoided a personal encounter. He hoisted his shirt up over his nose. Glass and ash crunched beneath his boots as he made his way to the cementlike vault where he'd stowed the Hayabusa. He struck a hunk of twisted metal, pain darting up his throbbing leg. He bit down on the curse that wanted to leap out. Steadying his breathing, he eyed the area beneath the stairs, which had collapsed. But the hole looked intact. He hobbled closer.

The sleek black form came into view. Besides some dents, the bike had survived. With a breathy laugh, he patted it. *Good. Good, now. . .weapons.*

He coughed and looked toward the locker room.

Correction. Where the locker room used to be.

The warehouse roof groaned and wailed as it gave up its final beam. It fell silently. A series of explosions ripped through the building.

Max dove under the cement well, stuffing himself beside his bike.

Boom! Crack! Pop-pop!

Metal and steel twisted as it descended, effectively caging him in the hole.

Not good!

Max shoved the metal with his foot. It gave a little.

He scooted himself down and shoved again.

Just a little more.

On his feet, he leaned against the steel rafter. It wouldn't budge. *God, I need a break here!* He coughed, tears streaming down his cheeks from the smoke and ash.

Grooooaaaann.

The beam swung out of the way.

Max stared, stunned. *What the. . . ?*

As he turned back to his bike, a form coalesced to the right.

Max threw a fist.

The form dodged it and came up, fists up, one foot back—ready. "What was that for, mate?"

27

Stumbling backward, Max blinked and coughed. "Dighton?"

The man nodded and waved him out. "Come on, let's get out of here."

Hurrying back to his bike, Max swept the kickstand free and rolled it backward. Sirens shrieked over the din of noise from the raging warehouse. Lights flashed and swirled, mingling with the fire and smoke.

"This way." Dighton tugged on Max's arm.

When he started away, Max saw the M4 slung across his back. Where'd he get that? The image of the collapsed locker room where they'd stowed their gear after the mission filled his mind.

They jogged toward what used to be a main wall. Dighton stepped over a steel brace and waited as Max popped the bike's front tire over the twelve-inch beam. Max doubled over, coughing, as he trudged forward with his bike.

"Phone," Max said with a gasp. Then coughed. "Lambert."

"Already sent the distress call." Dighton squatted beside a Dumpster, pinching the bridge of his nose.

Tires crunched. Not close, but then again, entirely too close. Fingers of light traced the buildings as if pointing to Max and Dighton.

"We need to move." Max straddled the bike, which wasn't built for two, but they'd have to make it work. They were all that was left of Nightshade, and they had to stick together. Figure this out. Get the team back. Make whoever did this feel a lot of pain. A whole lot. Dead was too good for these thugs.

With Dighton behind him, Max ignored the pain stabbing his leg and ripped the gear. They screeched down the alley, aimed to the right, away from the warehouse. In the side mirror, Max took one last, long look at the Shack. Burned down. Burned into his memory.

They rode up the highway for a dozen miles, then Max aimed into the national park, hoping for some anonymity and quiet to think and plan. At a picnic bench, he killed the engine and rolled to a stop. They sat on the cement bench, surrounded by the rustle of trees and insects.

"They knew who we were," Dighton said.

"My wife. Gotta call. . .my wife." Only as he straightened and hauled in a long draught of clean air and cleared his throat did he see the mess someone had made of Dighton's face.

Dighton rested his forearms on the table. "They tried to spill my brains. Took me for dead and left. The bullet only grazed my cheekbone." He smirked. "They're good, but I'm better." Cocking his head, he lifted his shoulder and smeared the blood off his face.

"I need to get to a phone."

Dighton slid a cell phone over the table. "They're probably being monitored."

"It won't matter." He punched in the number to Syd's cell. "We need weapons, too."

Dighton stood and lifted a Glock from each side of his pants. From the back, he drew out an M4. "When they dragged Colton out, I grabbed these and climbed out the window."

Unease slid through Max's gut. Was it too clean? Too perfect the way Dighton had escaped when the others said he was dead? That he came away with weapons?

As the call connected, Max stared at the Aussie for a long, hard second.

Squirt frowned. "What?"

"Whose side are you on, Dighton?"

Rrrinng.

"You must be out of your mind to question my loyalty." He pointed to his face. "Look at this!"

"Convenient graze."

Rrrrrinng.

Come on, Syd. Pick up.

"Hey, I'm a SEAL. An American. A member of Nightshade. Since when do I get the long walk off the short pier?" He punched to his feet.

So did Max. . .only he stumbled because of his leg.

"You don't trust me? Is that what this is about?" Dighton reached toward him.

Max brushed the hand away. "Step off, Dighton."

"Hi, baby. What's up?" Syd's voice sailed through the line.

"Syd"—Max pointed Dighton away—"Hey, babe. Listen—"

"No, Dillon. Hang on, Max."

"No, Syd." Max's pulse thumped. "Syd!"

She must've lowered the phone, because her voice sounded distant.

Dighton scowled as he stepped closer. "Hey, I'm one of us, remember?"

"Yeah?" Max angled the device away from his face. "Well, one of *us* just dismantled the team. And right now, I don't trust anyone."

"Bloody bad decision, mate. Our team has been skewered and set on the barbie. I'm ready to get them back. Are you?"

Chin tucked, Max glared. "Don't." Teeth ground, he flared his nostrils. "Those are *my* men. They followed me. Nobody wants them back more than me."

"What about their families?"

Max held his ground.

"Look, all I'm trying to say is you're not the only one pissed off by this."

Max met the guy's eyes. "Syd!" he shouted into the phone. "Syd, are you there?"

"Yeah, sorry. Dillon was trying to get—"

"Syd, stop talking."

Silence rent the line.

"Mrs. & Mrs. Smith."

"Who? Wha—" She sucked in a breath. "Oh my gosh, Max." Her words wavered with thick emotion. "Are you serious?"

"Do it. Get the kids and do what we talked about, baby."

"No. . ." A whimper, so unlike her, snaked through the line and coiled around his chest.

"Syd." He tried to be firm. But inside, a massive sinkhole was consuming his life. "Do you remember everything?"

"Y–yes. I. . .PIG."

Relief swept through him. "Yes, baby. Do it."

"But Max—don't you remember where I am?"

What day is it? Did she have plans? Tuesday, right? No, they'd been in Tunisia then. It was Thur—*Saturday*. The shower. *Oh God, help us.* "Syd, get them out. Get everyone out right now!"

CHAPTER 3

Wallens Ridge Federal Penitentiary,
Virginia

He'd missed Christmas.

Rubbing his fingers over his knuckles, Griffin stared up at the picture taped to the wall. Christmas. He rocked gently, working the tension from his back and shoulders. Missed Madyar's turkey and ham.

Missed Madyar. The memories unleashed with a vengeance.

"Uncle Griff, check out the news."

Griffin glanced at Dante—and froze.

A dark shadow passed in front of the see-through curtains.

He reached for his weapon.

Glass shattered. A round black object bumbled into the center of the living room.

Instinct told him to plug his ears, open his mouth, and squeeze his eyes shut.

Boom! Crack!

Even with his eyes closed, intense whiteness and the concussion of the flash-bang made him stumble backward. He blinked and tried to peer through the numbing brilliance. No good.

He heard the front door disintegrate under a ramming rod. Black-clad figures—blurred by the haze of smoke filling the room—streamed in.

"Get down! Get down! Get down!"

Hand fisted, Griffin squeezed it tight till the muscles in his arm trembled. Teeth grinding, he glared at the black-and-white pages on the thin mattress beside him. He'd battled PTSD as a kid. Gotten over it. Didn't need this. Not again.

Where was God when the SWAT team raided their home, treated him and Pop-Pop like criminals? Cuffed Dante, who was so terrified he tried to run? Phoenix and Madyar were in the kitchen. . .then came the knife in the gut—

"You're under arrest for the murder of Congressman Billy Jones."

"Where were you, God?" Griffin bit out quietly as he stared at the open Bible. He'd lived to the Code his whole life. Fought for a good life, a safe place for his family. Honor. Respect. He'd earned them. Now. . .gone. They were all gone.

Head down, he wrestled with the verse from Psalm 9 that said God was a refuge, a stronghold in times of trouble. Madyar died. Dante was traumatized. His family ripped apart. And him—in a Level 5 prison. Where was God's help?

I brought you to the end of yourself to bring you to Me.

That was the truth. There was nothing left of the man he'd made save the skin and bones stuffed in this prison. He'd never been a religious man. Not till he landed here, in a cell, alone with himself.

Griffin glanced at the pictures Phee brought—the family at Christmas, Dante's freshman photo, Dante's football picture—and lowered himself to the ground, gaze locked on the images as he began push-ups. He would never forget what happened. What the *in*justice system ripped from him. Hadn't seen Dante in six months. The boy turned fifteen last week. The thought twisted and knotted in Griffin's gut. The plan to give Dante his first car when he was of age collapsed on a misty night.

Out for a run to clear his head before bedding down, Griffin had seen two men sprinting out of a pedestrian tunnel. The scene just didn't sit right with him, so—being the Recon Marine that he was—he went to check it out.

A man lay in a puddle. . .of blood. The congressman.

Griffin had no sooner reached him than the cops arrived. He'd given his statement, and they told him he could go. A week later, all the demons of hell descended on his life.

He blew quick breaths as he rapid-fired through the push-ups. As a kid, he'd gone to counseling, worked through the trauma. *"If you don't deal with it, the pain will bury you,"* the counselor said.

"Got a visitor, Riddell," a voice shouted through the bars. "You know the drill—assume the position. On your feet."

He hopped upright, spread his legs, and placed his hands behind his head. Who was visiting? He'd seen Cowboy last week for their biweekly meeting. Phee came the week before. He was only allowed four hours of visitation each month. They'd had them planned because all too often the guards forgot to inform the prisoner and the visitation never happened.

Griffin detected Guard Acton's presence to his right. Shorter by a head and sporting a large belly, Acton wouldn't have a prayer if Griffin wanted to fight. But the man's height wasn't what kept Griffin in check—it was the fifty-thousand-volt stun gun that could jolt him into next week. That and his pride. He'd been an exemplary inmate and earned the visitations that had started last month.

Acton clamped a cuff around Griffin's wrist, drew it around and down, then did the same with his other wrist. Another guard tightened shackles on his ankles.

This—*this* is why he told Phee never to bring Dante here. He didn't want the boy seeing him like this, seeing the inside of a prison.

Cuffed and secured, Griffin shuffled around, the chain clanking. "You know we don't need these."

"Yeah, and the first time I believe you, boy, I'm dead." Acton nodded. "Let's go. Clock's ticking."

Boy. Griffin let the slur slide. Wouldn't do no good to object. He'd get shocked. Or shot with those rubber bullets. Besides, he wouldn't let some balding fat guy get a power trip on him. *On the battlefield, as in all areas of life, I shall stand tall above the competition.* The Marine Creed served to keep his mind focused, his actions controlled. His emotions deadened to incitement. Besides, he *did* stand above these fools—by at least a head.

With the reduced leg movement, compliments of the steel around his ankles, the walk took way too long. If someone had come to visit, something had to be wrong. Colton told him Lambert was working to get him out of Supermax, but the petitions were falling on deaf ears.

The whole system is deaf.

Through one door, locked in the exchange point, then through another, he lumbered. Acton pressed the call button on the door marked VISITATION. A click resounded through the sterile white hall, and the guard flipped the handle. The door swung inward. Bleachers flanked one wall, the only accommodation for sitting—to make sure the prisoners had no available weapon at their disposal.

"Phee?" Griffin shuffled in, hands going slick at the sight of his sister, who stood from the bottom step of the bleacher where she'd been sitting. Behind him, he heard the door slam shut and the locks engage. "What's wrong? Is Dante—?"

"I'm sorry." Her satiny skin wrinkled up, her nose pinched as she shook her head. "I tried to tell him, to explain. . ."

The air swirled behind him. Griffin turned—his cafeteria-fed stomach heaved at the young man standing nearby. "Dante." His breath caught. The boy was tall. Much taller than the last time he'd seen him. *Almost as tall as me.*

Dante's eyes fell to the cuffs, down the bright orange jumpsuit, straight to the shackles.

No. . .no, Dante couldn't be here. *Can't see me like this.*

Griffin jerked back to his sister. "Why did you bring him?" he asked between gritted teeth, shooting a sidelong glance to the guard standing in the corner. One wrong move. . ."I *told* you not to."

"I. . .I wanted to come."

The boy's voice had deepened. He was becoming a man, and Griffin wouldn't see it happen. He closed his eyes. "I don't want you—"

"Yeah, you made that clear," Dante said.

"No." Griffin turned to him, shaking a cuffed hand at him. "*Don't* put words in my mouth."

"Why not? You don't have any of your own. You don't talk to me. Don't write me." Hurt gouged a painful crevice through Dante's words and expression.

"What do you want to see?" Griffin heard the growl in his voice and tried to tamp it down. He raised his cuffed hands. "This?" He jangled his feet. "This?"

Phee came to his side. "G, please—let him talk." She placed a hand on his arm, her black sweater fresh with the scent of a crisp winter. And unusually noticeable in this dank room.

"Naw, forget it." Dante started for the door on the other side of the room. "I'm done."

"Dante, *please.*" Phee hurried after him, her boots clunking on the cement. "Tell him. Tell him why you insisted on coming today. It's important, baby. Please. . .tell him."

Hesitation held Dante at the door as he looked over his shoulder at Griffin. Broad shoulders were filling out the lanky frame of the boy Griffin would do anything for. *I wanted so much more for you, Dante. So much more.* But someone blasted those dreams into oblivion.

"Naw. Uncle G doesn't want me. Then I don't want to be here." Dante pressed a button on the wall, requesting to be let out of the visitation room.

Though the words hurt—bad—Griffin wouldn't stop him. The boy didn't belong here. Had no business being in a prison. "Remember what it's like behind bars. And don't end up here. You were raised better."

Dante's hooded eyes rolled as he pushed out of the room. "Whatever."

Phoenix stood at the threshold, glaring at Griffin. "You're a proud fool, Griffin Riddell. I'm ashamed, and Madyar would be ashamed." Her eyes watered. "He's getting scouted for football." Her voice cracked. "*College* football, G. And he just had to tell his uncle. Knew the man who taught him to play, who used to throw that stupid ball around the backyard every weekend, would want to know, that he'd be *proud* of him."

His shoulders slumped.

"Well," she said with a sniffle. "Now you know." She drew in a stiff breath, then wilted. "Please—let me bring him back in. Talk to him. Encourage him."

"Encoura—" He clamped his mouth shut and shook his head. "Phee! Look around you. It's Supermax. Why would you bring him up in here and do this? I told you—*told* you not to." Dante didn't need to see Griffin shackled and humiliated. He needed to forget that Griffin existed, move on with his life. Get scouted. Go to school. Make a name for himself. "Keep him in school, Phee, but don't bring him back here." He locked eyes with her. "I mean it."

Her brow tangled and her mouth opened. "You and your stupid pride!"

Secret Facility, Maryland

"Evening, General."

Olin returned the obligatory salute but barreled down the narrow hall to the command room. He popped a pill in his mouth and prayed it'd steady the erratic rhythm that had taken over his heart.

"Everyone's here, just like you asked. We've been powered up for about ten minutes."

"Good." Olin swiped his badge and punched the door, descending the half dozen steps into the command center. "Jernigan, what do we have?" He watched the door shut, then nodded to Colonel Bright. "Secure that."

The man spun and activated a code that would keep anyone outside this team locked out. As Olin stared at the box and the red indicator light, he realized how trivial a notion of security was at this moment. The team had been attacked. Men—no, not just men, but those he considered sons—had been attacked. At least one had lived long enough to activate the emergency signal.

"Not much, sir," Lieutenant Colonel Dale Jernigan looked up from a whiteboard. "Emergency signal came in approximately twenty minutes ago."

"Source?" Olin worked his way to the command deck.

"Snakeroot."

So, Dighton was alive. "What else do you have?"

"Nothing, sir. We're still—"

"I need data, people. Lives are at stake." When only the hum of machines answered, Olin pounded a desk. *"Now!"*

The screens covering the walls leaped to life.

"Those are news images." Lieutenant Jason Sparks punched on the keyboard. His fingers made typing look like aerial combat. Light reflected off his wire-rimmed glasses as he peered up over the monitor at Olin. "Glory One is coming online. . .now." The wiry officer pulled his gaze to the massive screens.

Haze danced over the gray screen, then crackled and blipped. An image taken from miles above Earth's surface revealed the nightmare. The warehouse, aflame, lie half in ruins. Emergency vehicles crowded the road leading to the pier.

Olin stared at the flames, still trickling up, as if reaching for the satellite that snapped the images. "What's the time delay on Glory One?"

"Fifteen, twenty seconds," Sparks answered.

Not good enough. He needed to rewind time. See what happened before the emergency crews were onsite. His gaze fell on the brunette sitting at a cluster of terminals as her digits flew over the keys. "Major, tell me you've got something."

"Sir," she spoke from her seat on the raised platform. "I'm accessing and pulling surveillance-camera feeds from the surrounding area. There are four." Her gaze struck his, then snapped back to her work. "I'm enhancing and isolating. . ."

Olin threw down his trench coat and briefcase, then stalked over to Sparks. He leaned down and very quietly said, "Can you get into the satellite feeds for tracking assets—without anyone knowing?"

"We don't have the clearance for that."

"I didn't ask if we did. Can you do it?"

The man's blue eyes sparkled. "Of course."

Olin nodded. "Do it."

Another few seconds and the lieutenant paused.

In a whisper, Olin provided four name codes. "Find them, Jason. I want my men back. But not a word." He clamped a hand on the man's shoulder, then blew out a breath as he surveyed the amphitheater-style room, the dull gray walls bathed in the bright glow of monitors. Hands on his hips, he watched the screens. Of the six, two showed images stuttering in from the satellite feed. A third filled with billowing smoke.

"That's from a Jet Ski outlet directly north of the warehouse," Major DeMatteo said. "I've contacted the owners and requested all recordings. Someone is working on feeding them into our—"

"There." Jernigan pointed to the bottom right screen. "That's the feed."

"Rewind it," Olin said. "Let's see this thing from the beginning."

"Yes, sir." DeMatteo went to work on the keyboard.

"Sir," Sparks spoke up. "I've been monitoring cell phones since the emergency signal was activated. Sydney Jacobs received a call from Wolfsbane's cell phone for less than two minutes."

"Did you get a location?"

"Not exact, sir, but I've extrapolated using known data. The call was made from somewhere along the Virginia coast to a cabin in the mountains." The man shifted toward him. "Our data verifies Nightshade Alpha has a cabin lease there."

"If we can figure that out, so can someone else. I want a chopper there ASAP."

"Already en route, sir."

The monitors went hazy. "There!" Olin said. "Start from right there." The haze was from the interference their jamming technology created during extraction and drop off at the Shack. As if to confirm his thoughts, the screens came back to life.

The windows took on a yellowish hue. A sliver of light narrowed, then vanished on the cement. Someone had hit the lights, then closed the main bay door. Then nothing. Conditions unchanged. The men probably headed in the back, showering up before going home.

Olin tried to stem the emotional squall threatening to drown him. "Fast-forward. We're short on time."

DeMatteo flicked a key and time warped. A light flickered in the upper level. *The office.* Who had gone into the highly secured room? Olin's heart chugged. Only two people had the code for that room. Himself. And Max Jacobs.

Was Max alive? Or had someone already broken in there when the team arrived?

RONIE KENDIG

"Oh my word," DeMatteo muttered.

And then he saw it—two vans and a limo. Tactical teams rushing the building. Twinkles of light through the grime-blurred windows. *Muzzle flash.* The light in the office winked out. In fact, all light vanished. Someone must've killed the breaker.

In numb shock, Olin stared at the screen as his worst nightmare unfolded. His men dragged out of the Shack in various conditions, one carried out as if dead. Fist to his mouth, he counted. The images were too blurry to say who was whom. But he saw four men. Three tossed in the van, one in a limo.

"I want the tags on that car."

"Yes, sir." Jernigan worked feverishly, then he looked up with a frown. "No tags."

A white flash shattered the night. Balls of fire shot out of the warehouse.

Jernigan cursed.

Others gasped.

Olin paled as his gaze drifted to the black-and-green satellite feed. His lunch dropped to his toes, then bounced back up and threatened to heave as he stared at the daunting information. "Dear God. . ." Sweat broke out over his brow and upper lip. This wasn't possible. How. . .how would. . . ?

"Who did this?" Heat spiraled, pumping inordinate amounts of adrenaline and fury through his veins. "By God, I'll kill them, strangle their ruddy necks!" Something in the footage snagged his attention. "Freeze it!" Olin shouted as he leaped toward the wall of screens. "What is that?"

Silence.

"Sir?" Sparks asked.

Olin stabbed a finger at a dark blur. "That. Right there. Enhance and magnify."

Before his eyes, the image tightened.

Olin chuckled. "Nightshade Alpha."

Flying through the air, followed by a volley of fire and debris. And if a call had come in on Sydney Jacobs's phone while she was in the mountains, then it was probably Max who'd called her from Wolfsbane's phone. Which meant Max believed a threat existed against his wife and sons or he wouldn't have risked the call. They watched Max haul himself out of the water, climb up the wall, then hustle back into the burning warehouse.

38

The man had more gumption than Olin realized. Nothing could keep him down. It was as if he didn't have a fear threshold. Minutes later, Max and another man— "Enhance!"

"Snakeroot, sir."

"I want the fastest chopper out of here." Olin grabbed his jacket and briefcase. "Okay, people. We've got six high-value targets who have been attacked and kidnapped—on American soil. I want our men back." Olin rushed toward the door. "Jernigan, use every surveillance you can to find out where those vehicles went with our men and get ID on that limo. DeMatteo, see if you can get a team on those images and get names. I want to know who did this."

Sparks motioned to him from his chair.

Olin hurried to his side and blocked the monitor and their discussion from the others. "What have you got?"

"Four signals, sir."

He'd run everyone's except Firethorn, who was wrongfully imprisoned for a murder he didn't commit. A fact that still infuriated Olin. "Who's missing?"

"Snakeroot and Nightshade Alpha."

Normally a dead signal meant a dead objective, but he'd seen both Dighton and Jacobs survive the warehouse attack. Had they been caught and killed after that phone call?

Okay, they needed to focus on what they had: four *live* objectives. He hurried from the secure bunker room.

"Sir," Jernigan shouted from behind. "Chopper's ten minutes out from the cabin."

Olin pointed toward him. "Then guard that location. Destroy anything that gets close without explicit clearance from me personally."

"Yes, sir." Jernigan turned back to the headset.

Sparks looked at Olin, who still hadn't moved. "I'll pulse the trackers in random increments so nobody is tipped off to where they are."

"It may not matter," Olin said as he gulped the acidic taste in his mouth. "If those trackers are right, they're as good as dead."

Acholi, Uganda

Show me."

Night embraced Scott Callaghan as he hurried into the blue-gray hues of dusk. Even in the early evening the lush green fields were apparent, evidence of the man-made lakes and the mountains rimming the plains on the northern side. He'd fallen in love with the land, then the people—even the young man jogging ahead of him. Scott thought of him as a brother. . . .

A familiar, lonely ache wove through him at the thought. He hadn't spoken to his brother in fifteen years. Regret stood as thick and taunting as the cornstalks that slapped his arms as he and Ojore ran to the mine. But Scott was here, helping those who could not help themselves. He wouldn't walk away as everyone else had.

Anger pushed him through the bean fields, forced him to keep quiet and harness the misplaced anger. Or maybe it wasn't misplaced. If what his apprentice had said was true, he had bigger trouble than venturing out beyond curfew and being angry over something in the past he couldn't change. Dembe had chastised him relentlessly for clinging to the past. But here in Acholi, he felt like he could make a difference for Ojore, for others who'd been roped into the Lord's Resistance Army. Help the young boys find meaning in life, help steer their paths toward good futures.

Like nobody did for me.

"Shake it off," he said in a low growl to himself.

Twenty minutes carried them down dusty roads, past another village, and beyond the border of the area that had provided an income for hundreds, if not thousands, of locals. Dirt and rocks crunched beneath their feet as they approached.

At the entrance to the tunnel, Ojore signed in—filling in their names and time of entry.

Hanging back to avoid giving the man behind the desk a line of sight on him, Scott waited. Unbelievably, shifts went round the clock here. No inactivity. No downtime. No doubt whoever owned this mine made a fortune. He couldn't begrudge the wealthy—the source of their gain also benefited the Ugandans, brought hope back to a bleeding, starving people.

Hope he'd never had growing up. Ojore—the age difference between him and Scott reminded him of his own brother. Half brother. When he'd needed the guidance, the advice, his brother hadn't been there. Told Scott he was better off on his own. It'd cut Scott to the core. The one person he thought would "get it," hadn't. He'd never do to Ojore what his brother had done. Scott was here, to the end, with the young man.

"Weebale." After his thanks, Ojore turned, producing two work hats with mounted lights.

Scott slipped one on, tugging it farther down his brow than necessary. Though he had dark skin, thanks to his father's Cherokee heritage and a decade at the mercy of the sun, his complexion was still considered "white" to the natives.

They stepped into a cage—an elevator that would take them down more than seven hundred feet. Groaning and creaking pervaded the wire cell, vibrations worming through Scott's boots as they stood in silence. He suppressed the questions racing through his mind.

Twelve years in the Lord's Resistance Army had forced Ojore to grow up fast, commit enough atrocities to last several lifetimes, and understand the importance of integrity and honor. So if Ojore said bad things were happening here, they were. But Scott needed to know what to report back to the UN and U.S. government.

The cage heaved and jerked to a stop.

Ojore pushed back the gate, stepped out onto hardened bedrock, and twisted on his headlamp. Scott did the same as he followed the man down a narrow tunnel, across a small bridgelike structure, then into another tunnel. Fumes and dust coated his face and nostrils as they moved deeper into the earth. Shinks, thuds, and grunts carried through the area. On the far side, men slung picks into the rock, hacking out chunks, while others searched the bin for precious gems. A conveyor hummed to life, the squeaking of the belts penetrating the dirty, thick air.

Amazed at the hundreds of feet of cored rock, striations marking ages, Scott let his gaze take in the surroundings. Several tunnels sprouted off the main atrium-like area. The muscles in his shoulders tightened at the thought that only one exit existed—the cage he'd just escaped. But they'd be fine.

Just as long as they didn't find trouble.

At a juncture, Ojore stopped and cranked off his light, and once again Scott took his cue. With only the shadows and crunching of rock underfoot, they slunk forward. Ahead fifty meters, light escaped a large opening. A droning sound grew deafening as they approached. The massive vents and fans drew his attention.

With a pat on Scott's forearm, Ojore pointed to the area that had already captured his attention, especially the man lifting a large chunk of rock. Several men clapped his back and laughed. Dread consumed Scott at the sight of the ore. He wasn't a geologist, but he'd seen enough reports and been briefed on the mineral during his stint in black ops.

"Watch out!"

It took two full seconds for Scott to realize those words had been in English. His gaze struck a suited man who stood amid Ugandan miners. By the slick suit, clean hands, and manicured appearance, he didn't belong here. Clearly American. Apparently checking up on his gold mine. And in charge by the way he shouted and ranted at the miners.

Better get moving. Scott nudged his friend and started backing up, out of sight. Out of the tunnel. Out of whatever snafu they'd stepped into. Because if there was one thing he knew—these miners weren't digging for diamonds. They were funding terrorism. Not because they were Ugandan. Or in a diamond mine. But because of what they mined: U_3O_8.

Aka yellowcake.

Uranium.

For nuclear weapons.

Thoughts colliding, he stared at the man—and tightened his muscles. The guy was staring back.

"*Yimirira!* Stop!"

CHAPTER 4

Log Cabin, Blue Ridge Mountains

Phone clutched in her hand, Sydney Jacobs turned and stared over the large living area of the log cabin. On the thick Oriental rug, McKenna Neeley played with her new best friend, Tala Metcalfe. Their mothers sat on the sofa, both holding infants and talking casually. Sydney had invited them up for the weekend to celebrate the birth of Owen Metcalfe, the newest Nightshade offspring. And now. . .she might have just killed them all.

Whatever happened, whatever forced Max to make the call and give her that code, it was really bad.

Oh Max. . . Would she ever see him again? She squeezed off the thought and strangled it. Of course she would. But not if she stood around, frozen stupid.

"Okay," she said, her voice cracking. Sydney cleared her throat. "Okay, listen." She swept her fingers over her forehead, thinking. "Something's wrong. I. . .I don't know what, but I know we need to move fast."

"Hey, dude, what's wrong?" Three-year-old Dillon came barreling toward her and threw himself into her legs.

Sydney caught him. Any other day, she would've laughed, but today the move made her cry. It'd been the way he greeted Max every time his father came through the door. The boy had twice the amount of energy and intensity as his father. She honestly wasn't sure she'd survive parenting him. And now. . .

"What do we need to do?" Danielle crossed the room with Piper, cupped little Owen's mop of white-blond hair, and angled him away, bringing herself closer.

43

"PIG—it was Max's code that I'm to destroy anything that can be tracked."

"Tracked?" Rel Dighton, sister to one of the newer Nightshade members, had joined them for the weekend after taking time off at the hospital where she put her superior nursing skills to work. "Who would be tracking us?"

"Doesn't matter." Dani hurried away as did Piper. Sydney retrieved her beloved iPad. "Dillon, come here. I've got a job for you, little man."

Her son climbed up onto a bar stool and stood on his knees.

She pulled a wooden mallet from the drawer, handed it to him, then set her phone and the others on the counter. "It's a game, Dillon. I need all these broken into tiny pieces so nobody can tell what they were."

Coal black eyes held hers fast. "Break them? Daddy will be mad!"

"No, not this time." She leaned closer. "Guess what? Daddy told me to break them!"

"No way!"

"Here ya go."

He hesitated, eyes wide.

Sydney knew he was grappling with being allowed to be destructive.

"We want to help," McKenna said as she stood hand in hand with Tala. Danielle and Piper returned quickly with phones and MP3 players.

Then with Rel, they dumped their devices on the table.

"Have fun," Dani said.

"Okay, while they're doing that, let's get the cars loaded."

"Wait," Dani said. "Can't they be tracked?"

"Max disabled anything that could be tracked on mine."

"I have no idea on mine," Piper said.

"We can use my rental." Rel stuffed her hands in her back pockets. "Nobody knows who I am, right?"

"I seriously doubt they don't know, but it's our best choice. Let's hurry. I don't know what our timetable is, and I'd like to be on the road to the safe house soon!"

"What safe house?"

"Less said, the better." Sydney met each woman's gaze and was relieved when they all nodded.

As she closed the rear hatch, a sound stilled her. Hands on the white SUV, she cocked her head. Listened. Then braved a look over her shoulder. Ice dumped down her spine. A helicopter loomed in the distance, heading straight toward them.

Sydney sprinted up the steps. "Move, let's go. Now! There's a chopper coming." She lifted Dakota in his carrier, caught Dillon's hand, and all but dragged him toward the front door, her gaze sweeping the living room. Piper had her son bundled up and reached for McKenna's hand, who sat playing with Tala, the Filipino beauty-of-a-child.

"Tala, come on, sweetie. Time to go." Dani rushed toward Sydney with her newborn son.

As Sydney hurried toward the door, she realized kids outnumbered available seat belts. She hesitated.

"What's wrong?" Dani cupped her hand around Tala's silky black hair. If anyone hadn't met the two before Dani married Canyon, nobody would know Tala wasn't her biological daughter.

What would she do? Sydney couldn't ask Dani to separate from one of her kids, especially if the vehicles got separated. "I only have five seats."

"Tala can ride with us," Piper said.

Dani's hesitation screamed through the seconds. She squatted next to the little one. "Tala, go with McKenna, okay?"

Tala's pale-blue eyes widened, and slowly she nodded.

Sydney cringed. The girl had a very rough early childhood and now suffered separation anxiety. Only recently had she begun to trust Canyon and Dani.

The drone of the chopper grew louder. "We have to go." Her own fear was mirrored in their worried expressions. But right now, she had one goal: get to the rendezvous site.

Dani scooped up the little girl in her free arm and stood.

They hurried out the door, armed with kids and terror.

Boom! Crack! The ground vibrated beneath her feet. The small blue sedan Piper had driven flipped into the air and landed, upside down, engulfed in flames.

Sydney shielded her face. The children screamed. The chopper hovered over them, wind, smoke, and fire whipping into a frantic frenzy. She lifted the carrier closer and pulled Dillon to her leg as she looked into the sky at the big black bird. Was someone leaning out of the side?

She sucked in a breath as he aimed a weapon at them.

Dublin, Ireland
One Week Later

Kazi stood at the pub counter, her fingers stroking the glass. *Squeak.*
Squeak. Tina was gone. Really gone. All because of Kazi, because
Carrick wanted her to remember all he had done for her. That he
could reach her anywhere, anytime, force her will to his. To remind
her that she owed him everything. Even the very breath she breathed.
For saving her.

And he had. Plucking her, a then homeless girl, off the streets
after two years of living as one of Boucher's girls. *Thanks to Roman.*

Laughter, smoke, and bodies pressed in around her. Kazi stared at
the foam head of her Guinness.

"It's got more head than Carrick," Tina said.

A smile pulled back the gray clouds that had formed over Kazi's
mind as the infectious, annoying laughter once again filled her
thoughts. Then, swift and deadly, like a trip wire, memories killed that
ray of sunshine.

Tina's dead. Murdered by Carrick.

I'll make him pay.

She didn't have a plan yet, but she'd struck gold yesterday in a
rendezvous with an American general. She would locate and retrieve
four missing men. Her prize? Millions. She could vanish. That would
do more damage and create more pain to Carrick than she could do
any other way. She'd amassed significant proof that could put him
away in a dozen EU countries and bury him beneath the White
House's ever-green lawns. The information she had, nobody would
want made public. And lording this over Carrick would force him to
stay away from her.

"She wouldn't want you to do it, you know."

Kazi blinked and glanced to the side, to the hand cupping a tall
glass of golden beer. "Leave me alone, Mick." She dumped some of the
warm stout into her mouth and braced herself. While it was a good
drink, she wasn't one for alcohol or the buzz that fried the synapses
afterward.

"Now, that I won't." He shifted on the stool, his hazel eyes peering
beneath a mop of curly brown hair. "She always wanted me to take
care of you, help you find your family." One leg propped on the bar,

one on the floor, he caught her fingers.

She shook them free. Stabbed him with a fierce glare for the comment about her family.

"Tina wanted you to be happy," he said, his brogue thick and quiet. "She wanted both of you to find fellas and start families." No doubt he'd volunteer for that. Mick had never been quiet about his attraction for her. "She wanted you free—"

"Tina was idealistic and naive." The venom was bitter on her tongue. When the shock registered on Mick's face, Kazi glanced down, ashamed for speaking ill of her only friend. "Sorry." She gulped more stout, pushed several euros into the tip jar, then patted Tina's brother on the shoulder. "Good-bye, Mick."

She spun on her boots and stalked toward the door with the stained-glass panes. Out in the cool evening, Kazi stalked down the hedgerow-lined path, bound by guilt and pushed by remorse. But even as she crossed the street clogged with small whining cars and strode up the slight hill toward the future, she heard steps behind her.

"Kacie, please. Wait."

"Forget me, Mick." Forget that Kacie Whitcomb exists, because she doesn't—not really. But she couldn't say that to him without giving things away. "Go back to your girl, profess your love to her, and live happily ever after." Stuffing her hands in the pockets of her jacket, she continued. Puffs of icy air swirled before her nose. The bitter weather matched the condition of her heart.

He hooked her arm and swung her around.

As he did, she swept her hand up and broke his hold. "You know better than to do that."

"Come back to the pub, sit and talk. Let's get things sorted."

The way he said that, the pleading in a voice that had always been strong and confident, tugged at the wrong strings on her heart. Kazi lowered her head. "Mick. . .please."

Surprisingly warm fingers traced her cheek, chapped by the cold. "Kacie."

Her eyes slid closed. Then she popped them open and stared him in the eye. "You know I can't do this."

He leaned in and pressed his lips against hers.

She let him kiss her again. And again. Then she leaned into the kiss and returned it. But only because she knew this could never happen again. She jerked and took a step back, gaze on her boots.

"Kacie, stay here. With me. He won't find you."

"You're talking without a brain now, Mick Kelley." That kind of stupidity put everyone's life in danger. "He's already found me, or have you forgotten who's lying up in Shanganagh now?"

"Her death was an accident." He reached out to touch her again. "Please—"

She slapped his hand away. "You're a bigger fool than I thought if you believe that."

"I don't want to be losing me sister and me lady in the same week." Mick's voice rose on the cold, bitter wind. "You're butchering me here, Kacie."

Irony plied a sad smile from her unwilling face. "No Mick. I'm saving you." She tiptoed up and kissed him again. "Good-bye, Mick."

Forever.

Somewhere in the Blue Ridge Mountains

The explosion shoved Sydney back into the house. *Not good.* Trapped within the house, they wouldn't survive if the chopper sent a missile through the roof. Shrieks from the children shuddered through her.

"What's that noise?" Danielle shouted over the children.

Sydney stared at her. What did she mean? The thunder of the chopper? The wails of the children? The roar of the fire? "I—"

"Feel it!" Danielle said, nodding to the ground.

Sydney hesitated, trying to train her mind past the wild, frenetic screams of Dakota. But then. . .then she realized what Danielle meant. It felt like a mini earthquake rumbled beneath her feet. Was that from the raging fire and bullets?

"Look!" Rel pointed out the rear window.

Two massive helicopters streaked through the sky, their rotor wash like a drumroll, signifying a grand finale. *Our finale.* Sydney tugged Dillon into her arms, fearing the end had come. And yet the only thing she could think was that she pitied whoever took her life, pitied them going up against her husband, who would be bent on revenge.

"Downstairs," she said, her brain and voice reengaging. "Everyone down into the basement." It was made of cement and would shield them. As long as smoke inhalation didn't kill them, they might survive.

As she glanced back to the window, to the two new choppers, her heart skipped a beat as a trail of fire and smoke burst from the chopper on the left. Then another. . .and another. Her eyes widened as the missiles streaked toward them.

She held her breath. Watching. Waiting.

Closer. . .closer. . .

She cringed and hugged her sons close, huddled on the floor, waiting for the final hurrah.

Boom! Boooom.

BOOOOM!

A horrendous crack resounded through the house. Something dropped from above. Landed a dozen feet away. Sydney jerked that way, then up—a massive hole gaped in the roof. And in the north-facing wall. Enough plaster and wood had vanished to allow her to see into the yard. All the cars blazed. No. . .not the cars—the commercial helicopter.

Through the hole, a blur of black whooshed into the battered home.

Her heart hitched. Tactical. Military. Fast-roping.

Three appeared in the doorway. "Sydney Jacobs! Danielle Metcalfe. Piper Neeley."

Sydney shifted around, terrified to be singled out by men she didn't know. Men who'd just blown a helicopter out of the sky.

Another soldier slipped between the first two. He flipped up his face shield. "Mrs. Jacobs, we have orders from General Lambert to take you and the others into custody."

On weak knees, Sydney rose. "I'm Sydney Jacobs."

He took a step forward, his weapon straddling his chest. "We need to go, ma'am."

Danielle joined them. "We're not leaving with you till we have proof you're who you say you are."

The soldier looked irritated. "All I know is to get you out of here, ASAP. Now, you can come on your own, or. . ."

"What about our husbands?"

He waved them out. "Sorry. I don't have intel on them. Let's move, people. We have incoming."

As they filed through the double row of men in tactical gear, Sydney heard a commotion behind her. She glanced over her shoulder, only to find two men holding Rel back. "What're you doing?"

"She's not on our list," the leader said. "Three women, six children."

"Well, she's with us."

"Sorry, ma'am. I have strict orders, only you and your children."

"She's my daughter." She bit down on the lie, but she would *not* leave the girl.

The man frowned at her.

"I just adopted her." It wasn't a whole lie, and didn't the Doctrine of Competing Harms cover this situation? After all, she'd adopted the girl as a part of the Nightshade family—just then. "Come on, Rel. We need to hurry." She felt a war of giggles and fear as the soldiers hesitated, scowling between them. "Can you prove I didn't adopt her?"

The man's face darkened. So much like Max when she'd cornered him.

"None of us are leaving without her." Dani put an arm around Rel.

"Sir, less than five." The man to the right of the leader tapped his ear mic.

"Move, people!"

Outside, Sydney jogged toward one of two waiting helicopters. As she reached for a handle on the side to climb aboard, she noticed two more choppers, hovering over the Black Hawks. They looked fierce and fast.

Sydney climbed in and sat on the canvas strap seat, and immediately the skilled hands of a soldier strapped her in. As the last one in, she sat near the door and two soldiers sat on the edge, facing out, weapons ready. She wrapped an arm around Dillon, who buried his face in her leg.

As the bird lifted, her mind drifted to her husband. *Oh Max. What's going on? Where are you?*

They veered to the right and came around. Movement to the side snagged her attention. The two soldiers snapped their weapons up and began firing. Only then did she see a truck on the side of the mountain. Sparks flying up.

No, not sparks. Shots.

The soldier near her left whipped back, then tilted forward. In that split second, several things came to Sydney: one, the soldier was shot and would fall to his death if she didn't help; two, she'd just released a grip on Dakota's carrier; and three, she was exposed to the very same gunfire that had struck this soldier.

She grabbed the man's vest and dug her fingers around the material. When she felt the carrier tip, she lifted her leg and tried to counterbalance.

"Taking fire! Taking fire!" someone shouted over the drone of the rotors.

"Man down. Man down."

The helicopter veered right.

The baby carrier lifted from her legs. Sydney gasped and jerked—only to realize Rel held on to the seat with Dakota in it. "Help her," she shouted.

Thank goodness someone had noticed she couldn't hold on to the man any longer. Her arm ached and her fingers felt like they'd break off. Just when she couldn't hold on anymore, two hands stretched into view and dragged the soldier onto the steel floor of the chopper.

Adrenaline pumping, Sydney swallowed. Lifted her trembling hand to the carrier, but as she did, she saw something on her hand. She frowned. What. . . ?

"Sydney, are you okay? Sydney!"

Her hearing hollowed. The edges of her vision ghosted.

CHAPTER 5

Wallens Ridge Federal Penitentiary,
Virginia

A loud buzz reverberated through the steel and cement block. Clanking somewhere in the correctional facility grated against Griffin's nerves. Bars that served to contain the less decent of society only led to more captivity. Imprisonment. Outside, voices and laughter carried on the cold wind. Squeaks and grunts. Shouts and laughter. Hoops.

God, You have got *to get me out of here.* He would lose his good mind here for forty more years. He grunted.

With one hand behind his back and the other palm-down against the cold floor, Griffin ignored the painful, numbing iciness of January seeping through his bones and up his arm. Eyes on his multilegged friend, he lowered his chest and board-straight legs toward the floor in another rep. Two-thirty-nine.

Sixty-one to go. Three hundred reps.

What else was there to do for twenty-three hours in a six-by-eight trap?

The spider skittered over the drab floor, its dark body contrasting the gray. Dark gray. Light gray. Striped gray on the pillows. Wool gray blankets. Every shade of the dreary color.

As he continued, thudding echoed through the narrow hall outside the steel door. Boots. With short, staccato breaths, he advanced through the repetitions, listening to the movement beyond his dank cell. Boots sounded like Guard Acton. That didn't make sense. What would he be doing this far down in the pit at this time of day?

Schink!

Griffin eyed the square of light that appeared on the floor to his right. The spider skittered back to his corner. Now why would Acton interrupt his private time? All 1,380 minutes of it.

"On your feet, Riddell, and get a shirt," Acton called through the bars.

Lumbering to his feet, Griffin peered through the small window. The guards behind Acton had their battle gear on, padded from head to toe, their faces protected by visors. The scene rolled over him like a bad dream. Griffin shook it off.

"We having a party, Acton?" He brushed off his hands. "What's the occasion? A birthday? Got some cake?" He snatched the shirt from his two-inch-thick mattress.

"Just do it, Riddell."

Eyeing the guards, Griffin threaded his arms through the sleeves. As he assumed the position, hands behind his head, he pressed his focus to Dante and reminded himself that extracting his vengeance would serve no purpose but to disgrace his family. But humiliation had cost him the last semblance of honor and pride he possessed. They'd deemed him a flight risk, a high-security risk, and a lethal weapon because of his training and skills. Lambert did what he could, but in the end, it wasn't enough.

The steel window clamped shut. Groaning echoed through the room as the door slid into the wall. "What's up, Acton? Where we going?"

Who was here? Phee knew better than to come back so soon. Colton had missed last week though.

Rough hands pawed at him, clamping metal and chains onto his wrists one at a time as they secured his hands. The tendons and muscles in his shoulders strained as they jerked his arms behind his back. He stared straight ahead at the barrel of an M4 one of the guards held trained on him. Another guard held a fully automatic. Even by the way the men held the weapons, Griffin knew they didn't feel confident. He scared them.

Good. At least they were smart enough to recognize the threat he posed. Of course he could take them. Take them all. He had the skills. The training. Get out of here, hide out. . .

And bring that humiliation down on Dante?

Griffin released the urge and let his shoulders relax. Chains jangled as his hands and feet were bound together to limit his range of motion.

Acton gave a hard pull, the tug stressing Griffin's shoulders. He grimaced and flinched.

Feet shuffled. Weapons snapped up. Shields nudged forward as the guards hid themselves, weapons aimed at him as they readied for a fight.

Griffin shrugged one shoulder. "They're cutting me."

"Sorry." Acton tried to play off the rough treatment, but Griffin knew it wasn't an accident. "Don't want you to wiggle out of those."

It was okay. The guy could save face if he needed. Thing of it was, if Griffin decided to start something, these fools wouldn't be able to stop it. It'd be too easy to take this midget out. Then again, Griffin wouldn't do that. Yeah, he'd been screwed by the system, but he still had his honor.

Never shall I forget the principles I accepted to become a Recon Marine. Honor, Perseverance, Spirit, and Heart. Times like this, the Creed served him well. He was a Marine. They couldn't take that from him.

Acton and the others hustled Griffin out of the cell. The head guard gave the signal, and another door opened.

"Who's my visitor?" Griffin eyed the seemingly endless rows of one-window condos lining the corridor. How many others had been unjustly relegated to the steel coffins by the judicial system?

"Psychologist."

A groan escaped. "Just take me back." The thought of another brain-digger tempted him to resist. "I don't need no shrink."

Acton grinned. "Hey, orders are orders. Government wants a peek inside your brain, they get a peek. Maybe this psychologist will put you under hypnosis and find out how you knew where the congressman would be the night you killed him."

Griffin glared down at the head guard. Did the fool really want to start something? Even with the wide glasses and droopy belly, he didn't look that stupid.

"In you go." Acton guided him into a room.

A massive one-way mirror lined the wall. *Easy, Riddell. This ain't war.* Two chairs flanked a table that looked as if it'd been used for torture.

Then again. . .maybe it was war.

"Take a seat, *boy*." Acton waited by a chair situated between two large loops set into the cement floor.

Griffin huffed. "Why you trying to make me mad?" Frustration always brought out his slang. Madyar would whoop him from here to the Mississippi and back if she heard him. *"You won't have a chance in life if you talk like that."*

"Just putting you in your place. Now sit nice for the psychologist." As one guard kept a weapon trained on Griffin, Acton and another hooked the chains to the reinforced bars looped into the ground. He patted Griffin on the shoulder and motioned the others out of the room. Two in, four out. As if he would go anywhere.

Sitting in the chilled room, his body cooling from the workout, Griffin huffed. "Like a dog on a chain."

Steel clanked the table as he set his head in his hands, elbows propped on the metal surface. Man, he didn't want no shrink digging through his mind. What was there wouldn't change anything that happened. Why bother? They'd convicted him of capital murder. Swiftest trial of the century. His attorney had been powerless against the evidence, and having a trial in Virginia with a black man who'd murdered the Republican party's rising star white congressman—well, he didn't have a prayer, even if he had sent up thousands to the Pearly Gates. Someone with a grudge must've had guard duty up there when his prayers floated in. He'd gotten locked up for the next forty years of his life. *"A threat to society,"* the judge had ruled.

Yeah, she got that right. Let him loose, and he'd show them how much a threat.

"Boy, you're better than that."

Madyar's mental chiding slapped a smile into his face. He missed his grandmother. His sister had written, saying Madyar had spent two weeks in the hospital before passing through those Pearly Gates, greeted no doubt by Mama.

They killed Madyar. Came into his home, assaulted his family, and murdered his grandmother. All for a crime he didn't commit.

"I'm sorry, maybe I didn't make myself clear."

The uniformed guard shifted. "Yes, ma'am, you did. It's just that—"

"I want that room emptied." She pointed to the steel door. "I will not speak to my patient with witnesses. Have you heard of privacy laws? Doctor-patient privilege?" She thumbed over her shoulder. "So clear out. You can stay here in the hall, but I'm going in, and I'm going in alone."

The mealymouthed guard sniggered. "Dr. Whitcomb, that's just not something I can do."

She stomped back toward the viewing room. "Fine, I'll call your supervisor and tell him you're breaking the law." She paused and glanced at him, throwing as much uncertainty into her face and voice as possible. "Wait a minute. Aren't you the one who just came off administrative leave?"

He paled.

Ah. "I'm sure you had a legitimate reason for all those images on your computer." She had him right where she needed him, so she played nonchalant. "What could happen?"

A hissing breath escaped as he opened the door and motioned the two guards out. Smiling her appreciation, Kazi Faron stepped into the room. Pen in hand, she clicked it. The lock thudded into place.

She shifted toward the prisoner and stilled. This man didn't look anything like the one in the photograph. Fluorescent light glinted off his shiny, shaved head. Had they brought the wrong prisoner to the interview cell? Lambert had provided her with a Marine Corps picture of a man in dress blues and a proud, defiant gleam peeking from under the shiny rim of his hat.

This man—the only word that came to mind: *broken*. No pride. No haughtiness. Six months in a Supermax would do that to even the toughest of guys. But one thing she hadn't counted on was his size. Arms as big around as rocket launchers. Neck thick as a tree trunk and nearly missing due to the bulk—toned, tight bulk; none of the flabby stuff—he'd accumulated. His knees banged the edge of the table as he shifted and looked at her. Even bent forward, he hulked over the table, which seemed dwarfed as if he sat at a child's tea table. Good grief—the size of those hands!

What if he was really guilty of capital murder? He could snap her neck like a twig with those enormous paws.

Rich brown eyes raked over her. He made a hissing noise. Shaking his head, he dragged his gaze back to the table. "You're wasting your time, Doc."

Oh yeah, this was him.

"Mr. Riddell, my name is Kacie Whitcomb." She still liked that alias, even after all these years. It sounded sweet. Disarming. She dropped her briefcase on the table. "I'm here to interview you on behalf of—"

Palms splayed, he lifted his cuffed hands. "Just go back to your padded office and tell them I'm passive-aggressive. Paranoid schizophrenic. Delusional. Whatever it takes so we can go back to our very fulfilling lives."

The attitude that rolled off him was as thick as his head. "Passive-aggressive, huh?" She folded her arms and stared down at him, because if she sat, she'd have to crane her neck to look up at him. "According to records, you brutally assaulted four men when you were taken into custody. Put one in the hospital. Cracked ribs of another."

His jaw muscle popped, the dark complexion rippling. Smooth, satiny. . .

She blinked, regathering her thoughts. They didn't have time for this. Speaking of time, shouldn't the—

Boom!

Three seconds behind. She'd have to fix the timing.

Feet scrambled outside the door, followed by two thuds.

Griffin jerked, straining at the smoke billowing in through the small cracks along the door frame.

"Hold your breath." She tugged back the edge of her briefcase, revealing a hidden panel.

He locked gazes with her, surprise dancing over his handsome features. "What is this?"

"Shut your mouth or you can call it your funeral." She peeled out a device, pressed it over her mouth and nose, then hooked it up to a small pouch she tucked in her pocket.

A curt nod later, she knew he'd cued in on the fact that she was in control, which often was an issue with military types like him.

Kazi lifted out the files. Digging her nails into the bottom of the case, she worked out a small bladder. She hurried to Griffin, strapped a breathing strip over his mouth and nose and slapped the oxygen bladder against his chest. The glue patch would hold it in place.

Using her pen case, she unscrewed the cap and knelt beside him. Carefully, she poured the searing chemical over the first links. They sizzled and snapped. Within seconds the acid ate through and the chain fell loose.

At the door, she poured the rest over the lock. More smoky sizzling. She tried to open it, but the thing wouldn't give. She yanked hard. Grunted. Why wouldn't it open?

Griffin reached around and gave a solid jerk. It pulled inward.

Two guards slumped into the room, unconscious. She dragged them inside and started undressing the man. One of the benefits of rescuing a black-ops soldier was she didn't have to instruct him in what to do next. He worked swiftly on the other guard.

The masks would only give them five minutes of the precious

element, so she worked quickly and stepped into the clothes. Being petite served her well. Silently, she thanked her lucky stars that the guard was a younger, fit man. Most men were larger. The uniform fit just right. Too bad the same couldn't be said for Griffin.

If only she could smile—two inches of ankle whistled at her. The shirt tugged taut across his muscular chest. Even with the seal taped over his mouth and nose, she could see the glowering expression stabbing her. That made her want to smile even more.

They hurried into the hall and rushed toward the cafeteria. They could slip through the serving area to the waiting service truck. Shouts pinged off the all-cement building as they hustled down one whitewashed corridor after another.

Rounding a corner, she saw a flash of black. Guards disappeared around the corner. They rushed past the spot where she'd set the plastique. The explosion had been enough to cause chaos and confusion, but not enough to unleash two-hundred violent criminals onto an unsuspecting public. She wasn't without scruples.

A variation of color on the floor registered one second too late. The sprinklers had come on. She tried to slow, but she hit the wet spot. Her feet spun out from under her.

Strong arms caught her, dragging her onward. Kazi scrabbled forward, using his momentum to launch herself on.

"Stop!"

She never did understand why they said that. Whoever stopped? Shots rang out.

Plaster burst out at Kazi as she banked right, through the double doors to the cafeteria. Zigzagging around tables. Twenty feet ahead a guard emerged from the kitchen, looking backward over his shoulder. He carried his weapon lazily at the side. He hadn't seen them yet. And if she had anything to say about it, he never would.

Deviating her course, she jumped onto a chair, then the table without missing a beat. She launched herself at the man, her right foot thrust forward. He whirled toward her, his gun coming up seconds too late. Her booted foot collided with his face. He whipped around.

She rolled out of the maneuver and came up running, then shoved through the kitchen door and aimed for a serving tower. Skidding up behind one, she grabbed both sides. A strong push sent it spinning toward the door—*thud!*

Griffin maneuvered another into position. The temporary barricade would buy them desperately needed time. She sprinted toward the back door. From inside her shirt, she peeled away a thin layer of latex, wrapped it to her finger and pressed it against the coded box. A row of round red lights flashed back and forth, then blinked green. *Click!*

Outside, she led him to the food van. They darted inside. She beelined past the pallets of food stuff, careful not to touch them and leave a DNA trail for the dogs. At the back, she squatted and palmed a panel. Griffin joined her, but she waved him back a step as she applied subtle pressure to the metal. At her feet—right where he'd been standing—the raised indentions glowed. She stroked one left, then another left, then one right. The back wall receded.

Kazi motioned Griffin into the narrow void, wanting to laugh at the way his shoulder blades touched the back and his pectorals brushed the front of the false wall. His face contorted. Was the big lug claustrophobic?

She moved in the cramped space, nudging him down a couple of inches. The door flashed closed. Darkness devoured them. Using her nails, she scraped the sticky oxygen mask from her mouth and nose. Had Griffin moved yet? That pouch would run out soon.

Unable to risk telling him to remove it, she reached up, her cool fingers tracking over his face. Smooth. . .stubble. There, the edge of the tape. She pried it back.

He caught her hand, making her spasm. The soft ripping of the tape drifted to her.

The sound of water spilling over the truck told her the plan was on schedule. Soon shouts reverberated around them. Dogs barked. The delivery truck rocked as the shouts seemed to devour the interior. The guards were inside, searching.

"Find anything?"

"Not a thing."

"Well, they came through the cafeteria. Larry's unconscious and the back door was open."

"They aren't here. Check for yourself, man."

"Didn't the dogs catch a scent?"

"Yeah, the scent of ground beef, I think. Stupid dogs."

"Yeah, and you're spoiling it," a guy complained. "That ain't coming out of my pay. Now, do you want to take the truck apart, or can I get going before I'm fired for being late with spoiled food?"

"Nobody's leaving. We have an escaped prisoner."

"Okay, guess I'll have to call my boss and explain about the ruined food."

"You sure you checked inside?"

"For cryin' out loud. Check yourself."

The bed rocked again, then shifted. Loud thuds boomed through the small space. Feet drew closer. . .closer.

Bang! Bang!

As the man knocked on the metal, clearly testing it for signs of weakness, Kazi remained calm. The false wall should give off a solid thud that matched everywhere else in the truck. But was *should* good enough?

"All right."

"I'm clear?"

"Yeah. Go on."

Kazi closed her eyes, listening as the driver climbed behind the wheel. Vibrations tickled her feet as the engine rumbled to life. It lurched forward—which pitched them toward the false wall. Or, at least it pitched *her*. Griffin was soundly wedged.

As the chassis lumbered onto the main road and gained speed, she relaxed finally. "In an hour, we'll rendezvous with a Cessna. We'll fly to the Caribbean—"

"Hold up!" Although he'd removed the strip of what felt like duct tape, Griffin still couldn't breathe any easier. Why on God's green earth had he just escaped a maximum security prison? "Who are you? Why did you bust me out? I mean, I appreciate your help, but now I'm a wanted fugitive." Madyar had to be shouting a few "Oh sweet Jesuses" right now in heaven.

"In two hours you would've been dead. A hit had been hired out on you."

A hit? Why? He was behind bars, immobilized, paralyzed. "Who wants me dead?"

"What you need to know is why you're out. They're all down."

This was crazy. "Lady, I have no idea what you're talking about." He couldn't believe he'd followed Lara Croft's sister out a Supermax without a second thought. The eyes. She flashed those innocent eyes at him and knocked him senseless. "As soon as we can, I'm hoofing it back. No way I'm going to let my respect—"

"Your team, Mr. Riddell. The team has been flatlined."

Nightshade? "Not possible. Nobody knows who we are."

"They found *you*, didn't they?"

Oh sweet Jesus.

"From what I've been able to uncover, Midas is imprisoned in Venezuela. A place, as you know, Mr. Riddell, is very unfriendly to Americans on the wrong side of the law. A place where nice guys like your buddy disappear and nobody hears from them again. The newest member, the assassin, faces execution one week from today in a Hamas safe house."

The news looped his heart into a knot.

"Cowboy was arrested in London and faces charges of terrorism."

The knot tightened. He couldn't breathe.

"Marshall Vaughn is hooked up to a machine and not expected to live. Someone found your Shack, grabbed the men, then blew the building into the Hudson."

Unbelievable. Griffin leaned against the wall, rubbing a hand over his face. No wonder Colton missed their weekly meeting—arrested. On terrorism charges. The Kid on life support? It made him sick to his stomach. Metcalfe. . . "Frogman. Where's Max? And Squirt?"

Her green eyes met his. "Unknown. Both disappeared two weeks ago. Frogman made a call to his wife, then vanished. His wife was shot, but it wasn't fatal. She and the other wives and children are safely tucked away, out of sight and mind."

Whoever had gone after the team hit hard and in a way that would decimate any chance of the team recovering.

A slow burn worked from his toes, through his legs, stoked by the sickening feeling of being hunted. It surged through his chest with volcanic fury. He'd handpicked the team with Olin. And he'd be among the damned if he let someone disassemble Nightshade. "What's the plan?"

CHAPTER 6

Winter had crowded out the heavenlies and silenced the familiar song of the cicadas as they waited along a barren runway. Griffin remembered sitting on the front porch with Madyar, rocking. Talking. Enjoying. Doing nothing but listening to one another. To nature. To God.

Strangely, God had been as quiet as the stark night that stretched before him. An icy wind rustled the tall, uncut grass waving under the dull glow of the winter moon. Eerie silence drifted through the starless sky. Pop-Pop had taught him to watch for God in the small things, the whisper of the wind, the smile of someone unknown. Was this woman sent by God?

No, Lambert sent her.

Griffin had to be a fool to cooperate with the escape—but Nightshade needed him. He had to get the guys back together. And the only way to do that was to be free. Wrestling with the notion that he served time for a crime someone else committed—well, God would have to sort that one out.

Cupping his hands over his mouth and blowing hot breath provided little warmth. Griffin remained quiet, ignoring the bitter cold worming through the thin scrubs. Beside him, Wonder Woman sat like a loyal guard dog, watching. Her wide eyes sat glued on a fixed point down the airstrip. She shifted onto her toes and crept forward a few feet.

"There," she whispered as two lights blinked in the distance.

Slowly, the thrum of a plane droned into his awareness. Red

wingtip lights grew brighter.

"Let's go." Kacie patted his shoulder and, in a hunched run, approached the runway. Staying close, Griffin prepared himself to overpower the pilot of the plane.

The moon peeked through drifting clouds, accenting the glossy body of a single-engine plane as it rolled into view.

Griffin anticipated Kacie's move and darted toward the craft with her.

"Other side," she said.

He whipped around the front, avoiding the pointed steel tip that guarded the propeller. The sleek hull was new, but it was still a single-engine plane. He hated single-engines. He'd been jiggled like Madyar's homemade butter on one too many flights. At the side, he tugged up the gull-wing door—and froze.

Kacie sat in the pilot's seat. Headphones on and pressing buttons. Her eyes darted to him. "What?"

He glanced to the backseat. Empty. "Where's the pilot?"

"You're looking at her. Now get in or I'll leave you."

Mind tangled, he folded himself into the ultracompact compartment and drew down the door. Before he could fasten the three-point harness, she was taxiing down the runway.

Even with the divider between their seats, her cool skin brushed his. Frustration wrapped him tightly as he squished his left arm against his side. He rolled his neck and pushed his thoughts to the team and away from the speed as they ramped up to take off.

Metcalfe holed up in a guerilla camp. No doubt held by someone loyal to Bruzon, whom Metcalfe had taken down. Torture. They would torture the man until he screamed and ratted out his friends.

Colton. His Recon buddy held by British authorities on charges of terrorism, which was asinine! Where was Piper? And his mother and daughter?

Aladdin would face a humiliating execution—and no doubt the men holding him would make sure to display the traitor's body for all to see. A week. He only had a week.

Max. . .Max. . . *Where are you, Frogman?*

Gravity pressed Griffin against the seat. He gripped the leather and clenched his teeth as the plane dipped to the right and—wobbled. "Did we just wobble?"

"It's called flying, Mr. Riddell."

He pointed to the panel where blue sat on brown. "J–just keep it straight, okay? That should stay straight." Again he wagged his finger at it. "Straight. Got it?"

"If I did that, we'd end up in China." Glowing under the lights of the instrumentation, her smile spiraled out at him and struck him in the chest. "Are we scared of flying?"

Clicking his tongue, he shook his head, doing his best to regroup his thoughts. And that's all they were. He wasn't afraid. He'd faced worse. "You're crazy. I hop flights all the time." He roughed a hand over his face. "I just don't like planes where my shoulder could push the window out." Her laughter did nothing to ease the irritation seeping into him. His fingers ached as the heated air chased off the icy coldness. "Where are we going?"

"Private airstrip in Texas. We'll gear up and head to Afghanistan."

"We?"

Another smile, this time as she read the gauges. "You have something against a woman helping you?"

"I—I—no—that's not what I meant."

Her laughter bubbled out, so light and infectious it finally dragged a reluctant smile from his own face. She punched a button on her left, then shifted and reached into the back.

"Hey!" Griffin reached for the stick on his side—only he didn't know how to fly this thing. "What are you doing? Shouldn't you be looking out there?" He jabbed a finger at the windshield.

"Why? So I don't rear-end a 747?" As she drew her arm back, she brought out a large black bag and dropped it in his lap. "Get changed."

He rummaged through it. Pants, a shirt, shoes. He eyed her. Probably had a full dossier on him, which explained how she knew. How was he supposed to change? He couldn't even stretch out his legs, his shoulder grazed the window and her elbow, and she wanted him to change? "Excuse me while I step outside. . ."

Her lips parted, another grin threatening. "Watch the first step. It's a killer."

He would not laugh. This was not funny. But the pressure in his chest built. Finally, he let out a breathy laugh and covered his mouth with his fist. "Baby Girl, what do you think I am? A conniptionist?"

She arched an eyebrow at him, her white-blond hair practically glowing from the instrumentation. "You mean a *contortionist*?"

Wring her neck. Strangle her. Get it over with. He knew how to parachute—if there was one in this thing. It'd been a long while since he'd mangled his words like this in front of a woman. He tried to tuck aside the irritation at the way she took charge, ordered him around, and gave no explanation, but it only made him angrier.

"Relax, Gunny." With a cheeky grin, she winked at him. "I promise not to peek."

How could the woman infuriate and amuse him at the same time?

Tugging up his shirt, he angled his body to afford himself enough room. He cinched up the material and hauled it off. He clamped his teeth together and drew out the silky polo and threaded his arms into the holes. "Man, Madyar would beat me." And if she saw him dropping his pants in front of a woman. . .

Kacie glanced at him and frowned.

He wiggled into the slacks and noticed her staring at him. "What?" Was that a blush? "Your records didn't mention the tattoo."

He placed a hand over his heart, as if he could feel the fire of the gryphon burned into his chest even now. "Got that in high school." When he thought he was a big, bad brother, ready to take over the local gang. As memories of Venus Washington violated open thought, he shoved them back and stuffed his feet into the shoes. He'd put that behind him long ago. No need to dredge it up now. "What about a shaving kit and cologne?"

She thumbed toward the back. "Right there with your cement parachute."

"You got some serious attitude, know what I'm saying?"

Her lips thinned. A slow, uneasy breath seemed to ripple through her. Without a response, she removed the headphones and dove partially over the backseat.

Heart in his throat, he grabbed the stick. "What're you doing? Someone has to fly this thing!"

"Autopilot," she grunted as she flopped back down with another, smaller bag.

Griffin glanced at her—but a flash of her bare midriff as she tugged off her shirt jerked his gaze away. Heat crawled up his neck and into his face as he registered the fact that she was undressing. "Baby Girl, you have no modesty."

"You've escaped a maximum-security prison, every law-enforcement agency in the nation is on the lookout, and you're going to gripe about modesty?" Soft angora bathed her torso but did nothing to deflect his piercing comment. Shouldn't matter. *Doesn't matter.* He was a job. An objective. Finish this, get his thick-brained team back together, and she could retire.

Five years too late. But who was counting?

"Is this thing. . .okay?" His eyes glazed as he studied the panel. "This looks new."

"It is." She rifled her fingers through her short hair, kneading the tension from her scalp. "Cost half a million." Yeah, talk about the equipment, the toys. Keep his mind—and *hers*—on safer topics. "Compliments of your benefactor." Her words faltered as she climbed back into the pilot's seat. Though she'd tried to put syrupy sarcasm into her voice, it didn't work.

His dark chocolate eyes came to hers, penetrating. "What's your name?"

"I already introduced myself."

"A psychologist introduced herself to me. What's *your* name?"

"You think I lied?"

"I *know* you lied." He chuckled. "I don't think you could hold your tongue long enough to listen to a lunatic's ravings. And I am sure you wouldn't sit there quietly while one of those hardened criminals decided you'd be their next meal or playmate."

She flashed a challenge at him.

More chuckles. "Go on."

He was baiting her. She wouldn't bite. "In my career I've put up with more egotism and testosterone than you could imagine."

He held out a hand toward her.

She furrowed her brow. "What?"

"Wanted to introduce myself." He could disarm a nuclear weapon with that smile. "Griffin Riddell. They call me Legend."

Dare she do this? Open the portal to her soul that she'd sealed off long ago? Ha! Not likely. Nobody, nowhere, no man. . . She thought she could trust a man once. Carrick had convinced her he was watching out for her, but in the end. . .well, that was just it. Everything ended. She wouldn't betray herself like that. Not again. Stick to the story, the alias. Stay safe. "Kacie Whitcomb."

A hissing sigh coiled around her conscience. "I see. Going to be like that, huh?" He nodded slowly, pursing his lips. "It's all right, Baby Girl. I'll win your trust."

Baby Girl? Something slithered through her stomach, burning. She bit back the harsh retort about not being anyone's baby or girl. Then again, it always worked to her advantage when men underestimated her.

Quiet monotony settled into the cabin like an iceberg. The thought pushed her attention to the wings where the automatic deicing seemed to be working. If only she had something that could thaw her life. She was tired of living like this. Tired of. . .

Shedding the gloom, she straightened and turned off the autopilot. Over the next twenty minutes, she guided the sleek craft toward the private runway. Without a hitch, they touched down and rolled across the tarmac. Kazi aimed the plane toward the hangar where a Learjet waited. She cut the engine and climbed out.

The stairs to the jet deployed. A man waved a phone at her. "He's asking for you."

"Thank you." She strode up the steps, took the phone, and moved into the narrow cabin. Working her way past the first two seats, she settled into the buff leather and pressed the phone to her ear. "Go ahead."

"With the chaos at Wallens Ridge that hit the news, I assume you have my man."

"Did you doubt?" Her gaze followed Griffin as he ducked to avoid grazing his head. His tall, powerfully built frame devoured the jet's interior. Muscles bulged as he lowered himself into the seat across from her, the leather seeming to sigh as he eased onto it.

"Then you're on schedule."

"Would you pay me if I weren't?" She closed the phone and tossed it on the chair next to Griffin. Tousling her hair, she tried to knead the tension that laced a tight band around her head as the high-pitched scream of the engines ripped through the cabin. Behind her, the door closed, the pressurization sucking at her hearing. She stretched her jaw. With a smirk, she finally met his gaze. "So, this more to your liking? More comfortable?"

Griffin smoothed a hand over his black tactical pants. "If I don't have Ripcord boots and an M4, I'm not comfortable."

The cabin steward delivered two Styrofoam trays and bottled waters along with a portfolio.

Griffin looked at the items and then at her. "Dinner and blueprints."

"What else for a perfect conclusion to breaking a convicted felon out of a maximum-security prison?" With that, she opened her box, then plucked the fork from the plastic wrap. Only then did she notice something about Griffin had hardened. He'd gone silent. Talking to the man was as useful as trying to extract information from a marble statue. "I hope you like Chinese. I gave the waitstaff the night off."

He opened the box of General Tso's chicken and started eating. Not a word. With his fork, he scooped a pile of rice and stabbed a chunk of chicken. Halfway to his mouth, he paused. He put down the fork, his gaze on the food.

Kazi slowed in her chewing, monitoring him. Was he having second thoughts?

The sound of his hand over his stubbled jaw sounded like sandpaper. His brown eyes met hers. "I didn't do it."

She swallowed. "Do what?"

His jaw muscle popped again. "I did not kill Congressman Jones." Delectable food steamed up at him. Comfortable, luxurious leather. A change of clothes—he had something besides numbered stripes. The only thing the man needed was a shower. And he shucked it all aside, intent on convincing her of his innocence.

"I don't care." The words caught in her throat. She did care. Although, why she cared she couldn't fathom. Caring was dangerous. Caring got operatives killed.

Griffin cocked his head. "You could be sitting across from a violent killer, and you say you don't care?"

Swiping her tongue along her teeth, she laid her fork aside and leaned back. Folding her arms, she locked gazes with him. "Mr. Riddell, I've been an operative for eleven years. I've outsmarted bigger, uglier, meaner men—and women—than you." She lifted the bottled water and took a sip. "I think you're smart enough to know I'm here to help you, so"—she shrugged—"no, I don't anticipate trouble from you."

Kazi resumed eating, hoping he'd do the same. When his gaze drifted out the window as the jet roared into the sky, she tried not to let his wounded expression haunt her. She had enough ghosts of her own. Which is why she kept her heart on ice.

Staying mission-focused meant staying alive. "I'm sure you've guessed that due to time sensitivity, we're going to extract Azzan Yasir from the Hamas." Savoring a bit of dinner, she glanced over the photos, diagrams, and intelligence reports. She plucked a couple from the file and handed them across the small table between them. "This is the satellite image of the building where he's being held."

His gaze slowly came back to hers as he took the photo. "Ironic."

She raised an eyebrow.

"I hate this man." A snort bobbed his head. "Never thought I'd care whether he was dead or alive."

The spark of hope in his eyes filled her with a strange giddiness, but one she had to tamp down. "Our reports are several days old. Since we have boots on the ground, it's delicate trying to retrieve the information."

He hesitated. "What're you saying? That he's dead?" His shoulders seemed to swell several inches. "Is Aladdin alive or not?"

Kazi swallowed, wanting more than anything to tell him his friend was alive. But she couldn't. Not for certain. "There are no guarantees."

CHAPTER 7

Somewhere over the West Bank

Forty-five minutes of prebreathing pure O_2. Now the plane climbed into the great blue, aiming for a grand thirty-three thousand over hostile territory. Hostile in its own right—a desert laden with IEDs, rocket-propelled grenades, and insurgents. Even in the dark, explosives had a way of finding their targets, but hopefully the high-altitude, low-opening maneuver would give him and Kacie an edge. Despite the risks of HALO jumps, this was the fastest way to insert. Let them descend upon the fools stupid enough to take one of his boys hostage.

The numbing vibration of the C-130 tickled through Griffin's free-fall boots. Dressed head to toe now in desert camo, he stared across the cabin at the enigma of a woman. Kacie hadn't wanted to give him private information. She'd stepped into that harness and his life like a pro. Even had to help him with a tangled strap.

Face framed by the thick helmet and the oxygen mask that covered her mouth and nose, she sat calmly, eyes on him. Was she plagued by as many questions about him as he was about her? She'd shown no fear as she extricated him from the prison. Dauntless as they sped through the air in the single-engine plane. On the Lear, she'd explained little of the plan, taken a nap, and made the transition from one country to another as if she'd been born to it.

Who is she? Where did she come from? He hadn't even questioned whether or not to trust the petite, take-no-mess woman. Her knowledge and assuredness had eliminated his fears before they took root. Olin sent her. Even though she hadn't named the general, this mission had the earmarks of the general's stamp of approval.

He glanced at the digital readout strapped to his wrist. Thirty-thousand feet. The six-minute warning bell rattled through his nerves as the bay door opened. Black night gaped. Earth waited some eight miles below that ebony void. Memories leapt to life. Taking his nephew to a private air school and tandem jumping with the then ten-year-old. They'd done it often in the last five years. The kid had adventure in his blood, to the point of boiling.

Warmth curled around Griffin's heart at the thought of Dante.

"You have to tell him, Griffin. He should know." Adamancy laced his sister's words.

But Dante *didn't* need to know. The boy had a good head on his shoulders, a solid home with two parents, loving great-grandparents. And an uncle who would always make sure he had what he needed, even if Griffin had to die to make it happen.

A hard pat on his shoulder brought him up straight. Swallowing and blinking back his thoughts, Griffin glared up at Kacie, who stood over him with the two-minute warning signal. She'd already disconnected from the oxygen panel and switched to her bailout bottle. The jumpmaster moved into position at the open bay door, and Kacie lumbered toward him and lowered her goggles.

Quickly, Griffin opened his bailout bottle, took a deep breath, and held it. Smoothly, he disengaged his O$_2$ from the plane's console. He let out his breath, then inhaled. That first burst of cold air shot through him, proof the bottle worked. He monitored the flow meter. All good.

The light flashed from red to green. The jumpmaster pushed their gear through the open portal. Another green light sent Kacie sailing into the black. Griffin leapt out behind her. Gravity grabbed and yanked him toward the earth.

Ecstasy defined in three minutes. Terminal velocity of over two hundred miles an hour!

Oorah!

Frigid air seeped around his collar and needled his neck. He thanked the Good Lord that polypropylene undergarments protected against hypoxia and the gloves from frostbite. He checked his altimeter and oxygen. Fifteen thousand. The pressure in his ears grew, and he forced an exaggerated swallow. His ears released and equalized.

Wind seemed to claw him downward. Kacie stayed almost completely even. The girl had skills. Impressive skills. Although she looked young, there was nothing young about the experience this girl owned.

Altitude check again. Five thousand. He reached back, fingering the rip cord. Glowing green, Kacie turned her head and gave a thumbs-up. No doubt a smile hid behind that oxygen mask.

She reached up and back, grabbed the rip cord.

Griffin did the same. They were in sync. He just hoped it stayed that way or someone would end up dead. And it wouldn't be him.

She hit the ground running. Kazı popped open the oxygen mask.

Thud! Griffin landed to the side.

She cleared the landing spot and spun around, pulling the nylon canopy down to avoid detection. Once she flattened the chute, she ripped out of the harness. Gaze tracking over the area to make sure they were safe, she stowed the chute, then buried the gear. She scrambled over the still-warm sand to where their conjoined sacks had landed.

Kazi separated the two rucksacks and unzipped hers. She grabbed two handguns and strapped a Glock onto her right thigh and an HK USP Compact at the small of her back. Threading her arms through the pack, she glanced at Griffin, who stood with his hands on his hips, smiling. Waiting. How had he geared up so fast?

He tossed her the CamelBak and started walking.

She hustled to keep up, quickly realizing that now that he had the game plan, the Gunny would probably take charge. But that wasn't how this worked. She hadn't told him everything. Never would. Too much information meant someone ended up dead.

Had he noticed they were five miles too far north?

"Head south, eight klicks," he said in a tight, controlled voice. His M4 dangled at his chest from the three-point harness. "Fast and silent." His last order snuffed the bitter retort dripping off her tongue.

Plodding across the desert proved difficult even without the weight of competition. Still, who did he think he was to assume command of *her* mission? She'd anticipated this considering his personality and career, which was why she'd only told him how to get to safety once they landed. She urged herself forward, trying to get a foot ahead of him. But the man navigated the shifting terrain without so much as a grunt. What was he? A sand spider?

Twenty-two minutes and a mouthful of tiny grains later, she trailed him as he came up on a palm tree. With the celery-colored image swaying against the black, she knelt and dusted off an area around the base. There, the brass ring. She pulled hard.

The trapdoor groaned and creaked. Griffin assisted, and the thing flew upward, powder-fine dust spraying her face. She coughed and sneezed, then glared at the beefy oaf. So intent on what was in the hold, he didn't even notice. He took the stairs two at a time.

She stepped in and closed the door. Darkness devoured them. She shoved up her night-vision goggles and twisted a shoulder lamp on. She took guilty pleasure in the grimace of pain from Griffin, who slapped up his NVGs and glared at her but quickly refocused on two small motorcycles propped against the wall.

Griffin leaned one toward himself, eyed it, then glanced at her. "No key."

Ah, the leather reins thickened in her grasp. She took a slow drag from her CamelBak, turned off her lamp, then flipped back down her night-vision goggles. Who knew if there were weak spots where her shoulder lamp would give them away? Kazi tugged a chain with two keys from under her shirt. "Do you know how to drive one?"

NVGs down again, Griffin snatched the key from her hand. If she could see his eyes, she'd bet he had them narrowed.

With a smile at the ire she'd drawn, she nodded. "Follow me." Straddling the bike, she stuffed the key in the ignition and heard the telltale sigh of grumpiness behind her. She let the bike rip and thrilled at the way she tore down to the end of the narrow, underground passage.

Guided by the lone light of the bike, she maneuvered through the tunnels, aiming straight for the Hamas-held village. If all went well, they'd grab his guy and get out before the first streaks of dawn hit the sky. Her heart raced as she sped toward one dark end after another. Lambert had put her up to a monumental task. Six missions all in one. And with spec-ops guys who knew their business. Which meant, if they'd been caught, the guys after them had known exactly how to take them down.

Which begged the question—did the bad guys know how to stop her?

She cut the engine and let the bike coast toward the exit. At the bottom of the makeshift steps, she eyed the crate. Great, her contact had made good on his deal. She swung a leg over the bike and started toward the wooden box.

Her arm caught. She whipped around, ready to punch.

"Whoa, chief." Griffin held up his hand. "Look." He pointed toward the crate. "It's rigged."

Kazi flipped her gaze to the box. Her heart skipped a beat. Then another. *No!* She darted to it, her eyes tracing the wiring under a wash of green. Resisting the urge to kick the wood and blow them to kingdom come, she took a step back. Schooled her reaction.

Think it through. Think it through.

"How far to the camp?"

If she told him, he could abandon her. Leave her to die.

He scowled. "How far?"

She lifted her head, heavy with the helmet.

Griffin's shoulders seemed massive under the NVG monochromatic display. *He* seemed massive. She didn't need broad daylight to know fire flashed through his eyes. "Tell me the plan," he said through gritted teeth.

"I'll tell you what you need to know."

"And I need to know what we're doing."

"Only as I say." She stood tall, refusing to back down.

"Who do you think I am?"

Defensiveness rose swift and solid, erecting an impenetrable fortress. "I don't really care who you are. I don't know you from Adam, and that means you're someone who can get caught. You're someone who can spill his guts when they cut off your ear. You're someone who can get me killed because your mouth leaks."

His head cocked to the side. "Baby Girl, I'm black ops, former Marine—Special Operations Command. The best of the best. Thirteen years. I'm trained to resist interrogations. You think I ain't never been captured? Never been tortured?" He pivoted and hiked up the back, right side of his shirt. A long discoloration glared back. "They tried to take a piece of me." He bent toward her, pointing to the scar on his neck. "Played 'how deep can the knife go before it would sever my head.' "

Kazi swallowed. His dossier didn't mention captivity or torture. Then again, much of his file had been blacked out. As he spun away, her anger leached out, squeezing her heart.

No. Not her heart. She didn't have one.

"So you're black ops. You still have a mouth. If they find me, I'm dead. If they discover my contacts, your benefactor and all your friends are dead." She stuffed her hands on her hips. "Is that what you want?"

"The plan, Kacie. I want the plan." He stopped. "What happens if *you* die? I'm stuck and have no way to get Aladdin or any of the others. I need to know what the game plan is so we can move without hesitation." He stepped forward. "I'm not here to steal your thunder. I want my men—alive. I want to go home to my family—alive." Veins bulging along his temples, he took another step. "This isn't a power grab, so stop acting like I'm the bad guy and tell me the plan!"

Tell me the plan? With him yelling at her? Sorry, Mr. Big-and-Bad, it didn't work that way. She started toward the door.

"Never worked on a team, have you?"

Foot on the first step, she paused.

"See, me and my boys, we a team. We talk to each other, depend on each other. That keeps us alive, know what I mean? Makes us friends. No, more than friends—*brothers*."

She hesitated at the emotion pulsing through his words and glanced to the side. "I'm an orphan." Without meeting his gaze, she climbed another rung.

Behind her, boots scratched against the tunnel floor. A light touch on her arm forced her to look at Griffin—thank goodness he had his helmet on or she'd cave faster than a tiger trap.

"*We* are a team, Kacie. You and me."

Being a team meant depending on someone else. That wasn't going to happen. "If the weapons cache is rigged, it means my plan's screwed. It means we're going to get caught."

CHAPTER 8

Baby Girl had issues. But that was all right by him. Griffin took hold of her arm and swung her around, simultaneously shifting until they stood almost nose-to-nose. Okay, nose-to-chest. For a woman who had more fight than most men he knew, she came in a tiny package. Even now, holding her arm, he was aware that his hand nearly engulfed her entire bicep—which was toned and stretched taut.

If he could see her eyes, Griffin knew there'd be fire pouring out of them. Under the glow of the moon, her white-blond hair seemed a halo. An angel stood before him.

"Kacie," he said, keeping his tone low but firm. "There's a reason Lambert had you get me out first." His heart pounded as she looked up at him, the moonlight reflecting off her milky-white complexion. She was determined to keep him under her control. That was okay. If she needed that, he knew how to work her to get what he wanted. "Promise me this—since you can't give me your whole trust, then just give me a leg."

She drew her head back. "What?"

"An elephant can only be eaten one bite at a time. So—just give me a leg." He nodded. "I need that—to know you've got my back and I've got yours. That if I go forward, you've got my six. Together, we work together, or we're done before we get started."

Man he hated her wearing those NVGs. Couldn't see what her eyes were doing, what her expression was. What was she thinking? What kept this woman bound so tight in a cage of fear? That's what everything boiled down to, right? Fear—fear of failure, fear of being hurt. And he had this really whacked need to know what made this woman tick, what hurt her so bad that she stared at him now as if he'd stepped off a Martian ship.

"Fine. A leg."

He resisted the smile, knowing it'd probably set her off.

"But know, so help me God, that if you double-cross—"

"*God* will help us, Baby Girl. He will."

"I need someone I can touch—or punch, not a God who hides out in heaven while we run amok on this planet."

He pressed a finger against her lips. "We're wasting time. Tell me the plan."

A curt nod. Her arm lifted, her gaze still locked on his, as she pointed east of their present location. "Less than a kilometer over that rise is the village."

"How many people?"

"At least a hundred Hamas. Their wives and children, too, that we know of."

"And who's 'we'?"

Her lips stretched taut. "That's not part of the leg."

"Okay." He planted one hand on his tactical belt and dragged the other over his face, already feeling the stubble. "Where's Aladdin being held?"

She nodded to the left, and he followed her out of the tunnel into the night. They went to their knees and crawled a few paces before flattening themselves against the sand. Hauling herself into position, she pointed out across the road to the village.

Shoving himself into place, Griffin eyed the location.

"Center map, see the antennae?"

Thanks to the advanced technology, the scene lit up and seemed closer. He focused on the building sprouting wire like a naked tree in winter.

"Two structures to its nine o'clock, a large squat building—it's an abandoned school. Two levels: ground and basement. Intel has your guy in the basement."

Scanning through the puke-green imagery, Griffin traced the perimeter, noting the heavy guns. "They're prepared for a fight."

"Just watch, grid red three—your upper left."

And he did. For the next fifteen, they remained belly-down on the rocky location. A sentry made its patrol, then returned to his location. Then the guard who held red three paced near a door. An arm reached out from the stairwell that descended into the dwelling. The guard went down. His booted feet dragged out of view. Who had—?

Griffin started to pull away the binoculars.

"Red two," Kacie said.

He had barely zoomed in on the location before the second guard vanished.

"It's time."

He shoved his mind and body into action, hustling down the incline to the city, following her lead. Either she'd bought out someone or had someone on the inside. Regardless, they were one roadblock less on the highway to recovery.

Boots crunched as he rushed toward the village. He slammed his spine against the first dwelling, taking position beside Kacie. He tapped her shoulder, indicating his readiness. She bolted ahead, then flanked left.

Griffin shouldered his weapon as he snaked through the winding paths of the village. He hated this—had seen this mazelike tangle snaking between homes and buildings in combat before. Clearing a village. Routing radicals. Seizing terrorists.

Following her with the aid of his NVGs felt much like following a firefly—her movements quick and agile. But his mind was on Aladdin. The guy had ticked him off more times than his sister, but he was part of Nightshade. That meant family.

Mind traipsing through the horrendous field of torture methods he'd seen and experienced firsthand, Griffin could only pray Aladdin was alive. The man had a resiliency that Griffin admired from day one, but even he knew what these extremists were capable of when hatred drowned their sense.

A man stepped out from an alley.

Kacie launched at him.

Griffin flicked his finger off the trigger—had he not, he would've shot the only person who knew exactly where Aladdin was and how to get him out.

In the space of two heartbeats, she had the guy out cold. She hauled him back into the alley and waved Griffin onward. Pace quickened, they rounded several corners.

Gotta be getting close.

As he took a hard left, Kacie stopped short.

Griffin rolled to the side to avoid knocking her into the open. Across a stretch of road wide enough for two cars to narrowly pass, he saw the building. Tucking his focus into a tight ball, he steadied his mind.

A scream shot through the night.

Kacie jerked.

Though she didn't look at him, Griffin read the body language. Drawn shoulders, hands to the side. Shoulders bunched. Ready for a fight. Which told him something in her plan had gone wrong.

Two shadows coalesced in the main doorway of the building.

Griffin sighted and fired with the silenced weapon. Once. Twice.

Thump.

Thump.

Kacie bolted across the street.

Staring down the barrel of his weapon, he hurried after her, aching for his team, for the reassurance of the bound-and-cover techniques they'd perfected. The precision with Frogman and Cowboy never missing a beat, seeing what needed to be done yet remaining cohesive and lethally effective.

Kacie tugged one of the men out of view. Holding the other man's shirt, Griffin dragged him back into the building. He flipped up the NVGs as the glare of fluorescents nearly blinded him. Inside, he crouched and swept his weapon around as his vision adjusted. But Wonder Woman was already halfway down the hall.

About to step into the open, he hesitated as a steel door at the far end groaned open.

Kacie did some sort of wicked somersault, launched into the air, and grabbed an exposed pipe. She swung herself up around it, straddled the pipes, then balanced her feet on it and waited in a tight crouch in the three-foot crawl space.

What was she, Spider-Man's sister?

Boots squeaked on the vinyl floor, nudging Griffin into the shadows as he locked his attention on the man stalking toward him. Voices skidded into his awareness. No, not *voices*. A voice. The man was on a cell phone.

About to take the guy out, Griffin noted Kacie's signal. *Don't shoot?* Was she crazy? If he didn't—

The man pivoted, punched a door open, and disappeared.

When the door shut, Griffin stepped out and scowled at Kacie, who dropped to the ground, knees bending as they absorbed the shock of her landing.

"What was that?" he whispered.

Without answering, she hurried through the first door the man had entered. They eased their way through, cleared left and right. Griffin's stomach lurched. A stairwell. Nothing said booby trap like a stairwell. Muzzle sweeping up, down, right, left, he eased himself down the stairs. Wonder Woman didn't seem so confident here either. Maybe she realized the danger, or maybe she knew something he didn't.

The thought held Griffin on the landing. Just past her, he spotted a steel door. What was beyond it?

More voices.

Griffin glanced back to the top of the stairs. Definitely coming that way.

"Psst!"

He darted a look to Kacie.

She slid across the landing and flattened herself against the wall, bobbing her head toward the door next to her.

Both doors? People coming through both doors? His heart rapid-fired. They were as good as dead!

Only as he leapt toward her, caught her hand, and whipped her around, did it register with Kazi that men were coming from both doors. Riddell spun her around and tucked her into the dank corner beneath the upper stairwell. Pressed into the darkness, his bulk shielding her, she closed her eyes.

This was too familiar. Too. . .

No, don't think about it. It's a job. You're in control.

She clenched her fingers at her side, mentally pushing herself away from his large frame. Focused on listening to the two men who'd just stepped into the fire well. A stream of Arabic flowed through the space, echoing. Leader informed Minion they were on schedule. That nothing unusual had come up. But Minion informed him the sentries hadn't reported in for their last patrol.

"I'll check on them." Team Leader spun and stormed up the steps.

Griffin lunged and reached through the stairs. He caught the man's ankles and yanked hard.

Realizing Griffin's intention, she launched at Minion. Leapt into the air and slammed her feet into his chest. Even as she did, she heard the loud *thwack* of Leader's head hitting the steel-grate steps.

Minion flopped back like a rag doll, no doubt wondering if he'd ever breathe again. His head snapped back—right into the stair support. *Crack!* He dropped hard.

Within seconds, she and Griffin were in the bowels of the facility.

Again, he caught her hand and tugged her toward the open door. "Let's move. Check over there, and I'll cover this. Find him and rendezvous back here."

Kazi jerked free. Took a step back.

Legend stopped and looked at her, confusion rippling through his brow.

He couldn't seize control. "This is my mission. We do this on my terms."

His jaw went slack. "You *got* to be kidding me."

She hardened her expression and stood firm.

He raised his hands. "Fine. Aw'ight." He motioned toward the door. "Can we go save my man now. . .Majesty?"

Anger tightened her chest.

"What?" Legend covered his mouth, gaped, then placed it over his chest. "Did I forget to bow? My bad. Here. . ." With a grand, sweeping motion, he bowed. Craning his neck at her, he cocked his head. "*Now* can we go?"

Heat poured into Kazi's face and neck. Two-handed, she shoved him. "This a game to you, Legend? Or did you get that name by being a legendary pain in the—"

"My man." He pointed to the door, nostrils flaring. "Now."

"You're going to get us killed." She rushed past him into the long, narrow corridor. The holding area should be straight ahead, well guarded.

But it wasn't.

She slowed, reaching for the handgun holstered at her thigh.

Legend frowned, signaled for her to ease back away from the door. He retrieved a canister, pulled a ring, then nodded at her.

Silently, she indicated with her fingers, Three. . .two. . .now!

She jerked open the door.

Legend tossed the flash-bang.

Tink-tink-tink.

Shouts erupted.

Boom!

Shielded from the concussion, she and Legend waited a two-count.

The door flung open.

Griffin kicked it back, ramming the steel into the man's face. The guy wobbled, then slumped to the ground. Griffin grabbed the door and yanked it open. Kazi rushed into the room.

Plumes of green smoke rose like a poisonous vapor reaching toward the low-slung ceiling. A light popped. Glass rained down.

Thwat! Thwat!

Knowing Griffin went left, she aimed right—

A dark form rose out of the green smoke.

She went for her weapon.

Thwat! Thwat!

The form seemed to be sucked back into the vapor. Only as he vanished did it register that someone had shot the person. She glanced back and spotted Legend, who turned and engaged with another guard. Had he shot the guy?

"Find him," Legend shouted.

Right. Kazi pivoted and scanned the long, rectangular room. Pipes snaked across the ceiling, intersecting and bypassing pendant lights—which were out, thanks to her contact who'd cut the power. As she held the weapon up, staring down the sights, she moved through the smoke. She stepped over a body, then skirted a table bolted into the ground. The floor dipped down, which told her most likely a drainage area—waterboarding?

Okay, so where was the objective?

She licked her lips and scissor-stepped, her senses pinging. As the haze cleared, she turned a slow circle, probing every dark crevice and object. To her right, she heard Legend's boots squeak as he approached.

Her gaze struck his.

M4 at the ready, he scoped the area. The right side of his lip was fat and bloodied, but he didn't seem to notice or care. His focus was singular. He wanted his guy back. "Where is he?"

Kazi took one more look around the room. "He's not here." The confession felt as if she'd sprung a leak in a tanker, her hopes sinking.

Like a storm moving in off the coast, his expression went from terse to hurricane-strength fury. "What do you mean? You said—"

She stomped to the far end then back to the middle. "This doesn't make sense."

"You're right it doesn't. I trusted you—"

Clang. Clang.

"Why did I ever think—?"

"Shut up."

Clang.

Acholi, Uganda

The shout felt like a sucker punch to the chest. Scott grabbed Ojore's shirt and propelled him back the way they'd come, away from the suit chasing them. Bake to safety. Back to where Scott had some semblance of control and wasn't facing yellowcake contamination. Sprinting through the tunnels, he listened to the chaos erupting behind them. Ojore stumbled, but Scott caught his shirt again, hauling him upright.

Something spiraled past his head.

Sparks flew off the rock edifice. Scott blinked at the machete that had narrowly missed his temple. He kept moving and retrieved the weapon, then bolted toward the gate.

They both dove into the mine's wire cage. Ojore slammed the gate shut and punched the button as Scott faced out, one fist tight around the handle of the machete, the other curled into a ball. All his training, all the years of combat. . .gave him the courage to face the battle.

But not Dembe.

He blinked at the intrusion of that thought. The shouts trailing them and the slow ascent of the elevator guaranteed they'd have trouble topside.

Braced for fighting, Scott pressed his spine against the wire side and waited.

As the cage rose and the opening slid into view, Scott grew uneasy at the empty tunnel. He frowned, probing the dimly lit corridor with his determination to seek out trouble before it found them.

"Where are they?" Ojore read Scott's mind.

As quietly as possible, he eased the cage back, his gaze never leaving their path to freedom. Adrenaline drenched his muscles. *God, go before us and prepare the way. . .*

Scott stepped out with one foot. He eased the boot down and

83

shifted, cocking his head to one side, then another. It made no sense, but the tunnel was empty.

He motioned to Ojore to exit. They walked close to the wall, covering their six so no one could jump them. At the L-shaped intersection, Scott held up a hand to Ojore. He eased the tip of the machete into the light and into the open, watching the dulled tip for indication of movement.

Nothing.

Holding the machete with both hands, he stepped around the corner. Eerily quiet. And again, empty. He frowned. A flicker to the side spun him in that direction.

The man behind the counter ducked, shaking his head. He didn't want trouble. Wouldn't stop them. Scott reached for Ojore and grabbed empty air. Where. . .where had he gone? Scott spotted Ojore's shrinking form racing toward the mouth of the tunnel. Toward freedom.

Just like I did. When nobody had bothered to help him find a way out of an abusive father's hold, he'd found his own.

Scott realigned his thinking. Shoved aside the specter of the past trying to overtake him. What was wrong with him? He hadn't thought about his brother in years. Why now?

And the mine. . .the breath of hell itself seemed to breathe down their necks. Something was wrong. Very wrong. The thought haunted Scott all the way back to their village and into the night. It'd been too easy to escape. Easy meant someone was cheating. And it wasn't them.

That night in his hut, unease knotted his gut as questions pummeled him. Who was that American? What was he doing in Uganda? No, worse—how had he hidden the yellowcake mining? Did the Ugandan government know about that? What about the UN and United States?

Over the years, as Scott had embraced his fledgling faith and entered Uganda not as a soldier but as a missionary—unofficially—he'd felt the hand of Providence on him. Protecting him. Guiding him. And right now he knew he needed to make contact with someone who could get this information into the right hands. But. . .who?

The *who* didn't matter if he couldn't get to a sat phone. Scott dropped back against the mattress and groaned. That meant going to the peacekeepers. Which meant he'd have to see Dembe.

He'd rather step on an IED.

CHAPTER 9

West Bank

He'd kill her. They'd come all the way into enemy territory only to find out it was a trap. Or a ruse. Either way, it didn't get Nightshade back.

Clang. Thud.

Griffin shifted toward the noise just as Wonder Woman darted toward a bay. Behind a metal gurney, she crouched. Checking their six, he made sure they weren't going to get ambushed. Then he turned and hunched closer.

Light flashed through his NVGs. He grunted and jerked away, flipping up the lenses. When he looked back, he found her digging her fingers into the wall.

"Help me. He's in here."

Heart in his throat, Griffin leaped into action. At her side, he coiled his fingers around the grate. "Aladdin. That you?"

"Yeah. . ."

The faint answer was enough to reignite Griffin's hope. With a hard yank, he freed the grate and tossed it aside. "Watch our backs," he said to Kacie. He used the SureFire and gauged Aladdin's position. "You stuck?"

"No." The man's blue-green eyes peeked at him, then cringed at the light and jerked away. "Just. . ." A hand extended. "Help me."

Clapping the guy's wrist, Griffin wrapped his hand around his forearm. Banging ensued as Aladdin freed himself from the vent. Tugging him to his feet, Griffin noticed he was light—featherweight. "Got your land legs?"

He traced the beam over the assassin. Bone thin, face gaunt, Aladdin nodded—reached for the gurney behind him as he swayed.

"Did they put you in that vent?"

Aladdin shook his head.

"What were you doing in there then?"

Another small smile. "A lot of people want me dead. When I heard the commotion and flash-bang, I didn't know who was coming. A nurse who was soft on me helped me in there, then she escaped." His gaze drifted to Kacie, and he studied her for a long while. Something shifted in his expression.

Noises drew them out of the reprieve. "We'd better move," Griffin said.

"That way." Aladdin drew himself straight.

"He's right," Kacie said. "It's a back route that should be less populated." She looked at Griffin as she nodded at Aladdin. "Help him. He's emaciated and dehydrated."

"You think I don't know that?"

"I'm fine." Aladdin stiffened. He took a step, and his leg gave out.

Hooking an arm around him, Griffin's awareness of how bad Aladdin's situation was hit him full force. "You know—"

"This changes nothing." Aladdin swallowed, sweat dotting his upper lip and brow.

"You're learning, assassin." Griffin took a few steps, heading toward the exit. Ahead, Kacie opened the door. She checked the passage, then gave them the all-clear. He aided Aladdin into the tight corridor. Two-deep, their shoulders nearly scraped the cement walls as they shuffled on. Aladdin's right side dipped and his foot dragged.

He jerked himself upward and shook his head. Coughed.

Though Griffin wanted to ask how he was doing, he wouldn't put him on the spot. Wouldn't embarrass him in front of the girl. Heck, even he was embarrassed at the way she moved through the tunnels while they both labored to keep going.

"Where is everyone?" *Scritch. Scritch. Scrrrritch.* Aladdin stumbled. Caught himself. Straightened and continued.

"Same mess like you." Griffin frowned at the sloppy gait—the man had been the epitome of stealth in their earlier days, so whatever was wrong, whatever happened to him here, he would need some serious medical treatment. Griffin trained his gaze and attention on the door at the end of the hall. Though roughly twenty feet, it felt like half a mile.

Aladdin grunted. "I'm sor—"

"Quiet." The guy didn't need to expend energy talking when walking seemed to take every ounce of effort. He'd offer to do a fireman carry and get them out in double-time, but the humiliation would do the guy in. Still—it was humiliation or dead.

Kacie stood at the end, watching. She looked at the door, then back to them, clearly torn.

"Find a vehicle," Griffin hissed as they made the halfway point.

Eyes wide, she nodded. Then disappeared out the door.

Shouts spiraled from their six.

Aladdin's grip tensed.

"Just keep moving," Griffin mumbled, his focused trained solely on making it to the door.

"Stop."

"No time."

"Stop," Aladdin growled. When Griffin hesitated, Aladdin shifted around behind him, used a strap to tie his hand into Griffin's vest, then hooked an arm around his chest. "Go."

Surprised at the man's quick thinking, Griffin shifted his M4 into both hands. He pivoted with the assassin strapped to his back and trained his weapon on the opening they'd just come through. A few feet farther and two men manifested in the hole.

Griffin eased back on the trigger. Once. Twice.

One guard dropped. The other jerked out of sight.

Griffin bent forward, arching his spine and lifting the assassin off his feet. Hurriedly, he back-stepped toward the exit, toward the route Kacie had disappeared through. His heart hiccupped at the thought of sending her off to find a vehicle. What would keep her from running and saving her own hide, leaving them to get killed?

Why'd he trust a spy? She clearly had no compunction against breaking someone out of a maximum security prison. She didn't even know—or care!—whether he was guilty. What kind of person doesn't care?

Aladdin drew in a sharp breath. Slapped a hand on Griffin's vest and yanked hard. The move spun him around. As his body pivoted, Griffin saw the muzzle of a weapon poke toward him.

It was too late. He knew as soon as he lifted the weapon that he'd never get a round off before the gunman.

Crack!

The man stumbled forward.

Griffin stilled, his mind ablaze. Then he saw the red splotch spreading over the uniform as the guard slumped to the floor at his feet.

Blond hair flashed into view. "Move. Now. We have a truckload of trouble coming our way."

Half dragging Aladdin to safety was slowing them down to the point of detriment. With a roll of his shoulder, Griffin reached back and hooked a hand under Aladdin's thigh. He hoisted him onto his shoulders. Let the guy hate him for embarrassing him.

Hustling sideways was the only way to avoid banging Aladdin's skull against the walls, but they made quicker time. When they broke out into an alley, he stopped short. Darkness enveloped them. Where was the car? He looked around, his vision adjusting to the lack of light.

Kacie stood to the side, holding something.

No. Not something. A piece of junk motorbike.

"Are you crazy? Three people won't fit on that."

"I know."

Griffin scowled. So, she was going to abandon them?

"Take the road out of town. Two klicks east there's a house, half blown. Meet there."

"Where are you going?"

She flashed her eyes at him, the light from the side of the building catching the whites. "Get him on there and move!"

Griffin clamped his jaw tight as he shuffled to the bike, then eased Aladdin to the ground.

"I'll kill you for that," the assassin hissed.

"It was my pleasure." Griffin bobbed his head. "Get on." He held the bars as Aladdin drew a leg up over the back. Then Griffin straddled it. He glanced around.

A Muslim woman flitted past them, long fabric billowing like phantoms of the night. Blue material wrapped her head.

Griffin ducked.

"One hour," said the Muslim—no, it was *Kacie*.

How—how had she done that?

"Wait." Griffin grabbed for her. "No! I'm not leaving you."

She scurried into the darkness, the shadows eating her form and blending her into its darkness. Everything in him ordered him to stay, protect her, not leave her side till they were all safely out of the city.

"She'll be okay," Aladdin said. "She's made for this stuff."

Surprised at the man's words, Griffin probed the shadows, the alleys, the buildings for a sign of her. But she was gone. He cranked the engine on the bike, skimmed the shadows once more, then raced into the night.

"I'm not leaving you." Sweet sentiment.

A lie told by every man she'd met.

Yeah, should've known this guy wouldn't be any different. Regardless, it was the best choice they had. She couldn't find anything but the bike for transportation, and Aladdin had to be transported to safety.

Phase one—complete. Now to give Lambert an update.

Kazi slunk through the dark alleys. As she hustled, she kept her head down but her gaze out. A woman out after curfew meant death, no matter who she was or why she was out. Which was why Kazi had to hurry, get to Tariq's before being spotted or before the swarm of police descended on the facility where she'd just freed a man wanted in a dozen countries.

Lights, people, and cars grew in number as she neared the hub of the city. That was good. She could hide better. Yasir had the great fortune of being held captive in a city familiar to her. She'd been able to work her channels and dig him out of the muck.

But that was also part of the problem—here people knew her. Knew her face. Could recognize her and remember her comings and goings. So, getting back to her objectives could put those very same people in grave danger.

She crossed the street and entered the hotel.

Tariq looked up from behind the counter, and his eyes widened. "Noor!"

"*Salam,* Tariq." She inclined her head in respect.

"It's been awhile." He reached under the counter and retrieved a key. *"Eshtaqto elaiki."*

"And I have missed being missed." She clutched the key, thanked him, and hurried for the stairs.

"We are having falafel in the morning. Don't be late for breakfast." He winked and went back to his computer.

Kazi took the steps two at a time, her heart racing. Tariq's reference to the falafel warned her that someone was looking for her. *Already?* How did they know? There was no way. . . . In the room, she locked the door and bolted it. Then she hurried to the far corner where a desk hugged the wall. With great care and quiet, she moved it aside. On her knees, she used her mostly broken fingernails to dig in between the plaster and the molding. She pressed harder and finally—*click!* She pried the wood back. It opened like a stiff drawer. There she retrieved a wad of paper and three passbooks.

Kazi stuffed the panel back, returned the desk to its place, then lifted the chair and carried it to the other side of the corner. On it, she reached up and loosened an air vent. She tiptoed up and stretched, her fingers coiling around nylon straps. With a tug, she freed a bag. It flopped into her arms.

In minutes, Kazi had changed into jeans and a black T-shirt. She strapped the HK USP Compact around her waist, then donned the jacket. She lifted the brick-of-a-phone and dialed.

"Tell me you have good news."

"I do not." Kazi ignored the hiss on the other end of the line. "I have Aladdin. He is not good."

"Just get him back here."

"That will be impossible. He is more dead than alive."

"Then I guess you do not want your money."

She ended the call, a winter storm moving over her heart. She'd been played and manipulated all her life. If men wanted something, they bought it. Roman wanted the farm. He bought it. With her soul.

She swung around and dropped hard on the bed, the springs creaking. How did one get a half-dead assassin, wanted by just about every EU and Middle Eastern country, out of one hostile country into another?

Shouts preceded feet pounding the stairs.

Kazi punched to her feet. Nothing was ever easy, but just once, she'd like a break. And not in her back. Pack slung over her shoulder, she hoisted up the window and climbed out. Clinging to the ledge, she toed the window closed and then inched along the facade and around the corner. To her left, she spied a truck. And grinned. It belonged to the police—but unmarked—and they'd left the door open and the engine running. *It can't be that easy, can it?*

She hurried along, fingers digging into the cement, which tore at her flesh, then eyed the spot and stepped off. As she did, light ripped through the alley. Kazi landed in a crouch. Shoved herself into the shadows.

Three men burst out a side door to Tariq's.

Gauging whether they spotted her and their distance from her,

Kazi knew she had little time. And less luck. Even if she could get into the truck, which she needed to get Legend and Aladdin out of here, she could never escape without being shot at or killed.

But they hadn't seen her yet. That was her advantage. All she had to do was sneak into the truck and voilà!

Of course, she knew better than to believe it'd be that easy. She'd lived too long and seen too much. Nothing ever went as planned. Which is why she had to be quick on her feet in more ways than one.

Nimble and low, she scuttled around the vehicle.

Crunch. Crunch.

Kacie dropped and rolled under the vehicle. With the engine running, the heat radiating from it felt like a warm sauna. As she waited, the darkness from the hotel vanished.

Feet crunched. The two men conversed.

Oh no.

They'd given up. Decided she wasn't there.

She watched, her stomach in her throat, as both men came to the vehicle and climbed in. *Thunk. Thunk.* The underbelly of the SUV dropped closer. The engine revved.

CHAPTER 10

Abandoned House,
Outskirts of West Bank

Unnerved didn't come close to what churned through Griffin's chest. Alone with a former assassin who looked to be Death's best friend right now and dependent on a covert operative with serious issues—*what* was he thinking?

And taking shelter in a home that only had two of four walls intact and no electricity. . . ? The dwelling must've been hit during a raid or something, because the furniture lay scattered across what was probably once the living room. In the back, he spied a wall with a torn curtain. A bedroom?

Aladdin tensed and gritted through a grunt as he pitched forward.

Griffin hooked an arm around the man's waist and led him over the open area to the curtained doorway. "Almost there."

With a hand fisted over his midsection, Aladdin said nothing, his every focus on putting one foot in front of the other. Only then did Griffin notice the blackened spot on his shirt. What good had it done to come after Aladdin in this shape? He wasn't any benefit to them like this. Of course, Griffin had always debated the assassin's usefulness to the team anyway. But that wasn't fair considering the situation.

They step-dragged through the doorway, and Griffin nodded at the lumpy mattress on the simple bed pressed against the wall. "Here we go." He angled Aladdin so the man could ease down.

But instead of easing, Aladdin dropped. Hard. The assassin's head bounced.

Griffin tensed. That had to hurt.

Aladdin groaned, twisted away, and curled onto the mattress.

He needed a doctor or surgeon. *No, a miracle worker.* And they had nothing. No water, no medicine. All their supplies were buried several klicks away.

Griffin stood over Aladdin, watching. Feeling completely useless.

"Going to watch me die," Aladdin said, a sweaty sheen covering his face. He coughed and lifted a knee toward his stomach, as if to ward off the pain.

"What'd they do to you?"

Agony weighted Aladdin's lids as he looked at Griffin for a second. Then closed his eyes and swallowed. "Nothing I can't"—another cough—"handle."

"Then why you so messed up?"

"Blood poisoning." He lifted his hand that covered a dark spot on his shirt. "I was shot"—cough—"at the Shack during the attack."

The attack! Griffin dropped to a knee. "The others, did they make it out?"

Rumbling quivered through the night. Griffin paused and hurried to the door. Through it, he saw a glint of metal bouncing across the field. He gripped his M4 and peered through the scope. A vehicle. He lined up the sights.

The headlights flashed twice.

Sleek and black, an SUV rumbled, popped up over the foundation of the house, over the debris, and straight into the living area, or what was left of it. Parked, it was effectively hidden from any passersby.

Kacie exited the driver's side, a scratch over her left cheek.

"What happened to you?"

Without a word, she eyeballed him as she moved to the hatch, lifted it, and grabbed a bag. She tossed it to him.

Surprise spiraled through him. She'd retrieved their gear. Baby Girl had more skills than he realized. But it bugged him. Something bad. She'd put herself in danger, had no one to back her up or bail her out.

"You going to stand there staring at me, debating whether to argue, or are you going to save your man's life?"

Griffin curled a fist around the nylon straps of the bag.

Kacie nodded to the bag. "Medical supplies." She pointed to the room. "Dying friend."

Cold-hearted, unfeeling. . . Grinding his teeth, he pivoted and went to work. He slid a wide-bore IV into Aladdin's arm and administered a painkiller that would take the edge off the pain but not off the warrior. Then he slid another one in that pumped antibiotics into his system.

As the drugs spiraled through his veins, Aladdin gradually relaxed. . .then went limp on the rusty pallet.

On his knee and spent, Griffin fought to hold down the power bar he'd eaten earlier as he cut away the soiled shirt and exposed the infected wound. Digging in someone's side and extracting a bullet did a lot to curb a man's hunger. And did little for one trying to hold down his cookies. He dabbed with the sponges, working to cleanse the wound. But something. . .something still wasn't right. He squinted around the swollen angry tissue as blood rushed over it. He reached for a cloth—

"Here."

The soft voice pulled his attention away. Kacie stood beside him, a clean wet cloth in hand. "It nicked an artery. You'll need to stitch it up."

"I know." Griffin worked around the area to find the artery. "This is why I never went to medical school. If I wanted meat to bleed, it'd be beef on a plate. Not a friend dying on a bed."

"So, he *is* a friend?"

Griffin ignored the comment and dug till he found the artery. He clamped it off, then finished cleaning up the wound. As he applied a bandage, he used his shoulder to swipe away the sweat dribbling down his face. "You're supposed to wipe my face."

"What?"

He stitched the wound up, his gaze never leaving it. "You know, like in the movies. The nurse and the doctor—you're supposed to blot my brow as I work."

"What, then we fall madly in love?"

"I like options, know what I'm saying?"

"How about I dump a bucket of water over your head instead?"

Grinning, Griffin pushed away from the bed and turned, hands raised and bloodied. "Don't think you could reach."

"There's more than one way to take a man down." Though Kacie stood at least a foot shorter, her attitude made up for it and stared him square in the eye. She toed a bucket of water on the floor. "Wash up." She spun around and strode into the other room. "We need to talk."

Scrubbed clean, he would never be able to wash away the images of seeing Aladdin in that condition. The nimble, stealthy man nearly dead. Even with the bullet removed and wound cleaned, there was no guarantee they'd gotten to the sepsis in time to stop it.

On the other side of the wall, he stilled, taking in what his eyes saw but his mind rejected. A command center, all set up and blinking and bleeping at him. Crates used for a table and chairs. Baby Girl had improvised. Camouflage netting covered the area, and the SUV sat just outside the door to the living area but still inside the house so it wasn't visible to aerial surveillance.

"We need to get out of here."

"He's in no condition to travel."

"We need to move," she said as she rearranged supplies.

"Did you hear what—?"

"If you want to guarantee he dies, we'll stay." She stuffed a duffel into the SUV. "If you want him to have a chance to live, we move."

Griffin pointed to the half-concealed room where Aladdin lay unconscious. "If we *move*, he dies. That wound—"

She snapped around, her white-blond hair appearing as the tips of flames in the darkness. "If they find us here, they won't take time for pleasantries like waterboarding and electrifying interrogations, which is exactly what they've spent the last two weeks doing to him. For you, they'll skip right to swords or Pin the Bullet on the American's Heart." She shoved her fingers through her white hair. "Look. We have to meet a plane in two hours. That is our only way out of here. Trust me, I want your man alive as much as you do, but staying here will get us killed."

Suspicion rippled through him. "What do you know, Baby Girl? What aren't you telling me?"

"They're looking for me—him, your assassin."

He hesitated then slowly shook his head. "You said 'me.' They were looking for *you*? Why?"

"It doesn't matter! We need to get out—now!"

Teeth grinding, Griffin eased back onto the crate, which creaked and cracked beneath him. "He's going to die." The thought burned his conscience. Could he stay here, find a place to hide out. . . ? Yeah, right. A black man hiding an assassin with a sucking chest wound. Aladdin's magic carpet would stall out—permanently. Gaze bouncing over the rocks and pebbles by his boots, he wrestled with making the decision. No, he didn't like the guy, but he didn't want him dead either.

At the crumbling wall, he planted his hands on the cement cinder blocks, dirt and rocks poking against his palms. Less than a week ago, he'd been caged, fighting a lethal case of boredom. Now he was back in action, fighting to save men he'd come to think of as brothers. All those years he'd spent building a reputation of respect. . .all gone. Now he would bear the stigma of not only being a supposed murderer, but an escaped convict. A fugitive of justice.

Fugitive of *in*justice.

"Medic!" a shout came from the kitchen. "We need a medic in here, stat!"

Madyar and Phoenix were in there. What happened?

With every last morsel of strength, Griffin pushed against the carpet pile crushed beneath him. A booted foot stomped down—hard. Griffin ground his teeth against the pain spearing his hand and wrist. The nightmare unfolded right here, in the middle of his living room, with his family. Voices squawked, cartoonish in the haze and ghoulish chaos that swallowed his hearing and thinking.

"Griffin Riddell, you will stand down."

His gaze locked with Dante's. Fury lit within Griffin. He pushed up again.

"Stand down!"

Why did this have to happen in front of the boy?

A hiss pressed into his thoughts.

The tight band that had woven around his mind snapped. He blinked.

Wide beautiful eyes framed by a halo of white stared up at him. "Do you need an extra hand?" Kacie looked down.

Griffin followed her gaze—his hand engulfed her petite one. Her fingertips were almost purple in his grip. He flashed open his hand and released her, startled. "Sorry." That's when her "joke" registered—*need an extra hand?*—and he realized she'd tried to help him save face, ward off the embarrassment of being lost in a bad memory.

Something strange squirreled through her chest as Kazi watched the mountain-of-a-man crumble into a valley of bad memories. Something horrible lurked behind his stoic facade of indifference and machismo.

If he was lost in the past, then he'd get them killed. "Are you with me?" She hated the hard edge to her question, but he had to get it together. Maybe she needed to ditch him, tuck him in a safe house only she knew about, then round up the rest of his adrenaline-junkie friends.

His expression morphed from dazed and confused to humiliated and angry. He nodded.

"Good. Now, please." She stepped back, out of his suffocating presence. "Stop fighting me. I'm not one of your men or part of your team, but I'm on your side."

He scowled. "My side?"

"For now."

Griffin looked at her again, those mahogany eyes unseating her, making her feel like he knew her every secret. Just like Carrick. *Don't let him get to you, Kaz.*

"How do I know when you're not?"

"Oh, you'll know."

He huffed and shook his head, running a hand over his bald scalp. As he pivoted and walked the length of the half-blown-up room, he cupped his hands behind his head. Unwilling to open the floor to discussion again, Kazi resumed packing the supplies. But she needed him *with* her, not just "with" her. If that made sense.

No, it didn't make sense. She knew better than to trust anyone. She'd let Tina in, and look what happened. But this gig with the general bought her out, bought her freedom. "Okay, let's load him."

Kazi followed Griffin into the bedroom. Surprise wormed through her as he lifted the man without a grunt or breaking a sweat and carried him to the SUV. She zipped the assassin into the waterproof sleeping bag and hung the IV drips from the clothing-bag hooks. From another bag, she pulled out a *keffiyeh* and tossed it to Legend. "Suit up."

She donned her own, then slid into the driver's seat. She almost laughed when the entire car canted to the right as Legend folded himself into the passenger side.

"How do your knees taste?" she asked with a laugh.

"Hey." He wedged himself in by closing the door. "This is all muscle, baby. If you'd choose a car that a man could actually fit in. . ."

She turned the engine over. "Tell me what car you *do* fit in, and I'll make it a priority to appropriate one next time."

He eyed her, then clicked his tongue.

The SUV trounced as they pulled out of the dilapidated house and aimed away from the town. "Thought you thrived on this stuff."

Griffin looked out the window, his face stern again. "Yeah, well, that was before. . ."

"Before what? Prison?" Why did she ask? It wasn't her business, and asking personal questions only opened up a sinkhole.

Thankfully, he nodded and let the silence swallow the journey.

Commander Greene, you wanted to see me?"

"Please, come in, Lieutenant." Greene waved the Coastie in. "And give us some privacy, please."

Olin watched as Range Metcalfe shifted to close the door, his gaze lighting on him.

A steel rod seemed to slide down Range's spine and granite overtook his face. "General Lambert." His hands fisted as he shot a look at the commander, then back to Olin. "What're you doing here?"

Greene rose and rounded the desk, hiking a leg up as he leaned back against it. "Have a seat, son."

Robotically, Range complied, though his acidic expression warned he wasn't happy about this setup.

And that's exactly what it was. As much as Olin hated to admit it, he'd used every connection he had left while flying under the proverbial radar to get here and get Greene to help.

"Do you know why I'm here, son?" Greene tugged off his wire-rimmed glasses.

"Fleet and routine inspections."

"Officially, yes." Greene nodded to Olin. "Unofficially, I'm here at Olin's request. This isn't a formal meeting, so let's cut the protocols."

"Okay," Range finally said through clenched teeth. "I have no idea why you're here, General Lambert, but—"

"Your brother has been snatched from American soil by enemy combatants. I believe his life is in grave danger."

Range's lips flattened.

"And while I know you have less than congenial feelings toward your brother, I believe you very much loved Danielle."

He flinched.

"And you should know that the same people who attacked your brother went after Danielle, too."

That drew out a reaction. He scowled. Shifted in the chair.

Olin moved closer to Greene. "Your brother was part of a high-level black-ops group. Their identities were, we believed, concealed. But someone put it together and took out the team."

"Is she okay?"

Olin nodded. "For now."

"Then I think this conversation is over." He punched to his feet.

Greene caught his shoulder. "Hold on there, son. I don't think you understand what this could mean for our country."

"Our country? What, are you going to tell me Canyon's going to save the president? Or stop a nuclear weapon from hitting strategic sites?" Range's sarcasm hung thick on those words. "Please. I know my brother doesn't know that much. He's not that important."

"On the contrary; he has been involved in some of the most secretive and sensitive missions. Remember Mauk? Remember Obigambwe?"

The implication swept across the young man's face, then vanished. "I guess your golden boy proved beneficial."

"He's about to prove dead. And while I know you hate him, I seriously doubt you want him being brought home the way your father was."

Range lunged at Olin, but Greene held him back. "How dare you! My father was a hero. He was the best of the best!" He shoved a finger at Olin. "Don't compare my self-absorbed, coward of a brother with him."

Surprise wove through Olin at the hatred spewing from those words. "Do you realize what Canyon went through to bring Danielle home, *alive*?"

"And what good did that do me?"

"So, your anger isn't because you loved Danielle, it isn't because you wanted what was best for her, but because you were beat out by your brother." He ached, thinking of his daughter in these terms, of a pawn wedged between two brothers. "Then I guess I came to the wrong man. I thought I was coming to a hero."

Blue eyes blazed. "If Canyon is what you call a hero, yeah, I guess I'm not that man."

Ticked, Olin dropped a file on the desk. "If you discover that you wouldn't be able to face your mother again, or see Danielle and your nephew ever again knowing you had a chance to save your brother's life but did nothing because of your own pride and arrogance"—his pulse thumped against his temple—"Greene knows what needs to be done if you grow a conscience."

CHAPTER 11

Unknown Location

Warbling and indistinct, voices swam through the darkness. Taunting. Daunting. Haunting. Fingers reached through the thick fog, clawing at him. Flashes, sparkling—no, it wasn't sparkling, stabbing. Shooting! They were shooting.

Marshall jerked. Pain sluiced through the haze clouding his mind. He groaned and shifted. Brightness flashed against his corneas. He groaned again and turned from the light. Only it wouldn't go away. Why wouldn't it go away? He tried to lift his arm. It wouldn't budge.

What. . .what was wrong? Why couldn't he move?

"Why isn't he awake yet?"

"It takes time."

"But why. . . ?" The voice faded, dancing and wobbling on the edges of a nightmare. Marshall felt the talons of something sinister pulling him down, down. . .down. . .

Secure Underground Facility
Lynchburg, Virginia

"This is ridiculous!"

Ignoring the pain in her side, Sydney Jacobs didn't look up at the woman pacing, holding her wailing newborn son.

"We've been in here two weeks—*weeks!*" Danielle Metcalfe pushed a hand through her long, dark hair.

The first week Sydney had tried reason, encouragement, even her

100

status as "wounded" from getting shot during the escape—anything to help them maintain a semblance of sanity in a facility with no windows, few toys, hard mattresses, and absolutely no visitors. Nobody would tell them why they were here or what was happening. They were alive. And for now, she held on to that thread of hope, thin as it was.

"Is it legal for them to hold us like this?" Piper sat in a chair, her son and stepdaughter playing on the large carpet that anchored the four bays that served as "rooms," if you could call a curtained-off twelve-by-twelve space with a bed and dresser a room.

"Legal or not, we're here. We can't get out, and there's nobody to complain to." Dani laid her tiny, swaddled son in the swing and set it in motion. She shifted and looked around the room. "We have to do something."

"What?" Rel Dighton asked. Her expressive brown eyes and chestnut hair framed a youthful face. "They have cameras, and we're half a mile below ground."

Sydney closed her eyes, thinking about the trip down here. The choppers that ferried them here, the men in tactical gear—so like her own husband—who escorted them into the elevator, then down the elaborate tunnel system, past one secure barrier after another, to this. . .place. A doctor had come and tended the wound in her abdomen—it'd been so close—but other than that, they'd been alone in what could resemble a gymnasium with its semihigh ceiling and a play area, the only good thing about this place with six children in tow.

Chink-chink. Thunk. Hissss.

The sound snapped Sydney's eyes open and to the eight-foot steel barricade that served as the front door. Dani looked at them, then turned to see who had come visiting.

A Marine stepped into the room, glanced around, then stepped to the side. As did another. Then a man in a suit.

"Dad." Dani hurried across the carpet to him. "What's going on? Why are we being kept here?"

The general's presence brought Sydney to her feet.

He pointed to the dining table, a long metal table with bench seats. "Let's talk. I don't have much time."

"Well, we have all the time in the world, apparently." Dani folded her arms.

Sydney joined the other three women and the general. Cold metal made her forearms ache.

"I am truly sorry for the situation as it is, for keeping you here under such conditions," the general said. "It is for your own safety, as hard as that probably is to hear."

"What about our husbands?" Piper asked. "I can endure just about anything as long as I know Colton's okay."

"My brother, too," Rel injected.

The older man's face looked beleaguered. "Little is known. I cannot say much without placing them, all of you, and myself in grave danger. Since I don't know who is responsible, I don't know where the threat lies. That's what I'm working on." He looked down, and something heavy pulled at him.

"General." Sydney touched his arm. "What's wrong?"

Seated, hands folded on the table, he looked at each one, then his gaze rose to the ceiling before dropping back to the table.

Sydney was about to turn and look when she remembered the camera. A tiny black rubber stopper–looking thing she'd noticed the first day they were down here. *Watching and listening. He doesn't even think we're safe here.*

She curled her fingers around his hand and gave a squeeze. "We trust you."

Wizened and experienced eyes met hers. "Have you ever wanted to take a vacation on a deserted Caribbean island, like doubting Thomas did? To relax on a beach and contemplate origin and sky-white clouds?"

What on earth. . . ? The intensity in his eyes bore through his bronzed face carved with hard experience. But there was something else there, too.

"Excuse me," Dani said from the other side of the table, snapping them both out of the moment. "We're in lockup, our husbands are missing, and you're talking about a vacation?" Her voice pitched. "On a *beach?*"

"Of course," he said as he squeezed Syd's hand again then let go. "Terribly inconsiderate. We're in hard times, and I won't always be around, so it's good to be thinking on your feet, Danielle. Well done."

Sydney's pulse skipped a beat. Something was very *off* about the general's visit. She'd never seen him this. . .flighty?

"We are searching for your husbands"—he looked at Rel—"and brother. We will find them." He stood. "I'm afraid I don't have more news, or better news."

"How long are we supposed to stay locked up like criminals?"

The general moved to his daughter's side and leaned down and gave her a hug, whispering in her ear. Sydney's throat tightened at the tears in Dani's eyes. What was he saying? After a kiss on the cheek, he straightened and walked to the door.

"Wait," Sydney said as she rose from the bench. "How long do we have to stay here?"

"It won't be much longer," he said. "Rel, would you come with me, please?"

The twenty-one-year-old joined him, then they both left.

Thunk. Clank. Hisssss.

Somewhere in the Desert of Palestine

Little. Little information. Little respect. Little reason to go on. Little woman, as in, she didn't reach his chin. But he wouldn't underestimate Kacie. In fact, with her quick moves and sassy mouth, he'd want her on his side——any day.

"I'm on your side."

Yet she kept control firmly in her hands.

Hand. . . Humiliation still poked at him over that incident. In the dark of night as the car jounced over the low-lying ravine, which she assured him was the quickest route to the airstrip and the best way to avoid being detected or spotted, his gaze flicked to her hand. Or at least to where he imagined her hand would be—with the instrument-panel lights killed for safety, he couldn't see anything. But he remembered squeezing her hand tight. Had he heard a crack? Or was that just his mind messing with him?

"This pilot we're meeting," Griffin said, staring through the moonlit terrain as they clung to the shadows and crevices as much as possible. "How are you buying his silence?"

"You assume he needs to be bought."

"I assume he'd squeal like a little girl if someone asked him a few questions with the business end of an M16."

She glared at him. "Well, you're wrong."

"And why's that? Why would a man I don't know be willing to put his life on the line to protect me?"

"Do you always talk so much?"

Griffin arched an eyebrow at her. "If you wanted me quiet, you should've told me the plan, told me what's next, so I can be focused on that, not on the fact that I don't know anything."

"Not knowing anything keeps you alive."

"And stupid."

"Like you need my help for that."

Her comment punched the breath from his chest. "You did not just say that." A noise from the rear drew Griffin's attention to Aladdin. Was he okay? He leaned over the back and stretched to see the guy. Though he wasn't sure, Griffin thought there was a smile on the assassin's face. " 'Bout time you woke up and pulled your weight."

Aladdin coughed. "I like her," he wheezed out.

Griffin could relate. "Save your foul breath for breathing. You don't do us much good dead. And not much more alive, but we take what we can."

"IV," Aladdin said, his voice a whisper.

Eyeing the bag, Griffin understood. It now hung empty. "Okay, we'll get you hooked up to a new one in the air."

The man's shaved, bruised, and bloodied head nodded. So weak he couldn't change out his IV, his lifeline. This was bad. Much worse than Griffin realized. He shoved his attention to the road, his nerves clamped tight. Losing the assassin wouldn't be good. They had to get him to a doctor. He peered through the windshield. How far out were they from the chopper?

A flash about a klick to the northeast punched through his thoughts. "Stop!"

Kacie nailed the brakes. The back of the car fishtailed. Rocks crunched and popped. Griffin braced himself as the car skidded to a stop amid a plume of dust.

Seconds later, a bright light ignited the sky.

CHAPTER 12

A curse sailed through the air, and only after the dust and ringing in her ears died down did Kazi realize the word had come from her own lips. She stared at the flickering flames in the distance, her pulse jackhammering.

"Get out of here," Legend ordered.

A loud, painful groan came from behind them.

"Aladdin?" Legend stretched into the back, and when he did, his barrel chest pressed into her personal space. "Aladdin!"

Kazi threw her attention to the flames roaring into the sky.

"Come on, assassin, do your thing, know what I'm saying?" A hand dropped on her shoulder. "Kacie, get us out of here."

She rammed the gear into REVERSE, automatically checked in front of them—and froze. She pulled in a breath and slowly drew forward. There, silhouetted by the flames. . .

"Look!" With both hands she gripped the steering wheel. "It's not the plane that blew up." Defying his order, she shoved the gear into DRIVE and gunned the pedal.

"What. . . ? What're you doing?" Legend dropped back into his seat.

"It wasn't the plane that blew up. It was a car." Her pulse thrummed. If the plane was still there, if it was not going up in flames, then they had a chance. . .

"You better be right about this," Legend said.

She shot him a sidelong glance. "I thought we were sharing legs."

"What?"

"An elephant—one leg at a time." But what did she expect? For him to appreciate her for what she'd already accomplished?

As the car crept farther along the ravine, which slowly ramped up to surface level, she saw the plane intact. A vehicle—Jeep, if the burning hulk was a clue—served as a makeshift bonfire. Or homing beacon. They'd need to board quickly and get airborne before backup arrived.

Movement between the two vehicles made her apply the brake.

"Is that your man?"

"I can't tell."

Legend lifted a weapon, checked the barrel, then reached for the door.

Kazi parked and climbed out. As she reached for her weapon, a tremor of pain in her fingers made her wonder how she'd do pulling the trigger. When Legend had gripped her hand tight, he'd crushed her fingers. He might've cracked one or two, but it wasn't anything debilitating. She'd endured worse.

Her boots crunched over the dry, rocky desert as she closed the distance between her and the plane. Under its belly, she saw feet. Not moving.

She eased around, searching her surroundings. Confident they were alone, Kazi stepped into view. "Kaled?"

He jerked toward her with a raised M16.

She raised the palms of her hands toward him. "Whoa."

Under the tease of the fire, his face bore a sweaty sheen. "Noor, you. . ." Relief loosened the taut expression, and the tension seemed to seep from his pores. He blew out a long, hard breath. "Hurry. There are more coming where they came from."

"What happened?"

Kaled whipped around, his weapon trained on Legend, who quickly—and extremely easily—disarmed her friend. Kaled went into fight mode.

"Kaled, *qef*! Stop. *Sadiq*—he's a friend." Kazi rushed between the two men, who'd gone to blows.

Suddenly, Kaled twisted and dropped.

Kazi plunged toward him. "What did you do?" she shouted at Legend and shoved him with two hands, which had no effect. His hands came up, and after years of being an operative, every muscle tensed at the movement, but. . .he didn't touch her.

"I didn't—"

"Don't"—she pushed him again—"do that"—once more—"again!"

Hands up in the same fashion in which she'd shown hers to Kaled, Legend back-stepped. "I didn't do anything except disarm the man."

Her friend writhed on the ground, reaching toward his back.

Legend squatted. "There's blood on his back—he's been shot."

Kazi darted a look at Legend, then quickly turned Kaled over. Heat bathed her back from the burning car as she sucked in a breath at the stain covering his back.

Kaled groaned and pushed up off the ground. "Is okay." He swayed. "Get me in the plane. Hurry."

For a second she hesitated but also realized they had no other way to get out of here. Gently, she helped him to his feet.

"He *cannot* fly that plane," Legend said. "He'll kill us."

"Do you have a better idea?"

"You can fly this thing."

In his native tongue, Kaled said, "He worries, but I have gotten you out of worse, yes?"

"You always do," she replied in Arabic. They climbed up the four steps, and he stumbled toward the pilot's seat with a hiss and grunt.

Kazi patted him on the shoulder, said they'd be right back. Out in the night, she stormed past Legend to the SUV. "Get your friend. We're out of time."

"You trust him? In that condition? We'll fall out the sky."

"Only if I push you out of the plane." She stomped to the back, opened the rear hatch, and grabbed her pack. "Consider this my next leg."

Greenwich Village
Home of Senate Majority Leader William Parker

Rich and rich alike swirled around the marble floors of the mansionlike home that had belonged to Senator Parker's family for generations. Slinky dresses, ample bosoms, plentiful liquor—it had all the makings of some great elbow-rubbing. Stretching his neck beneath the pale-blue silk tie, Warren Vaughn moved deeper into the crowd.

A delicate touch to his arm slowed him. To the side he found Amberlin Parker giving him a sad smile. "Oh Warren, I am so sorry to hear about your son's accident. We're praying for him."

"Thank you, Mrs. Parker." He nodded and kept moving.

Finally, he spotted the pale-blue curves he'd been looking for and headed that way. He slipped an arm around her small waist.

With a quick intake of breath, Lis turned—and smiled as she eased into his touch. "There you are." Hair up, her neck lay exposed and inviting.

Warren kissed it. "Sorry I'm late."

Lis gestured toward her companion. "I was just talking about all the benefits coming out of your Green World efforts in Uganda, which are spreading throughout other states in Africa."

"Indeed," he said as acknowledgment to Shannon Stanton, a relatively new senator from Texas.

Thick, dark coiffed hair accented her tanned complexion. No doubt Nathan would want to meet the single woman who'd devoted her life to politics. Then again, Nathan would have as much in common with the Republican sweetheart as Warren had in common with his own son.

"It's astounding what you have accomplished through that organization. The infant mortality rate has lowered 30 percent!" Stanton shifted, her black dress elegant yet conservative. "If we could just replicate your success there in other third world countries. . ."

"Getting the necessary medicine and nourishment was the key." Warren lifted a flute of champagne and offered one to his wife and one to Stanton, who refused it. He sipped it slowly before continuing. "The African Affairs subcommittee found a way to do it, and I'm proud to have been a part of it."

"I'd like to sit down with you soon and discuss just how you managed that. The United States has tried for decades without success, but you've done it."

An uneasy feeling squirmed through his stomach. She seemed to be digging. "Maybe one day we can do that."

"Just give me one tip, how did you work it out to get the money to fund all the supplies? What's your secret?"

"Hello, sir."

As dependable as the sands of time. Warren shifted and extended a hand to Nathan Sands, whose sandy-blond hair bore subtle streaks that already showed the toll his role in the Senate had taken over the last ten years since the man had interned with him. "Evening, Nathan."

Nathan inclined his head and nodded.

"Senator Stanton, I'd like you to meet my secret, Nathan Sands. Nate, this is the GOP sweetheart, Shannon Stanton." Warren said, tipping his champagne glass toward her. He enjoyed the flame he detected in her demeanor. She hadn't gotten what she wanted. Good. He'd have to keep his distance.

"It's a pleasure, Miss Stanton," Nathan said as he offered his hand.

"It's *Senator* Stanton," Shannon corrected with a tepid smile. Something flickered over her face, but Warren wasn't quite sure what.

"Excuse me, Senator," Nathan said as he leaned closer to Warren. "Could I have a word with you?" His gaze struck Lis's. "Privately."

"Oh, relax, Nathan." Lis laughed, linked arms with Stanton, then the two sauntered off.

Nathan pointed to the back veranda where a fountain sparkled and tumbled into a large pool that spanned the ornate lawn.

After he set down his glass, Warren trailed his one-time apprentice out into the sultry evening. A breeze danced over the waters, carrying with it the crisp scent of winter.

"What's got you so riled up you'd pull me away from my wife?"

Nathan turned, shoved his hands in his pockets, and cocked his head down. "Sir, I'm afraid. . .that is, I think we might have trouble."

Warren laughed. "Son, we're in politics, remember? Big Trouble is our middle name."

Though it was a joke, Nathan seemed to glower.

They'd taken a really big risk shutting down the black-ops team, but it'd been done—and effectively. The rogue team was operating without official U.S. consent. He knew for a fact that no government agency authorized the missions. They had to be shut down before they damaged U.S. relations with a foreign power. And he had Marshall back. Now maybe he could groom him into something respectable. It wasn't the first leap they'd taken that had paid off, but it wasn't without a few hiccups. He could handle hiccups. "Go on."

"Someone went after the women, the wives of those men."

Warren frowned. "Who would be stupid enough to do that?"

"Sir, they missed a few, and someone managed to kill the mercenaries. Now the remaining women and children are missing."

"I'm not seeing the problem. Seems it cleaned itself up. We have no connection to that incident, son." Warren patted the man's shoulder. "You really need to relax, take things in stride, or that gray at your temple will overtake your head." He laughed, wishing someone had given him that advice twenty years ago.

"Yes, sir. But there's also the village."

"What village?"

"Nkooye village in Uganda."

"Our epicenter." When he'd first visited it, the deplorable situation had literally sickened him. After unloading his lunch behind a hut, he vowed to make changes. But those people, the vacant expressions, the bloated stomachs haunted him. So they applied the Green World, a program he established with Nathan's help to Nkooye first, impacting the villagers' lives and preventing deaths. From there, Warren had been hailed a hero. That success was duplicated in several villages before the wind caught and he sailed to success. The results legitimized his presence in the United States and his position on Capitol Hill and among the Foreign Policy Committee, which he now chaired. It established him as a formidable senator and vaulted him to Senate minority leader. Guaranteed his future.

Warren blinked. "How?"

"The details are sketchy, but preliminary reports suggest some of the villagers got greedy, started a revolt of some kind. They wanted more benefits, more food."

Warren bit down on the curse sitting on the edge of his tongue.

"When the uprising erupted, soldiers went in and quieted them."

Warren's mood darkened. "Quieted them *how*?"

Nathan arched an eyebrow.

They killed villagers. The curse slipped out.

"We were able to put a lid on things—"

"That's not a lid. That's a ticking time bomb that will blow up in our faces!" Weighted by the news, Warren paced. "We need to prep a statement, preempt the negative publicity that will no doubt come out of this."

Green World had been his ticket to the top. Although he'd left most of the details to Nathan, then a stellar attorney with aspirations of seeking a seat on the Hill, Warren had put countless hours into the effort.

"If this hits the news. . .can they blame us?"

"I'm sure they'll try."

"But things were done legally, so we don't have to worry about that." The only element in this whole thing that gave him peace right now. Nathan reassured him years ago that they'd come out squeaky clean.

"Sir, there's more."

He pulled the handkerchief from his breast pocket and wiped his forehead. "What?"

"There's a village about two hours north. One of the women working under Green World was the sister to a woman in this other village. They are making all sorts of accusations, saying the women are being used in slave trades, that the people are selling bodies for goods."

"That's outrageous!" Warren tugged at his tie. "But the authorities are on our side, right? We're returning strength and vitality to the country." When Nathan didn't respond, a chill traced down Warren's spine. "They killed them too?"

Nathan nodded. "Some of the villagers fought back. It was. . .ugly. An American missionary living there—without the consent of the Ugandan government—is the cause. He told them to fight, gave them weapons. He fired the first shot on the soldiers when they arrived to enforce a curfew."

Warren dropped onto a stone bench and cradled his head in his hands. "It can fall apart in a heartbeat." He looked at his friend. "Can they trace this back to us? You said everything traceable would clear us."

"Well yes, on paper." Nathan scrunched his shoulders. "But this missionary, he's former spec ops. He knows his stuff, knows how to survive."

"By all that's holy. . ." Warren shook his head. "It's going to come and bite me in the backside, isn't it?"

"It could. If he is allowed to talk."

"Then let's make sure he can't talk."

Acholi, Uganda

Wraiths. *Black, bloodied, and shrieking, they swarmed around him, taunting. Flitting around, their wispy tendrils traced icy trails down his spine.*

No! Not again. They'd come after him before.

Scott Callaghan took off running. Through cornfields. His legs slogged through the narrow rows, stalks smacking his face as the ghouls gave chase. Don't look back. Don't look back.

He looked back.

Children screamed after him, reaching for him. Crying out to him.

No. . .no. . . He plunged through the shoulder-high stalks, gasping. Mouth dry, eyes filled with sand, he pushed on. Looking for escape.

Something scraped along his hip—a hand, no doubt. Trying to stop him. "Scott!"

With a glance back, he slowed. No way. Not possible. The man looked like him, yet didn't. ACUs camouflaged him in the fields, but not from Scott's trained eye. "Brother?"

"Go, run!" his brother shouted.

Jogging, Scott couldn't stop to look. Disbelief choked his mind. How could his brother have found him? Scott double-checked that he wasn't seeing things. His breath backed into his throat as his brother went down, an ax sticking out of his back.

Horrified, Scott burst into a run. He pressed himself onward. And burst into the bean field. He stumbled, fingers sweeping the dirt and large leaves. Onward. Had to keep going.

"Please, Akiiki!"

Another glance over his shoulder revealed dozens of prepubescent boys. Some missing lips. Some ears. All missing hope.

"No!" Scott lunged upward, sweat drenching his body as he shook off the heavy weight of sleep. He looked around the dark thatched hut. A subtle shift of movement to the side. He snatched up his weapon and blade from either side and aimed them in that direction.

At the tip of the machete, a streak of moonlight glinted off the blade and reflected in the whites of Ojore's eyes.

"Akiiki, hurry," came the urgent whisper. "They're coming."

The fog of sleep vanished. Scott swung his legs over the low-slung metal bed, his mind keen on the young man crouched by the door. They'd been foolish to think they wouldn't be identified. It'd been his earnest desire to keep things low-key, stay off the radar so he could continue helping others. Wouldn't God give him a break?

A sound spiraled through the night, stilling both of them. Rumble. Like thunder. Only. . .it wasn't thunder. Not in the middle of the hot dry season of February.

He lunged for the door and ripped it open.

Whistling spiraled through the air.

Scott spun around and dove on top of Ojore at the familiar sound. "Down!"

Boom!

Screams raped the peaceful night.

CHAPTER 13

USCGC Fallon
Sector San Juan

Y ou know—"

"Please. Don't talk."

"I'm sorry. I thought *I* was the commanding officer on this vessel."

Range Metcalfe swallowed hard and met the gaze of Lieutenant Arianna Connors. They'd gone to school together, and when he'd bailed on staying anywhere around Canyon and requested an assignment on Sector Galveston, she'd won command for Sector San Juan after Browne's promotion.

"Sorry." Range gripped the rail as he stared out over the churning waters. It wasn't too long ago he stood aboard a similar cutter. With Canyon. "Just not. . .in the best frame of mind." He shot her a glance and a halfhearted smile. "I'm tired of hearing platitudes and lectures on how and why I should be doing this. How I should just forget how he betrayed me."

She pursed her lips and nodded, then leaned against the rail. "I was here, ya know, when your brother was aboard."

Range shot her a look, tension knotting the muscles at the base of his neck.

Arianna was undeterred. "I could tell you two were at odds, but there was something. . .deep between the two of you."

"Deep hatred."

"That, too." She laughed a nice laugh that seemed in sync with the waters the cutter sluiced through. "Look, rumors get around—"

He straightened. "This is why I said not to talk."

"Well, I guess it's a bad habit, being commanding officer, that I don't take orders from those under me in rank."

Low blow. He'd taken a demotion to get Galveston. It'd been the farthest he had been willing to relocate at the time. Someone else landed Alaska, and California had no openings.

"Listen." She touched his arm, her brown hair snapping against her face. "Don't let it eat you, Range. I remember the quiet kid back in the academy. Back then, I saw a young, handsome, promising Coastie."

His heart pounded with the waves.

"Now I see a man willing to throw away everything, just so he can cling to bitterness."

Bitterness? Yeah, maybe that was what coiled his stomach in knots. *Disregard.*

She didn't know what Canyon had done. How he'd ripped the heart right out of Range. "That's pretty easy to say for someone who has sailed through life."

Arianna shifted and leaned back against the rail, the sun twinkling in her eyes. "I guess it might be. But the only sailing I've done has been in Hawaii." With one eye pinched closed, she looked up at him. "Not to belittle your pain, but. . .she's not the only fish in the ocean, Range."

With that, Arianna pushed off the rail and left.

What did that mean?

Did it even matter? He was out on a fool's errand and would most likely end up dead. He'd even told Greene this was asinine because he wasn't spec ops like Canyon. He was a Coastie, trained in water maneuvers and rescue. Not land rescues.

And yet, here he was, about to sacrifice it all for a brother who nuked him.

Somewhere over the Middle East

There was only so much a man could be expected to tolerate and not lose his good mind. *And we are way past that.* Back pressed against the interior of the small plane, Griffin sat with his feet all but pressed to his hind parts, the toes of his boots touching Aladdin's ribs. Sardine in a can came to mind, but since he didn't eat the nasty things. . .

Loud dialogue from the front made him look up at the cockpit. Kacie—if that was her real name—shouted across to the man she'd called Kaled, who was slumped to the side, his head against the window as he talked to her in a weak but tight voice. The pilot's minutes were numbered.

Great. We'll die up here, plummet to our deaths, and it will be all over.

Elbows propped on his knee, he threaded his fingers and poked his thumbs against his forehead, against the headache pounding worse than a bass beat. He wanted Kacie to trust him, to allow him to work out the plan. Her methods were intense and her mouth scathing. But she got the job done.

Though he'd rigged a new IV for the assassin, it didn't seem to do no good. Aladdin had been unconscious for the last hour. The plane banked down and tugged him, as if pulling him into its hull. Vibrations wormed through his legs and back, numbing him. Was this a good idea? Escaping prison, snatching Aladdin back? Now headed to find another Nightshade asset?

Truth be told, he didn't know.

They'd saved Aladdin's life. He couldn't argue that. Wouldn't. For that reason alone, he'd been glad to be free. But really—did Lara Croft's sister even need him?

No. In fact, nobody had needed him. In a long time. Not even Dante—which was a good thing. It was. Griffin had put together Nightshade by watching the news, monitoring military channels to pick the best of the best. The men who had the *oomph* to own what they did.

Now those men, his *brothers*, were scattered across this messed-up world. Who did this? Who went after Nightshade? Someone who had a powerful need to die, because he and the others, once back together, would ensure their attackers kissed the grave—fast.

Hands loose, he let them dangle over his legs and focused on the powerhouse sitting in the copilot's seat. She had it going on—good mind, quick moves—but she had issues. Trust issues. And so did he—but his were because *she* wouldn't *trust* him. Would she ever? They had four more guys to snag back.

Max. . . *Where are you, man?* He'd been the one to find the shortest path from A to B in any given scenario. Sure could use that genius now.

Shouts from the front drew his gaze. Kacie arched toward Kaled, tugging on his arm. Her gaze shot back to Griffin. "Do something!"

He pushed himself to his feet, hunched to avoid thumping his head against the ceiling as he did when he first entered, then shuffled toward the front. "CPR isn't going to save him."

"How do you know? You haven't even tried." Her frantic response stilled him.

She *knows* him. That was the only logical reason she would be

116

acting crazy. "Because he is riddled with bullet holes. His breathing earlier—you could hear the fluid in his lungs. Up here, in the air, there's nothing I can do."

"We're only twenty minutes out. Just revive him. We can keep him alive."

"We can't, Kacie." Griffin set a hand on her arm. "I don't have equipment to bag him or give him an IV unless I unplug Aladdin."

"So your friend lives and mine dies?"

"Aladdin can breathe on his own. He's stable."

"Then do CPR. You can do that, right? I mean, you have some usefulness besides taking up space, right?"

Griffin glared. "To do CPR, I have to lay him flat—there's no room."

"Do it!"

"No room!"

She nudged the controls.

The plane pitched to the right.

A tight hold on the seats kept him from sliding into the thin wall. Really thin when you considered that was all between you and twenty-some thousand feet of air.

"Woman!"

Both hands on the controls, Kacie worked them. She turned it to the left.

Once again the craft banked, this time in the opposite direction.

"You trying to get us killed."

That green-eyed glare raked him again. "Are we afraid of heights?"

"Heights?" He could not believe his ears. *"Heights?"* He stabbed a finger toward the windshield. "That's not heights."

"Save Kaled. Give him CPR."

Griffin bit his tongue, looked away to stop from shouting what he'd said repeatedly already. He bent his knees—

The craft dipped.

"I can't do nothing if you keep flying like a crazy woman." He eased Kaled down, tilted the guy's head back—knowing full well it was too late. There was nothing he could do. But this man meant something to her. So. . .he'd show her he wasn't a heartless jerk. Griffin blew into the man's mouth. The chest rose. Fell. Nothing. He repeated it, then pumped on the guy's bloody chest. Nothing. The plane again canted to the right.

"I thought you knew how to fly."

"Relax, it's a stripped-down Piper. We have engines, so we're fine. I know where we're going—"

"And where is that? I mean, you can decimate that information, right?" Forearm resting on the back of her seat, he leaned closer. "Or don't you trust me yet?"

Her gaze flicked to his. "Do you mean *disseminate*?"

Heat chugged through Griffin's veins, but he tried not to let it show. Instead, he stared her down. Waited for the answer to his question.

"One leg at a time, remember?"

"I'm pretty sure our elephant is a quadriplegic by now. Location."

After letting out a frustrated growl, Kacie jerked back to the front and dropped against the seat with a grunt. "Greece."

"Greece," Griffin muttered. Why on earth would they go there? He eased onto one of the two seats still anchored to the floor, wiping his hands on his tactical pants. Glad she didn't ask about her friend, hoping she accepted that it wasn't his lack of trying—that the man had been dead before Griffin even tried to save him.

Bending forward nearly had his shoulders touching the front seats. "Listen, Baby Girl. We're on the same team. We have the same goal— get back the men from my team." He shook his hands for emphasis. "Now, I don't care what sort of business you're trying to protect or if you're trying to protect yourself, but you need to understand—these are my boys." Was it his imagination, or were they descending? "I will do whatever it takes to get them back, and part of that includes protecting you when and if I have to. So let's put this ornery nature behind us, all right? Let's play pretend: You like me; I like you."

She stared straight ahead, the blue dust of dawn caressing her jaw.

"Like one big happy family, you"—he touched her shoulder—"and me. Got it?"

"Families aren't happy."

Griffin pushed himself backward onto one of two seats directly behind the cockpit, frustration rippling through his muscles. He smoothed a hand over his head and resisted the urge to dump her out of the plane. They'd dunked the Kid for less frustration.

He lowered his head to his hands. *Lord, You have got to help me. This woman is getting on my last nerve. I want my boys back. I want them alive.*

When nothing but the roar of the engines met his prayer, Griffin lumbered back to Aladdin. In the darkness, he could tell that the assassin still hadn't gained consciousness. As he eased himself along the hull to sit, a puttering sound flicked into the drone of the engines. . .which slowly died.

Silence voided the engine noise.

"What happened?"

"I don't know. Maybe a fuel or line leak. Engines are down, but we still have electrical."

"How are we—?"

"Secure him and then get strapped in," she called over her shoulder.

Griffin went to work. He propped gear around Aladdin, used a bay tether to hold him in place but not hurt him more, then he dropped into the chair.

"Hold on!"

Unknown Location

Burning radiated through his chest and back as if someone had set it afire to grill steaks. And his arms, why wouldn't they move? Marshall groaned and opened his eyes—much easier this time. White blasted through his field of vision, and though instinct nearly slammed his lids shut, he resisted. He had to get oriented.

The room had the look and smell of a hospital.

A hospital? Why did that feel wrong in every way and sense of the word?

He stretched his neck up to look around, but pain prickled his chest. He slumped back against the mattress, pulling back his chin to peer down at his chest. A white bandage covered his right pectoral.

Snap. Did he get shot again? When did that happen?

They'd been to Tunisia. In and out. The mission had problems— Legend was definitely an asset, even if the big thug did drop him in lakes and pools—but they'd come back.

Pulse ricocheting through his temples, he groaned when he realized he couldn't remember coming back. Not even the flight back. He remembered the heinous firefight, and him wishing like nobody's business Griffin had been there to assist with Cowboy's sniper skills, since they'd plugged Marshall into the middle of the chaos, but. . .

Why couldn't he remember coming back? What happened? Why did his legs feel like anvils?

"Augh!" Marshall fisted his hands—about the only thing his hands *would* do.

This was wrong. Everything was wrong. In the back of his mind, something pinged and reverberated through his soul. A soul that would never get the Saint of the Year nomination, with his tendency to rebel against his father and established institutions, but he wasn't *rebellious*. There was a difference. He'd seen it in other kids growing up. But his dad couldn't. All Senator Vaughn saw was that his son wasn't following in his footsteps.

Not in a million years. Okay, yeah—he found a raucous pleasure in defying his dad in that area. If that made him a rebel, then cool. He wasn't a James Dean or even a Max Jacobs.

As if an arrow had been shot through his temple, pain spiked through his skull. Marshall jerked and slammed his eyes shut as a million different images and a horrendous sense of doom swallowed him. Wracked with guilt and intense pain, he squirmed in the bed, the sheet stretched taut over his body, tucked in on the sides. Foul and wicked, black formless beings chased him into the darkness.

His heart rate soared. They weren't real. Couldn't be. But he could *feel* them. He ran toward the Shack. Safety. Home.

BoooOOOOmmm!

"No!"

"Here," a stern voice broke through the adrenaline-laden dream.

Marshall squinted around the haze of sleep. When had he fallen asleep?

A woman stood beside the bed. She was older, laugh lines cutting into her mouth and blue eyes, which matched the scrubs she wore. She injected something into an IV, and only then did he notice the line planted in his arm.

"What is that?"

Without answering, she turned and left.

Wow, some bedside manner. But even as she disappeared through the door, Marshall felt a chill rush through his veins, relaxing his body. *Yeah, this is nice. . . No cares. No pain. Just. . .*

CHAPTER 14

Over the Greek Isles

H ang on. This is going to hurt!"

Griffin tucked his head between his knees, and somewhere in the wicked silence of no engines and yet the roar of the wind pushing the aircraft, he heard Madyar crying out, *"Oh Lawd, protect us. Send those angels, Jesus!"*

Amazing peace rushed through him. And he knew—*knew* it was going to be okay.

He peeked through the two cockpit seats and saw the terror etched into Kacie's face. Her white-knuckled grip. "Kacie."

She didn't flinch from her rapt attention on trying to make them survive.

"It's okay, Baby Girl. God's got our backs."

In the second he spoke, a sea of blue rushed up at them. His breath backed into his throat. *Mercy, Lord. Don't make a liar out of me.*

Head down again, he folded his arms around his head.

Bam! Whoosh!

Inertia threw him forward. He jerked back. Groaning and creaking erupted throughout the cabin. A gurgling noise drew his gaze up.

Kacie launched over the front seat, landing practically in his lap. "Grab the seat, it's a flotation." Something dark covered her temple and part of her hair.

"What's on your—?" Blood. She must've hit her head on impact.

"Flotation," she snapped, pulling out of his reach. "Unless you have gills hidden in those mountains of muscles." Kacie pushed around him.

Plunk! A drop landed on his face. Water. Sea.

121

Drowning. He might be able to take down Hercules, but facing Poseidon was another thing. Griffin swung around and ripped the bottom seat free. He grabbed the other for Aladdin as Kacie shoved open the door.

Like a demonic presence, water rushed into the cabin, and she leapt into the seat. Aladdin grunted at the cold water swirling around him and peeled himself off the floor.

"Nice of you to join the living again." Griffin helped him to the door. He tossed the first seat out, then the second.

Holding his breath, he jumped into the water, submerged, then pushed himself upward. When he broke the surface, he saw Aladdin leaning against the portal where the door flopped. His knees buckled and swayed before he caught himself.

"Come on, assassin! I'll catch you." Griffin grinned. Taunting the man would push him to man up. He shoved a cushion toward the assassin. "Here's your life preserver. Sorry, all the pink sea horses were taken."

Aladdin groaned and slumped into the icy liquid.

Griffin dove and ringed an arm around the man's chest and pulled him up, coughing. He swam to the cushion and waited till Aladdin had himself stretched over it.

"I. . .kill. . .you."

Treading water, he patted the man's back. "Whenever you think you're man enough."

"Why do you antagonize him? He's injured."

Griffin blinked away the water that splashed in his face and reached for the other flotation device. He wouldn't answer that. He didn't expect her to understand. So it shouldn't bother him that she thought he was mean. "Where do we head?"

Grooooannn.

Griffin pushed away, dragging Aladdin as the plane dropped below the surface, leaving a wake of bubbles and hissing.

"Beautiful." Griffin clenched his teeth, thinking of all the equipment plummeting to the ocean floor. Good thing none of it was marked.

"Yeah. It is. Our trail is gone."

Thanks to the moonlight dumping over the water, he saw a hard, angry edge locked into her face. "Then what's wrong?"

She snapped a look at him but didn't answer.

Again with the not trusting. If he wanted her trust, he'd have to show a little, wouldn't he? Swallowing his pride and a mouthful of seawater, he let go. "Okay, Baby Girl, lead on."

Her eyes widened for a split second. And in that expression he saw not only the obvious surprise, but appreciation. "We. . .we need to get out of the water."

"Astounding."

Another glare as her gaze raked their surroundings. He might not be trained in facial expressions like some spooks, but her face was as easy to read as Dante's kindergarten primers.

"Are we lost?"

He wasn't sure, but it sounded like she cursed.

"Did that help?"

"Look," she snapped. "Get off. . ." She bit down and treaded water. "Let's get to shore."

"Com. . .ny," Aladdin mumbled.

Griffin frowned. "Say what?"

"Boat," Kacie hissed from behind. "Dive!"

"We can't. He can't go under. He'll die."

"That's the authorities."

Griffin hesitated, then an idea seized him. He nodded. "Dive."

As the boat roared closer, a spotlight blinked on and stabbed the waters.

Nose pinched, Griffin let himself drift downward. As he kept his movements small to stay below but enough not to sink all the way down, he felt a flutter at his side. Kacie remained nearby as the wake of the boat churned the waters into a furious foam.

Engine rumble slowed.

From his spot, he watched the bottom of the boat. Aladdin's legs dangling below. Then his right leg drew up. . .out. Gone. Completely gone.

They'd taken Aladdin.

"Are you out of your mind?" Kazi shouted as she spit water from her face. "They just took your man!"

"To a hospital." Legend swam away without another word.

Kazi pinched her lips together and threw her anger into swimming. How could anyone abandon a friend like that? What was wrong with this man? One minute he was cracking jokes at the expense of someone whose hands he'd put his life in, then he was saving him, then he let the authorities pick him up without batting an eye.

Just goes to show she couldn't trust anyone. Especially men. She had a slew of them as proof—Roman, Boucher, Carrick to start—so why it surprised and angered her that Legend joined that crowd, she didn't know.

When she finally dragged herself onto the pristine beach of Cyprus, she plopped down, breathing hard. She pounded the sand. Why. Couldn't. Anything. Go. Right? The workout from the exertion made her lungs burn. Her head throbbed as if someone were using it for batting practice. A knot had already formed above her right eye.

Legend stood propped against an overturned boat, holding his knees. His black shirt rippled with each breath thanks to the caress of the moon against his wet shirt.

Kazi shook her head. This mission couldn't be over soon enough. She punched to her feet and stalked away up the sandy stretch.

Legend caught her arm.

She jerked free. "Let's get this straight—don't touch me."

"I get it—you have trust issues."

"Yeah, I do. Starting with you."

He cocked his head and furrowed his brow.

"How could you abandon him? He was one of your own, but you were so ready to dive. I've seen you treat him with contempt, talk to him with utter disregard for his feelings. At the first chance, you ditch him." She should calm down. But the more she talked, the more fire raged within. "I thought you were a team. I thought you stuck with your *boys*?" She batted the hair stuck to her face. "But the first chance you get, you sell him out. That boat came, and you could've saved him. We could've done it together—protected him, taken them. But you *knew* they'd grab him. And what is it with you people? Are you cursed? How can so many things go wrong?"

His expression remained unchanged.

"You don't care. You honestly don't care." Unbelievable. Did the man even have a heart?

"Are you done?" Something simmered just under the surface of that question.

"Oh yes. I'm done. Completely."

"Good." His lips were tight. Stretched taut over his stubbled face. "Let's move."

"Where? Where exactly are you planning to go? In case you haven't noticed, we're not in Greece. My contact? No good." She stabbed a finger over the Mediterranean. "He's over there. We're here. Not much help. So tell me, mighty Legend, where are we going?"

He shifted, his shoulder muscles swelling and cording around his neck like a blood pressure cuff. "Out. Of. Sight." A terse breath escaped through his nose. "Somewhere we can make a plan."

Kazi stilled, reeling. What caused her to go mental on him? She'd lost focus. Lost control. Not good. *Wrap it up, tuck it away, Kaz.*

An awkward stalemate stretched around them like the darkened waters that lapped at the shore. Only as she stood there did she feel the tremors in her arms. Too subtle for him to see, but with the way he stared her down, Kazi had no doubt Legend recognized the panic that burned through her veins like wildfire.

"We should get some cover." His tone had changed.

But the anger that gripped her hadn't. It clenched her by the throat and refused to let go. Strange, almost sinister, the thoughts screaming through her mind, demanding Legend admit what he'd done. That he had given up his own man, abandoned him.

What's with this? Who cared what he did? Completing this operation was all that mattered. Quietly, they hiked up toward a cluster of tight-knit buildings that bled into the darkness to the left and toward the sea to her right. In an alley, he dropped onto a set of stairs.

Swiping his face, he heaved a sigh. "Do you have a contact or safe house here?"

"I have. . ." She licked her lips. "We can make it." She would figure something out. She always had.

"No." He slowly came off the steps. "No good." But then he paused. "Hold up." Turned a quick circle, hustled back to the beach, and looked up and down its length. The moon reflected off his shaved head as he looked around. "We're in Cyprus?"

Where's he going with this? Kazi gave a slow acknowledgment.

A subtle shift, like gears grinding into motion, overtook Legend's expression, which became determined, confident. "Okay, let's keep to the shadows. We'll hoof it along the coast."

Oh nice. He was taking over her mission. Kazi folded her arms. "And just where are we headed?"

Legend rounded on her. The intensity had returned. He opened his mouth, then stilled, and his gaze dropped to the sand. Finally, he looked at her. "I won't ask you to trust me—I know better. Just give me one hour."

Kazi resisted the urges pinging through her system. Panic. Fear. Vulnerability. She didn't have any better plans, so an hour of walking might just net her some ideas on where they could hide out. Being flexible kept her alive and her options open. Teeth clamped, she nodded. "One hour."

He returned the nod and started walking.

With his six-foot-plus stature, he had a long, quick gait. For someone not used to a lot of walking, it might be a problem. For Kazi, keeping pace felt like a comfortable, confident stride that gave her the overall sense of getting somewhere. As if they knew where they were going.

Twenty minutes into the hike, Legend scaled a stone wall and stood atop it, turning and checking around them.

"You do know where we're going, right?" The teasing died on her lips as she saw the consternation take over his face. "Legend?"

He stepped off the wall and dropped in front of her as if he'd stepped off a curb. Angling toward her, he held up his left arm. Pointed to his wrist. "One hour." And started walking again.

Brushing the hair from her face, Kazi cradled her head and closed her eyes. Why did she agree? Sixty minutes would have been better spent scouting out somewhere to lay low until they could find out where Aladdin had been admitted—because Griffin might just walk away from friends, but the general had paid her too well to leave a man behind. She needed that money to buy her freedom from Carrick. To buy a new life. She wasn't going to let some thick-skulled antisocial Marine ruin her best-laid plans.

"Keeping up?"

Warmth spread across her shoulders and down her spine at the taunt. Unconsciously, she skipped a step. *Don't let him get to you.* Yielding to the rebellious streak she'd inherited from her mother, Kazi slowed, watching him as they continued on.

A few minutes later, he looked to the side—no doubt to check on her—and made a *tss* sound before shaking his head but never breaking his stride.

"You know—"

"Fifteen minutes still."

And it struck her. When he'd pointed to his wrist earlier, there was no watch, no imprint of any timekeeping device. "How do you know that if you're not wearing a watch?"

He chuckled.

He's playing you! Stupid, foolish girl. Would she never learn? Putting her life in a man's hands only got her—

She barreled into Legend, who had stopped and pointed through a small huddling of white and terra-cotta buildings. "There."

Secret Facility, Virginia

"It's time for you to leave."

Sydney Jacobs stared at the black suit and his two minions, disbelief choking off her brain. "Excuse me?" She glanced down at her sons playing on the thick, plush circular carpet that spanned the quarters they'd shared for going on three weeks now. "Leave? But General Lambert—"

"Is missing."

Sydney blinked, stupefied.

"What do you mean General Lambert is missing?" Dani stalked toward the three men. "How exactly does a member of the Joint Chiefs go missing? What are you doing to find him?"

A metallic taste glanced across her tongue as she watched the distress coat Dani's face.

"Find him?" The suit laughed. "Miss Roark—"

"Mrs. Metcalfe. That man is my father, and he's missing. Considering someone's trying to blow us off the face of the earth, I'd think you'd be searching high and low for a key member of this country's military system."

The man sighed. "General Lambert has vanished—as in he packed his bags and walked into the sunset. There is nothing in his home or office to indicate foul play."

"Are you insane? You think he just left?" The shriek in Dani's voice bounced off the cement walls and ceilings. "My father wouldn't leave his grandchildren! Or his wife—"

"Yes," Sydney said, gathering her wits and stepping forward. "What about Mrs. Lambert? Where is she?"

The man held his arms wide, as if answering them was as ridiculous as the question. "She's right where he left her."

Sydney and Dani shared a look. A look that said something was really wrong here.

"Now, if you'll please get your bags and your brood, it's time for you to stop sucking up taxpayer dollars."

Again, Sydney blinked. "Excuse me?"

"Why are we being chased out of here?" With elegance and grace that Sydney had always secretly admired, the taller Piper came forward. "Regardless of General Lambert's actions, we were attacked. Nearly killed when someone fired an RPG from a helicopter at us."

"I'm sorry. I really don't have the authorization to discuss any of this with you ladies. So, please"—he waved a hand over the room—"gather your things, and let's be quick. I have a meeting in ten."

"What if we don't?" Dani's stubborn streak reared its head.

Sydney touched her arm, mind already pinging through their options, formulating a plan to get them to safety, to somewhere they could figure out what was happening and what to do. How to find Max. She could only hope Lambert would take care of Rel since the girl wasn't here. As she gathered up the boys' clothes and toys, she fought back tears. She felt lost without Max, confused with the insane twisted-up events.

"Mommy, what's wrong?" Dillon threw his arms around her neck as she tucked Dakota into his carrier.

She drew him close and kissed his cheek, inhaling the scent that was so like his father's. "It's time to leave. Are you ready for another trip?"

Wary, dark eyes held hers. "Are we going to see Daddy now?"

She dusted the silky black hair from his forehead. "Maybe. I don't know." She cupped his hand in hers, lifted the carrier and her purse, then turned toward the others. All similarly armed with two children, bags of belongings they'd accumulated in the weeks of solitary, the ladies of Nightshade once again faced the unknown.

Eight heart-thumping minutes later, they were escorted back down the cement tunnel, into a secure elevator, and across a parking garage. Sydney hoisted the carrier up higher, the ache radiating through her abdomen, shoulder, and arms at Dakota's hefty weight.

Past a guard hut loomed a chain-link, barbed wire–topped gate. The two Marines flanked it as another Marine exited the hut and unlocked it.

Sydney stepped outside, the bitter air tracing her neck and face. "Can I use a phone to get a ride to my home?"

"Sorry, government use only."

She wanted to smack the smug look off the man's face.

"And I hate to be the one to tell you this, Mrs. Jacobs, but you don't have a home." He slid his hands into the pockets of the too-expensive suit. "In fact, none of you do. Not anymore. They've been seized."

"Come again?" Dani snapped. "What do you—?"

"Until certain questionable activities conducted by General Lambert are investigated and cleared, including any involvement of your husbands, all assets are seized until further notice."

CHAPTER 15

Cyprus

Really? Did she have a brain? Trusting this *man*? It was no wonder she ended up owing Carrick the very air she breathed with stupidity drenching her brain cells.

Calves burning as she pushed her way up the sandy and rocky incline, she glared at Legend's back. At the broad shoulders that seemed to bear the weight of the world without so much as a flinch. Despite it all he had not complained. He'd ribbed her, prodded her, even taunted her, but even she knew most of it had been a form of stress reduction.

The thought gave her a mental pause. The image of her first encounter with him skidded into her memory. And oddly enough, she realized that he'd already changed. The man in the prison scrubs had stood hunched. This man stalking up the beach toward a gorgeous Cyprian home moved with purpose and determination.

He's got a mission.

Or at least she seriously hoped so. He'd just hopped over a waist-high white wall that encompassed an expansive property. To be on the coast and have *this* much—the owner must have a shiny shilling. She vaulted over the wall.

"Hold up," Griffin whispered and crouched in the anonymity the shadows provided.

"What's wrong?" Even keeping her voice down, it felt like a scream in the quiet.

He shook his head, gaze locked on the home.

Kazi traced the plaster glowing a peaceful blue under the caress of the full moon. Now this was a place she wouldn't mind calling home. A sense of community nestled amid other terraced homes, yet an ocean of freedom was just a short walk back. But someone like her didn't belong in domestic life. The idea of staying in one place more than a few months made her skin crawl. Too easy to trace.

"Not home. Security system," Griffin whispered.

"I can probably disable it."

Griffin shook his head and indicated another home. There, cresting a slight incline on the other side of the road, the home overlooked an expansive estate. A bank of windows revealed a gorgeous interior. All lit up. Wide open.

We'd be seen.

He dropped to a knee and slumped back.

Great. He intended to wait. The longer they stayed in one place, the greater the chance of being discovered. Surely Legend knew that. Surely he didn't expect to sit here for hours on end.

As she slid against the wall, hugging her legs, she glared at him. "Your hour is up."

He eyeballed her.

Kazi looked away because in his expression she read the dare to offer something better. And there wasn't anything better. Not exactly true—anything was better than sitting here waiting for death to come to them.

She pushed away from the wall. "I'm going to scout out the area."

He caught her arm and tugged her down.

Kazi shoved a hand into his chest.

Griffin grunted, then snatched her hand free. "We wait."

"Waiting gets us killed."

"We *wait*."

Tremors zipped through her arms and legs, both out of weariness and agitation. Kazi threw herself back against the wall with a grunt. Wait? Wait for what? Someone to walk up and gun them down? Someone to call the authorities?

If they'd just landed on Greece. . . . Over there, across the sea, she had options, knew people. Here, nothing. What they needed to do was take a boat. Jet across the waters. And she'd be back in control. She'd make contact with the general again and figure out the next step.

His somber eyes begged for her to provide the solution.

She couldn't.

"I'm going to knock on the door."

When he started to push up, Kazi's heart jumped into her throat. "Wait!" She touched his arm. "Let me go."

"No."

"I'll knock, and you stay by the date palm tree. Check out the house, and if it's clear, then speak up."

"If not?" Warning simmered in his dark irises, the Cyprian moon glinting off his eyes.

She smirked and strode into the open.

"Kacie," he hissed after her.

After a quick check of her surroundings, Kacie stepped into the small covered patio and knocked. A few seconds later, light burst out from under the threshold seconds before it flooded her.

Training kicked in and pushed one foot back.

The door creaked open a couple of inches. Bushy, graying eyebrows hooded intelligent eyes. "Yes?"

"I'm sorry." Kazi planted a hand on the door, as if bracing herself, and reached for her shoe. "Sorry, I think I stepped in—" She intentionally stumbled and pushed into the door.

It swung wide.

The older man stumbled backward.

"Oh!" Kacie steadied the man and let her gaze sweep the interior of the home. Simple but lavish all the same. And empty. "I'm so sorry!" What about the kitchen? "Forgive me." Empty as well. "I thought—"

"Dr. Golding," Legend's voice boomed from behind.

Golding. . .a doctor? *That's interesting.*

The man straightened. His eyes went wide as he took a step back. Confusion yet a flicker of recognition. "Do I—?" He gasped and waved Griffin into the home. Quickly, he shut the door. "Yeshua is at the center of this, *nachon*?"

Griffin hesitated. So did Kazi. But she'd let the lug work this one out on his own. The two obviously knew each other, and both seemed to have faith in God. She'd had it once. Or rather, her father had. He'd been devout in his faith. When he died, so did her desire for anything related to God. Not that she didn't believe He was there. She just didn't get why He let the things happen that happened. If He didn't have time for her, to keep a man alive who devoted his every move to pleasing Him, then she didn't have time for Him either.

"As much as I'd like to agree, I'd be a liar if I did." Griffin smoothed a hand over his head. "Listen, Dr. Golding, we are in one messed-up mess."

Golding stroked a neatly trimmed beard. "Yes, yes."

Griffin glanced at Kazi, his large frame filling the small doorway. Or maybe it wasn't that the door was so small but that he was so big. "No, no." Griffin scowled. "I don't think you understand."

"He understands more than you could know, Legend," came a voice.

Griffin pulled straight.

Kazi spun. "General!"

Relief roiled through Olin as he stepped into the sitting area. But then it hit him. "Where's Aladdin?"

"They took him." Kazi sneered at Legend.

"He was messed up—bad. The authorities have him, probably at a hospital."

"I will make a discreet inquiry and locate him." Dr. Golding lifted a phone from his pocket and stepped out onto the terrace.

Olin saw the anger, the confusion, the frustration rippling through the face of the man known only as "Firethorn" in his above top-secret reports. Reports that seemed to have been somehow exposed.

The man who'd helped him put the Nightshade team together stepped closer, hovering over him, his voice low but angry. "General, *what* is going on?"

Olin touched the man's upper arm, mentally noting his fingers did not even make it halfway around the muscle. "I share your anger."

Legend stared at him for a while. "If you shared what I was feeling right now, you wouldn't be standing still. You shouldn't be here. *I* shouldn't be here." His deep brown eyes resonated with conviction. "But I knew—*knew*—you wouldn't break me out if it wasn't bad."

The unspoken warning that Legend had just risked everything he valued—respect and honor—to do this came through clearly. "It is. In fact, it's worse." Olin pointed to the long arrangement of chairs and low tables. "There is much to discuss. Let's sit."

Soft light from the living room danced along the popping muscle in Legend's jaw. Finally, he gave a single nod, stepped back, and stretched a hand toward Kazi, directing her to the seats.

Surprise leapt over the milky complexion of the girl. And it was only then that Olin realized he'd never thought of Kazi Faron as a *female* so much as a very skilled and effective Polish-born operative. And yet the pink tingeing her cheeks awakened an awareness in him—and apparently in another man in this room.

Or was that Legend just being the Southern gentleman he'd been raised to be?

Once Kazi sat, Griffin took the chair to her right and Olin lowered himself onto the sofa, then met Kazi's green eyes. "The final payment has been made. I will depend on your integrity and reputation, Kazi, to fulfill your obligation."

Griffin stared at her hard, no doubt questioning that integrity. He knew nothing of the woman except the obvious—she'd broken him out of prison and orchestrated Aladdin's extraction from the hands of Palestinians intent on ripping the betrayal from his chest.

Kazi said nothing and did not respond to Griffin's nonverbal questions.

"Legend, we are beyond protecting our identities. Someone knows who we are." Heaviness pulled at his limbs, rife with exhaustion, agitation, and exasperation. Olin scooted to the edge of the cushions. "Things have gone downhill fast. We must figure out who's holding that basket and pry it from them. A week ago, Charlotte had a dream—"

"It was more like a nightmare." The soft, gentle voice drifted from the room where his wife had gone for a rest. Charlotte glided into the room, pulling him to his feet.

Griffin stood.

On his feet, Olin extended a hand to his wife, looking at the others in the room. "Legend, you've met Charlotte before."

"Mrs. Lambert." The big, surly former Marine nodded.

This time Olin extended his hand toward Kazi. "And this is—"

"Kacie Whitcomb." She stepped in and offered her hand.

It did not surprise Olin that she wanted her identity concealed. Olin watched the woman, an enigma of a covert operative, ever impressed with the way she maintained a strong presence despite her diminutive size. And next to Griffin the height difference seemed comical. With her white-blond hair wet and askew, she looked much younger than her midtwenties, more childlike and vulnerable than he'd ever seen her.

"The dream." Undaunted, Griffin pressed them.

Easing onto the sofa, Charlotte wrapped her arms around herself. "I awoke drenched in sweat. I'd never had a dream like that—as if I'd already walked through a day of unimaginable horror. It was so clear and alarming that I immediately awakened Olin. In the dream, I saw Olin and me hurrying through the night to a waiting plane. On board a waiter arrived and handed out small plates of baklava, as if it was the most natural thing in the world. As the plane taxied, I looked out the window. There I saw my home, my friends, my entire life—and they vanished as if someone had swiped an eraser across a chalkboard."

Olin held his wife's wringing hands, offering a vain thread of comfort. "I hadn't told her about the events of the previous few weeks, though she detected my distress and angst, so this dream was not something I could dismiss." The older couple shared a look before Olin focused back on Griffin. "We were on a plane out of the United States within two hours. I won't bother with specifics, but know that Charlotte and I are here under false identities—we can't be traced."

"*Everything* can be traced if someone wants to find it badly enough." Kazi met Olin's gaze with a fierce determination. "I found Aladdin, and he was buried deep."

"Exactly." Griffin swiped a hand over his face. "You bought us time, but that's it. Tactically, the smart thing would be to hide out, let us finish our mission, get the team back together."

"I had to amend our plans when things spiraled into utter chaos." Intense dark eyes held his. "What happened?"

"Someone is turning my life inside out, trying to find evidence of treason, espionage. . . . I don't know what. I saw it coming, so I created a false trail and left, but not before sending another asset to retrieve Midas from Venezuela and another to the Kid."

Griffin hung his head and hooked his arms over his head, hands resting on his shoulder blades. With a groan, he straightened. "What about Frogman, Squirt, and Cowboy?"

"Frogman and Dighton are MIA." Olin eyed Kazi. "Max made contact with his wife to warn her, then both he and Dighton vanished."

Griffin peered up at him. "Cowboy?"

"He's your next assignment."

"Okay, wait." Kazi sat straighter, her expression knotted. "This is my gig. You paid me, so why exactly are we dividing up the jobs?"

"When I hired you, I needed an operative who could work under the radar, report back to me as progress was made. Since you left, someone escalated the situation. They came after me and the wives of my men."

Griffin drew back, as if a warrior drawing in his strength and focus to unleash on a foe. "Wives?"

"Yes." Olin ground his teeth. "They tried to kill them. I got them to a safe house, but that's when things collapsed around me. I have no idea where the women and children are now, and I cannot find out. My normal means and access are completely shut down." Each breath felt like fire. "We need this team back together. Now."

"Isn't that dangerous?" Kazi finally looked at Griffin. "If they want you dissected, what's to stop them from blowing you off the planet if you guys go after them?"

Griffin's shoulders seemed to swell with purpose and fury. "Because we're going to blow them away first."

CHAPTER 16

Unknown Location

A voice warbled through the maze of discordant images. Burning buildings. Marble halls. Water. Fire.

Marshall, can you hear me?

Where was she? He could hear her, but only a gray smokescreen separated them. A strange warmth spiraled through his blood. He moaned.

"Marshall?"

He blinked. An angel stood beside him. Beautiful, amazing. "Narelle."

She quickly pressed a finger to his lips, then checked over her shoulder. "Shh. I'm using a jamming device."

He loved the sound of her voice, the Australian lilt to her words. But she wasn't making sense. "What. . . ?" He shook his head, trying to clear the fog from his brain. "Why? It's a hospital."

"It's not. I can't really explain much right now. I'm going to find a way to get you out of here. You have to call me Kim. That's the name I gave them as a nurse, okay? Got it?"

He frowned.

She squeezed his hand. "Please trust me. Things are really stuffed up."

"Huh?"

"Stuffed—messed up."

"Oh. Okay, sure." Did he really care as long as she was here with him? "I don't get it."

"There's too much. You were shot, and. . ." Her brown eyes danced over his face, then dropped to his arm.

"Shot? When. . . ?" What wasn't she telling him?

Slowly, she looked at him, her voice quieter this time. "Just get better, okay?" She snapped her head around. "Quiet, someone's coming." Quickly, she went to work. With both hands poised on the tower, she looked over her shoulder.

His father bled from a blurry image in the background to one more in focus.

"Hey." Weird. His father had never cared the other times he'd been in the hospital, even that first day after the accident when Mom died. Melanie had been there, faithful and loyal sister that she was. Until she married Nathan Sands, ticking off Marshall in a big way.

"Evening, son." Even a simple greeting sounded formal, as if part of a speech given on the floor of the Senate. His father strolled to his bedside. "I thought I'd drop by the hospital and see how you were doing."

Blinding flash of the obvious, Dad.

"Besides killer pain and another victory badge, I'm fine."

Hold up. Hadn't Rel said he wasn't in a hospital? Then why was his dad saying he was in one? The confusion swam a mean circle around his mind.

A strong pat on his arm. "Well, get better, Marshall."

"Sure, Dad."

"You're his nurse?"

Rel angled herself toward him, her attention fastened on the charts. "Yes, sir. I. . .I started today." She turned and offered her hand.

His father accepted the greeting. "If he needs anything, just let them know. It'll be taken care of."

Without a good-bye or another word, Warren Vaughn strode out of the room. And as he did, in the seconds between the door closing and his father moving out of view, Marshall saw the wood paneling that lined the upper attic of their home.

So, Rel was right. They were keeping him in his own home. But pretending it was a hospital. Why? He lifted an IV-taped hand to his head and rubbed his temple. "What's. . . ?"

Rel withdrew a syringe from her pocket and slid the needle into the tubing of the IV. "They are keeping you heavily sedated. I'm weaning you off the drug, but if you are too coherent too soon, they'll get suspicious."

Marshall swung out a hand. "Wait. Why. . .why is he doing this?"

She gave a sad smile, her beautiful pale face twisted into what looked like agony. Her brown gaze jumped to his, then back to the sheets. She shook her head, as if pleading with him. "You don't remember?"

Panic streaked through him. He caught her hand. "What? Tell me, Rel—*please!*" Swirls and swoons surfed his brain waves. He fought the lure of the drugs she'd injected into his IV. "What? What don't I remember?" He tightened his hold on her arm. "Tell me, Narelle. I need you to help me."

"Okay, okay, be quiet." Her eyes watered. "Someone attacked the Nightshade team. Max and my brother are missing. The others are. . ." Her chin trembled. "They're gone, Marshall. I don't know where. They're just gone."

No. . .

His body sucked him into a dark chasm.

Kyrenia, Cyprus

"I've located Azzan," Dr. Golding said as he returned from the terrace. "He's at the state hospital in Güzelyurt. It is not far from here, and I have a friend who is the head of surgery." Golding ran a hand through this thick mop of slightly grayed, curly hair. "Not too far from here, and I believe it will work for our favor, yes?"

Griffin stood.

"No, it is good that I do this alone." Kindness oozed from the man who stood as tall as Griffin but had the gentility of a lamb. "I believe my position will grant me unfettered access, but showing up with strangers will beg questions we'd rather not have drawn up."

Fingers curling into fists, Griffin probed the man's eyes, searching for the thing he'd seen in many faces that warned him to withhold his trust. What position? Who was Dr. Golding?

"Thank you, Jacob."

The man inclined his head, then left. Griffin stared out the door, wondering what he'd find. Was Azzan alive? They would've told Dr. G if the assassin was dead, right?

"I know there is much to discuss," the general said. "But I think you both need a shower and a good night's rest."

A caged lion paced within Griffin's chest. Rest? At a time like this? Yet his experience in the field told him the suggestion came from the voice of reason. But with his men, his friends, out there, in

God-knows-what kinds of situations. . .

"Jacob's home has many bedrooms," Olin said. "Charlotte and I have the first room on the right. There is another on the left, then three more rooms upstairs, as well as the rooftop terrace."

The lion paced more. Sitting here, doing nothin', having no plan. . . *It's like flinging mud and hoping something sticks.* He'd go out of his good mind. "We need a plan."

"We will."

The reply took Griffin by surprise. Had he really spoken out loud? He ran a hand over his face and scalp.

"For now, shower and rest," Olin said firmly but softly.

Griffin stared at the man.

Laugh lines crinkled the Old Man's blue eyes. "That's an order, Marine."

"Oorah," Griffin muttered, not feeling the oomph that normally went into that word. He glanced at Kacie—but Olin had said her name differently, like Kazie. Was that her real name? Or just another pseudonym she used?

Kacie eyed him. "I'll shower first."

He nodded and held a hand toward the hall.

Her chin drew up, and this expression overtook her face. What is that? "I need to speak to the general."

I see. She needed to talk to the general but still didn't trust Griffin enough to speak in front of him. Fine. "Then I'll shower first." He trudged down the hall and stepped into the bathroom. There, two sets of clothes, neatly folded, sat on a bench next to the sink. Griffin lifted the black shirt of one and held it up. Pressed it shoulder to shoulder with his large frame. Perfect. The pants—nobody ever got that right. He might be built like a train, but he took care of his body. The Good Lord told men to buffet their bodies, and Griffin took that literally. He didn't have a tire for a waistline. With hesitation, he lifted the black tactical pants. Held them up.

And grinned.

Perfect. Had to be the Old Man to get this right. But. . .how'd he know? That question and many more trailed Griffin beneath the pelting spray as he scrubbed down. Amid the steam and hot water, he let the tension drain from his limbs and from his mind, right down the drain.

"I. . .I was thinking of going into the Marines, like you, Uncle Griff."

Hand on his nephew's neck, Griffin gave a playful squeeze. "You got a better head on your shoulders than I do. A good, strong family who's got your back. Go to school."

They moved to the steps of the back porch and sat. "But," Dante said, *"I thought you said I could be whatever I put my mind to."*

Thump-thump. *A black object tumbled into the center of the living room.*

Flash-bang! Curled into a corner, he obeyed the instinct that made him plug his ears, open his mouth, and squeeze his eyes shut.

Boom! Crack!

Griffin jerked. Slapped the water off and stepped from the shower. Hands on the edges of the sink, he braced himself, hauling his mind from the edges of the nightmare. He stared down at the tactical pants. Being a Marine, being a warrior, that's what Dante thought made a hero. Shooting people. Chasing down bad guys.

And look where it got him.

Chest tight, Griffin snatched the clean shirt from the bench and ripped open the door. He stomped upstairs, ignoring the lull of conversation in the living room. They didn't want him down there anywhere. Kacie—Kazie—didn't, and in this mood, it was the right thing to separate himself.

Anger destroys. Anger kills. Nothing good comes of anger. Taking the steps two at a time helped him expend some of the pent-up frustration. At the top of the stairs, two options existed: right where three doors opened into two bedrooms and a closet of some sort, then to the left—a glass door provided a view of a rooftop terrace.

Griffin flipped on a light in one of the bedrooms, checked it— bed, dresser, nightstand, couple of nice paintings—before he pulled it closed, then headed to the roof. Early morning dawn streaked the sky with midnight blue. He eased the door open and turned. On the far wall, he set his shirt. Stepped back. Closed his eyes and drew in a slow, deliberate cleansing breath.

With practiced moves, he swept his right arm out and simultaneously spread his legs shoulder-width apart and bent his knees. In wide arcs, he pushed the tension out with his right hand, then drew his hand in. Tai Chi had been the one outlet that allowed him to release the storm within him, find some semblance of peace.

"Peace comes from the Lawd, boy. Don't you forget it."

Madyar never would let him forget it. And though he tried it her way, tried to draw on the strength of God, it seemed he repeatedly hooked his claws in demons of fury instead. Controlling his anger was tantamount to peace. Without the harness, without the purification, he could become one of the demons that had plagued his father.

Griffin stumbled. He blinked out the image that came with the mention of that man. Unheeded, they came. Shouting. Pleading. Screams. A loud bang. Then. . .silence. Horrible, terrifying silence. *Bang!*

He went to his knees. Pebbles dug into his flesh. Dropping onto all fours, Griffin drew in a ragged breath, feeling as if something had hold of his chest, squeezing. . .twisting. . .strangling. Two paces forward brought him to the wall. He turned and slumped against it, elbows on his knees, head in his hands.

God, make it go away. Please. . .

Griffin lifted his eyes heavenward, panting. Just like that night. Fleeing the house. Wishing with all the fervor of a six-year-old boy that he'd been the real creature his mother had named him after, the gryphon. The noblest of noble creatures, head and claws of an eagle, body of a lion. A powerful beast who could've ripped through that stormy sky and stopped the nightmare. But he had been all of sixty pounds.

A shadow to the right danced, blocking the light from the interior hall.

Click.

Kacie stepped into the predawn morning with a grace and style all her own. In fact, the way she moved, the way she strode toward the wall, she *owned* it. She wore the clean clothes that had waited for her in the bathroom. Eyes on the sparkling sky, she moved to the opposite wall. In seconds, she stood atop it, walked to the far edge. With one look over her left shoulder—he stilled, waiting for her to spot him— she looked to the house. Then refocused, held her hands straight out in front of her.

Was she going to jump? Ditch them now that the money was in her account? If she lost her balance, it was a solid ten, maybe fifteen feet to the rocky beach below the house. If he said anything, he might startle her. He reached for his shirt and pushed to his feet, keeping his eyes on her.

Kacie, graceful as anything he'd seen, did several backflips on the twelve-inch ledge.

You have the heart of an Olympian, Kazimiera. Now tell that to your body. Train! Train! Train!

After three back-handsprings, she reached the wall and pivoted. Toeing the ledge, she repeated them till she stood on the lip, grateful for the solace, the chance to relax and unwind. As if on the balance beam, she swung around, her right leg out behind her, then dipped down and brought it up. Toe touching the warmed plaster, she held out her arms. She didn't make the Olympics, but she'd never surrendered the one love in life she'd excelled at. Forward into a tuck, then a handstand, relishing the gentle whoosh of the cool February air around her body as she moved. She stood straight again, arms out, graceful, light, and she threw herself forward— A sound from the side broke her concentration.

She wobbled on the edge, then sat to prevent injury to herself. Kazi spun and faced the darkness. Heat swirled through her stomach as Griffin emerged from the shadows.

"Baby Girl," he said with admiration in his tone and gaze. "I thought you had moves earlier, but you have *moves!*"

"What are you doing out here?"

Griffin frowned, threading his hands through his shirt. As he did, the light from the corridor traced a tattoo on his chest. Some eagle-looking creature. "Same thing as you."

"You should've said something." Kazi jerked to the wall, bent, and retrieved her shoes.

"I was afraid I'd startle you off the wall."

She snapped toward him. "I'm a big girl. I can take care of myself."

"Agreed. You handle yourself with more skill than a lot of men I know."

Warily, Kazi eyed him, waiting for him to make the comment a backhanded compliment. She slipped on her shoes. Only the soft moan of the ocean came to her. *Play nice, Kazi. Think. Change gears.* "Earlier, you didn't ask the general why he was here."

With a sigh, Griffin strolled to the far edge of the overhang and shifted around, leaning back against the half wall, and folded his arms. As he crossed his ankles, she couldn't help but notice he was barefooted like her. What had he been doing out here?

"No, I didn't. But neither did you."

On the ledge, she shrugged and hugged her legs. Mentioning that she'd taken her cue on that point from Griffin, from the fact that he didn't question his superior, she'd reasoned there was no threat. Liking Lambert's presence here was a different thing. She didn't appreciate him stepping in on her game.

"You know," Griffin said, slowly bringing his gaze to hers, "we can spend a lot of time keeping things from each other, pretending we don't care, or we can work as a team and get this done." He angled his broad shoulders toward her. "Did the general surprise me being here? Yes. But questioning him—we were beyond that. I knew when you showed up and told me the team had been hit that if Lambert sent you to break me out of prison—he knows, he *knows* how much respect and honor are foundations in my life—if he needed me to break my code and flee that prison like some criminal from the 'hood, that told me things were beyond broke. So I left with you."

"Yet you've fought me at every chance."

"No." Griffin swung around and straddled the wall, one leg dangling over fifteen feet of air. "Not fought you. Sought an accord, cooperation."

"You're a team player." She shrugged, feeling so very small in his presence. "I'm not. I work alone."

He inched forward. "Even if you aren't a team player, Kacie, if you think about this with logic, with that brilliant mind of yours, then you'll see that working together makes both of us stronger, more capable for whatever comes. Whether you want me here or not, I am doing this. And I'm not leaving till my boys are back."

"So that's what matters to you." Where did that come from? Kazi pushed her gaze to the sea sparkling behind him. Why had anger suddenly tangled up her mind? Minutes lapped the silence around them, but she wouldn't look at him. Those eyes were probing for weak spots, for ways to get in under her radar. She wouldn't let that happen. Not now. Not ever.

"Where'd you learn those moves?"

First volley. Ask an innocuous, quiet question, and he learns a bit about her past.

Not if she had anything to say about it. "In a gymnasium."

"How many medals did you win?"

Kazi's gaze bounced to his of its own will. Blue-green waters still dark beneath the subtle tease of dawn's fingers silhouetted his large frame. The tide pulled on her mind—not the tide from the sea reaching for shore, but the one in his eyes. Why did he care? Was she just a thing he could conquer and overcome? What would he do with the information from her past, a cemetery of fallen innocence and dead dreams?

She blinked at the idea she'd even considered opening that crypt.

She swung her legs over the side and stood. "Good night, Griffin." As she pivoted and strode away, she heard his heavy sigh.

That's right—I'm hopeless. Just give up and go away.

"Kacie," Griffin said, her name a whisper on his lips.

Holding the door handle, she paused before her mind had a chance to catch up with the mistake.

"Don't lock me out." His deep voice resonated through her like the gong of a bell in a tower. And yet he'd spoken so quietly, so gently. So close.

She glanced up at him and felt the flicker of a frown tie her brows together. "I wasn't—" *Oh*. He didn't mean the door. He meant. . .something else. A weird taste leapt across her tongue, and she swallowed. In a fluid move, she swirled into the small foyer and flipped the lock.

Then she looked at him with a smirk. . .and that was her second mistake, because the warm glow of the foyer bathed his face. And what she saw there, in his undaunted eyes, in the face lined with determination amid that smooth latte skin, speared its way through the midnight hour of her heart. Past the broken and chipped headstones of fallen hopes, broken dreams, and certain fear, and straight at the vault.

Though she spun on her heels and stalked down the hall, the pained expression on his face haunted her. Where she'd expected anger, she found. . .sadness.

Don't weep for me, Griffin. There's nothing left to cry over.

Kazi closed the bedroom door and traced the small gap where the door and jamb didn't quite meet. *"Just brill, Kazi. Just brill. You scared off another fella."* Tina's voice sailed past the gates of paradise and into the present. She had to, didn't anyone get that? Keeping the walls up, keeping her mind focused meant she stayed alive. But. . .what would it be like to know a man who didn't give up, who didn't abuse, who didn't seize on her weaknesses?

Like Mamo and Tata.

As if a bat hit her head, Kazi stumbled back. With a choked breath, she fought the stinging in her eyes. She turned, hands on her hips, staring, searching for whatever had brought them to her mind. All these years, she'd pushed them down, suffocated the memories till they lay dead in that crypt. Her heart beat faster, pumping twice the amount of fear as blood through her veins.

She brushed her short, wispy hair from her face and let out a ragged breath. She would not—*not!*—go there again. They were dead.

Buried. Not a part of her life. Roman had sold her. Discarded her as easily as toilet paper. And. . .Kazpar. . .*my twin*.

A half-choked sob punched through her chest, seeking relief.

She covered her mouth. Something hot slid down her cheek. She batted it. Curse Griffin Riddell. He'd brought this out in her; he'd slipped under her radar, under her defense. But it'd never happen again. Renewed resolve transfused the fear in her veins.

The only victims would be the ones she created. Not her. Never again. She didn't care what it cost—even if it meant this mission.

Acholi, Uganda

*B*oom!

Crackling raced along the roof. Fire licked and devoured the grassy covering. Thuds outside the hut reverberated through his mind, the sound indicative of a slaughter. Smoke swirled down into his one-room hut as if seeking out victims to strangle.

Scott pushed himself off a coughing Ojore. "Stay along the perimeter." He clapped the fifteen-year-old's shoulder. "Just like we practiced."

As Scott slipped out of his hut, the roof roared. Seconds of blaze brought it down with a *whoosh*. He seized the distraction of the noise and sprinted into the tall grass, his gaze locked on the two trucks that had borne the soldiers hauling sleeping people from their homes. Children screamed. Women wailed.

A lone figure on the other side of the village, beyond the trucks, skittered between two huts. *Ojore?*

Scott glanced back to where he'd expected to find the young man. But he was gone.

A fist punched Scott's stomach into his throat.

Raging fires lit the night almost like daytime. And there. . .darting between thick clouds of smoke and burning hulks was Ojore. Going after Kissa.

A guard turned in Ojore's direction.

Scott leapt into the open. *"Kikati?"* Okay, asking what's up wasn't exactly the best way to confront a Ugandan soldier in the middle of a raid. But he needed them to think he was unprepared. *"Sikitegeera.* I don't understand." He repeated the phrase a few more times as dark-skinned men rushed him. He let them secure his arms.

Hands up, he noted that in his periphery, Ojore, Lutalo, and Taban secreted their families out into the fields to safety. Despite the

147

smoke and ash clogging his tear ducts and throat, Scott focused on the colonel who strode toward him.

"You are training these men for an army, to raid our cities. You were also seen at the mines last night."

In Lugandan, Scott said, "We are peaceful and living here as farmers. Some men work the mines—and as you know, my funding comes from the UN. I don't work in the mine." A little deception proved vital. "There is no army here. Only men and families."

"Someone saw you at the mine." The colonel poked Scott's chest with a club.

Scott laughed and shrugged. "I'm not the only American in the area"—he noted the flicker of acknowledgment in the colonel's eyes—"but again, why would I be in the mine? Even if I were, is it illegal to visit it?"

"You were in a secured area."

"Secured area? For what reason? I'm just trying to help these men and their families."

"These men are demons; they fight in the Lord's Resistance Army! Why would you help men who kill their own people?" The colonel hesitated, a sneer curling his lip. "You are American. Your help failed last time. Why do you think it will be different this time?"

Scott cringed at the reference to the 2008 effort when the United States sent advisers and tactical men—like him—to help eradicate the Lord's Resistance Army. A miserable failure thanks to fog and other factors. Spies, he believed but could not prove.

"These men are murderers!"

Scott let his gaze rake in the scene, then he slowly locked onto the body of a woman—Nabiyre—strewn across the threshold of her home. Her thin linen dress was darkened with the stains of her own blood, of injustice. Taming the fury swirling through him took a great effort, but he would make his point.

He waited till the colonel followed his gaze. Then, "Isn't that what you're doing, Colonel—killing good men who were ripped from their families and forced to do horrible things?" Scott sighed. "We both know I'm not raising an army. Your own son lived here for a few years." Though he had the training to take out the ill-trained soldiers, he wasn't that man anymore. He'd given it up to help the villagers, teach them to protect themselves, but always—*always*—try peace first.

A tremor spirited through the colonel's dark skin, lit by the fires ravaging the village.

"Who told you to come out here, Colonel?"

Hesitation held the attack hostage.

"Tell me who did this. What are they protecting?"

The man blinked. Rubbed a hand over his mouth, a subconscious indication he didn't want to speak what he was thinking. A thought struck Scott. One not far-fetched in a world ravaged by disease and poverty. "What did they offer you, Colonel? What price did you put on coming out and razing this village?"

Outrage blazed through the colonel's face, lit by the fires that ravaged eight years of hard work. "Take him!"

In the seconds it took for the men to respond to their superior's order, Scott reacted. Training long repressed surged to the forefront. Took over. He slashed out with a flat-handed "blade" and dropped the colonel. The man gasped for air.

Scott heard boots behind him. He pivoted and threw a roundhouse right into the man's groin, doubling him. He slammed a fist into the man's nose. On his knees, the man wailed as blood gushed down his face. Shadows flickered to Scott's left and right. He threw a right hook to the left. A grunt warned him to duck. The familiar *tsing* of a machete swiped over his head.

Scott shoved his boot into the man's knee. Bones cracked and collapsed the other opponent while Scott wrangled another. In a choke hold, he dropped hard on a bent knee. The guard went limp.

Shouts jerked him around. Like ants from their hill, Ugandan soldiers flooded out of more trucks. From the far field beyond where a truck ground to a halt to disembowel itself of more soldiers, a light flickered. If Scott noted the position right, that came from the buried rocket launcher. It'd buy him time to escape.

Incoming.

CHAPTER 17

Cyprus

Hot coffee and an early Mediterranean sunrise warmed Griffin as he stood just inside the house at the bay of windows overlooking the sandy beach. A lot had happened in the last few weeks. Whoever did this to the team, whoever took a bead on his friends—they'd pay for this.

"You can't do this!" The Kid yelled as they hauled him up the beach to the pier. He writhed as Griffin and Cowboy wrangled him.

"Say it again," Griffin said. "Say Army is better."

Silence dropped on them.

Had the Kid finally gotten some smarts?

Then. . .

"I cannot tell a lie. . .Rangers lead the way!"

With Cowboy, he swung the Kid back and forth, sent him sailing into the air cursing and shouting.

Movement on the sand lured his mind from the past. Kacie trudged alongside the wall and turned into the courtyard. What was she doing out there? Didn't she realize she could expose their location? He frowned as she met his gaze, then hopped over the barrier. He flicked open the door and let her in.

"What are you doing—?"

"Finally woke up, huh?" She arched an eyebrow and stalked to the kitchen where she lifted a mug from the counter, dropped in a tea bag, filled it with water, then placed it in the microwave. "We leave Friday for London."

"Did I miss a conversation with the general? When did this plan

150

happen? I thought we were going to lay low and wait for Aladdin."

She smirked. "I touched base with my London contact. The general's presence here does not alter my plans. We proceed as planned."

He set down his coffee and moved to the kitchen. "Don't you think you should consult me about these things? Or did that knot on your head from the crash affect your brain more than I thought?"

Fearless, unaffected pale-green eyes held his. "I am talking to you."

"*Before* you make plans."

"Do you have a contact in London?"

Griffin bit down on the ear chewing he wanted to give her and flared his nostrils.

"Look, relax." When the microwave dinged, she retrieved her tea and sauntered into the living room. She tucked her feet under her and sat on the sofa. "This is my gig. Lambert hired me to get his men back. That's what I'm doing. Lambert will stay here with Golding as a hideout and to monitor Aladdin's progress."

It made sense. And that's part of what infuriated him. She was right, but she was going about this in a cavalier, nose-snubbing way. She'd fight for control on this. And the more he resisted and demanded cooperation, the worse she got. So. . .

"Okay." He held his hands toward her. "Fair enough." He eased onto the coffee table in front of her. "So, London—we're going after Cowboy?"

She peeked over the rim of her cup as she sipped the brew and gave a slow nod.

"Good. All right." He sloughed his hands together. Two more days pent up in this house. With her. Would he strangle her before they were en route?

Griffin pushed to his feet. Fisted his hands. What could he say? What could he do? Nothing. He'd never met anyone like her, anyone so closed off and bullheaded. No one so determined to be in control and have things their way.

No one so much like you.

He needed space. Smoothing a hand over his head, he moved to the windows again. Tugged back the door and stepped into the cool Cypriot air. It grated on his last nerve, knowing the men he looked on as brothers depended on *him* for their survival, but he depended on her. A her who wouldn't give him the time of day without a fight.

Bent forward, he rested his forearms on the wall. *Lord God, give me mercy.* The sitting, the waiting, the green eyes. . .

He roughed a hand over his face. Stood straight. She would drive him out of his good mind before this was over. Why couldn't he get past that barrier of hers? Last night, he'd seen something dart through her delicate features that gave him pause. Fear. Not of him. Fear of punishment. Or rejection. It was like. . .like she'd told a secret she wasn't supposed to tell.

It didn't make no sense. He'd never seen anything like her on that wall. Except maybe on TV during the Olympics. Phoenix loved watching the competition. And then Kacie or Kazi or whatever her name was froze up like a Popsicle when she realized he was there. Even his compliment had evoked more anger.

What's with that?

Palms planted on the half wall, Griffin stared out at the sea. "And why do you care, Riddell?" Seriously. What was he doing standing here wasting breath and energy over a girl? A white girl, even.

It wasn't like that. He just. . .she was smart. She had a mind that amazed him. She'd outwitted guards. Outmaneuvered bad guys—and him! But there was a girl hurting inside there. She'd been the one to figure out where Aladdin was.

She could rescue everyone but herself.

The thought stopped him cold. What happened to her? That was it. She was pushing him away, afraid he'd get in her head, figure out her secrets, the path to her heart. Hadn't he done the very same thing? Closed off his heart, his feelings, his thoughts? Keeping people at a distance kept them from seeing what he was really like.

Exposed by the revelation, Griffin lowered his head.

God. . .

He had no idea what to pray. Or why he even wanted to pray.

No, he did know. He wanted to help Kacie. Something about her pulled at him, at his sense of honor. Sort of the way he wanted to help his little sister, protect her.

Yeah. . .protect her. Like his sister.

Stomach knotted, Kazi watched through the glass door as Griffin paced, then stood still staring up, then paced again. Hands pressed together as if praying, Griffin looked upward. Muttered something. Shook his head. His chest rose and fell, then his shoulders sagged. She'd upset him by going around him to talk to her contact. And why it bothered her that it bothered him, she didn't know. It wasn't the first time. Probably not the last.

Yet her insides hurt.

Oh Tina. Where are you when I need you? Her steampunk friend had an uncanny way of balancing the forces of Kazi's life in a way that made each day manageable. Carrick knew that. Which is why he'd cut the support out from under her.

"I own you, Kazimiera!"

She closed her eyes, blotting out the memory of that day. The day she'd tried to assert herself, wrestle her own life from his deadly grip. She'd tried to tell him that he didn't own her. That the years of work and the horrible things she'd done for him had more than repaid her debt. He disagreed. Violently.

A swirl of air and a shudder lured her back to the present. Only as she hauled her mind into line did the colors and images before her take shape into the large mass of Griffin Riddell. Inside, he rushed past her to the front door. He yanked it open.

Surprise rippled through her seconds later as Golding and Lambert carried in a stretcher that bore Aladdin. The former assassin, a man she'd met two years ago on assignment, rolled his gaze to hers. His heavily hooded eyes told of the painkillers that numbed his mind.

"Why is he here?" Kazi asked as they moved him into the lower bedroom on the left. "I thought we were letting him get the medical care he needed." She met Griffin's gaze briefly. In that split second, she knew he didn't know what was happening, but he trusted them.

Trust. There's that stupid word again. Her dad had trusted God, she had trusted her brother. . . . Trust was highly overrated.

Golding spoke through huffed breaths, "He was not safe."

When the elder men eased the stretcher toward the bed, Griffin climbed up on the mattress, knelt, and hoisted Aladdin onto the comforter. Then he eased off again. Griffin stood at the foot of the bed, his hands stuffed on his belt as he stared down at one of his teammates. Worry dug into the angular face, hardening his expression. The sight forced Kazi to take a mental step backward. She saw the potential for an explosive temper but also his great effort to harness it.

"Did anyone see you leave with him?" Kazi's heart pounded. This could completely blow this mission.

"Please." Lambert guided her from the room. "Trust us to do our jobs. We trust you to do yours."

Effectively removed, Kazi stood in the hall, disbelieving, as

Lambert closed the door in her face. Shut out. The stinging reminder that she was alone in life left her eyes burning. She lowered her gaze. *Just gut it up. It's better this way.*

But how would they care for Aladdin? He'd had major surgery, hadn't he? Didn't that require extensive follow-up and monitoring?

"Sometimes," came a soft voice, "it does not make sense, the things they do. But trust them, my dear."

Kazi looked over her shoulder to Charlotte Lambert. *I don't know how to trust.* "I'm fine."

Charlotte gave a sad, sympathetic smile. "It hurts, but you learn to understand that when they're in 'mission' mode, they're doing what they do best." She shifted and motioned toward the kitchen. "Would you like some tea?"

Tea? Seriously? She wanted Kazi to sit and drink tea when all of her internal alarms blared? If they'd brought him here, fearing it wasn't safe, then shouldn't they be clearing out?

"Tea?" Charlotte repeated.

"I. . ." Where were all her pithy remarks? Her razor-sharp wit? "Sure." What did she have to lose? The men weren't rushing around packing up. So that meant there wasn't a dire threat, right?

Five minutes and a cup of hot green tea later, she sat at the octagonal glass table in the kitchen next to Mrs. Lambert. Minutes ticked by without a word, without any indication that the woman even wanted to talk. Maybe she didn't. Perhaps it was just a form of social alliance. Supporting each other by being together. Some women did that. Hung out. Went to malls. Sat at coffee shops drinking expensive lattes. But to do that, you had to have friends willing to waste time. Kazi didn't have friends. Not anymore. . .

So she sipped her tea. Tried to calm her racing mind. What was happening back there? Why were they all in there? Were they conspiring about the mission?

Kazi pushed up. "I think I'll—"

Mrs. Lambert's hand coiled around Kazi's. "Just"—blue eyes came to hers—"trust."

Unnerved at the steel that seemed to ram itself through Mrs. Lambert's eyes and down Kazi's spine with the terse yet gentle command, she lowered herself to the chair. Wow. She hadn't seen that coming from the genteel woman. Kazi stared down at the pale-green liquid, feeling disoriented. Disjointed. As if her world had tilted two degrees off its natural orbit.

"Trust them, Kazi."

Her pulse sped. A viper of a reaction whipped its ugly head up. "That's not how I work."

Charlotte squeezed her fingers. "I know." The emphasis on that last word seemed to hang in the air. "You work alone, keep yourself alone, afraid you'll let the wrong person in and get crushed again."

How on this whacked planet the woman knew that, Kazi didn't know. But she braced herself against reacting, against showing Charlotte Lambert that she was right, that she'd read Kazi like an open book. Yet she couldn't tear the shock off her face. She felt it— her eyes wide, her mouth slightly agape, her pulse thumping in her throat. . . . Finally, she swallowed.

"I *know*. You're not the only girl Olin has rescued, you know." A soft smile smoothed away the age lines that graced Charlotte's face. "Give yourself a chance to risk freedom, Kazi."

Breathing became a chore. She had to get out of here before someone heard this woman.

For an older woman, with long, delicate, fragile-looking fingers, she had a death grip on Kazi's hand. Why was she saying these things? What could she mean? And in the heartbeat of a space between those two questions, the truth unveiled itself: Charlotte Lambert knew of Kazi's past.

Kazi snatched her hand free and drew back. "Leave me alone." She stalked out of the kitchen, up the stairs, and across the landing to her room. Inside, she locked the door and turned, staring at it, as if it'd open. As if Charlotte Lambert could read her mind through the wood.

No, she couldn't read minds. There was only one way Mrs. Lambert could know those things—the general. Anger replaced the panic that had widened the gap that led out of the graveyard of her life.

"You're not the only girl Olin has rescued."

What did that mean? She hadn't been rescued. She'd been *hired*! Paid in full. Lambert was in desperate, dire straits and came to her. He *needed* her.

The thought flickered through her mind about his being here. Stepping in on the mission.

Thud! Thud!

Kazi flinched and blinked at the knocks. Why did she feel trapped, cornered? Everything in her told her to run. Get out of here before it was too late. Before someone connected a few dots too many and she ended up a slab of meat like Tina.

"Kacie," Griffin's voice boomed from the other side. "Downstairs. Change of plans."

Change of plans? Was he kidding? She reached for the handle. Kazi yanked open the door, but Griffin was already halfway down the steps.

"What change of plans? We leave Friday. I talked to my contact," she said, hating the growl to her voice as she followed him. He turned the corner and out of sight. No answer. No explanation.

In the living room, the general and Golding conferred quietly and looked up when she entered.

"What's going on?" she demanded. "Why the change?"

Griffin stood off to the side, arms folded over that ridiculously large chest.

"I cannot explain how or why we must do this, but believe me when I say, there is no choice." The general pointed toward a chair and eased himself into a seat opposite.

Kazi remained standing. "If you can't explain it to me, then I proceed with my plans."

"Then you'll be two days too late and fail your mission," the general said. "Please, sit and listen. This once."

Her heart plummeted to her toes. Failing meant he'd take the money back. Meant she'd never be free of Carrick. *Give yourself a chance to risk freedom.* Involuntarily, she swallowed. Pushing butter through ice would've been easier than yielding, but Kazi lowered herself to the sofa.

"I have intel that says Cowboy is being transferred to American custody tomorrow morning. We must stop that from happening." Lambert looked at her. "Since we can't prove who did this to the team, we *cannot* risk Cowboy being remanded into American custody."

"Agreed." Griffin came forward in his chair and assumed that standard pose of his—forearms on his legs, fingers steepled. A rippling in his jaw spoke of the muscle he worked, the tension she'd noted earlier. Finally, his mahogany eyes came to hers. "Are you with us, Kacie?"

Curse the ground the man walked on. She had no choice before his question, but now, if she said yes, he would think she was doing it for *him*. "This is my gig. I'm getting paid. Of course I'm doing it."

Griffin's gaze stayed on her, unchanged. No disappointment. No anger. No. . .nothing.

Kazi shifted, then looked at Olin. "What's the plan?"

"Two CIA operatives are being sent in to retrieve Colton."

Spy against spy. Made things tougher, more adventurous. It wouldn't be the first time.

"We'll delay them while you and Griffin pose as the agents, get Colton, and get out—"

"Wait a minute!" Kazi took a step forward, tucking her hair behind her ear. "An operation like that requires fake IDs, countless hours of monitoring their movement to know the best place to hit, to have backup in place, coordinated efforts with other operatives to cover a trail. . . ." She huffed. "No way that can be ready by morning."

"Things will be ready. I assure you." Golding stared at her with unfazed, dark eyes. "But the question is, will you be ready?"

"I don't have weeks to prepare. And how are things 'ready'?"

"You are quite correct, there is little time to explain or prepare."

"Then—"

He rose. Towering over her, Golding tapped her temple. "In here, Kazi. Will you be ready to save this man?"

"You haven't answered my question." She leaned away from him and sought Lambert out. "How is this ready? How can you be ready when you hired *me* to do this mission?" A tsunami pummeling her wouldn't have hurt as much as the revelation that assaulted her at that moment. "You never planned for me to extract him."

"That is where you are wrong." Lambert stood. "It was my full intention for you to do this. But when I found out the Brits had Cowboy, I talked with Jacob shortly after hiring you. He has been working on a contingency plan." He eyed the dark-skinned man. "Golding has some contacts in the UK."

"Contacts?" Her pulse sped. "How do you—?"

"Kacie," Griffin hissed as he came to her side. Voice lowered, he leaned in, his crisp, clean scent sailing through the one-foot space between his strong jawline and her nose. "Stop trying to control this thing. Work with us—with *me*."

The planet tilted another degree with him so close, so in her face. "I . . ."

Golding went on. "There is a club in the South End of London called Bread & Butter."

Someone set her world to "spin." "South. . ." The name died on her lips. "Bread—" She tucked her head, a flood of incongruent and throbbing images bombarding her mind. Strobe lights. Pulsating bodies. Thick air that wasn't breathable let alone maneuverable. Screaming music and patrons. Annoying, infectious laughter. . .*Tina*. No.

God. . .please, no. Not there.

Warmth pressed against her back, soft and subtle. Yet strong.

"Kacie?" Griffin whispered, touching the center of her back. "You with us?"

Raising a hand to her forehead, she bought time. At the trembling in her fingers, she fisted her hand. "Ye. . .yeah." She cleared her throat. Only then did she realize that less than two inches separated her from Griffin. When had he closed in? She looked up—straight into soul-stirring eyes that in an instant seemed to penetrate her every defense. Her every secret. Down, through the sod of her made-up strength. The dirt of her life. Past the lying worms, the slugs. . .straight to the va—

Hands on his tight abs, she nudged him back. Took a draught of the cool air and inhaled Griffin's crisp scent again. He'd gotten close that time. *Too close. Seal it off. Push him away.* Especially if they were headed to the B & B.

She looked at Lambert. "Why are we changing plans again?"

"The exchange is unexpected and quick—it wasn't scheduled until next week. But something happened. We don't know what, but they're trading him tomorrow. We're convinced if we don't extract him now, we may never see Colton alive again."

Miranda, Venezuela

"Agua, por favor." Range eased onto the stool at the bar. Elbows on the counter, he pushed his hands through his hair. A week. Seven long days and he hadn't gotten any closer to finding Canyon. It made no sense. Who would do this? And why? Granted, Canyon had a way of ticking people off. Range had a lifetime worth of experience.

How many times did I swear I'd kill him?

And now, if somehow by some miracle he didn't find him, Canyon would be dead. Groaning, Range fisted his hands in his hair and tensed his muscles. This was asinine. He wasn't a fighter, a warrior like his brother. That's why he'd gone into the Coast Guard.

Where was that water? He lifted his head and glanced around. The bartender leaned against the counter talking with another man.

"Agua, por favor," Range said, raising a finger.

Eyes hooded with disgust, the bartender stomped to the sink, grabbed a glass, and flipped the tap. He swung around and planted the cloudy water on the counter. Water splashed over the rim as the Latino glared at him.

Come to think of it, Range was probably safer drinking beer than water. But he wouldn't compromise every moral fiber and the Metcalfe name—not that anyone here knew him. "*Gracias,*" he muttered as he set money on the counter and left without touching the drink. Even as he pushed his way out the door, he chided himself. Another hour in here, sitting, listening, and maybe he'd hear something. Or someone would walk up and say, "I hear you're looking for a cocky, yellow-haired American."

Range snorted as he crossed the street and entered the motel. Exhaustion weighted his limbs as he trudged down the threadbare carpet to room 114. He passed a vending machine and eyed it wearily, patting down his pockets. Empty. He'd need to get some money from his duffel, so he pushed himself toward the room that lacked in every area imaginable. As he pointed the key toward the lock, he paused. His breath backed into his throat.

The door stood ajar, the wood splintered.

He took a step back and eyed the frame. Range reached behind and lifted his black sweatshirt. His hand closed around high-impact plastic, stippled grip. He eased the Glock from its holster at the small of his back. Toeing the door, he tilted his head and peeked into the darkened interior.

Light from the hall stretched into the room. Farther. . .farther. . . A T-shirt lay strewn across the floor. His belt next to it. Pants. Coins. Toiletries.

Weapon at the ready, he sidestepped into the room. The small bathroom—he'd never again complain about how Canyon left their bathroom—to the right. Keen senses alighted on the ghost of a shadow drifting across the carpet.

A flash of movement to the left.

Range swung toward the assailant. Too close, too fast. Light exposed the man as a hairy ape of a man. Ape's shoulder rammed into his chest. Drove his spine into the wall. *Ooph!* Range jerked the Glock up and slammed it into the guy's skull. A sickening thud echoed in the darkened room.

Ape stumbled back, cupping his head.

Range steeled himself against the warmth that slid down his head, mirroring the dark liquid dripping down the man's face. Rage flooded the face. Eyebrows went down. Lips snarled. He hulked.

If Range didn't shoot him now, Ape would beat the life out of him. Range aimed and fired. The man still came. Stumbled. Crumbled.

Adrenaline surged through Range's body, but he had no time to catch his breath, his mind tripping over the earlier shadow he'd noted. Where—

Air swirled near his face, a meaty fist narrowly missing his nose. He whipped around.

A hand flew at him. Connected with his jaw. Range stumbled back. The weapon flipped backward, but he clung to it, refusing to yield his only defense. Knees wobbling, he forced himself to remain upright. To focus. To fight. These guys weren't playing hide-and-seek. This was life or death.

Another right hook came at him.

He jerked back. The punch rammed into his shoulder, throwing him off balance. He hit the floor hard. The breath knocked from his lungs. He blinked. Saw the man looming over him. This was it.

Gun!

His fingers tightened around the stippled grip. He yanked it up and eased the trigger back. The report clapped through the night. *Splat!* Something wet and warm hit his face. The man fell on him with a wheezing groan as the air left his lungs. He was still. Dead still.

Pulse hammering, Range lay there, gulping air. Shock pinned him to the floor.

Shouts erupted from somewhere outside. The strengthening surge of adrenaline lit his veins afire. Would that be backup for the bad guys? Or the authorities? Either way, finding an American with two dead Venezuelans wouldn't look good no matter how they cut it.

He shoved the guy off and leapt to his feet. After bolting the door, he grabbed as much of his stuff as he could and stuffed it in the emptied duffel. At the window, he peeked around the curtain. The street lay empty and dark. Perfect. He freed the latch and tugged it back. Metal screeched against metal. Halfway open, it wouldn't budge. Ramming his elbow against it didn't help.

Banging at the door made him jerk.

Crack! The door flew open.

CHAPTER 18

Larnaca International Airport, Cyprus

Clearing Cypriot security had been a lot easier than Griffin expected, especially with Golding's powerful presence. The man walked them through the checkpoint without so much as one armed guard batting an eye. What was with that? Who was Golding?

There was more to the man than being the friend of a Jew who saved Israel two years ago. He had influence, connections, and prestige. The way he'd stepped in, removed Aladdin from exposure, and hidden him in his home told Griffin something.

He just wasn't sure what that something was.

Probably because Kacie had him distracted. She hadn't been the same since Golding and Lambert mentioned that club. He'd seen the reaction, even if the others hadn't. Her hands shook, and her breathing went low and deep. He expected her to fall out cold. But she hadn't. She rallied. For the most part. The other part hadn't recovered from whatever blow that news delivered.

He'd find out. Everything instinctive and protective rose up as he watched the color drain from her face. He inched closer, ready to pull her into his arms, hold her tight—whatever it took to make that fear and panic go away. She wore attitude, spunk, and feistiness. That's what he liked on her. Not this collapsed shell sitting across from him on the private jet—another of Golding's benefits.

"Nice digs," he said as he smoothed a hand over the cream leather armrest.

Kacie kept her gaze on the portal to the outside world. No recognition that he'd spoken registered in her eyes. Light stretched through the window and bathed her face in the orange glow of sunset as they streaked toward the UK. Halfway through the flight, a light meal was served along with drinks. She didn't touch any of it.

"Come on now, Baby Girl. You need to put some meat on those bones."

Elbow propped on the arm, she rested her lips on her knuckles, her gaze still on the great beyond. Griffin set aside his tray and slid across the small space into the seat beside her.

Still no response.

He angled toward her. "Kacie."

Though she didn't look at him, her gaze drifted to the carpet of the plane.

"I saw it, Baby Girl." *Take it slow, Legend. She's spooked as it is.* But he knew he had to call her on this.

"What do you *think* you saw?" The seething tone warned him he was on the right path. But to be careful. Tread carefully.

"Fear. Panic. At the mention of that club."

Her gaze flitted back to the window. Her milky-white throat rippled as she swallowed.

"I'm going to be there with you. I got your back. Know what I'm saying?" He leaned down, trying to peer into her eyes. "But if I need to know something—"

"You don't." She whipped toward him, her white-blond hair sparkling under the tease of a stray ray of sunlight.

Mere inches separated their faces. Flecks of gold glimmered in her green eyes. The black circle that encompassed the irises. But he saw so much more. Pain. Crushed dreams. "A'right." He nodded. "You're right. I don't need to know. But it doesn't change that I'm going to be there for you." He tucked his chin, meeting her eye to eye. "Whatever happens, I'm there."

"Your focus should be on getting your *boy* back."

He might not read people the way some could, but he didn't need an interpreter for that one. "You're a spy. I get that you might not understand a cooperative effort, but working together benefits me getting my boy back. I am not so narrowly focused that I can't widen my scope."

Finally! She looked at him. "I don't need your sympathy or your pity. I know my job. I'll get it done. Don't worry about me."

"Oh, I am." More than he'd ever admit. Deep, grievous wounds had gouged hope from her heart.

He'd give her some time to get her bearings, to reset her focus.

Griffin eased back in the chair, intentionally not returning to his own seat. He folded his arms over his chest, fully aware that his elbows pressed into her space, leaned his head back, and closed his eyes.

Funny how a week ago, he would've gnawed her backside for this attitude. A little time and an inadvertent glimpse into her life—that footwork on the wall at Golding's he'd *never* forget—and Griffin knew there was more to Baby Girl than she'd ever open up about. If he'd figured one thing out about the spritelike girl, it was that talk was cheap. And apparently handed out with every male encounter she'd had, like pocket change for beggars. Bread for the homeless. Water for prisoners.

Prisoners. She'd freed him from that prison. Granted, it hadn't exactly been a legal act. Necessary, but highly illegal. What would happen when this mission was over? What penalty would he face back in the States? They'd already given him life for the congressman's death. Which was messed up in every way the mind could drum up. He hadn't been nowhere near that man's home or life. Who cared if some rich white boy wanted to run the country but couldn't even lead his own family? Not Griffin Riddell. He had family. Respect. Honor.

Had. He *had* it. Not anymore. They'd destroyed his life. All he'd worked for flushed down the drain and straight into the sewers of failure. His life stunk.

A sharp pinch on the soft flesh of his underarm snapped his eyes open. He jerked to Kacie.

She stared back unrepentant. As if daring him to get angry or lash out.

Intentionally, Griffin turned his attention to the galley. "Have they brought dessert yet?" With a half yawn, he resettled in the chair.

"Are you comfortable?" Her tone was civil, but he heard the sarcasm, the aggravation behind it.

"Yeah." He lolled his head to the side and nodded. "I'm good." Arms folded, he pressed his side into the arm that separated them, making sure to edge into her space more. Eyes closed, he yawned and let out a groan-moan.

Aw man, he really shouldn't mess with her like this. But the girl made it worth the guilt.

Beside him, he heard the tinkling of ice in her water glass.

She'd get along well with Phoenix. They both had that insane common sense and obsessive nature. *Why can't you act like a grown man, Griff?* How many times had his sister shrieked that at him after he'd pulled some fool stunt?

An ice-cold sensation stung his legs and thighs. Wet.

Griffin leapt up. Out of the seat. On his toes as water ran down his legs. Mouth agape, he stared at the slick black spot on his black tactical pants.

"Sorry," Kacie said, her words completely void of regret. She locked eyes with him as she set the glass on the tray on the table between the two sets of seats. "I guess I bumped your arm."

Nostrils flaring, he fought for something to say—something civil. Not that words didn't come to mind. But those weren't words a good ol' Southern boy said in front of a lady. "Are you out of your fool mind?"

"What?" She sat back, playing the wide-eyed innocent. "Oh, did I spill?"

Griffin gritted his teeth. An idea hit him. He stomped to the galley.

Mustering all her skills not to laugh at the way Griffin Riddell exploded from his seat when she dumped her water in his lap had proven near impossible. But she'd done it. Played off the prank. Though ire screamed through his expression, he'd hidden it. She allowed herself another small laugh, watching as he disappeared into the rear of the plane. To the bathroom, most likely, trying to dry off his pants. She snickered.

But really, what was his problem? That thick bicep had bulged into her personal space, right under her nose. Then after she reprimanded him, he'd gotten even closer. She never mentioned that for a split second she'd seen herself resting her cheek against his arm, relaxing. *Ha. Like that'd ever happen.*

Griffin's large frame emerged from the rear. Alarm spiraled through Kazi at his expression loaded with retribution. Shoulders taut, chin tucked ever so slightly, those deep, rich eyes pinned her. Then she saw it. The water decanter in his hand.

She punched to her feet. "Put it down."

"What?" He stalked up to her so close that if he took in a deep breath, his chest would bump her nose. Slowly, eyes on her, he bent and retrieved her glass. "I'm just going to refill your—"

"No." She snatched it from him and flung it on the leather seats, afraid if she turned her back on him, he'd dump that ice-cold water on her. "Put it down, Griffin."

"Oh." He jutted his jaw. "What? You afraid I might *spill* it?"

This would not end well, especially in the confined space of a private jet. "Okay." She raised her hands in surrender but also to enable herself to fight him off quicker. "I'm sorry. I shouldn't have done that."

He stuffed the decanter onto the table. "Done what, Baby Girl?" He inched closer.

Whoa. He smelled good. His chest larger than the width of her shoulders. He was bigger—*much* bigger than her. Her defenses skittered up her arms like spiders seeking refuge.

"You should've stayed on your side."

Arms out, he shrugged. "I'm a big guy. I need space."

"More like your own planet."

His eyebrows rose. "No, you didn't. . ."

Someone laughed. Kazi blinked, realizing it'd been her.

"What, you think this is funny now?"

"Fine." She backed up one step. "I'll give you space."

"Aw, now it ain't that easy." His head cocked to the side. "You drowned my pride, Baby Girl."

"Stop calling me that." It unhinged her in too many wrong ways.

He came forward.

Her hand spiked out.

Griffin deflected the strike.

She struck out with her left.

Again, he defended himself, his gaze never leaving hers. It spurred her on. Made her angry that he was trying to unnerve her, gain the upper hand. That wouldn't work. It wouldn't get him what he wanted. She wouldn't yield. Wouldn't show her belly like some dog in submission.

A roundhouse kick.

Blocked.

She spun—a seat knocked her off balance. But she used the mistake to swing the confrontation in her favor.

Griffin motioned with his hands as if to say, *Bring it!*

She hopped forward, then threw her feet toward his abs. Midair, in the seconds before she actually struck him, Kazi saw him step back and snap up his hands.

He whipped her legs around, spinning her straight into the ground. Metal collided with her head. Stars sprinkled over her vision. She stayed on the industrial-grade carpet. Waited for him to feel bad about nearly knocking her down. Then use his compassion against him.

"You givin' up already, Baby Girl? Had enough?"

Kazi glared up at him as she pushed to her feet. "You're not like most men." Get him distracted, get his mind on the verbal assault, and she could nail him. Take down the giant.

He grinned.

"You don't have a heart."

Face awash with dejection, he placed a hand on his heart. "Aw, that hurts."

Bingo.

She had seconds to seize on his weakness. But a somersault—no room. It'd have to stay hand-to-hand. Kazi threw a right hook at his jaw and connected.

But it was like connecting with a cement wall. Fire spiraled down her wrist into her elbow and up into her shoulder. She cordoned off the pain and focused on the fight. On beating him. She stomped his foot—a steel-toed boot. No effect. Frustration coated her every thought. She swung around, grabbing his wrist as he deflected another punch from her, rolled around, and flipped her left arm back—straight to his face.

Another hit!

In a second that felt like an eternity, Griffin caught her hand, twisted it behind her. His right arm hooked up and around her neck. He squeezed, shoving her forward. She blinked and found her face sandwiched between one of the seats and his solid pecs.

Grip tighter and harder than cement, Griffin whispered, "What's got you running—put this fire into beating *that*."

The way his deep bass voice tickled her ear sent swarms of panic rushing through her stomach. She wrestled her shoulders, trying to free herself, but only met with pain. A grunt escaped then morphed into a whimper.

"You can beat it, Kacie." His face leaned in nearer.

She darted a look and found herself falling into the richest, brownest eyes. Blood dribbled down his chin. She'd busted his lip, hurt him, but he'd not flinched or complained. The realization unseated her. She yanked her gaze forward.

"Imagine what it'll be like to stop running."

She pushed away—and miraculously, he released her. Even stumbling and putting two feet between them didn't release her from the invisible hold he had on her. "You have no idea what you're talking about."

"I see that fear in your eyes every time someone gets a little too close to the truth. What about the club? You ready to go in there and—"

"Yes."

"No, you're not. It's why you're on edge. Why you've been silent for the last three hours. Why I drew you out to get your head in the game."

Drew me out? He did this. . .on purpose? A violent crash in her chest made the cabin spin. *Have. . .to. . .get away.* "Stay out of my head." She turned and stalked to the bathroom, calling over her shoulder, "I don't need you or your help."

"You can't get rid of me with tough talk."

His words chased her into the lavatory. She slammed the door shut, flipped the lock, kicked the door. Again. Banged it. Crazy-mad, she slumped against the steel door and growled. Anger wrapped its lengthy tendrils around her heart.

Oh Tina. . .I need you. . . This was where that magic friend bond helped her escape the frenetic raving of her mind and heart. A stabilizing force, Tina had always known how to talk Kazi off the ledge.

It felt like Griffin pushed her off it.

He'd pushed her in more ways than that. Around him, she was unbalanced and unnerved. Her stomach twisted and knotted, her mind even worse. Which meant they had to go their separate ways.

A soft knock came to the door. "We're on approach. Landing in ten," a female voice announced.

Standing, Kazi looked in the mirror, surprised to find a ragged, worn-out version of herself staring back. She smoothed her hair and shook her head. No wonder Griffin only saw a petulant, angry girl. She'd wait out the landing in here, thereby limiting her time with the beefy guy. Once the tires screeched on the tarmac, she opened the door. And froze.

Arm over the top of the door as if hugging it, Griffin rested his forehead on his arm, looking miserable. Eyes held fast to hers.

"Get out of my—"

"You can hate me, but we're still working together."

"That's your mistake." The words were automatic. The standard response when a man tried to inject feelings into a situation to manipulate her into his court, his power. "I don't need to have any feelings for or against you to complete this mission."

"True. My point was that we need to be on the same side. Ready to defend each other."

Oh.

A long hesitation ensued.

She should say something. Tell him to get away. Tell him they had to get his boys back—his only real priority. But something had shifted inside her. Scared her. No. . .*petrified* her. As if someone had stolen into the graveyard and dug up the casket.

"You know this club, so you can probably anticipate trouble. I need to know you're going to have my back. That you won't abandon me to the wolves."

"Aban—" Her pulse stampeded over his words. *She* had never abandoned anyone. *Everyone* had abandoned *her*. "I don't work that way."

"You look out for yourself, Baby Girl. You've done it every second since you sprang me from Wallens Ridge. Convince me." He lowered his arm and leaned against the wall, affording her an exit from the musty lavatory. Hands stuffed in his pockets, he sighed. "Convince me when we go in there, you got my back, Kacie."

Agitated at his words, she understood the deeper meaning. He was afraid. Afraid of being abandoned. Of getting strung up again. Fiery slivers of surprise rippled through her to think that this undaunted mountain of a man was afraid someone like her would leave him, as he said, to the wolves.

"Convince me, Kazimiera."

Mentally, her eyes shut at Carrick's sickening words. He'd wanted so much more than words or a promise. Her gaze traced the lines of Griffin's angular features. Is that what he wanted, too?

No. He wasn't like that.

Of course he is. He's a guy.

Fine. She'd played that game for years. No loss. No worries.

She tiptoed up, planted her hands on the corded muscles that bulged so his neck and shoulders almost appeared as one. Then she leaned in.

His eyes locked on hers so fast and hard she thought she heard a click. Worse—she felt something like the Loch Ness monster swimming through her belly as the moment in time froze. So close, his scent tingling her nose, she felt like a small child facing a giant. A big. . .muscular. . .beautiful giant.

Do it fast before you lose your nerve. All part of the game. Keep him where she needed him.

He hauled in a fast breath, and his eyes widened for a fraction of a second. Catching her arms, Griffin pushed her back. Hard. Eyebrows drawn tight, nostrils flared, he drew away from her. "*What* are you thinking?"

"I—" The growl in his voice tangled her thoughts.

"*Don't* do that again." He shook a meaty finger at her. "Not ever! I'm not—" His chest heaved. The muscle in his jaw worked as he lowered his gaze. "Forget it. Let's do this."

She watched him, watched his shoulders, watched the broad biceps that forced his arms out so that his elbows couldn't touch his trim but still large waist. That man carried the weight of the world on his shoulders. Carried it without a complaint. Without a grudge.

And it dawned on her that he'd been willing to carry her load, too. But now. . .

I'm on my own.

Just like always.

In reality, that was the best place to be. Nobody got hurt. Nobody got killed. Keeping things to herself, discarding feelings meant those around her and connected to her remained business acquaintances. Nothing more. And that meant they stayed alive. If Carrick could peek through her carefully guarded crypt of feelings. . .she feared what he might see examining it through the lens of Griffin Riddell.

CHAPTER 19

Vaughn Residence, Virginia

W hy are you keeping me here?"

"Son, you're not thinking clearly."

Marshall shoved the glass of water off the bedside table. "I'm thinking just fine."

A nurse rushed forward, but the glass—which turned out to be plastic—clunked against the linoleum floor and splashed water all over the wall.

"It's the drugs talking," his father said, oozing condescension. Which in and of itself was wrong, since his father had always had short conversations and an even shorter temper when it came to Marshall. "You're at the hospital, Marshall. It was that blasted job of yours—you were injured again, almost killed. I keep telling you to get a respectable job—"

"Defending our country is the most respectable and honorable career that exists."

With a huff, his father shook his head again. "I'll come back when you're more reasonable." He stood, stuffed his hands in his pockets.

"I'm done." Marshall ripped the IV from his hand, savoring the prickling fire in his hand and arm. Pain was good. Reminded him he was human, that he wasn't drugged out of his mind. He tossed them down deliberately in a dramatic display so his father would have no doubt where he stood.

The door opened, and Rel stepped in with a gray bin propped on her small hip. Her eyes widened when she saw his father. "Oh, I'm sorry," she said as she backed out.

"No, no. Kim, you're just in time with that medication." His father motioned to Rel and sighed. "I think he's overworked. He's having fantastical delusions." Hand on her shoulder, he said, "Make sure he gets some rest—do your job and do it right. He's a bit too feverish right now." He turned a taut expression to Marshall. "Straighten up, son. If you continue making irrational assertions, they'll never let you out of here."

Why was his dad so hell-bent on keeping him drugged and imprisoned? What was his father protecting? "I'm as straight and clear as they come, Dad."

Disdain dripped from the graying man stalking out of the room.

Rel came to the bed. She bent and retrieved the IV needle. "What are you doing?" she hissed as she worked on the tubing. "You're going to give it away."

"Testing him." Marshall's heart hammered. "Do you still have it?"

Her gaze hit him as she reconnected the tower. She lifted a pen from her pocket, twisted it, then wrote on his chart. "If we keep using this, they'll figure it out."

"After today, it won't matter."

She paused.

"He's playing me, Rel. Thinks I'm an idiot." He clamped his jaw, thinking back through the conversation. How his dad had played stupid, tried to steer the conversation constantly away from the "accident," as his father had called it. "Nothing's changed. No matter what, I can't make that man happy."

"Then stop trying," she whispered so softly, he wasn't sure she'd spoken the words at first. "You're a great guy, crazy-smart, and. . ." Her gaze dropped.

Marshall pushed a hand through his hair, then scratched the several-days' growth of beard. "Yeah, well, he's never satisfied. He wanted an Ivy League son, and I didn't follow that path, so he's still trying to force me into that mold."

"He's a fool if he can't see how amazing you are."

Like a dead weight, silence dropped between them. He caught her gaze, but she pulled it away, pink tingeing her cheeks, as she rolled the clear plastic between her fingers.

What was this? He searched her face, disbelieving. Whoa. Had she really said all that? About him? A beautiful girl. . .talking about *him* like that. In earnest. Not joking? What did he do with that? Nobody liked him. Nobody thought he was amazing. He was the butt of jokes, the comic relief. Not the hero. He'd never be fierce like Max. Or charming the way Cowboy was with the ladies. Or slick and smooth-talking like Midas. And Legend had that quiet, brooding manner that sucked women in like a vacuum.

But. . .Rel. . .a gem in a pile of coal—he didn't want to risk letting her think he wasn't interested. And yet they didn't have time to sort out their feelings. What if he was completely misreading this? *Dude, that could hurt.* Marshall wrapped his hand around hers, pulling those brown eyes to his. "Get me out of here."

"I am." She looked to the door. "We need more time. You're not strong enough yet."

"No, today. I can't stay here with him drugging me, lying to me. I've had time to think about it. He has to know something about what happened." Marshall motioned to the room. "How else would I be here?"

"Someone he knows. . . ?"

"Right, and they'd bring me to him with two broken ribs, a concussion, and just say, 'Oops'?" He shook his head. "My dad would come unglued. He's got to be in on it."

The facts were never simple. Through Rel and her counter–drug administration over the last few days, Marshall's brain fog had lifted. Now he could process—or at least try—what had happened.

Fact number one: His father explicitly knew Marshall had been injured in the attack that wiped out the team.

Fact number two: His father or someone associated with him had Marshall brought back here, erected a pseudo hospital to trick him into thinking he was getting real medical care for grievous, near-fatal injuries. Yet as far as Marshall could tell, he had a few cuts and scrapes to go with the healing ribs that no longer felt like he was breathing fire. The doc said he had a concussion, but who knew if that intel was legit?

Fact number three: His father wanted him sedated so he either couldn't remember what happened or couldn't leave the room.

What's he trying to hide?

If there was one person who would know what was going on, it'd be the Old Man. "What's Lambert saying?"

She hesitated. "The last few nights, I haven't been able to reach him, so I left messages."

Lambert out of touch? At a time like this? That meant the situation had escalated and either Lambert was dead or in hiding. *What's going on?* Urgency sped through his system. "Okay, get me clothes."

Rel smiled and reached into a bin she'd brought into the room.

She lifted a pair of jeans and a T-shirt. "I guessed on sizes."

He swung his legs over the edge of the bed. The room spun. He jabbed out a hand to steady himself. "Whoa."

"Did you miss the part where I said you're still too weak?"

"Didn't miss it. Just irrelevant." He tested his sea legs as he hovered near the bed. A little shaky, but already the surge of adrenaline was filling in the gaps the injuries had left.

As he reached for the pants she'd set on the bed, a wave of heat washed over him. Shouts. Shots. Like an undammed river, the memories flooded him. The locker room. Reaching for his change of clothes. Azzan sprinting into the room shouting, "Take cover! Under attack."

Doors burst inward. A stream of men in tac gear. The chaos. Deafening noises reverberating off the metal roof. Watching Azzan flip up into the rafters with a rifle. Marshall swung around with a left jab at an assailant. A right hook. Then a sharp pain in his back.

A half-dozen men converging on the team. Being dragged out into the main bay. Shoved to the cement, his face kissing the ground. Midas flying through the air into the room. Colton erupting like a volcano in one incredible last stand.

One bad guy firing at Dighton. *Crack!*

Marshall?

Two men emerging from a car. One an oversized figure. One an oversized ego.

"Gecko," he breathed.

"Marshall?"

He blinked and stared into the pale-brown eyes of Rel Dighton. Was her brother dead? Marshall had seen the man shot down in cold blood. Just like Azzan. Were the two men gone?

"What is it?" She touched his shoulder.

"I know who took us down. Gecko."

Confusion screwed her face tight. "I'm sorry?"

"A man who has worked security for my father for years. He's slippery and quick, so my sister and I nicknamed him Gecko." But the reinstated memory unleashed a whole new bevy of questions.

Namely, why was his father trying to kill his friends?

Heathrow International Airport, London

Griffin hustled down the metal steps, his heart hammering in his chest like a misfiring Gatling gun. He roughed a hand over his face and head, working himself down after the kiss she'd nearly planted on him. What was she thinking? Did she really think the only way to him was through his pants?

Was that her way, what she'd done in her life, to fulfill her mission?

His respect for her fell through the earth. Straight to China. He wanted to pace, but his pulse did it for him, rapid-time. No, he didn't want to think of her like that. She had more honor than that. Had to.

A black SUV screeched around a corner and barreled toward them. Griffin slunk back toward the stairs to use them for cover as he reached for his weapon.

Kacie emerged and stalked down the stairs, straight toward the SUV, right into its path. It lurched to a stop directly in front of her. She reached for the handle and glanced over her shoulder, amusement in her expression. So, this was their ride. Griffin toned down his tension and crossed the ten-foot space to the vehicle.

Once the doors shut, a vacuum pulled at his ears.

"Bjorne is waiting." A male voice cut through the darkness as they slid around planes and luggage carriers, racing toward the gate. The zigzagging around pylons and construction made it feel like they were in a pinball machine.

A hand offered bottles of water.

Griffin twisted the cap, listening for the crack of the safety seal to know he wasn't going to be drugged or poisoned. He heard the sound and opened the drink, then took a long draught. "When will the exchange be made with our man?" He squinted at the dials on the control panel, hoping to feed some AC into the rear. Too warm.

"I do not have that information. That will be provided by Burgess." The man gave a humorless laugh. "I'm sure you'll understand data like that is heavily protected. Too many hands in the pot and all that."

Griffin took another swig. "You don't have a British accent."

"Neither do you."

He glanced at Kacie, who hadn't moved or spoken. Not the best plan to be at odds immediately before a pivotal part of the mission. But no way would he let her think that kissing him would buy his confidence.

Sweat beaded on his brow. Using his forearm, he swiped it. Took another drink. "How long to this club?"

"Are you warm?"

"Yeah." Why did his tongue feel five sizes too big for his mouth? He lifted the bottle. . .and stilled. His gaze flicked to Kacie's water. Unopened. Her gaze was on the window.

Gray washed in around his field of vision. Griffin shook his head—but it only seemed to feed the haze devouring him. He cursed as a white sheet dropped on his mind and vision.

Kazi cupped Griffin's head as he slumped toward her. She eased him down, swiveling around to lower his bulk onto the leather seat. As she drew her hand from under his face, she traced the smooth but rugged angles of his jaw. The face of a steadfast man.

He'd trusted her. Completely. Fed right into her hands. Just as every target had. When she'd tried to kiss him, his reaction had been utterly unexpected.

Then again, so had hers. A funnel of hot fire zapped down her chest, straight into her belly. It'd startled her. Then he'd reacted so. . .angrily. Not with the physical response she'd typically elicited from men. He shoved her away. As if she were dirty. Contaminated.

Not a revelation to her, but to see it on his face, to experience his rejection, stung. Why, she had no idea. She wasn't interested in him. Not like that. Not in a relationship. They never worked, not in her profession. Besides, she and Griffin had no vested interest in each other beyond the mission. Which was good—she didn't want him to end up like Tina.

Thus the reason she'd betrayed him, not said anything when Andrez Bjorne handed her the water bottles. It was better for him to be drugged than dead. *I am so sorry, Griffin.*

"You impress me yet again, Kazimiera."

Kazi pushed up onto the edge of the seat, blocking Griffin from Andrez's view, and lowered her chin. "I work alone. You know that. It's better this way." She brushed the hair from her face, hoping he didn't see the tremor in her hand. "What's the gig?"

"Naturally, you cannot expect us to expose our resources and methods to Americans just because one of their operatives got sloppy."

"Sloppy?" Kazi bit her tongue on the error. She shouldn't care. Or show that she might.

Andrez leaned forward. The dome light glistened on his slicked-back hair. "Kazimiera, what is this? Taking sides?"

"Wouldn't you like to think that?"

He sniggered. "Indeed." Straightening, he released the buttons on his jacket. "Relax." Andrez propped his elbows on his knees. With the heavily tinted windows and dull illumination, the interior shaded the already-dark circles under his eyes. "I'm not here to hurt you."

The inevitable "but" to that statement lurked in the darkened interior.

He said nothing.

Neither did she.

Andrez clapped and dropped back against the seat. "I'd forgotten how delicious you are, darling. So uptight, so ready to chop someone's head off. Too bad Carrick isn't here to see you fawning over a man."

Kazi's heart caught. "He's not here?"

Andrez's smirk told her the answer. She allowed herself some mental room to breathe a little easier.

"Does he need to be, pet? Is there a reason he should be concerned that loaning you his assets, his people, will come back to haunt him?"

Kazi worked a colossal effort at tempering her frustration. Andrez had one intention with showing up at the airport, a menial task typically assigned to the underlings who could be discarded at the slightest whim. "Get on with it. You wouldn't be here if you didn't have a message."

He nodded. "Be aware, Kazimiera: he knows. Carrick is monitoring your every move. He is curious about your involvement with these men." Again, he leaned into the light, and this time she was convinced he did it intentionally to backlight his muddy brown eyes. "He finds it. . .*amusing* that you did not clear this with him."

In other words, Carrick wasn't pleased, but he was going to let the offense slide—as long as she cooperated. Which meant he had a plan. He wanted something. He always wanted something. Would she *never* be free of his grasp?

"Noted." She kept her tone even and her words neutral. A small miracle. "I'm waiting."

Andrez pursed his lips, then rubbed his hands. "The Americans have requested delivery of their citizen immediately, making all sorts of grandiose agreements and pleadings. That, of course, concerned the spooks and MI6, which in turn alerted Carrick Burgess."

Translated, someone in MI6 fed information to Burgess.

"When and where?"

Andrez smirked.

The car slowed. Kazi's pulse sped.

"It's nearly teatime. It'd be terribly impolite to discuss unpleasantries before a drink," he said as the door opened.

Kazi wanted to curse as the enormous warehouse loomed over them. It'd been a virtual prison for her—mentally—for the last ten years.

Having exited, Bjorne extended a hand. "Come along, Kazimiera."

She glanced down at Griffin, heart in her throat. What would they do to him? What would *he* do or say to her when he came to?

"Don't worry about the black man. We'll take good care of him."

Good care—right into the Thames? She narrowed her eyes at Andrez. Threatening him would only heighten his suspicion and increase the risk of Griffin returning to America in a box. She stretched her leg and stepped into the bitter cold of London's February. A thick fog curled around the buildings and added to the preternatural feeling.

He tucked her hand into the crook of his arm and took a step forward.

She took one backward. Staring at the doors that once hung on a German castle, Kazi mustered all the courage she had left. But going in there. . .it almost certainly meant no going back. Never being free. She had to force herself to take comfort in the fact Carrick wasn't here. He was off gallivanting, spewing money and making power grabs. Pressing some poor puck beneath his finger.

"If you don't want to tarnish Carrick's reputation," she said, "you'll make sure that man in the car is not injured."

Andrez arched an eyebrow at her. "Are we making demands? Have you forgotten what he's done for you, how much you owe him, *love*?"

Pulse thrumming, she worked to steady her nerves. "These men are Americans. He should remember he wants *allies* there, not enemies. Besides, that man in there is incredibly trained."

With a laugh, he said, "So incredibly trained we took him out with a doped bottle of water?"

That's my fault—he trusted me. But she had to focus on her point, on pushing the attention of Andrez and Carrick away from the men they were saving. "Carrick has long wanted a foot across the water."

Andrez's head tilted back as he seemed to consider her words.

"It is to his benefit to make this happen."

"It is not for you to say what benefits Mr. Burgess." He turned to the driver, who stood at the boot of the car. "The Revelry."

Kazi's fear bottomed out. They were going to put Griffin in a suite on the upper level of the club called The Revelry. Andrez gripped her upper arm and led Kazi into the Bread & Butter as if she were a petulant child. Inside, music pounded as they moved along the main wall. He used a key card and accessed a hidden door that slid into the wall. With a thrust, he pushed her ahead. Behind them the door hissed shut, and the deafening music muted.

Kazi walked, knowing full well they were headed into what those on the inside of Burgess's vast network called the Underground. Here, there were passages that led to more passages that led to government buildings, the rooftop, secret rooms, and bunkers. She'd even heard a rumor once that Carrick had vanished into a room and turned up on a boat miles from here. He had more tunnels than the Eurostar.

"How's it to be back with the family?" Andrez's snicker bounced along the cement passage as they headed to the rear lair via elevator and a set of stairs.

"Just grand," Kazi mumbled. She could handle Andrez. The guy was a mouthpiece, not much more, for Carrick. And by family, he meant the Underground. The shackle on her life that freeing Lambert's men would obliterate.

That is, as long as she pulled off the mission. As long as Carrick's interest in her involvement with Lambert and his team didn't go beyond just that.

Andrez led her to a door that led to an underground facility. Unusual. "Where exactly are we going?"

"I've got a team set up below."

They were going to let her finish the mission. Alone. Her mind whirled. She hadn't expected them to cooperate so freely. How had Golding or Lambert pulled this off? Nobody worked Carrick this easily.

"We've replicated everything from the uniforms to the vehicles, right down to a couple of American agents we've brought in to help us."

As they veered down another hall, Kazi stopped short. "No, no Americans."

He raked an eye up and down her. "Why not?"

He didn't need the reasons. "No Americans." Especially since he'd pulled all this cloak-and-dagger stuff with her.

"Very well. Have your way."

She stepped into an underground parking garage where two black SUVs waited. The six armed and suited men stood looking more like thugs with their bulging biceps and attitudes than American operatives.

"Sloan and Gray," Andrez said as they crossed to the other side. "We won't need your services after all. Talk with Smithers for compensation of your time."

The two men cast a long, hard glare at Kazi before departing without a word. By their reeking attitudes, she'd made the right decision. She shifted to Andrez, watching over his shoulder as the two exited. Once the door closed, she turned to the others. "Play it safe and cool. Security Services is expecting the exchange, so we let them expect it. And we fulfill it." She met each man's gaze. "Understood?"

A young man with black hair scowled and looked at Andrez. "Who's this?"

The guy had a mouth on him. She could handle that as long as he realized she was in charge now. "Who I am doesn't matter. What we do, does. Are we clear?"

Andrez stepped forward. "Let's be crystal, gentlemen. The lady here is your boss. You do the job, you do it well. Any problems will be reported directly to Mr. Burgess."

They grunted their understanding.

"Good. Let's move." A jerk on her arm swung Kazi around. She found herself facing Andrez.

"Let's be *clear*, Kazimiera," he said with a sickening sneer. "Get it done, get back here. Then he'll decide if you can have your black friend back."

"Who?" She didn't mean to play dumb, but she prayed to God that warning wasn't what she thought it meant.

Andrez backed away. "Carrick will be waiting."

CHAPTER 20

Somewhere in Miranda, Venezuela

Fire trailed down his leg and thigh as Range hauled himself through the narrow window. Glass shattered under the impact of bullets and peppered him. Shouts chased him into the thick night.

While his legs were dangling over the sill, hands pawed at his ankles.

He kicked free.

And dropped. Hard. Packed dirt collided with his shoulder. He scrambled to his feet and spun around. He lunged forward—and fell on the dusty road. Range pushed up and started for the trees but fell again. Only as he got up once more did he feel the warmth sliding down his leg. Glancing down, he saw the tear in his jeans. The dark stain. Shot?

Rocks crunched and popped, pulling his attention to the front of the hotel. Six or seven shapes swarmed under the yellow lamplight.

Clamping a hand over his leg enabled him to limp-run for cover. Heavy footfalls warned of the authorities right on his heels. Range pushed himself harder. Farther. Down the street. Toward the line of trees that bled into one massive green field along the mountains. Though darkness shrouded the trees, he knew they were there. He'd memorized their location in case he needed to escape.

"Stop him," they yelled in their native tongue. Six years as a Coastie in Sector San Juan demanded he learn the language.

Shots fired. Dirt exploded around him.

But he kept going, grunting, panting.

Something snagged his pack. Panic swirled through him. He

swung around and used the momentum to barrel into the man with his fist. The guard stumbled back. Range let another hard right fly. The uniformed man went down.

Range hobbled around, registering several more guards within a yard of him. He plunged onward through the night, his pulse and thoughts erratic. How had everything gone wrong? What choice did he have but to flee into the mountains? He wasn't a mountain man though. Not like Canyon, who used to disappear for weeks at a time, return home with a Grizzly Adams beard and looking more at peace and refreshed than before he left. The thought of spending weeks in the bush tightened against clear thought. There had to be another way.

God, help me! I can't do this.

Ahead, something shifted under the moonlight. He squinted, trying to make the form coalesce into something recognizable. A wet leaf? A tree? He couldn't. . .

Who cared? He had to get to safety.

A dozen more feet.

Behind, the pounding of boots closed in. He could hear grunts, smell the sweat of the jungle and stink of beer on them. The nauseating odor pushed him.

A weight crashed down on him. Realizing they were on him, Range punched. Thrashed. But went down. They pinned his arms. Grabbed his hair, spitting and shouting at him in Venezuelan Spanish.

"Get off me," he gritted out as dirt puffed in his eyes and mouth.

Writhing, Range tried to free himself. *There's no hope.* Cornered by more than a dozen rebel guards, caught in a hotel room with the bodies of two men, and trapped in a foreign country when nobody back home even knew he was gone—

I'm as good as dead.

They hauled him to his feet. "Okay," Range said in a huffed breath, his leg burning. He tried to clamp his hand over it again, but they yanked his hands back. "Wait. Por favor. I can explain. . ." Oh yeah. That would go over real well.

The small crowd parted as a shouting officer stormed toward them. Range waited to see his life flash before him. His panic was palpable, his regret deep—but what about Canyon? If he died. . .who would find him? Range swallowed, realizing Lambert was right. He didn't want his brother dead.

The man to his left tripped, spun, and landed on the ground. Face up, he stared at the moon.

A weight slammed into Range's back, shoving him forward. He looked back and found the guard from behind sliding off him and crumpling into a heap on the ground. What on earth. . . ?

"He's dead," one man whispered.

Startled, Range looked at the fallen guard to his left. A dark stain blossomed over the man's chest. Range pivoted, his pulse thrumming. The guard behind had two over his heart. Who was shooting them? He hunched, looking around as the guards and soldiers did the same. He'd been warned the area was a hotbed for guerillas vying for domination. Insane in a country that generally held its own against the power-hungry militants.

Range twisted around, staring down the road that rose up and over the slight incline before vanishing into the trees.

Hands pawed at him amid a flurry of shouts and commands from the center of the village. They wanted him taken in, ordered to hurry before anything else happened. No. . .no, he wasn't going down like that. He broke free and barreled toward freedom. At least, he hoped it was freedom. Something was there—he could make out the shapes on the crest of the hill. Friend or foe, he didn't know. But that was his only escape.

Lights exploded ahead, blinding him. Range skidded to a stop. Glanced back. More than a dozen men, law enforcement badges glinting under the bright light, rushed up to him. They captured him, avoiding the brilliant beam. Shielding his eyes from the glare, he tried to peer around the brightness to what lay beyond.

"Move away from him," a voice boomed through the darkness.

The police held fast, but their feet shifted, rocks popping beneath their feet. When he checked them, they were casting glances backward, as if looking for direction from their superior.

"Release him. *¡Ahora!* Or join your dead compatriots," a voice boomed through the darkness. "*Norteamericano*, walk." The thickly accented English didn't veil the warning.

Being caught and accused of murder was one thing, but being captured by guerillas and held for ransom all but guaranteed death.

"Soldiers, do you want to join your compadres?"

Grips loosened. Some fell away. Range straightened, his confusion compounding the pain throbbing in his leg. His toes squished in his sock. Mentally, he chided the soldier who dared to advance.

Dust plumed at their feet. Dirt peppered Range's face and needled his leg through his pants. Instinct pushed him back, not wanting to get hit by the threatening bullets.

"Norteamericano, walk!"

Fear—or was it wisdom?—rooted his feet to the ground.

"Norteamericano," the disembodied voice grew mean. "Walk forward. ¡Ahora!"

More dirt sprayed his legs, dust spiraling into his face. He coughed and took a step closer. If he went with these rebels, he may never be seen again. At least not alive. And he'd never find his brother. Canyon would die. Indecision halted his progress.

Something touched his arm.

He glanced to the side.

Thwat!

A guard fell over the first one.

"Move, or more will die because of you."

Range snapped his attention to the lights, his heart thrumming. "Who are you? Stop killing these people!"

"Then save their lives and walk."

Hands fisted, he shuffled forward, the blood coagulating and making his pants pull against the wound in his thigh.

"*Bien.* Ahora, *policia y soldados*, walk backward, hands up, or we will shoot."

As the lights grew brighter, Range wondered how they'd inform his mother that both of her sons had died in Venezuela at the hands of mercenaries. Why had Lambert ever asked *him* to come down here? He wasn't qualified. He didn't have the skills. He'd failed. . . . Dani would never speak to him again—that is, if he made it out alive. And if he did, he'd have to explain to his niece and nephew why he didn't save their father.

Just as the shadows overtook the light, Range squinted, able to make out a form standing in the back of a Jeep.

Black-clad men rushed him.

A hood dropped over his face.

London, MI5 Rendezvous

Cars emerged from the underground garage and leapt into the afternoon sun.

Kazi shifted in the rear of the lead vehicle, angling to catch the eye of the driver in the rearview mirror. "You familiar with London, driver?"

"Name's Davies. And yes, grew up here."

"Then you know another route to the exchange point, Davies?"

He hesitated, then nodded.

"Good, I need you to take an alternate route."

Wary eyes bobbed to hers. "We were told to hold to the plan."

"And you had two American spies in on that plan." She gripped the armrest as he swung around a corner. "Is it worth your life to find out if they had an ambush waiting?"

The car yanked right. Then a sharp left. Trounced down an alley. Kazi struck out a hand to brace herself as they took a curb and sped over a one-way street, narrowly avoiding a delivery truck. Frantic movements slowed as they swung onto the main thoroughfare and bled into traffic. Less than two miles off, she saw the roundabout.

Kazi glanced back, relieved the second vehicle had made the diversion with them. By the time her heart rate evened out, they glided into a driveway. Guards, poised and facing in the opposite direction, swung around at the screech of the tires as her car rounded the corner. Metal glinted at the maw of the parking garage. Security spikes dropped into the ground at the entrance, clearing the way.

The driver whipped into the garage, to the left, then curled around the wide cement supports and squawked to a stop in the middle. At the other end of the first level, a blue, heavily tinted sedan waited. Two armed men stood guard on either side.

"Flash them three times and wait." Kazi threaded her arms through the suit jacket on the seat.

A soft click sounded. Then another. And the last one.

As Kazi reached for the door handle, both the passenger and rear passenger door of the other car opened. Two suits climbed out.

Kazi exited her vehicle and motioned to her secondary unit to bring their exchange. A man emerged with a prisoner. The average-looking man who stood with his hands bound sauntered up to her.

Eyes back on the blue sedan, she waited as MI5 retrieved the package. Head covered, hands bound, the man was taller than those holding him. Maybe a bit bigger in build, too.

Kazi took possession of the operative beside her and walked him to the midpoint, where she waited for the Brits to transfer their captive. She couldn't help but think of the times she'd been the subject of such transfers. Carrick had bought her back every time. Thousands, maybe millions, paid to get his agent back. *How can I ever be free?* Her stomach churned.

Shoes clicked closer, and she drew in her faculties, noting the hooded man had no broken limbs or noticeable limps or injuries. She nodded to him. "Remove his hood."

When the hood came off, the man squinted, blue eyes shadowed by green and yellow puffy skin and a swollen, crooked nose. A scab arched over his upper lip. Dark hair curled around his ears and neck—longer than the picture she'd been given. But despite the disfigurement, she recognized him. "Is there an explanation for the abhorrent treatment of an American citizen?"

"An American *terrorist*," one Brit said. "Let's remember we're doing you a favor transferring him so quickly and quietly."

"Innocent until proven guilty, gentlemen. We'll remember this treatment when considering future engagements." She wrapped her arm around Colton Neeley's forearm—or at least tried. The man's bicep was wider than her thigh. And yet, with the littlest force against his muscle, she guided him away from Security Services. Each click of her shoes against the cement sounded as a homing beacon. So far so good. They'd managed to get their man without tipping off anyone. At the black vehicle, she opened the door.

"Who are you?" he asked, his voice low but tight.

Hand on his head, she tucked him into the cabin.

Thud-clank! Feet pounded.

Kazi pushed Neeley, fearing they'd been blown.

"Stop them! They're not Americans!"

Suspicion confirmed, she bulled Colton into the SUV and lunged in after him. "Drive!" The door flapped open, then closed as the driver gunned the engine.

Crack! Tsing!

A spiderweb spread through the front windshield.

"The other team's down," Davies shouted as he roared toward the exit.

"Keep going!"

"Spikes!"

Sunlight glinted off metal barriers that seemed to growl at them from the mouth of the garage. Glass cracked.

She shifted onto the seat. "Keep going!"

"If we hit those, we can't drive."

"Just do it."

Leather seemed to sizzle as a bullet ripped through it, narrowly missing the driver, who ducked and cursed. Another bullet whizzed past her head—and seared the flesh off the driver's shoulder. He shouted. The car swerved, but he righted it.

"Give me a gun," Neeley demanded.

Remembering his dossier was the only reason she slapped the Ruger into his palm. *Sniper.* Neeley angled around, bracing himself against the back of the seat, and took aim. Another bullet shattered the rear windscreen. He didn't flinch. The chain linking the cuffs jingled as he seemed to hesitate. With him being a meticulous sniper, she knew it wasn't hesitation but a calculated, controlling breath. At least, she hoped so.

He fired once. Twice. And switched back to the seat.

The spray from behind ceased.

When she surveyed the damage, Kazi smiled at the MI5 agents taking cover. They were as good as free.

"This is going to—son of a. . ."

Kazi jerked around. The grate slid into the ground. Their SUV vaulted out of the garage. Cars dove out of the way. Tires screeched as they found purchase and propelled them away from the Security Services exchange point.

"Stop the car."

Kazi flinched at the barrel staring her down. She lifted her gaze to the clear blue eyes that meant business in a way she hadn't seen before. "Not happening, Mr. Neeley." Right now, she really wished Andrez hadn't drugged Griffin. It would've been helpful to have the giant waiting in the vehicle to allay Neeley's fears. But having the big lug here would've tipped off the authorities.

Neither his grip nor intensity lessened. "I don't know who you are, but right now, I don't trust anyone. And I'll do what it takes to stay alive so I can figure it out."

"That's my goal as well." Kazi worked to steady her pulses, knowing if this man chose to put her down, she didn't have a prayer—even if she hadn't darkened a confessional in years. "I'm taking you to Griffin."

Fire flamed through his expression. "Bull. He's in a state pen."

She shook her head calmly. "He's about ten minutes from here." Drugged out of his mind and unconscious. But here.

The gun remained steady and his gaze fierce. "Who are you? Never mind—I don't care." The barrel of the weapon drifted toward the back of Davies's head. "Stop the car."

"Davies, keep driving." Kazi angled toward the big guy—man, did they grow them all this big in the States? "Listen, nothing makes sense. I get that. Someone disassembled your team. Almost three weeks ago, I extracted Griffin from that prison you mentioned. We retrieved the assassin from a Hamas camp. He's not dead but not far from it either."

Neeley swallowed. "The Brits said I was going home."

She assessed the handsome man, lingered on the way he said that last word. His eyes told the tale of one too many battles, but a softening around those words bespoke a depth that was. . .startling. *He's testing me.* "I'm pretty sure you already knew they weren't sending you home. And if you were going home, think about what happened. It's not safe there till—as you said—a few things are sorted."

Steady, unwavering.

"I'm here to help," she said as the whooshing in her ears lulled. Since Davies wasn't a known asset, she had to be delicate with information. "The general is waiting. I think you've figured that out, too, but you're too freaked over what's happening to trust yourself or anyone else. That's where you're being smart. If you believed I was a threat, you would've already pulled that trigger. So holding a gun on me isn't smart."

A grin tweaked a dimple in his cheek. "Reckon you're right." After dropping the magazine and clearing the chamber, he removed the slide and handed the pieces to her.

Kazi blew out a laugh, dumped the dismantled gun on the seat, then held out her palm as she produced a key. Neeley lifted his arms, and she freed him from the cuffs.

"Thanks." Rubbing his wrists, he fell silent as Davies wound through London with an experience and expertise that helped Kazi focus on the next phase—getting Griffin and sneaking both men out of the country before Carrick could say hello.

The car glided into the underground structure behind the Bread & Butter, dropping back into anonymity. As soon as they stopped, four armed thugs appeared.

"What's with the armory?" Neeley asked, the warrior in him sizing up the threat.

Kazi purposefully met his gaze. "It's nothing I can't handle. And that's just it—let *me* handle it. Go along, play nice. I'll get us out of here before nightfall."

"What if you don't?"

"Then playtime is over." Kazi climbed from the car and shifted so Neeley could emerge. When he did, he towered over her. As big and barrel-chested as Griffin. *A matched set.*

She started for the entrance, determined to make it known to these buffoons that she was in control. Not the other way around. But as she moved between two of them, they accosted her. Behind, she heard a scuffle. The unmistakable crack of bones. A scream.

She strained to see over her shoulder, past the three men now *escorting* her into the building. Her pulse ramped up. *No no no!* Neeley had neutralized two of the three remaining guards, fire roaring through his gaze.

"Hey!" she shouted to him. Aggression wasn't the route to take here, not at the B & B. There were a hundred more of these apes where the others had come from.

Neeley's gaze flicked to hers.

"Nice work, but let's take it down a notch." She wrested her arms free of the two beside her. "These men know if they so much as bruise me or you, Carrick will make sure they get *severance* benefits."

A voice, hollow and sickening, snaked out from the shadows of the past. "You sound as though you miss me, love."

CHAPTER 21

Bread & Butter Club,
South End, London

Don't worry," Griffin whispered. "It'll be over soon."

"He seems mad something fierce, Griff." Phoenix pressed her face to his shoulder, snuffing out her tears. "I ain't never seen him this ma—"

A scream rent the musty air of the broom closet.

Griffin stilled.

More wails. A sound of banging. An angry growl. As if the dog had gotten loose. Bungie? Yet the growl didn't—

"Please, Reggie. . .please. . ."

Griffin ground his teeth as Phee's quiet sobs drenched his shirt.

Shuffling and banging stumbled into the hall.

His heart hammered. Momma and Daddy were in the hall now. Fighting. Again. Through the slats, he made out his mom pinned against the wall. His father hovering over her petite frame.

Phee lifted her head. Griffin tightened his hold, pushing her face into his abdomen. As if watching between bars, he saw his dad ram his fist into his mom's face. She crumpled. He dropped on top of her.

"What'd I tell you, b—"

A scream sliced straight through the narrow slit and into Griffin's heart. As he realized it'd been Phee's scream, the door swung open.

Griffin hauled in a breath as the image before him scalded a permanent imprint in his mind—his father's wild, enraged eyes, fury reddening his already dark skin; his mother on the floor, covered in blood, shaking her head frantically. Her beautiful eyes pleaded with Griffin. She reached a dripping hand toward him. "Save me. . ."

Griffin jolted and thrust out his hand and caught hold of someone.

189

Wide green eyes registered in his mind.

A ripple of sanity washed through him, and he released his grip. "Kacie." A deep bass boomed through his skull.

Hold up.

Not a bass. His heartbeat. Griffin groaned and rolled onto his side, then peeled himself off a creaking bed. Sitting up, he cradled his head in his hands and beat his way through the sludge called a brain.

"How you doing, Legend?"

He squinted through the piercing brightness at the hulk against the wall. "Cowboy?" Now he knew he was dreaming. Or having a nightmare. "I have lost my good mind. How. . . ?"

Kacie slipped back into view. "If you're done with your nap—"

He shoved to his feet and felt as if someone drove a spike through his skull. "Nap?" He glowered at the nymph. "You *drugged* me."

"Wrong." Her lips stretched taut. "You drank the water."

"The same water you had but didn't drink—you knew it was laced with something, but you didn't warn me."

She smirked at him. "I actually expected you to have a brain. I know better now."

Griffin drew up his shoulder.

A hand landed on his chest. Cowboy wedged between Kacie and him. "Hey," he said, his voice low and strong. "Stand down. Let's get our bearings."

"I'll give you bearings"—Griffin stabbed a finger in Kacie's direction—"I'll bear right down on that woman. Don't trust her."

Cowboy nodded. "Already got that message."

"Look, I don't care what you think about me. But if you intend to get out of here alive, you'll listen to me."

Though her words were terse and putrid, something about her posture ripped the anger from Griffin's chest. "Hold up." When he started for her, Cowboy fielded the move, but Griffin clapped the guy on the shoulder. "I'm good."

"You said that once, then went for 'better.'"

"Bigger problems right now." Griffin stepped around him and closed in on Kacie. "What's going on?"

She sidestepped him and diverted her gaze. "Nothing." Defiance coated her expression and word. "Just remember, here at the B & B, the path to enlightenment—read: 'staying alive'—is nonaggression, especially with Carrick here."

Griffin hesitated, his mind bounding over Cowboy's tension and something. . .something he couldn't put his finger on. "Is that a bad thing, that he's here?" Was he the reason Kacie had been skittish on the plane?

The weight of the world trickled into those green irises. "Only for me."

"Which translates to us." Griffin knew the game. Saw the fear she wore plain as red lipstick on her pale face. The change in her when Lambert mentioned coming. And the flicker of. . .whatever flashed through her eyes before she said she didn't care if they trusted her.

He closed the space between them. "What's he got on you, Baby Girl?"

Vulnerability coated her features, haunting her and turning her milky skin an even whiter shade. Almost as quick, the tough mask reappeared. "Don't worry about it." She removed herself a half dozen feet away. She made it look like a natural maneuver, part of her discourse. But was it? "Tonight there's a big event, a premier of sorts." She swallowed. "I have to be here. After it—we'll be on our way."

"Just like that?" Right. *And I'm white bread.*

Kacie didn't miss a beat. "Stay here, stay quiet. There will be more guards than you can count—all armed. So don't try anything stupid." Again, more of whatever lurked in those irises flitted again. Like she was trying to tell him something.

Cowboy shifted and hooked his hands through his belt loops. "Pardon, ma'am, but I don't know you. And considering what's happening to me and mine, that means you're disqualified from mission briefings that include me." To Griffin he thumbed toward Kacie. "How is she in charge, and why do we trust her?"

"We don't."

Kacie bristled. "Trust doesn't matter. Staying alive does."

"Naw," Griffin said, once again closing the distance. "See, that's where you're wrong. I need to trust that you got our backs, that you won't sell us out. Spike my water."

She wet her pink lips. "It was better for you to be drugged than dead"—something flickered in her eyes—"at least in theory. But right now, I'm wishing I'd gone with the latter."

Even he could tell she didn't mean that. It was talk. To protect herself. Though he admired her efforts, Griffin found himself wanting to dig under her radar with a backhoe.

"In the future, let's remember not to choke our allies." Her words filled his face with heat. "Mumbling in your sleep. Grunting and grimacing. Then you come up swinging." She quirked an eyebrow at him. "Something we need to know?"

"Only that one squeeze could've ended your life." He hated that he could've hurt her.

"In your dreams."

"Every night." Griffin felt a smile slipping into his face.

Kacie's lip curled up on one side—and it wasn't a snarl. "You're a train wreck, Riddell."

He let the smile take hold. "You're the driver, Kacie or Kazie or whatever your name is."

She smirked. "Does my identity bother you?"

"Not an aorta."

A laugh jumped from her throat.

What?

More laughter amid the words, "You mean an *iota*."

Fool. How did she manage to muddle his brain so he did stupid things like that? "Just keeping you on your toes, Baby Girl." Fingers traced her jaw—and he stilled, realizing they were his own. Where that move came from, he didn't know.

Surprise spilled into her eyes, illuminating some of the brilliance that laid behind them. Her lips parted as if to say something, but her eyes bounced around his face. Could she feel it? The electric fence that seemed to protect her? The same one that drew him like a bug to the light zapper? Yet, it scared him. Someday he'd get zapped.

Shink-thunk!

Griffin turned, aware the others did the same, as the door opened.

A man with meticulously styled blond hair angled into the room. With two fingers he motioned to Kacie, a withering glare shot at Griffin, then Cowboy. Carrick. Had to be Carrick.

Kacie walked by, her white-blond hair rimming crimson cheeks. Without a word, she walked out.

Fury wormed through Griffin at the obvious death hold the man had on her. He fisted his hands, staring through the door, imagining her walking the dark halls with him. Showed no regret. No hesitation leaving him. This wasn't what it looked like. Couldn't be. Or was it? Was she the coldhearted operative she pretended to be?

Cowboy turned to him. "Can we trust her?"

His gut twisted and collided with his instincts. He wanted to trust her. Wanted to protect her. But she'd already abandoned him—twice. She wouldn't hesitate to do it again if she felt it benefited her or the mission. "No." And he had a bad feeling about her being able to move about. . .on a leash. And Carrick held that leash.

That's what spooked her in Cyprus.

"She's in trouble." Why did he feel powerless all of a sudden? What could he do that she couldn't do for herself? She didn't need him. Didn't want him. And the stab of that revelation cut deeper than he'd ever admit to anyone, to himself.

"What do we do?"

"Get our own plan."

The metallic sweetness of blood squirted through her mouth. Kazi flinched as pain radiated up her cheekbone and into her temple. She grunted, suffocating her urge to fight back, find a way to break the hand that pinned her neck to the glass desk. With her own palms, she gave counterpressure so he couldn't push her face through the glass.

"What, did you think I wouldn't figure out your little game?" Carrick's chest formed against her bent body, his hot, liquor-drenched breath skidding into her nostrils.

She winced at the foul odor as the years of being under Boucher's grip, then Carrick's, leapt through her mind. *Tina. Remember, Tina. Remember what he did to her.* Resolve coiled around her panic, swirled into anger, and hardened into a heated, burning retribution.

"Have you forgotten, love, that I know everything?"

Kazi's jaw clenched, pushing against the skin-warmed surface. Fog bursts formed on the glass. "I have not forgotten anything." Her gaze surfed his desk, the notepad he never wrote on, the Waterford ashtray clock, a watch—he never did like actually wearing one, but the Rolex added to his appearance—the teak pen and pencil set. One hole in the wood block sat vacant. *Letter opener.* She searched for the matching item. There. Too far away. She'd have to distract him.

"Especially Tina," she said with a growl.

Carrick's nose pressed into her cheek. "Now there's an example of a puppet. . ."

Kazi blocked his soliloquy regarding his power. The man was drunk on himself. She didn't care. As long as she could sever his hold on her. Permanently. Her fingers trickled across the top. But even as her fingers made the trek over the surface, she reminded herself she couldn't kill him. Not here. It'd be like trying to steal the crown jewels in broad daylight.

Cold metal met her fingers, which closed around the opener. She fought the muscle in her face that almost smiled against her will.

". . .so terrified. Hickson tells me she screamed till the last drop of blood fell from her lips."

Fury tightened her hold on the opener. She shouldn't kill him, but she'd give him one doozie of a wound to write home about. Her arm raised.

Thud!

Pain exploded through her forearm and squeezed a yelp from her chest.

Carrick jerked. His weight lifted, and Kazi twisted, her other hand reaching for the fire licking through her arm.

Hickson stood with a death hold on her, pinching the soft spot under her arm. He ripped the opener from the soft flesh of her palm, cutting it. Fire raced through her hand, followed by warm wetness.

Kazi hissed at the searing pain—like a paper cut with lemon juice—as he shoved her backward. She stumbled but caught her balance.

"She nearly drove this into your neck." Hickson passed the bloody weapon to Carrick.

Shock never looked as good as it did on the face of the man who had suffocated her life. Controlled her every move. Hammered a stake through any hope of a happy ending to her story. "I see I have yet to make my point to you."

She narrowed her eyes. "But I made mine."

With an incredibly graceful but powerful move, he flung the letter opener in her direction.

Kazi refused to flinch as it flew, end over end, past her head and thunked into the wood paneling. She wasn't worried about that blade, or the blood dripping off her hand. What worried her was the unnatural calm that washed over Carrick as it left his hand.

Wariness clutched at her as he plucked the handkerchief from his impeccable suit pocket, strolled toward her, and took her wrist. He wrapped the linen around the wound, his gaze never straying from hers. "Who are these men, Kazimiera?"

When he tugged on the ends, pinching her injury, she knew better than to wince and kept her face neutral. "A job."

"I watched him take out two men in less than five seconds. They are *skilled* warriors. They move with intent, with decisiveness. Not ordinary men, absorbed in their own world. Those men are prepared—and no doubt preparing—for a fight." He tugged the ends tighter. "Now tell me who they are."

"Men with more honor and skill than you have in your pinky."

He clucked his tongue in a chiding way. "Shame, Kazimiera." Carrick pouted. "It's unlike you to resort to petty insults." He motioned widely with his hands. "Action! That is your mantra, or it was."

"I act when it's necessary." Her insides shifted.

Tidying his appearance, he sauntered to a liquor cabinet. Poured himself a drink, his blue eyes combing over her, assessing, dissecting. . . After a whiff of the gold liquid, he lifted a snifter from a shelf. "You've changed, Kazimiera." Ice clinked in the glass. "And that concerns me."

"The only thing that should concern you is that I do my job." She flashed her eyes at him.

And Griffin's little confession to the cowboy about not trusting her made things oh-so-much easier. He thought she was in trouble and was ready to cut ties to save her own skin. Why did it hurt so much? Men who'd done that were countless.

Featherlight, the touch against her cheek felt like a punch.

Kazi flinched.

Carrick's chuckle weeded her resolve. "One of them has gotten beneath your skin, hasn't he?" He drifted around her. "The man you lifted today from Security Services is named Colton Neeley. He'd been picked up at Heathrow one month ago before boarding a flight to Dulles. Charges were terrorism." Remote in hand, he aimed it at a wall-mounted television, accessed a secure menu. Seconds later, a video sprang to life.

The grainy, low-res image showed the man Griffin called Cowboy clearing security, donning his cowboy hat, then striding down the concourse, duffel in hand. Calm, casual. Nothing about him should've set off the authorities. She should know—she'd had similar training to recognize body language to protect herself. Yet halfway down, a dozen Security Services agents swarmed in, weapons pointed. Cowboy dropped the duffel and eased his hands skyward.

Carrick tossed the remote on the desk. With two fingers, he rubbed his jaw, then motioned to his bodyguard. "Hickson, what amazes me is that from our vast network of connections, other than being a ranch owner in Virginia, this man is as loyal and American as Yankee Doodle. In fact"—Carrick slid his hands into his pockets—"his record is clean. Pristine."

With a grunt, Hickson said, "Too clean."

"Precisely." Carrick circled back around to his desk and leaned against it, folding his arms and crossing his legs. "Which tells me that this man means a lot to someone."

"His family," Kazi offered.

"I'm afraid not. This man is an arsenal of trouble, and someone wants him out of the way." Rubbing his chin again, he sighed. "Whoever it was, they went to a lot of trouble to create problems for him. They weren't willing to kill him. That intrigues me."

"The person was just too scared to draw the fire back to himself. These men just want to protect their own"—Kazi tensed realizing she'd given a morsel away. Quickly she added—"families."

"I agree that he wants to protect *something*, but I am not convinced it's family."

"Why?" She spun to him, emotion choking her. "Because you've never had family you wanted to protect."

Carrick sneered. "No, love, that's your story, not mine."

His dagger nailed her heart. She turned back to the Thames. Her thoughts zigzagged to Carrick. He hadn't flinched over her mention of their families. Which meant—

"Why are you drilling me full of questions when you know who these men are?"

Quiet draped the office as she watched traffic lumber across Waterloo Bridge and the muddy-looking waters of the Thames. Beyond there, the London Eye seemed a portal to another dimension. But it wasn't that obnoxious circle that captured her thoughts. It was the beast-of-glass-and-steel station below it. Waterloo Station could spirit Griffin and Neeley to safety. If she could somehow get across the murky river. . .

First, they'd have to escape Carrick.

"Death is the only 'out' once you belong to me, Kazimiera." Air shifted close by as the ghost of that moment repeated Carrick's warning, chilling her.

Manila and thick, an envelope slid into view. "Here, love." Once she took the proffered propaganda—that's all it could be coming from him—Carrick eased around in front of her and propped himself against the window, watching. Waiting.

Peering up at him through a tight brow, she worked the fastener, easing her defenses up, preparing herself to see the worst. Dumped the contents into her hand—photographs, by the feel of them. Her stomach cinched. She hated being a pawn, hated being played, and that's exactly what he was doing. After Tina, she dreaded what truth or consequence the images held. No matter how long she glared at him, he wouldn't tell her. Games kept him in the position of one-upmanship. In control. The way Carrick liked it.

Finally, she dropped her attention to the pictures.

Heaven and earth shifted as she took them in.

Green, rolling hills on the perimeter. At the center, a column of trees leading to the white fence. . .rather, it used to be the color of snow. Now brown and in disrepair, it sagged like an aged sentry.

Kazi steeled herself for what would be next. Slowly, she drew the picture aside and tucked it at the bottom of the stack, letting the envelope flutter to the ground.

Breathing became a chore. The farmhouse. Nothing immaculate or fancy. Her father had built it with his own hands, growing it with the family. As memories assailed her, Kazi slid her eyes shut but forced them back open. *"Don't let him win, Kaz."* Tina's warning was little help against this. The home wasn't blue, Mamo's favorite color, but black. Blistered. Destroyed and consumed by fire.

"What did you do?" she ground out. Instead of handmade shutters dangling from the second story, embers drooped into what had been the living room. Or was that the kitchen?

Her hand trembled as she forced herself to look at the next one, her mind ravaged. Were they alive? Had her mother and siblings survived?

"Why. . . ?" Her voice cracked as she went to the next photo.

A sob leapt from her chest at the charred doll. Face half melted, the purple velour outfit—unburned—a stark contrast against the black-white-gray of the ash and debris. Hair singed but still white-blond.

"She looks like you, dziewczyna," her father said, dragging a thick finger over the doll's long blond hair as they sat on Kazi's bed late one night after he'd returned from the city.

Her sisters Izolda and Zuzanna. "Are. . .are they alive?" What of Kazpar?

"Don't do this, dziewczyna," Kazpar begged as they walked to the fence. "We can pay it back. This is not right."

She spun to him. "How, Kaz? We have not been able to even buy grain for bread since Tata. . ." She let the words fade from her lips about their father's death as she tugged up the torn collar of his well-worn wool coat.

"Besides, this is better, yes? I am free of Boucher."

"But you are not free.*"*

Snow crunched behind her before the man's voice reached out and smothered hope as threadbare as the coat her brother wore. *"Kazimiera."*

Like a time warp, she snapped back to the present. To Carrick. Her chest rose and fell like the heaving waves of the ocean. "Are they alive?" She held up the pictures.

Carrick remained impassive.

"Did you kill them? Are they dead, Carrick?"

He stood, slid his hands into his pockets, and came toward her. "It is good to remember who we owe, is it not, my love?"

In a quick move, she stepped back, braced on her left leg, and drove a roundhouse kick into his chest.

Crack! Eyes wide as he flew backward and face screwed in pain, Carrick cursed.

A force shoved Kazi sideways. Pain exploded across her face. Into her stomach. By the time she blinked, she lay pinned to the cement floor beneath Hickson.

Holding his side and grimacing as he picked himself off the floor, Carrick spit. "Maybe I have your attention now, Kazimiera. Your family is dead, and if you don't follow my every instruction, I will make sure those men die, too."

CHAPTER 22

Vaughn Residence

*T*hunk. *Plunk.*

Marshall's gaze dropped to the hardwood floors where the mirror tumbled. He jerked to the safe. Alarms shrieked through the house. "Get the pictures!" He closed the safe, spun the lock, and reset it to the numbers he'd noted when opening it. Behind him, he heard the scritching of Rel stuffing pictures back in the envelope.

When he pivoted, he froze. His heart dropped to his toes as he looked across the rug imported from Tunisia. The hand-carved oak bar sitting along the right wall. Past the relief of George Washington. To the door, slowly closing under the watchful eye of Melanie Sands.

Click.

Marshall flinched so visibly as the lock bolted that he felt an aftershock. Then another when his sister smiled.

"Melanie, what are you doing here?" He hurried to her side, concern flooding him. Where were his nephews? And Nate? Why wasn't she being attended? "You should return to the house, stay with Nellie."

"Smellie Nellie all about. Hatin' Nat'an beds about. Angry, beatin' he unleash. Killing to save, the beast."

Aching over her fractured mental state, Marshall coiled his arms around his sister and pulled her close, smoothing her hair. "Shhh." He held her as she sobbed in his chest once, then pushed back, repeated the rhyme, and spun toward the door. "Melanie, please—go home to the children."

"Gone, gone away to school. He's the one who is the fool." She giggled, then her face went serious. "It's about time someone figured it out," she whispered.

At his side, he felt more than heard Rel. Something pressed into his hand, but he could not tear his gaze from his once strong, beautiful sister. The one with their father's wit and favor. The Vaughn said to take Washington by storm. The only family member who had ever believed in him—completely.

"Here." Rel shook the envelope in his hand.

Marshall stuffed it in his shirt, then started for his sister. He couldn't just leave her here. What if she told them he'd been in here? With Rel? It'd be over before they could hit the road.

"Out for a spin, out for fun, time for Marshall to run," Melanie said as she tossed the keys to him. And with that, she tossed a thumb drive. "Run, Marshall, big brother Marshall. Only come back to end it all."

If a meat cleaver ripped through his heart, it would not have hurt as much as seeing the state to which his sister had been reduced. "Melanie." He started forward, reaching for her—

Thud! Thud!

He stopped short as she spun toward the door, eyes wide, fingers curled around her lips.

"Go," Melanie hissed and nudged him.

Marshall darted to the door and flung it open. He and Rel sprinted into the dual hedgerows lining the sprawling lawn. Pain tightened like a vise around his ribs and side. Fire leapt through him, but he pushed himself. Anger and agony writhed within. His father had said Melanie wasn't feeling well, that she wasn't herself. But this. . .this was madness. Literally.

Why? Why hadn't his father told him?

Right—just like the pictures?

More of the same. His father was a monster, so consumed with his career that he didn't care what happened to his own children. He'd never been a hands-on parent, but *this*? Melanie falling apart beneath his own nose and nothing was done?

There—ahead he saw the white colonial home looming against the still-barren landscape of winter. Leaf-stripped branches waved craggy fingers toward the stately home. Breathless, Marshall paused where the hedgerow stopped at a grassy knoll that seemed to desperately escape the black-paved driveway that arched back toward the home.

"Are you okay?" Cold, delicate hands touched his as Rel gasped. "You're flushed."

He grinned through a heaving breath. "A little exercise never hurt me."

"It might with those injuries."

"You can dote over me when we get back to the team." He scurried across the lawn. Gravel crunched underfoot as he half limped toward the rear door to the garage. Through the side door, they slipped into the pristine interior of his sister's Lexus SUV.

As he reached for the key, Marshall paused. Looked at Rel, then grinned again. "Can you drive—on the *right* side of the road?"

She rolled her eyes. "I've lived in the States for the last ten years, Marshall."

"Take the wheel." He dove into the rear.

"Are you crazy?"

"You look like my sister. They won't stop the car." He pressed himself against the floorboard. Vibrations wormed through his back and legs as sunlight spilled into the vehicle. The gears shifted, then pulled forward.

"Two men are waving me down."

"Just honk and make a lot of hand motions."

"Uh. . .okay. . ." Soon, a nervous laugh carried through the car, then tires gained traction and screeched away from the house.

Marshall hauled himself into the passenger seat as they sped down the road. "Don't stop for anything."

"I don't know where I'm going."

"Crazy," he muttered and plucked out the photos again.

"No, seriously, Marshall." Her hands tightened around the steering wheel. "In case you've forgotten, everyone's missing—including Lambert."

Roughing a hand over his face, he groaned. "I forgot he went MIA, too." He sighed and looked out over the road. Where would they go? What resources or unknown locations did the team have that he could tap into without alerting every combatant after them? Somewhere the team could go without heavy eyes. . .

"There!" He stabbed a finger toward a sign.

Rel darted him a look. "An airport? Marshall, we can't—"

"Trust me. My bad boy days are about to pay off."

"You mean they're over?"

His laugh faded as they turned onto the private, two-lane road leading to the hangar. If only Mario was here. . .

"Last building on the left is his."

"The whole building? How can he afford that?"

Marshall laughed. Did she really not have a clue how much *he* was worth, that men of the same color—green, as in greenbacks, in this case—stuck together? Of course, he'd tried to keep the rich-kid persona hidden with Nightshade. He wanted to be respected, to have value beyond the stock markets he'd dabbled in. The fortune he'd made copying his father's moves. He might not be into politics the way Warren Vaughn was, but Marshall had inherited one promising thing from his father: intelligence.

"There." He pointed to a sleek plane, his blood chugging through his veins. It'd been years since he'd spoken to Mario. "He's here." Out of the car, he strode into the hangar. Darkness descended upon him, momentarily leaving his vision affected.

A curse from the side flung him around. Dressed in an OD flight suit, an Italian stalked toward him, a part clutched in grease-slicked hands. The olive-drab garb made his friend look like a jungle monkey, especially with the jet-black hair dangling in his face.

"Mario."

Another curse. "Should'a known."

"That I'd come to collect?" Marshall kept the smile in place, determined not to let his friend know this was more than just a pleasure visit.

Mario hesitated as his gaze hit something behind Marshall, who checked his six. Rel stepped from the car, the sun glinting off the red in her chestnut hair.

"That's screwed up, man. Even for you. Getting a chick involved." Mario shook his head. "But don't think that will change my mind."

"What mind is that?"

"They told me not to help."

Marshall's gut tightened. "Who?"

Mario shook his head. "They all over you, man. Said they'd make me beg if I helped."

"*Who?*"

"The cops. . .your dad."

"That never stopped you before."

Mario's gaze bounced between Rel and Marshall. The toothy grin that had been the preamble to many illegal adventures gleamed in the midafternoon sun. "I know, right?" He thunked Marshall's gut with the steel part. "They said not to take you anywhere in my *planes*."

Marshall chuckled. "Still got that Black Hawk?"

"Yeah, but if you want fast and stealth, I've got something better.

Picked it up off an Arab prince."

Marshall followed him around the plane graveyard and straight toward a beauty of an aircraft. Boeing 727. Glittering in the sun, it sat as if ready to spirit them away to safety. Finally, something had gone right.

✦

Bread & Butter Club, London

Griffin stalked the halls pulsating with bodies and revelers. Too many people. Too many witnesses. This wasn't a good place to enact their plan. 'Sides, where was Kacie? Then there was the muzzle pointed at his back. That wouldn't be a problem if it were the only one. But there were two armed men to his six and twelve. And Colton had more of the same.

It'd been four or five hours since Kacie had left their cell. No word of her since. No sight. Had she abandoned them? No, she wouldn't do that. Even if she didn't have any loyalty to a person, to him—why did that bother him?—the girl was hard-core focused on the mission, the money she got for saving his black hide.

Directed through a low, narrow door, Griffin tucked his head and stepped through. It was like a door to an attic in Madyar's old 'hood house. Light dimmed and stank rose. Griffin slowed, his hackles rising, automatically drawing his gaze upward. He stopped, stunned that the entire wall rose fifty maybe sixty feet. About every ten or twelve feet a pipe poked out one side and stabbed the opposite wall. Beams supported the building without interruption. A rat hole—the man had an escape tunnel to get out of the building. That meant they were probably taking them out the back alley to shoot them and dump their bodies.

"Keep moving," a guard said.

Griffin shot him a sidelong glance and felt something shift in the air. He hesitated.

The guard shoved him. "I said move!"

Two steps forward and he heard Colton behind herded through the same shrimp entrances. Where were they taking them?

A soft noise thumped nearby.

Training awakened, Griffin jerked to his left. The guard gasped, then slid along the wall to the floor. A feathered dart stuck out of his shoulder.

Thump!

Soft and quiet yet decidedly unnatural, he heard something above him. He glanced up—*Kacie!* She leapt from one beam to a pipe, catching it and swinging around as if she were in a gym. She swung up and around, her foot nailing the guard in the face.

The guard stumbled back.

Griffin seized the man's confusion. Rammed his fist into his gut. Grabbed the man's weapon as he did. Griffin yanked it forward while driving his arm backward. The man's face connected with his elbow. The HK 9mm popped free. Griffin spun and aimed the gun at him. The man raised his hands.

In his periphery, Griffin saw Kacie approaching with a weapon in her hand.

The guard went for something.

Kacie fired a dart into the man's neck. He sucked in a breath and went limp. "Secure them. We don't have much time."

Colton gathered weapons, stuffing one in the back of his pants, another in his boot, then he tossed another to Griffin.

Beside him, Kacie fired a dart into each guard's thigh. Retrieved a weapon.

Stretching to his full height, Colton looked at her. Then Griffin. "Remember our conversation?"

Griffin nodded. He couldn't forget it. He'd been convinced Kacie had given up on them.

"So do I." She turned to them both. "I get you not trusting me, but if you want to debate it, then you'll have to wait."

"Trust is one thing; believing in you another."

"Semantics, Griffin."

"What changed, Baby Girl? Why are you here, putting your life in danger?"

"I'm not in danger." Her cool green eyes hit his. "You are. Both of you. These men"—she motioned to the unconscious guards—"were under orders to bury you. Permanently."

"So you care?" Griffin asked.

"I care about making sure Carrick doesn't kill people I'm charged with protecting. That he doesn't kill anyone I. . ." She wet her lips. "Are we going to chat all night, or are you ready to get out of here?"

"Let's go," Colton said.

She hurried down the hall that dumped into another door. She kicked it open and crouched through it. Griffin folded himself through the opening and made room for Colton as he came through. Kacie was already in motion as Colton closed the gratelike door. They jogged over the steel grate walkway that rose steeply.

"We going up?" Griffin glanced below his feet, seeing several walkways through the tiny octagonal holes. "Why up? I thought this led to an alley."

"It's one of his escape routes. Unexpected, so it goes unnoticed." She hauled herself forward.

She moved quickly onward and upward. . .still going, not slowing, as if the thing were going *down* instead of rising. His thighs burned as he dragged himself onward.

"Woman, what are you made of?" He gulped as they rounded a corner—nothing but a hundred-foot drop to the right. No wall bracing the catwalk. Only steel girders that rose into the ceiling. They were wide open.

She glanced at him over her shoulder with a wry expression. "I thought you were blue ops, Riddell."

"*Black* ops," he grunted.

"By the lack of oxygen you're suffering from, blue fits better."

He stopped and looked up at her. "You messin' with me?"

She smirked and moved on. "Just watching out for your aorta."

No. He would not smile. Would not.

Tsing! Thunk!

Cement coughed in his face. Dribbled down, tinkling against the grate.

"Taking fire!" Griffin shoved himself to the grate, realizing with the holes in the grate and the open drop, they were exposed. "Go, go!" Scrambling, he lunged forward, eyes locked on the door at the end.

Bullets sprayed along the wall, raining down dust and cement. Ahead, Kacie ran hunched, moving quickly. Almost to the door she went down. Yelped. Then pushed on, plunged through the door, and vanished into the darkness.

Griffin plowed through and pushed to the right to clear the path for Colton, who dove through. "Kacie?'"

"Here," she said with a hiss.

He groped to the left, to the sound of her voice, and caught her shoulder. "You hit?"

"A graze. I'll be fine."

"But you're not now," he said, sliding closer.

"We have to move. I saw them—they're one level below us." She toed the door closed. As she did, light erupted, illuminating the room.

Griffin saw the streak of blood on her leg. A little deeper than he'd have preferred, but she was right—a graze. A few inches to the right and it could've shattered the femur.

Kacie stood and pointed down the small hallway. "That leads to the roof. There's a hidden door in the pool supply shed. That will take you down and out the alley. Get to the Thames—the Eye. I'll meet you there."

Griffin's hardwired protective instincts erupted. "Meet us? No way. We're all going."

"No." The stance she took, the determination sparking in her green eyes, told him she would brook no opposition. In so many ways she reminded him of Madyar, though a league of differences separated them. "I'm going to finish this."

"That don't need to happen. Get out of here, get out alive."

"I have to."

"Why?"

Kacie looked toward the far door.

He waited for her to answer, to come clean. Something had changed. He wanted to know what.

The floor vibrated and they all turned toward the grate they'd just traversed. She threw herself against the door. "Do it. Go!"

"Not without you."

"I have to stay."

"Why?"

"My brother is here." She raised her chin as if to ward off the feelings that bubbled to the surface. "The only one who *should* have died is working with Carrick—if they find you, he will execute you right here, right now. Let someone else be the hero for once, Griffin."

What did that mean? Was she expecting to die here?

The door banged.

"*Go!*" Kacie flinched. "I'll meet you at the Eye."

"I'm counting on you. . ." Griffin backed away as Colton tugged him onward. "Don't let me down, Baby Girl."

But somehow. . .walking out of there, leaving her behind, he felt like he was letting her down. As he slipped through the final door, he glanced back.

Kacie opened the steel panel. Men flooded in. Pinned her to the wall.

CHAPTER 23

Airfield in Maryland

The jet hummed, waiting for a chance to leap into the sky and spirit them to safety. Like the numbing vibration coming off the wake of the engines, another vibration wormed through Marshall—worry. Could he get this done, get out of here before the cops or his father figured out his plan?

If his dad had no compunction against trying to kill the only friends—no, *family*—Marshall had known, then it stood to reason his father wouldn't hesitate to kill him. Right? The thought pushed him around in the hangar. He paced. Raked fingers over his stubbly jaw, a groan working its way up his throat.

"They'll be here," Rel said.

"It's been nearly thirty minutes." He shoved his fingers through his hair and paced some more. "If we don't bug out. . ." His father could catch up with him. Stop him. Interfere. Or. . .worse.

Rel came to him and touched his arm. "Sydney said they had a tail. Her brother would lose them, and the rest would get to the airstrip."

More trouble. Caused by his father. Why? What was the point? What did his father seek in this venture? He'd never approved of the military, even though it was the one thing Marshall felt clicked in his life.

"What is he doing?" Misery coated every word, and even though he felt weak and ashamed of what his father had done, Marshall didn't care that Rel saw him like this, raw. "He's always hated me, but this. . .this is insane. It makes no sense. Why didn't I see this?"

She caught his arms as he raked his fingers through his hair again.

"Marshall, stop."

The strength in her words stilled him.

"You can't take the blame for what he did."

"Yes." He huffed. "I can—I have to. What if one of the guys is dead? What if I could've stopped him, seen it—"

"Don't look back," Rel said. "Look *forward*, at what you're doing now. You're getting them to safety. You're protecting the families of the men you love."

He choked down the emotion swelling in his throat. "Would you want to face Max and say, 'Dude, I let your wife and kids die'?"

Rel smirked. "Your tough-guy talk doesn't work with me." Her fingers traced the side of his face, blazing a path straight into his chest. "You're a hero, Marshall."

"Tss," he muttered and stepped out of her grasp. Heroes didn't come in packages like him.

Mario burst out the side door. "Dude! We got heat. Bing called—the whole boulevard is swarming with lights and—"

A siren rent the air. Then more. . .and more, until the whole of his hearing seemed devoured by emergency howlers.

"They comin'." Mario pointed to the idling plane. "You'd better go."

"The women. . ."

"No time, man. We'll barely get you off the ground—"

"Look!" Rel shouted, jogging out into the open.

There, a black SUV barreled down the road, hot-tailed by a dozen or more cops and unmarked vehicles.

"It's them."

Oh God, help me. . . No way they could get on the plane without intervention.

A blaring horn broke through the din, snagging his attention on a train barreling down the tracks. His heart dove into his throat. The train wasn't slowing. . .and neither was the SUV.

"Get in the plane," Mario hollered, dragging Marshall by the sleeve across the open area.

He stumbled up the five steps into the plane, crouching to watch through the portal windows at the chaos unfolding. He gripped the leather seatback. "No. . .no, no. . .they won't make it." Pulse thumping, he leaned closer. "No, stop! Don't do it. No!" he shouted. Begging angels, God, anyone to stop them.

The train lurched from between two buildings into the intersection.

Boom!

Black metal twisted and hurtled through the air. Flipped once. . . twice. . .three times.

Bread & Butter Club, London

Hands grabbed her. Kazi used the chest of the man behind her as a counterbalance and whipped her legs up and shoved her feet into the chest of the nearest man. She snapped her head backward.

Crack.

"Augh!" Hands freed her, and she dropped to the grate with a thud—the sound masked thanks to the throbbing music and deafening din of the crowd almost a hundred feet below them.

When she started to straighten, Kazi found herself staring into the muzzle of a Beretta M93. She followed the arm up as she pulled herself straight. Disbelief churned in the wake of her fury. "Roman."

"Little sister." His blond hair was cut short against his broad skull. The shoulders had widened right along with the insipid calloused nature he'd developed. He motioned the barrel at her. "Hands."

Obeying, she raised her arms out to the side and pushed her gaze to Carrick—gloating, sickening Carrick—who stood behind Roman with a sneer. "I see you let one rat get away."

Though she saw him laugh, the throbbing rhythm vibrating the walls and floors swallowed it. It sickened her that he found pleasure in dismantling her life. Ruining all that she had built. He knew her weaknesses and exploited them all to his benefit. *Quite the contrary to Griffin.* He'd discovered her weaknesses, but rather than pushing them in her face, he gave her room to figure things out.

"Move," Roman shouted over the noise.

Kazi looked to the side. Noticed a pipe. Then another across. . .her gaze hopscotched over and over the club, her pulse ramping as her gaze took her lower. Would they support her weight? If she dropped on one too heavy or hit it wrong? She might be able to. . .

"Kazimiera." Carrick stepped forward.

She moved her right foot back a step. Drew her arms to her side.

Roman angled the gun at her again. Motioned with a bob of his head toward the small hall where she'd last seen Griffin. To her left a possible escape—which could also kill her if those pipes didn't hold—to her right, Carrick's lair.

Inside the twelve-by-twenty area, Kazi stopped just over the threshold and took up a defensive position with her back to the wall and her hand within reach of the door. "I thought you said my family was dead."

Carrick laughed. "You told me years ago he wasn't your brother anymore."

To her surprise, Roman shifted. His eyes bounced around. *Avoiding me.* What, did the truth hurt? Did he expect her to still care about him after all he'd done?

Arm around him, Carrick squeezed her brother's shoulder. "Roman and I are partners."

Brown eyes so like their father's met hers, then darted away. Roman lowered the Beretta, but just as quickly, Carrick leaned in and nudged it back up.

Thudding drew her around, heart in her throat—had they captured Griffin and Colton again? Two guards, sweat sliding down their temples, shook their heads.

Amusement gone, Carrick glowered at her. "Where are they? I want those men."

"On the roof."

Carrick scowled. "My men just searched it—they're not there."

She shrugged. "I told them to go to the roof."

He checked with Roman. "Is she telling the truth?"

"Like he would know." *Calm down. Don't let him get to you.* "He hasn't seen me since he handed you the thirty pieces of silver."

"Tsk tsk, Kazimiera. Religious overtones have never been your forte."

"Still fitting, wouldn't you agree?"

Carrick's hand encircled her arm. "Where are they?"

She wanted to fight him. Kick his slick backside off the rooftop, the same one that had ferried Griffin and Colton to safety—she hoped.

He yanked her to himself, his grip burning. "Where?"

"Not. Here." Grinding her teeth radiated aches through her jaw and neck, but it was of little concern anymore.

Carrick shoved her toward Roman, who clamped his meaty paws on her forearms. "Take her down and lock her up. I'll deal with her after the premiere." With Hickson, his personal guard, Carrick strode down the hall and disappeared through a door that led to an elevator, which would dump him into the main lobby—right into the lap of his loyal dogs below.

Nostrils flaring, Kazi struggled against her brother's hold as he wrangled her toward the rear entrance. "You are a coward, Roman."

"Don't waste your breath, little sister. I've heard it all before."

"Oh, that's right. I forgot you were the only Faronski born without a heart." She wrested free and jumped back. She knew better than to run—the armed guards were her reminders.

Roman's eyes blazed. "We had Kazpar; there was no need for you—it only meant more mouths to feed."

"Dad would—"

"He's dead, Kazimiera!"

"And you're nothing like him."

His face reddened. "I did what I had to."

"Easy money. Judas said the same thing, I bet." She hauled composure back into line. "Tell me, will you hang yourself when it's over?"

He surged forward. "Do you know *why* I went to Carrick?" His blond brows creased over his brown eyes.

Her stomach swirled. "He had a thing for young girls."

"No, not used-up little girls."

His words seared what was left of her heart, her hope that Roman's actions would somehow make sense, that someone held a gun to his head or some—

"I went to Carrick because I hated myself since the day Boucher took you. Because I wanted a life for you, a chance for you to—"

"To what? Be someone else's property? Do you realize what he's made me do?"

"When Carrick learned that Boucher was going to burn the farm and have Mamo thrown in jail, he offered to settle the bill because he had seen what you could do. It wasn't a bad thing—it was the answer!"

Kazi struck his groin with her foot. When he doubled over, she drove her hand toward his face, determined to push that lying tongue through his throat.

Somehow, Griffin's face flashed into her mind. And she knew. . . *knew* he'd be disappointed if she killed Roman. She whirled around, swept her palms over the dirty floor, and drove her heel into the chin of the other guard. As he fell, she jumped through the opening. Sprinting down the catwalk, she eyed the first bar. *Please hold. . .*

She jumped to the right, toed off the wall, and hurled herself over the flimsy barrier.

"Kazimiera!" Roman's shout chased her into the air.

Dread iced her veins as she sailed down through the chilled, smoky atmosphere. Above the lights, above the chaos, nobody would even notice if she fell to her death. Freedom clutched at her as she dropped. Gaze locked on the pipe below, she prayed there was enough dirt on her hands to coat them so she didn't slip from slick palms.

Thump! Her fingers coiled around the bar. Tingling wove through them. *Hot!* It was a hot-water pipe. She ground her teeth as she swung around for a front-hip circle, using the momentum to gain her balance on the pipe. She straddled it, then rose up, ignoring the heat radiating through her shoes. Arms out for balance, she gauged the distance to the next one.

"Kazimiera!" Roman shouted again. "Stop!"

She thrust herself into the air again. Down. . .down. . . As gravity yanked her to the next bar, she begged for a cool pipe. *Thump!* Relief chugged through her veins—not hot. She swung.

Grrooan!

Her breath hitched as she swung.

Pop!

The right side dropped. So did she.

But in a full arc, she twisted her body in a roll, searching. . . The other bar. Where was it? She was off balance now.

Shouts drowned out her fears.

A blur of white.

The bar! Kazi snapped her hand out. Caught it. The jerk rammed through her body. She reached up with her other hand, only to feel the slipping—her palms were sweaty. Adrenaline had coated her skin. She would fall to her death.

Quickly, she wiped her hand on her pants. Switched hands, her legs dangling fifty feet above the crowds—the shouting, chanting crowds. She looked straight down, past her feet, to the sea of bodies. All still. All watching.

Which meant Carrick had probably spotted her, too.

And he'd catch her. Stop her.

As she drew her attention back to her plight, Kazi spotted another pipe. Bigger, stronger. It'd be harder to swing around, but it would hold. And it was farther down. Which was both a danger—she couldn't get her fingers around it to aid in her movement—and a blessing, she'd be closer to the ground. To escaping. Below it and behind but directly under her position now was another bar. She'd have to swing around, crisscross, and do a three-quarter giant to launch to the other one.

A lot of moves. On untested pipes. Over a crowd of hundreds, if not thousands.

What if she didn't make it? What if she died? Griffin would be on his own. But if she didn't make it out of here, he was on his own either way.

Do it.

"Imagine what it'll be like to stop running." His words on the plane snaked down through the thick smoke and strobe lights, coiling around her dead dreams and soul.

She leapt.

"No!"

Midair, she heard Carrick's shout through the speakers, over the din, over the simultaneous screams. She hoped beyond hope that she didn't fall to her death. Although. . .it'd be better than having his noose around her neck for the rest of her life.

First bar. Clear. Crisscrossed her wrists and swung in the opposite direction. Completed a three-quarter giant and launched through the air. Her fingers hit steel. Slipped. Down. . .down. . .

Screams blended—hers, the crowd's.

Groan! Crack!

Falling, she thought only of Griffin. Of the fact he'd never know what she felt. That she would never have the chance to tell him he made her want to be *That Girl.*

Arms and bodies buckled beneath her.

Blinding pain shot through her ankle.

Acholi, Uganda

Brilliance pierced Scott's corneas. He moaned and squeezed his eyes tighter.

"Finally, the mighty warrior wakes."

Scott moaned again, suddenly remembering. . .everything. "You shouldn't have come."

"Trust me, I've already had that conversation with myself a thousand times over." Delicate fingers plucked open his eyes. A brighter light erupted.

He flinched.

"Don't be a baby, Callaghan."

His siphoned-off energy slowly returned. As did his mental faculties. "I need a phone."

"A brain is more like it, but you can't have either."

He pulled himself up, blinking through the blinding sun streaming into the. . .building. He froze his upward movement and jerked his head around. "Where are we?"

"My clinic. I'd think you would remember after all the time you spent here."

Her clinic. A day's journey. . ."How?" He shifted thoughts because asking how he got here was stupid. "How long was I out?"

"Just long enough to get you and others here to safety, get briefed on what happened, and for me to cut up your back and leave my mark."

If he had any doubt that she hated him, she'd just erased it.

"I removed two bullets from your back. Ojore said you found something at the mines. Want to fill me in?"

Bullets?

Shoulder-length brown hair framed one of the prettiest faces he'd ever encountered. *Don't let it fool you.* Yeah, he did that once. Regretted

214

it till. . .well, forever.

"Dembe—"

"No." She shook a dainty finger at him. "You're not allowed to call me that anymore."

He hung his head, too tired to fight her. Not this time. "I just need to use the phone."

"Scott?"

That she'd called him by his right name, that her tone wasn't laden with venom and hatred, drew his gaze to her blue eyes.

"What happened back there?"

He traced the cracks in the cement floor. All those years of work down the drain. Had he been idealistic and stupid to think it'd work? That he could rescue the unrescuable? He'd been a killer and hired gun—employed by the U.S. government—for years. He'd wanted to make a change for the better. As he stared down, the dried blood on his knuckles caught his eyes.

He'd never be anything but a killing machine. It kicked in without compunction.

Graceful fingers curled around his.

Scott clenched her hand in his, unwilling to speak or move. Not trusting himself to do so without falling apart.

Demb— *Marie.* . .sweet Marie. . .touched his face. Crouched to look in his eyes. "Scott?"

I must look stupid.

He swallowed and shook off the misery still unwilling to meet her gaze. "I just need a phone."

She cupped his face with both hands. "Who are you calling? Last I knew, you had nobody Stateside."

He dragged his gaze to hers. "My brother."

Faith is the evidence of things not seen. . .

And he hadn't seen his brother in more than fifteen years—and even then, the encounter had been brief.

An hour later, Scott sat alone in the communications closet, agitated by the mocking cursor. The one that said he didn't have the courage to send the e-mail. To reach beyond animosity and hatred.

No, not hatred. Intense hurt.

His brother rejected him. For reasons Scott had no power to affect or change. Yeah, he got it. Were their positions reversed, he'd probably do the same thing. Then again, he wanted someone to identify with. Someone to make proud. And his half brother was the only one who'd been a role model to him. Well, except the anger part.

Roughing a hand over his stubbled jaw, Scott heaved a sigh.

He had to get help. Had to talk to someone who would understand the situation, know what to do. And the only person he could trust right now. . .

Scott hit SEND.

"Thought you'd never do that."

He gave a soft snort as his brain chugged into the present and noticed the tawny figure leaning against the doorjamb. Should've known she was watching him. "I told you I'm not stealing anything."

"So you said." She ambled to his side and set down a cup of coffee. "Think he'll come?"

That was what hurt the worst. "Probably not."

CHAPTER 24

Somewhere in Miranda, Venezuela

A shock of light blasted through Range's vision.

He jerked and groaned, tucking his chin to shield his eyes from the intensity as it registered that straps around his chest, waist, and legs bound him to a wood chair.

"Why are you here?" a voice boomed through a speaker, warping the sound and thudding into Range's chest.

Shifting in the chair, he tensed, expecting the injury in his leg to pull against the material. When it didn't, his gaze shifted downward, but the light devouring every particle of darkness worked against him. *Where am I?* His mind backtracked to the village, to being taken captive. Driving through the night. Being roughed up. Pushed around. Punched. Shouted at. Then the darkness of exhaustion and blood loss gulped him down its greedy gullet.

"Why are you here?" the voice repeated.

Answering them would only give them information, and he certainly wasn't about to do that. They'd caught him, and he'd end up dead. He'd been a Coastie long enough to know what guerillas like this did to prisoners held for ransom—they demanded more ransom, often got it, but never produced the prisoner. Besides, his family didn't have money, nothing that would satisfy these types. And the government would disavow his presence here. So Range would just make sure he went down in honor, protecting his country.

"Norteamericano, why are you here?"

"Like the location," Range muttered.

Whack!

He flew backward, the chair tipping over. Pain fired through his jaw and neck seconds before his head thudded against the ground.

"What is your purpose here, Coast Guard spy?"

Range blinked, his heart skidding through the revelation that they knew he was a Coastie. That wasn't possible. He brought nothing with him that indicated his service with the USCG.

"I'm just visiting," he said, louder, clearer.

A figure loomed over him as a boot drove down onto his throat. "I don't think so," the man hissed in Spanish. "Now, answer me, and I might let you breathe. Why are you here?"

Straining against the pressure, Range grunted. Outting his real purpose would just get him—and Canyon—killed faster. "Just. . . visiting."

More pressure.

He could take it. Had to. If he couldn't get past the first barrier of defense, he had no hope of finding his brother.

The pressure lifted. Range hauled in a breath—water dumped over his face. He gagged. Choked. Writhed against his bindings. To the side, he vomited.

"Tell us why you are here!"

Fire spiraled through his chest. *Thud!* A sudden impact in his side kicked a scream from his throat. Legs bound, hands tied behind the chair, Range couldn't fight back. And dying wouldn't help him or Canyon—although, the latter was less of a concern at the second.

More water.

"My br. . .ther," he squeaked out.

A smack to his face startled him.

Range looked up.

A man hunched over him, one arm propped on his leg. "That was your first mistake."

Oh God. . .help me.

The man straightened and motioned over his shoulder. "Haul him up."

Three or four men in khaki uniforms rushed forward and pulled Range's chair upright. Confusion raked over him as they adjusted it, then walked out of the small tent. The big guy, the one who'd roughed him up, stood at the tent flap, eyes locked on Range.

"You're not quite what I expected."

English. Why was he speaking perfect, unaffected English? "I'd like to claim the same, but I don't think I was expecting you."

"Oh, that was evident." The man grabbed a chair, swung it around, and straddled it. "How did you expect to get your brother back? You don't know standard tactics. You can't even defend yourself against a simple interrogation."

"Simple?"

The man flashed a deadly smile. "You have all your body parts intact."

Range refused to look down. He didn't know how he would get Canyon back. He just knew he had to try. Or at least, he'd been guilted into believing that.

No. . .no, he did believe it. Guilt wouldn't have brought him down here and made him fight it out. He'd have turned back long ago.

"Your brother is one of the strongest warriors I've ever met." The man's voice held no malice, no anger. Only admiration. "But he's in one screwed-up situation. He needs help, but I'm not sure you're the help he needs."

"I would agree with you." Quiet resolve hardened in Range's chest. "Almost."

The man arched an eyebrow, then straightened, arms out to the side. "Enlighten me."

"You might have the tactics, the skills, but I have the same blood pumping through my veins. He's my brother. Same blood." He tightened his jaw. "I'm not going home without him. I'm not going to face our mother or his children or myself for the rest of my life and say I failed."

"At the rate you're going," the man said with a laugh, "I doubt you'll see next week, let alone the rest of your life."

"Perhaps," Range said, feeling the truth of the words. "But I'll die trying."

"Am I supposed to be impressed, Coastie?"

This time Range laughed. "Not if you really know my brother."

"Huh?"

"I am his complete opposite. Canyon is impressive, doesn't talk a lot, and hard hitting. I have none of his skills, but I am. . . dedicated."

"Deluded is more accurate." He squinted as he watched Range, then slowly he stood and produced a knife. "Do you realize who has your brother?"

Range shied away from the blade as the man squatted beside him. "No."

The man sawed through the bindings, freeing Range. "The men he severed power from—the VFA—have him. And every day they have him, they're shaving a year off his life." Brown, intense eyes met his. "These men, there is a foreign hand that's feeding their frenzy, promising all sorts of things that won't be delivered."

Range stretched his leg, surprised to find the material cut away from the knee and his wound stitched up. He grunted and hissed as his muscle rebelled.

"Don't be a baby."

Range glowered and directed the conversation back to Canyon. "Who has him?"

"Do you know what your brother was doing down here last year?"

Besides stealing Danielle and getting her pregnant? The thoughts pushed Range's gaze away.

The man chuckled. "I didn't think so. You are still hung up on his marriage to the senator's daughter?" Another laugh as he walked to a small cooler and lifted a dripping bottle of water. "Your brother brought down a very powerful man, one forming deadly alliances. Venezuela—some people are against the government here. Americans might not understand our leaders, but it works for us. For most of us. That is, until men like a certain U.S. senator steps in, arranges alliances to create coups. . ." He took a swig of water, then sighed. "I got too close to the truth, too close to exposing them, so they throw everything at me. Decide they better off me before I can do it to them."

He guzzled a bottle of water and grinned at Range. "Which brings us to why I am out in this jungle, not in our facilities in the city. And now, the same man who is trying to take me down is also trying to kill the men your brother works with. I stumbled on his dirty work—his involvement with Senator Roark. He didn't like that. This isn't some tap dance, Coastie. This is nothing but pure hell." He finished off the water. "You ready to face that kind of evil?"

"How do you know so much about me and my brother?"

"Because, unlike you, I look past the end of my nose. You came down here, stepped into a big pile of you-know-what." He seemed to snarl at Range, then grabbed another bottle and held it out to him. "Now, you ready to do what it takes? Or should I ship you home in the first available coffin and save myself some time?"

"You don't like me."

The man laughed. "I have no need to like you, Coastie. You're in my territory. If I didn't think I could use you, I'd have let the VFA take you last night." He shook his head. "Gotta hand it to you though. How you made it this far into the den of lions is beyond me. But now—now the real fun begins. Let's get the job done."

Awareness skidded into Range that he was on borrowed time. "And what job is that?"

A danger lurked behind the man's eyes. "Getting your brother out, killing the man who did this, and walking into the sunset."

Thames River, London

Dodging cars on the wrong side of the road, Griffin and Colton jogged down the street. He glanced up as the streetlight caught the sign. Northumberland. Good, good. They were on track according to the directions a man had given them a block or two back. The Thames should be just ahead.

"What if she doesn't come?" Why he asked, he didn't know. Didn't care. The burning ache in his thighs matched the one in his chest that feared she hadn't made it out of there. That he'd left her. Just like his mom. Griffin paused to take a breath, clear his mind. This wasn't the same thing. But what if Kacie was back there? What if Carrick—?

"Don't go there," Cowboy huffed. They crossed the street and angled toward Victoria Embankment. "She told us what to do; we did it."

Griffin knew what his buddy wasn't saying. She'd found them and given them a way out. What Cowboy was also saying was that she never gave any indication that she would come. And her going back to deal with her brother, with Carrick—that just didn't sit right with him.

The bigger question loomed and pushed in on him. If she didn't show—could he leave without her? Yeah, he could, but *would* he?

They hustled toward the river, his gaze groping for her halolike hair. Surely it'd glow in the evening moonlight, amid the lights that streaked up and down the embankment and pedestrian footbridges. From the wrong side, they searched those gathered around the Eye, watched the occupants of the various trams that rose into the sky. Then the theater.

"I don't see her."

"She's probably lying low," Colton said.

Keyed up, Griffin eyed the white suspension cords that anchored the bridge to the pylons. Was she down there by the pylons?

"Let me check it out," he said already in motion. He hustled down the steps, jogging up and down the river, around buildings, quietly but quickly searching. Praying God would open his eyes to find her. As he retraced his path, Griffin fought to maintain hope. As he took the steps back up to Colton, who lounged casually watching the river, he groped for a reason. "Maybe she's running behind. Or caught. What if that perv—"

"We give her time to come. Let's agree on a time frame."

Griffin couldn't pry his gaze from the bodies teeming by the Eye. His gaze stretched across the body of water to the large white Ferris wheel. The largest one in Europe and situated on the south bank of the Thames. "Let's check it out." He scurried back up the trio of steps he'd taken down to the river and scaled the steps up to the footbridge, using the rail to propel him faster.

Up top, he and Colton simultaneously slowed, not wanting to draw attention to themselves or their location. Two men running across an open bridge were prime targets for anyone following. In the darkness, with the lights of the city illuminating the river, they had little hope of seeing Kacie from this distance. But his heart pumped and churned all the same. How did a woman get his mind so fouled up?

As they reached the platform to the steps, sirens and lights scraped the night. The noise and chaos pushed them down the steps into the darkened areas beneath the bridge. Amid the crowds and staying in the shadows, they scoured the faces for hers.

"See anything?" Griffin asked.

"Nothing." Colton nodded to two uniforms strolling their way. "And those bobbies won't be much help."

Hands on his hips, Griffin waited for his breath to even out. "We can't stay down here all night."

"No, but we're not in a rush either." Colton propped himself against the pylon. "Give the cops time to move on. We're not going anywhere."

"But what if she does?"

"She's a spy. She knows about waiting things out."

Griffin glared at his partner. "You'd better be right."

Colton folded his arms and frowned at him. "What's with this girl? I mean, you've known her, what? Two weeks? Three at most? What's she mean to you?"

"Nothing." The answer tasted like acid, burning a hole through his lying tongue. "I don't know," he muttered, his voice hoarse. "It don't make sense—what I feel, what I don't feel. It's not like with other women, with Venus or Treece." He swallowed, scared. Both of those women had ditched him at the slightest hint of trouble or complication. Since Treece divorced him, he'd promised to stay true to three things: God, the team, and himself. That's it. Nobody else. "My life don't have room for a woman. 'Specially not one like her."

His fire buddy remained unmoving.

Shame pushed Griffin's attention to the ground. "I was angry that I hadn't seen it, you know? Getting drugged was my own fault. If she'd said something, interfered, her position would've been compromised. That could be deadly for her. I get it now, I think. One wrong move and she's dead."

"Or we are." Cowboy readjusted, settling in. "You realize she could have sent us down here to attract the attention of the local authorities. We could be walking right into a trap."

Clapping a hand on Colton's shoulder, Griffin let an idea take hold. "Trust me?"

"With my life."

"Good." He nodded toward the steps leading up toward the wheel that hung out over the water. "Follow me."

Griffin stalked toward the stairs, up the path, and around the corner to the right. Toward the throng of bodies gathered at the theater, the sidewalk café, and the Eye. With practiced moves, he probed the faces, those occupying chairs, the corners.

He angled toward an alley that sucked light into oblivion. Walking into that would put him on the disadvantage. What he wouldn't give for NVGs. But then. . .something Madyar had said long ago wormed from the recesses of the past. *When you can't see what God's hand is doing, trust His heart.* It hadn't been God who'd spoken the words leading him tonight, but couldn't God use this girl who tied his mind into a complicated, tangled knot—one surrounding his heart? Griffin couldn't see what would happen. But. . .he trusted—*trusted!*—Kacie wouldn't lead him into danger on purpose.

The thought pushed him into the dark alley.

"Legend," Colton hissed in a quiet whisper.

He struggled to let his eyes adjust but no go. Too dark. He strained every other faculty—smelling, hearing, tasting the musky, dank air.

"Legend—"

"Shh." He took another step, led onward by a stillness farther in. By a strange, quiet noise. It sounded like. . .sniffling.

He took two powerful steps forward.

Something slammed into him.

CHAPTER 25

London, England

She'd done dumber things in her life, but this topped them all. Kazi threw herself into Griffin once he'd come deep enough into the alley. Fingers coiled in the sides of his shirt, she held on for dear life, ignoring the stabbing pain in her ankle. Though the crowd in the club had cushioned her landing, it hadn't been enough to prevent an injury. But the frenzy afterward was exactly what she'd counted on to escape—because Carrick's men opened fire trying to stop her. And that unleashed the panic-fed crowds. She'd hobbled through the chaos and slipped out the front door like everyone else. Now fire blazed through her ligaments and tendons. Swollen like crazy.

Carrick betrayed her. He'd held power over her forever, and she had no delusions that he'd cut her off when he was through, but there'd been an unspoken alliance, a silent bond that said he needed her too much.

But the real pain, the agony that swam circles around her mind, was Roman's appearance. He truly believed he'd done her a favor. Saved the family. High on himself and his savior persona, Roman could not see the damage he'd inflicted.

Everything was over. *Everything*. Ties severed. Family dead. Heart. . .empty.

Clinging to Griffin, Kazi buried her face in his chest, waiting for the memories of Carrick, Andrez to go away. And Roman. . . Why? Why had he come back? Carrick said he'd killed her family—why leave Roman out? The one person in her family who deserved death, a very painful, lingering, excruciating death, and he was still alive?

She thudded her forehead against Griffin's pecs.

Arms enfolded her, holding her close, tight. Griffin shuffled to the side with her in his arms.

Shame and guilt forbid her from moving, from looking into his eyes and seeing rejection or pity the way every man who knew anything about her did. She didn't need that. Didn't want it. Not from Griffin.

The thought stilled her but sent her mind spiraling. What. . .what did she want from him?

Nothing. I don't need anyone.

Wearied by the thought that kept her going for these many years, she let her shoulders slump. She was tired of being alone. Tired of being betrayed.

And if you stay here in his arms that's what's going to happen.

Slowly, she lifted her head and took a step back. As a brackish breeze swept the hair from her face, several strands stuck to her cheek. She shuddered. Brushed her hair back and felt the dampness on her face. Tears?

Her eyes locked with Griffin's.

Cupping her face, he swept away a strand with his thumb. "You did good."

"I. . ." *Brain blank? Seriously?* A single thought suffocated all others. "You knew where I'd be." She forced a half smile into her face, realizing he'd had the chance to ditch her, to escape—but he didn't. He waited. The thought thumped against her fears. "I didn't think there was much under that shiny dome of yours."

He smirked and nodded, but something had shifted. In him. Between them. In life.

Oh no. . .

Snap into gear, Kaz. "Right, okay. Good—you made it. Any slower and we would've missed our ticket out of here."

"What do you mean?" Neeley shouldered into the tension.

"We're booked on the Eurostar to Paris. From there I have a friend who can get us to Greece quickly. But our train leaves in fifteen." She bobbed her head toward the theater. "A friend will drop us at the station, but we're short on time."

"And passbooks, wouldn't you say?" Neeley asked.

"Taken care of." She motioned toward the end of the alley, where a light flickered. "That's Bobby. Let's go."

She quickened her pace and hurried to the car, leaving the near-breach in her self-imposed walls. She climbed into the rear, knowing her face would be easily recognizable if Carrick had his way and notified the authorities. And he always did. In the car, she beat back the flurry of troubles that stormed her life. Carrick would be after her with a vengeance since she bolted the way she had.

But she'd gotten away from him. Again. It didn't mean much, but if Carrick revealed her identity, she'd never be a spy again. And that possibility always existed. It'd be the quickest route to the grave. That jeopardized the mission with Griffin and his men. It jeopardized her life. Their lives. But it was so much more than that—even though that was enough—she suddenly no longer felt like Kazi Faron. Or Kacie Whitcomb. Or anyone else she'd ever been.

The car shifted under the weight of the men, and she found guilty pleasure in the fact that Griffin had joined her in the rear. His size, his strength, his honor. . .

"Is this safe?" Neeley asked as the car pulled onto the street, heading for the station.

"Nothing is safe." Not anymore. Kazi swallowed. A tightness wove around her shoulders, stretched down her spine, and cinched at her waist. It felt as if life were folding in on itself. On her. Anger, hurt, fear swirled through her with a new vengeance, leaving her. . .

Scared.

As the car bobbed and weaved through traffic, curved roundabouts, and peeled around turns, Kazi braced herself with a hand on the seat. At one turn, her palm slipped—and nudged something. She glanced down, surprised to find Griffin's hand resting beside hers.

With the streetlamps and blue-green glow of the dashboard, the contrast of their complexions struck her for the first time—and the sheer size of that paw. So large. So strong. The memory of him holding her, safely and securely, crawled through her mind. It'd been stupid of her, really, to fling herself into his arms. And she hadn't been doing that. Well, not intentionally.

Her fingers spread toward his on their own will. *Stop!*

She fisted her hand and drew it back into her lap.

"Here we are, Kaz." Bobby eased the car to the curb and passed back three brown envelopes.

Kazi handed one to the guys. "Okay, we'll enter the station through different doors and in thirty-second intervals. Each person grabs a backpack." Kazi stepped into the night air and moved to the boot of the car. Flanked by Neeley and Griffin, she lifted the small blue case. "Each bag has clothes, some euros, and—"

"How in blazes did you manage to pull all that together between the time we saw you on stage and the time we met up?" Neeley balked. "She's better than the ruddy Boy Scouts—'always prepared.' "

Kazi ignored their banter and pushed on. Time wasn't on their side. "Remember, get in there; get on the train."

"I *don't* like this." Griffin scowled at her.

Heat spread through her chest as she took in his meaning. "We'll hook up on the train once it's moving."

Griffin yanked a bag from the boot and stalked toward the station. In seconds, he fell into the teeming bodies that poured through the doors and streamed into the station. Even the late hour did not deter travelers. Thank goodness.

With a nod, Neeley trailed his partner.

"Do you know what you're doing?" Bobby whispered as he eased the boot closed. "Those men—I can get you out of here without them knowing. It's messy, Kacie. That black guy looks mean."

Nah. That wasn't mean. She'd seen mean in Roman. In Boucher. In Carrick. In Griffin, she saw. . .

Well, it really didn't matter as long as he wouldn't put her in danger or betray her. And of those two things she was confident when it came to Griffin Riddell. "I'll be fine." She strolled into the station mindful of but not bending to the pain in her ankle, determined to see the mission through to the end. And it would definitely be the end. . .of everything.

Somewhere in Miranda, Venezuela

Surrounded by more than two dozen armed guerillas, Range cradled the AR-15 rifle. Blood, laced with ungodly amounts of adrenaline, sped through his veins like an uncapped fire hydrant. *Is this what Canyon thrived on?* Range's breathing sounded hollow in the gear that had been provided. Shots sounded hollow. The muzzle flash seemed fake. Like some grisly, animated computer game—but it wasn't fake. It wasn't a game.

This is for keeps.

The lethal precision of the men around him propelled him yet also repelled him. They had experience that tightened their response times, practiced in killing and breaking into a facility like this. Guilt clung to him thicker than the heavy air and sickening stench of sweat as they plodded down the cement corridors.

A man jumped from the side.

Range pivoted and fired. In the space of a heartbeat, as the man fell and the blood squirted, he realized he'd made his first kill. The thought rankled him. Pulled at him.

The space narrowed and the confrontations lessened. Ahead, three or four men rushed farther into the cavelike structure.

"The Colonel," as the rebels around him called the man who'd recruited him, slapped his shoulder and pointed. "They're leading us straight to him, yes?"

The words seemed to haul Range's mind back into gear, out of the gruesome events unfolding. He chided himself—what did he think? He'd come down here, do a waltz, and they'd go home, happy, safe, alive?

A barrage of shots and fights erupted ahead. Guards and guerillas clashed. Bodies filled the bottlenecked hall. Double pocket doors slid open. Five or six men backed into the area, firing and defending their position. One swatted toward the wall, and the doors slid shut.

"Stop them!" the Colonel darted forward.

Range stayed with him, eyes glued on the closing doors.

Behind the guards, two more doors opened. That split-second opportunity rammed all the oxygen into the back of Range's throat. On a dingy table lay a man in bloodied, tattered rags. He looked Latino, dark hair, tanned skin, wraith-thin.

Until he turned his head.

In the three seconds it took his brain to reengage, Range realized the brown skin coloring was actually bruises. The dark hair was oily and matted. The weight. . .starvation. Blue eyes swollen from abuse locked on Range.

"Canyon!" Range lunged forward, the shout of his brother's name a gargled mix of frantic fear and adrenaline.

With a whoosh, cement slammed together, severing his visual connection.

"No!" He pushed forward.

Shots pinged through the wood door.

Range ducked to the side, a blaze of fire searing down his arm. He winced and checked the spot. A thin line of red peeked out from the sleeve.

"Frag out!" came the shout.

The leader shoved Range backward.

Red-hot fire and wind blasted across his legs and arms.

"Go, go, go!"

On his feet, Range lurched into the smoldering debris. Around the corner. Three men pried at the other doors, shouting, grunting.

"Power's down," the leader snarled.

Range stuffed his grazed arm through the strap of the weapon and pushed his way into the others. Through the wood and cement came a large crash. Shots.

Range stilled, an acidic backwash coating his tongue. *God. . . ?*

Fingers digging into the seam, he quickly saw the futility. He spun toward the control box and ripped it open. After removing a few screws, he tugged out the wires.

"You can't hotwire it."

"No, but if I fry the circuits, the power lock will disengage." He spliced through two wires, stepped back, grounded himself with his rubber boots, then pinched the wires together. Voltage shot through his hands. . .his wrists. . .his arms. His teeth clattered.

"Oy!" came a torrent of cheers.

He stumbled around and saw the men prying the door open.

The Colonel clapped his shoulder again. "*¡Muy bien, mi amigo!*"

Back at the doors, he aided the others, his ears trained on the sounds of fighting from the other side. Grunts. Thuds. Chains rattling. "They're killing him!" He hadn't come this far to have Canyon die within feet of him. Range threw everything he had left into dragging the door open.

Finally, he pushed himself through the narrow divide. He stumbled but righted himself. And stopped cold.

Clothes hanging off him, his right arm dangling at an unnatural angle, blood coating his chest, a gaping wound near his neck that oozed, Canyon stood, his legs wobbling as severely sunken yet swollen eyes came to Range. His body swayed. A smirk slid into his face as blood dribbled down his chin. He staggered and grinned.

His eyes rolled into the back of his head. Canyon dropped hard.

Green World Health Compound, Uganda

"Marie!" Scott lunged forward, pushing her to the ground as wood peppered his face. He rolled, holding her against himself as he maneuvered them into a safe position. Scooting off, he probed her for injury.

She winced and groaned. "I'm. . .okay."

"Bull." He pinned her to the ground. "Stay." He scrambled to the shed, dragged two M16s out, stuffed a handgun in his belt, and filled his pockets full of magazines. Crawling back to her side, he locked on to her. "How're you doing?"

"Bleeding."

He smirked. "And they wonder why you're the doc."

"I'll be fine. It's just a graze, I think."

Trusting her word, he did a press check on the handgun, then drew up the M16 and scanned the perimeter through the scope. "I don't see him." He whistled and waited for the response.

Ten yards ahead, a flutter of movement bristled just seconds before a whistle.

Good. Ojore was in the school. He shouted a code and his apprentice answered.

Marie gave a soft laugh. "You're like Robin Hood and his merry men with your whistles and codes."

"It keeps us alive," Scott said. "Think you can make it to the school?"

She lifted her head off the ground and looked in that direction. Head dropped back down, she grunted. "Yeah."

"I can carry you."

That riled her. "Only when I'm dead."

"Promises, promises."

Supporting her, Scott helped Marie to her feet. They slunk around equipment and buildings, moving much slower than he'd prefer. The threat lay before them—a twenty-foot stretch of open area. They had to cross it to get to the school. But that would most likely expose them to the sniper. *Where is that devil?*

Vibrations wormed through his feet, stilling him.

Then the monotonous thumping.

"Chopper!"

A strange howl filled the day.

Screaming, a missile shot toward the school.

BooOOOOoomm!

Maryland Airstrip

The wreckage seemed ripped from a bad action movie. Marshall used two leather headrests to propel him toward the door.

"No!" Mario rushed into his path. "You can't do anything."

Marshall tried to shove past him, but the energy drained from his legs. His head spun. He hesitated.

"Company straight ahead," the pilot shouted from the cockpit.

Marshall and Mario jerked toward the front. Another SUV. The vehicle banked right. Doors flew up. Marshall went for cover, but as he did. . . "Wait. . .wait!"

People dumped onto the tarmac. Not in suits. Or uniforms.

"It's them!" Rel said. "That's got to be Sydney and the others."

Sure enough—three women armed not with weapons but with children. Face alight, Rel spun to him. "She said her brother was creating a distraction!"

He checked the accident. "I hope he got out." With the train barreling through, it effectively formed a barrier, preventing the cops from getting to them.

"We've got time." Marshall hurried to the front where the door still sat ajar. To the pilot, he said, "Ease up to them. We'll get them on board, then get out of Dodge."

"You got it."

With that, Marshall scrambled down the steps. He sprinted to the women. "On board, now! Now!"

He scooped up two children and turned, surprised to find Mario at his side. His friend gathered a child and scampered back into the plane, passing the child to Rel. Marshall handed a little girl to Rel, then another, reaching back for another hand. An adult hand took hold, and Midas's wife, Dani, surged forward, her baby strapped in some harness thing. Cowboy's wife, Piper, ambled up right behind her, then Sydney. He followed her up the five steps and into the jet. As he turned to shut the door, two things happened—a bullet whizzed past his face followed by another that narrowly missed his shoulder, and Mario shouted for the pilot to take off.

With a grunt, he grabbed the door handle, yanked it closed, and slammed down the bar, sealing it shut. He tumbled back and to the side as the craft ramped up for takeoff. Stumbling, he made his way past the others. . .the women, crying children—the families of Nightshade.

"Thank you," Dani said as he dropped into a leather chair.

"Don't thank me yet. That was the easy part." He huffed only then noticing the tears pouring down Sydney's face. He eased forward.

"Her brother was driving the other SUV."

CHAPTER 26

Cyprus, Golding Residence

You should be resting," Olin said as he set a hand on Aladdin's shoulder.

"If he is anything like his uncle," Golding said, "he will rest when he's dead."

Azzan Yasir's head sagged, his eyes dropped, but he typed. Clicked. Continuing his efforts to surf back channels and hidden networks in search of the team, of Max, of Dighton. Hours, countless hours, spent digging in a cesspool of data and history.

"Rest awhile, Aladdin." Olin ached for the team as much as the young man. "Your mind needs to recuperate. You are probably missing things—"

"I'm not." Azzan scrolled down a page, his blue-green eyes reddened from the punching bag they'd used him for and from deprivation. "Every minute out there is a minute they could face death." Brows tense, he flipped to another screen. Then to a separate monitor.

Olin met Golding's gaze in surrender before he ambled to the kitchen where Charlotte handed him another cup of tea. He sipped the hot brew. He should not be giving up. The men were the best. That's why he'd recruited them. Why he put the money behind their training and missions, convinced the chairman to fund vital interventions. And now that the team was in hot water, nobody blinked or cared.

"Legend and Cowboy are on the way back."

Olin nodded as he set the mug down.

"I've got a couple of eyes on them," Golding said.

Though Olin shouldn't be surprised, he couldn't fight the feeling.

"You always did have more connections than Waterloo station."

Golding smiled beneath his trim, thick black beard.

"Now, if we could just get those connections *connected* to the rest of the team."

"Patience, my old friend." Golding nodded to the assassin. "You think I have connections—wait till—"

Aladdin sat straight. His fingers flew over the keyboard.

Golding rushed to his side. "What is it?"

"Authorities in Virginia. Air Traffic Control is flagging a rogue jet." His fingers, unbelievably, moved faster over the keys. Clicks, groans, and a few more keystrokes. "It took off from a Maryland airstrip. Registered to a Mario Santana."

"We don't know him," Olin said. "Wait. Angel Santana at one time owned one of the most lucrative airlines, and he was friends with many senators. He may be our link. I'd bet my life that's the Kid."

"Stupid enough a move, taking a jumbo jet. . ." Aladdin grumbled as his eyes probed streaming data. "Ground reports are several dead at an accident involving a train, all racing to the airstrip. ATC and the feds are not happy."

Calmly, Olin placed a hand on his shoulder. "Don't let that happen."

Thudding at the front door brought Olin around.

Golding strode to the foyer with confidence and opened it. He stepped back, and in flooded ten men, all bearing laptops or large cases. "Gentlemen, welcome."

Again, surprise lit through Olin as the Israelis entered. Curtains were drawn. Folding tables erected. Systems unloaded, plugged in, networked. Fifteen minutes later, Olin's ears buzzed from the din of quick, quiet conversations on coded frequencies, secure channels, and clacking keyboards.

Golding's amusement filled his olive complexion. "Nightshade rescued our homeland." A deeper sense of satisfaction rolled over his face as he considered the men. "Now, we rescue Nightshade, nachon?"

"Sydney's brother is alive," Aladdin announced.

A man next to Aladdin spoke, his voice commanding and authoritative. "Santana aircraft, Kilo-Bravo-Foxtrot-two-one-three, this is Oscar-Mike. Switch to encrypted channel four. Repeat, channel four."

Nerves buzzing, Olin watched the data sliding down the screens of the monitors.

"Is that safe?" Charlotte's soft voice seemed to boom from behind him. "Talking to them so openly?"

"Yes," Olin said as he waited for the man's fingers to move, for him to speak, anything to show the Kid had picked up the message.

"But can't someone else get in on that call or overhear it? What if they figure out where we are?"

The agent looked at her, his deep brown eyes piercing. "They won't. And the only intercept," he spoke quietly but firmly, "would be from inside the aircraft. But let's assume your men are smart enough to take care of any unfriendlies. The channel is encrypted to that aircraft only."

"But there is a risk," Olin said. "They might be able to track us here."

The man's eyes flashed. "Unlikely." He jerked back to the console and repeated his command to the plane to switch to an encrypted channel.

Static washed through the blue monitor haze-drenched room. "Oscar-Mike—it's about time. This is Kilo-Bravo-Foxtrot-two-one-three."

Intense relief knocked the pent-up breath from Olin's chest. A half groan, half laugh escaped with it. "Praise God!"

Shouts erupted as the agent nodded. "Kilo-Bravo-Foxtrot, what is your status?"

"Good. . .good. We had a couple of wingmen. They flashed us then left. I take it we have you to thank for their sudden departure."

"Roger that," the agent said with a smile that lit his face. "What is your fuel status?"

Seconds lingered between the question and answer, making Olin worry. Didn't the Kid know he had enough gray hair from this mess? "Enough to get us where we were going—the Caribbean."

The agent frowned. "Who is your pilot?"

"Uh, some dude Mario knows. Hang on." Muttering overtook the connection before he returned with a name.

Several hands went to work accessing the man's name under Olin's watchful eye. Within seconds, two other agents shook their heads. Attention fastened on the monitor in front of him, which tracked the movement of the aircraft, the first agent resumed his dialogue with the Kid. "How many are in your party?"

"Elev—twelve, I think. A lot of kids."

Olin hesitated. "He must have the wives and children with him as well." Acute and warming, the relief was unlike anything he'd experienced. Putting a team of experienced men in danger was one thing—they were trained for it—but when the women and children were indirectly involved, a new depth and wave of grief transferred to his shoulders. Olin glanced to Golding. "You are about to have a very full home."

Though Golding offered a smile to Olin, it did not reach his eyes. He bent forward, his gaze locked on some data. He spoke in a hushed, foreign tongue to the agent handling the air chatter. In seconds, a flurry of action erupted around the room.

Olin inched closer. "What's wrong?"

Aboard Santana Airline Flight KBF213
On Approach to Caribbean Airstrip

Sydney Jacobs held a sleeping Dakota in her arms. Dillon stretched out on the laid-back seat beside her. Thoughts of Bryce threatened her conviction that escaping like this was the right thing. Had her brother just sacrificed his life for hers? She just could not accept that. She would believe the best. Believe *God* for the best.

She brushed the silky black strands from Dillon's face, eliciting a small shudder. It'd been a nightmare of a day, and yet he'd borne up like a trooper. Peace hovered over the flutter of his dark eyelashes against his olive complexion. So like Max—peaceful when asleep, a veritable storm awake.

Like a Navy SEAL.

Yeah, he had as much fire in his belly as his father.

Marshall stood as the tires squawked on the runway. He turned and locked gazes with her. Something alarming whittled away what little courage she'd regained since the Air Force jets banked off. She drew straight, internal alarms blazing.

Subtly, he motioned with his hand, then moved to the door. Once they'd taxied to a hangar, he opened the door.

As he stepped back, she saw glints off cars outside. Four sedans screeched to a stop around the plane, and a sea of men disembarked. Dressed in suits and expressions grim with business, they strode toward the craft.

Sydney looked at Marshall, who was locked in a confrontation with his friend. Rel stood beside them, her pale-brown eyes wide with concern.

Marshall seemed to grow a few inches. "Mario—relax."

"Who is that?" The Latino raced up and down the plane, staring out the windows. "This is bad. Real bad. Who are they?" He threw his hands up. "We can't just let them come up in here."

Marshall strode toward him. "I don't know who they are. Just relax. Don't do anything stupid."

"Stupid?" The man stabbed a finger at him. "That's exactly what I did when your dad said to take you—"

"My dad?" Marshall's voice pitched.

His friend hedged.

Eyes ablaze, Marshall threw a hard right. It nailed the man square in the jaw. The door opened, and men—all Middle Eastern—glided into the plane as if they owned the jet. A man dragged Mario off and stuffed him in one of the cars. Another pounced on Marshall, pinning him against the hull.

Sydney rose, ready to object, demand to know what was going on.

Marshall jerked toward her. "No." He sliced a hand through the air. "Don't."

Bitter acid coated her tongue as she returned to her seat, holding her infant son tighter, checking on Dillon. . .on the others.

"Sydney."

A whispered call from across the aisle drew her attention to Danielle, who cuddled a sniffling, red-eyed Tala. "Outside," she mouthed.

Sydney craned her neck to look through the window. Her breath caught in her throat as men crawled into the belly of the plane. A giant tanker pulled alongside and began dumping fuel into the jet.

The sound of sure, confident steps down the aisle snagged her attention. Three men stalked past her. She half expected them to wear hoods or masks, but they clearly had no fear of being recognized— or worry that Sydney could identify them later. Maybe because they intended to kill everyone.

Thwat! Thwat!

A strangled cry came from the cockpit. There, a man hauled the body of the pilot out of the cockpit and, with the help of a second, ferried him off the plane and into one of the waiting vehicles, which pulled away as quick as it had arrived.

She eased back into the seat, the leather hissing beneath her. Dakota lifted his head for a brief, bleary-eyed moment of confusion, then snuggled back into her neck. She savored the sweet innocence that stood in stark contrast to the skilled, lethal men who'd taken over their plane.

The man holding Marshall glanced at her, stepped back, slid his weapon into his jacket, then climbed into the pilot's seat. Sagged against the curved wall of the interior, Marshall drew in a ragged breath, touched his ribs gingerly, then straightened.

"What's going on?" Sydney hissed to him.

"Just. . .wait." With a look of regret—or was that relief?—Marshall slipped into a chair beside Rel and took her hand. "I think it's going to be okay."

Think? He *thought* it was going to be okay? But then. . .even if he had concerns that they weren't, what could one man do against eleven? Gravity pressed her back in the seat, and only then did Sydney realize they were on the runway. "We're taking off." This time, her own voice pitched.

"It's okay," Marshall said.

"Okay? How do you know?"

"Who are they?" Rel asked the question hanging on everyone's lips and in the cries of Tala and McKenna.

Marshall swiveled toward Sydney, Dani, and Piper. "I. . .I think the Old Man sent them," Marshall said, adrenaline cracking his voice.

"Why didn't you tell us?"

"I couldn't—the message was vague. I knew something was up but didn't know what. I thought it was the pilot, but—if it wasn't, I couldn't risk speaking out." He ran a hand through his hair.

Piper scooted to the edge of her seat. "They are Mossad."

"How do you know?" Rel asked.

"The way they move, the way they. . .*are*—it's very much like my cousin Azzan." Despite the words she offered, there was no peace about her. "If they are helping, we will be okay. But make no mistake—do not get in their way. Do not argue."

"Are we safe?" Sydney asked.

Piper hesitated, her gaze tracking over the half dozen suits now poised around the aircraft. The plane began moving before she offered a soft, "Yes. More than you would be anywhere else. As long as we do not interfere. They have a mission. They *will* complete it."

The takeoff was seamless and quiet, clearly executed under experienced hands and operatives. As the plane rocketed across the world, Sydney allowed herself to relax, her mind speeding through scenarios and questions—mostly, why hadn't she heard from Max? And Bryce—

A sob leapt through her throat. She covered her mouth, the image of his SUV twisted and gnarled in a heap of flames squeezing the last vestige of strength from her. *Please, God. . .don't let him be dead. Or Max. . .*

Was it too much to hope for? Too big a miracle? Quietly, she prayed as the hours slipped by with meals, naps, and very little discussion. The children played and talked, hardly noticing their thirty-two-thousand feet in the air adventure. It was good for them, but Sydney could not tear her mind from Max or Bryce.

As the cabin lights dimmed and children slept, Dakota and Owen went full wail. "I'll get the bottles ready this time." Sydney pushed out of the seat.

In the galley, she ignored the man whose sidearm bulged through his suit as she prepared the bottles. Capping the bottles, she turned to leave. Two steps later, she heard voices and turned. The guard slipped through the curtain to a small room that boasted a table, six chairs—all occupied—and a bank of computers.

Heart in her throat, she moved forward.

"Mrs. Jacobs," the man at the head spoke. "How may we help you?"

Startled by his clear, unaffected English and impeccable manners, Sydney hung between the curtains, bottles in hands. "How do you know who I am?"

With a breathy laugh, he held her gaze but did not answer.

Right. *Okay, get on with it before you lose your nerve.* "Are those"—she motioned toward the computers—"secure?"

"Of course."

She set the bottles aside and tucked a strand of hair behind her ear. "Could I. . .could I try to send a message to my husband? It was too dangerous at my brother's home." She shoved the mental image of that SUV out of her mind again. "I think I know how to get hold of Max."

The man stepped aside and placed a dark hand on the black seat. "Please."

She hurried around the table, her mind reeling.

He leaned across in front of her and closed the laptop then pointed to the man beside her. "Tell Yusuf where and what you want to type. He'll do it for you."

Of course. They wouldn't let her have unfettered access to all this equipment and technology.

"It's an old forum," she explained. "When we were dating, he used to leave me messages when he couldn't tell me where he was." Was she exposing Max—would telling these Mossad agents about this put her husband in more danger? Desperation clung to her, forcing her forward. She had to know if he was alive.

With a few deft keystrokes, the man accessed the forum. They scanned the messages, her heart dipping with each click and scroll. Thirty minutes netted them nothing. Hopelessness coated her defenses, weakened her, and left her feeling drained.

New tears sprung to her eyes.

"Do not fear," Yusuf said. "We will keep trolling and dissecting the data. We will also plant a message, one that will flag your husband's attention should he revisit the site. Is there anywhere else he might check?"

She shook her head, dislodging the gloom, which she attributed to hormones and stress. "Knowing him, he wouldn't send regular e-mail because it'd be monitored or interfered with."

"We've already planted messages there."

Sydney widened her eyes. "Why? He wouldn't use that. It's too exposed."

The man offered her only another plaintive smile. "Which makes it the perfect place. They won't suspect it. We have added others as well."

She turned back to the monitor as Yusuf brought up four or five sites with what seemed a single keystroke.

"Your Flickr account, yes?"

Mutely, Sydney stared at the images. But one snagged her attention. "Wait—that's not. . .where is that?" An image of her, Dillon, and Dakota on the beach stared back at her. "I—that's not. . .I've never been there."

The man closed the browser and another sprang up. Twitter. A string of messages showed up, but she looked for something different, unusual. "I don't. . . ?" But then she noticed words wrongly placed or misspelled. She darted a gaze to the man and found a smirk on his lips as he X-ed out.

Behind her, the leader spoke, "As you can see, there are myriad ways to plant messages. Your husband is skilled, trained to use his mind as well as his body, yes? If he is out there, we have left a trail he can find."

If. . .if he is out there. "What if he can't access a computer?"

For the first time, the man's arrogance slipped.

A shout from the far end severed the conversation.

"Shut it down! Hacking!"

Computers thrummed on the electric current as monitors blurred and fizzled to death. Silence hung like an anchor.

"What was the source?" the leader asked.

"Not sure," a smaller man at the far end said. "But. . .I think. . ."

"Where?" the leader shouted.

Wide, unfocused eyes came to his. "Texas."

Sydney frowned. "Texas?"

"You perhaps heard of the virus planted in Iranian computers that disabled them?" The man raised bushy eyebrows. "It is rumored they were started in Texas."

"What does that mean?"

"We are not the only ones looking for your husband or trying to stop the others who are."

Green World Health Compound, Uganda

In a surreal nightmare that felt drug induced, Scott lay on his back, staring up at what should've been a beautiful afternoon. Hearing hollowed, vision blurred, he saw something streak through the sky.

Fire and smoke engulfed the chopper lazing overhead.

A wall of pressure slammed into his chest. The world went dark.

Rain pelted his face. *Drip. Drop. Drip. Drop.*

Scott turned his face away. Wait. Not rain. He pried himself off the ground, the thunk of rock and debris prickling his skin. Rolling over, he searched for Marie. His mind warped into action, remembering the explosion that threw him into the side of the main building. Like being sucker punched by a blast of wind with a serious attitude.

Groaning, he pulled himself onto all fours. Cradling his side did little to help the agony twisting through his gut. Like a ghost, a vision of men rappelling from another chopper drifted into his awareness. That meant they'd been overtaken.

"Marie," he said, ash and smoke filling his lungs. He coughed. Choked. Panic grabbed him by the throat. "Marie!" Gravelly and strained, his words sounded foreign even to him.

Crunch-crunch.

A combat boot stepped into view.

Adrenaline spiking, Scott lunged. Wrapped his arms around the rebel's waist. Took him down. He slammed a hard right—into a helmeted face.

"Augh!" Pain stabbed through his wrist. Up his arm. Right into his shoulder. Even as he growled, he felt the fresh squirt of blood down his arm and chest. But he didn't care; these animals had taken over the compound. Taken Marie.

Scott growled and lifted a weapon.

Something cracked against his skull. He tumbled sideways, head and mind reeling.

"Scott, no! Stop."

The soldier he'd straddled flipped onto his feet and shouted, "Stand down!"

Confusion shuddered through him. He squinted up, the glare of the sun bright and silhouetting the man hovering over him. Dressed in combat fatigues, the man wasn't here for coffee. Scott snatched the handgun from his belt. Amid Marie's scream, he whipped it at the soldier.

A booted foot flew into his face.

CHAPTER 27

Eurostar Bound for Paris

One hundred eighty-nine miles an hour. Two hours, thirty-five minutes. Phenomenal speed and distance covered, and yet Griffin felt a gaping hole in his chest, burned into him when Kacie buried her face there and cried.

Cried.

He'd let her shed those tears, silently willing her to shed a few for him. He'd lost enough in this nightmare that had accosted his life. But now, as he sat in the last seat of the train rocketing away from the snake-of-a-Carrick, he wondered. Did Kacie get on the train? Or had she sent them off on their own?

He shifted in the seat. Maybe she was just trying to put time between them. Not make it look so obvious that they were traveling together. He bent forward, forearms resting on his knees. Glanced over the seat, back down the narrow aisle toward the front of the Eurostar.

"She'll be here," Colton said, eyes closed, head back.

Sloughing his hands together, Griffin peered down the cabin. They'd been in motion for forty minutes. More than enough time for her to find her way to him. He pushed to his feet.

Colton's chuckle and the pressure of the high-speed travel pulled at him as he stalked through the train to the next cabin. Through the other car, he entered the café-style cabin. Decked out in highly polished stainless steel and checkers, the place seemed like a sixties throwback. His gaze skipped over the seven passengers to the body angling out of view on the other side. Kacie. He stormed after her, weaving around the pole-style bars that littered the cabin. As he stepped through the door, he saw a door closing. Bathroom.

He lunged and sliced his hand in between the door and jamb.

A woman gasped.

Using all his upper body strength, he pushed open the door.

Red-rimmed eyes stared at him—*fumed* at him. Kacie batted her white-blond hair from her face. Her mouth formed a perfect O as he pushed into the ultracompact bathroom closet.

His shoulders rubbed the wall. He angled left. Banged a light fixture.

"You big oaf! There's not enough room for two."

Stuffed in the corner, he gripped her waist, lifted her, and set her on the counter that was barely as wide as her small hips. He dropped back against the wall that made him feel like a cement block wedged into a round hole.

Arms folded, he nodded. "Talk."

As if someone had pressed a knob and ignited a gas grill, fire erupted in her green eyes. "Talk?" Her lips tightened. "What do you think I am? A vending machine?"

Something had wounded her—deep. That's part of what he'd noticed earlier. Just didn't expect it to come with tears. "I'll wait." She needed to get this out, deal with it.

Kacie reached for the door.

He shifted and plopped against it, planting a booted foot on the commode, and peered at her out of the corner of his eye. "Cozy, huh?"

"Griff—" She bit her lips and tossed her head back, smacking it against the mirror that lined the bathroom wall. *Thud. Thud-thud.*

Quiet held them captive.

"What changed, Baby Girl?"

Rolling her head to the side, she looked at him with red, puffy eyes. Something strong and powerful snaked through his mind, through his muscles, through everything in him—He'd do anything to make whatever it was that tore her up so bad go away.

"I'm missing something," he said. "We escaped the club, you made it out alive, but something. . .changed. I want to know what."

She gazed at the opaque square window as if she could see anything through it. "What does it matter to you as long as you get your boys back?"

That was reaching a ways back, even for her.

But then, as if someone had pushed a button, the fight leeched out of her. She slumped and let out a long, stuttering sigh. "He killed my family—everyone except Roman. The one person I wish he *had* killed.

But the ones that matter. . .they're all dead now."

Griffin came up off the wall, arms spread.

Kacie met his gaze. "Burned down our home." A lonely tear streaked down her face. "I gave up *everything*"—her thin pink lips trembled—"so Mamo and the others could go on."

"How do you know? Carrick seems like the type to like mind games."

She shook her head, wiping away the tear. "Pictures. And Roman. He was there. Didn't even act like he was sad about their deaths." She pursed her lips and straightened. "Carrick actually took pictures of the house. Showed them to me."

"Doesn't make sense."

Kacie laughed, a hollow, empty laugh. "Nothing he does makes sense."

"No." Griffin leaned closer. "If he killed your family—what can he hold over you now?"

"Everything." She furrowed her brow. "Don't you get it? He's cutting anything and everything that's important to me. At the club, he made that very clear. It's why I escaped." Watery eyes met his. "I have to bury myself. Every job I did was connected to him—so he'll have eyes around the globe searching for me. I am not safe anywhere. My career is over. If he's angry enough, I'll be dead soon." She slumped again. "Just as well. I have nothing left and nothing to go home to. They're all gone. I have no one."

"You got me, Baby Girl."

Her eyes flicked to his.

"Hold up," he said. "I didn't mean it like that." He most certainly did mean it like that. But he was a fool to think anything could work between them. She was a spy—she'd go her way when things were over. "Don't jump ship on me just because one slick Willy tries to play his cards. Just stick with me, see this through, okay?"

Confusion tightened her smile lines. "Don't you get it—?"

"Yes. But do you?"

Kacie drew back. "Do you have family, Griffin? People who matter to you, outside of this team you're trying to salvage?"

Dante rushed to the front of his mind. Then his mom. . .Venus. . . Like a mighty, angry river, the images tumbled over him. No, no, he couldn't go there. He had to realign her with the mission. "All I'm saying," he said, trying to navigate around the intrusion of memories, "is what we've got here is your freedom. You're not—"

"My *freedom*?" Her intensity caught him off guard. "Griffin, he killed my family, and you're going to talk about freedom?"

"But you're free now; it's not holding you back—"

"How dare you! That's my brother, sisters, mother you're talking about. Gone!"

Griffin settled back. Let her talk.

"Up in smoke because that man decided I had outlived my usefulness, after all I'd done for him, all those years sacrificed. Doing things I abhor and things that could get me killed. Burning one person to save another. . .all because he had a noose around their necks. He bought my soul through them."

But as if they had been dammed up, the waters of the past stopped.

Indignation colored her flushed cheeks. "I don't know how you just did that." She looked down, toying with a thread on her jeans. "What do you know about losing family, loved ones?"

"Family is our core," Griffin said, his thoughts jumbled by her vulnerability and the thinly veiled accusation. "People we love, people we're willing to put things on the line for—they keep our honor intact because we know how we behave affects them. Every now and then we have to stop and take record of what they mean to us or they lose their value. We lose the will to fight for them."

"But they're dead."

"Maybe."

She frowned.

"He showed you pictures—of bodies?"

Kacie's face slowly shifted from distraught to disbelief.

"Okay"—he held up a finger, not wanting her to get her hopes dashed again—"just hold that thought. And think. What if he just wanted you to think they were dead?"

She shook her head. "Why?"

"God knows, but. . ." In the dark, cluttered recesses of his past, a connection formed with Kacie Whitcomb that suddenly felt irrevocable. But she didn't know about his past. Didn't know about. . .so much. 'Sides, this was about her and her family, her fight. "What would you do differently if they were still alive?"

"I. . .I don't know. Eventually, I planned to go back there, live out the rest of my life in peace." She wrinkled her nose. "But that's not realistic."

"Maybe, maybe not. What would you do then?"

She shrugged. "Keep working."

Griffin grinned. "That's it—he wants you to quit." He wagged a finger at her. "There's something he doesn't want you to figure out."

Kacie dropped her chin.

"What?"

"Or maybe he knows I have enough data to put him away for the rest of his life." She smiled weakly. "I took this job with your team so I could fund myself into retirement. I have plenty to incriminate Carrick. I just had to find a way out of his hold."

Dread drizzled through his brain. "Kacie. . .whatever it is you think you have, don't do anything with it."

Again, she frowned.

"He knows." A bad taste rolled across his tongue. "That's what he wants—for you to go public with it. To think you have nothing to lose, so you risk it." He placed his hands on either side of her and pressed into her personal space. "He's not through with you."

If she knew Carrick Burgess, he'd never be through with her. Not till she was a rotting, bug-infested corpse. Even then, he'd probably find a way to draw out the last drop of blood from her body.

But Griffin. . .his intensity, his strength, his adamancy drew her like an arrow to the heart. Tripping and falling into the man's gaze was stupid. Sitting here, in a high-speed train's bathroom, practically nose to nose with the man and trying to form a coherent thought that was clever enough to buy her time and space, was impossible.

Those brown eyes. . .rich, deep mahogany with flecks of caramel. . .

"Stick with me, Kacie."

Fire had nothing on the heat that flashed through her knee when he set his hand on it.

"Help me get my boys back and bury whoever did this." He ducked, trying to capture her eyes again, but she avoided him. "I meant what I said. You got me. I'm not leaving you out in the dark. We finish this mission, and I'll do whatever it takes to help you get this ape off your back."

She braved those eyes once more. He believed the words he spoke, which meant he was sincere. But deep down, she knew he was sincerely wrong. Nobody could get Carrick off her back in a permanent way. Yet. . .mentally, she traced the strong angles of Griffin's cheekbone and wanted with everything in her to believe that someone really had that kind of power. That ability to sever the talons of Carrick's hold on her life. If anyone did have that, it'd be the man standing before her.

"What do you say, Baby Girl?"

"Kazimiera."

His face softened.

"My name is Kazimiera Faronski."

He smiled. "Nice to meet you." His gaze dropped to her mouth, and though she felt the tidal pull of attraction, all she could remember was the moment when she'd tried to work him to get her way. He'd been repulsed. Was it because he wasn't interested in her that way? Would he think that's what she was doing this time? It felt like someone had a bungee attached to her chest, drawing her to him.

His smile slipped as his head tilted to the right, his eyes tracing her lips. Was he seriously looking at her lips? His breath dashed against her cheek.

A knock on the door severed the electrical current between them.

Griffin hung his head, then pressed himself to the wall, misery contorting his face as he pried open the door. Taking the cue, Kazi slipped out—and sucked in a breath as Neeley stood there, glowering. She ducked her head and headed toward their seats.

Despite having four hours in virtual silence sitting across from the matched set of musclemen as they made their way back to Greece, Kazi felt neither composed nor collected by the time they reached the safe house. Though Neeley hadn't spoken or asked why they'd been in that loo together, she'd be a fool to think he didn't know something happened between her and Griffin. In fact, she felt as if she were wearing a neon sign declaring their guilt.

What guilt? You didn't do anything.

But she wanted to, and that thought alone made her cheeks flame.

At the same time, Griffin seemed unaffected, talking to Neeley calmly. Even as they had grabbed a cab and headed to the airstrip, the men chatted as if nothing had happened. Griffin neither seemed inclined to touch her nor avoid her. Griffin remained stoic as always, as if they hadn't almost kissed. As if she hadn't given him the most intimate thing she owned—her identity.

Was it just me?

Had she been so worn down and emotional that it'd been her imagination, that she'd naively believed he had an interest in her beyond this mission? Yes, she had been emotional. No, she didn't believe she imagined it. Physical attraction to a man wasn't something she battled, because snakes came in every size and package and she no longer weighed appeal with interest.

True, Griffin Riddell had a lot going for him—handsome, big, muscular—but. . .it didn't matter.

Okay, perhaps not the complete truth. External appearances did matter, but not—

"Kazi?"

As if she'd been zapped into the middle of a conversation and location without warning, Kazi looked up. Griffin stood with Neeley and the general, waiting. "Excuse me?"

The general placed a hand on her shoulder. "I will work to find the truth about your family."

She snapped straight. Her family? How did he know about them?

"The others should be here any moment. We're going to have a full house." He pointed toward his wife, who was bustling about the kitchen. "She's been baking since word came."

Behind them, a door opened. A sea of bodies pressed into the home. Involuntarily, Kazi moved up onto the first step leading upstairs. Then another as more people streamed into the home. How could so many people fit? Griffin rushed forward, pulled a young man into a strong-armed greeting. A woman's yelp dragged her attention to where Neeley clutched a tall, beautiful woman to his chest, muscles straining as he held her tight. Her arms wrapped around him tightly as a small girl hugged his legs.

"Daddy, we missed you!" the girl said in a squeaky high voice.

"I missed you too, darlin'." Neeley lifted the girl, then kissed her and the bald baby the woman held. Then he angled in and pulled the woman tight, buried his face in her neck. An intimate exchange that pushed Kazi's gaze away.

Suddenly, Kazi felt pushed to the edge of reason, of belonging. When was the last time she'd hugged someone like that? When was the last time someone *wanted* her, loved her so wholly?

A woman with brown hair and matching eyes locked on to Kazi as she bounced a baby with a mop of black hair in her arms. Another woman with near-black hair and a newborn swaddled to her eased toward Lambert and hugged him. An awkward tension sifted between them along with quiet words. Neeley and his wife moved to Golding, then to the assassin Kazi had rescued. Tears spilled down the woman's face as she hugged the man.

"I am well, Lil—Piper." Aladdin tucked his head in a quiet nod. "As is your husband, cousin. Be at peace."

She nodded, smearing her tears aside as the baby gawked at his mom, then reached for Neeley, who lifted the boy. Family. Love. Thick and deep. She'd know what that felt like if things in her life hadn't been turned upside, ripped out, and churned.

Something tugged at Kazi's pant leg. She looked down.

A little boy with black eyes and hair climbed up onto the step next to her. "Who are you?"

Nobody.

The woman with the black-haired baby caught his hand and drew him away. "I'm sorry. He's not afraid of anything." She smiled. "I'm

Sydney, by the way."

"Kazi," she said, realizing her mistake too late.

In the twenty minutes of chaos as greetings were exchanged, visits to the bathroom were made, and beds claimed, Kazi wished harder than ever that she could vanish.

The young man Griffin had first greeted came toward her with an extended hand. "Marshall Vaughn."

She shook his hand but said nothing.

"And you are?" he asked, smiling.

"Nobody."

Griffin loomed over her. "This is my angel."

Taken aback, Kazi looked at him.

"She pulled me from prison, saved Aladdin, and extricated Neeley."

Vaughn grinned, a boyish charm that no doubt had the girl behind him clinging worse than plastic wrap. "Then that makes her Nightshade's angel, not yours, right?"

Griffin smacked the boy's gut. "Ignore the Kid. He's got a mouth but no brain."

Nerves pushed the words from her mouth. "Then he fits in, doesn't he?" Kazi wanted to bite her tongue for teasing Griffin in front of the others.

The Kid slapped Griffin back. "Legend, you caught a live one! I vote she stays."

Amid the laughter and banter that ensued, Kazi locked on to the woman with brown hair and two sons, who had sidled over to the general. "Have you heard from him?"

"What about my brother?" a young woman with Vaughn asked.

"I'm sorry, Sydney and Rel." The general nodded to the two long tables littered with computers and Mossad agents. "They've been working nonstop to locate Max, Midas, and Dighton—that's our priority, of course. But we're also working to figure out who did this and how to stop them from doing more or permanent damage."

Marshall said, "I can answer that."

CHAPTER 28

Golding Residence, Cyprus

Hands on his belt, Griffin stole a look at Kazi while they waited for the Kid to rifle through his rucksack. Still the smell of her—not fancy perfume but something light and clean—wormed through his brain, infected since he'd lost his fool mind in the train and nearly made good on that kiss last week.

Week. Got it? You don't know this girl. You can't feel this way. Get stupid equals get killed.

Marshall cut off his line of sight as he stood and returned to the table. He tossed a handful of pictures on the table. "Found those in my father's safe at home."

"Your father?" Griffin growled, lifting the pictures. His gut writhed as he took in the images. "It's. . .us."

"Sydney," the Kid called across the din of activity. He waved her over. "These the pictures you told us about outside Mindanao?"

With Dillon propped on her hip, she looked over the images. Her face went pale. "Yes." She looked at Cowboy. "That's them. Where did they come from?"

"My dad, I guess." Marshall scratched his head. "But something bugged me about them."

Griffin thumbed through them. "A lot bugs me about them."

"Nah, I mean. . ." With a finger, the Kid spread them over the grainy white surface. "Look at them. Notice anything?"

Cowboy's shoulder pressed against Griffin's as he leaned in. "What's your point?" He handed his baby boy back to Piper.

The Kid bent over the table, palms spread wide as he peered up at them through a knotted brow. "Who's not in the pictures?"

Flashes of memory, heat, humidity, and smells vaulted out of the images. Things he knew. But nothing unusual. Griffin reached through the tangle of bodies and lifted one. Then another. "You." He snatched up another. Sorted through the others quickly. "You're not in them."

"Bingo! Give the man a sucker." Torment darkened the Kid's face. "I remember this village—I would've been standing right here"—he motioned holding the picture out and placed a hand in front of it— "which means somehow. . .the images came from me. I don't know how, but my dad must've planted a camera on me."

The assassin braced himself against the table, his skin clammy and bruised, but his eyes alert, intelligent. "All images are taken from about chest high."

"Button camera," a soft voice said.

Griffin looked over his shoulder, surprised to find Kazi there.

"I've had diamond stud earrings that were cameras," she said. "You'd never notice it."

"Cameras can be the size of lint," Aladdin said. "This has been going on for a while." He held up two pictures. "Before I joined the team." He tossed them down. "I can't believe we didn't catch on sooner."

"I'm the reason the team's been disassembled," the Kid said. "It's my fault."

"Bull." Cowboy shook a finger at the Kid. "Don't go there. None of us are to blame for this. Somehow, Nightshade stepped into your dad's line of fire."

Griffin shifted his attention back to the team. "We just have to figure when and where."

"And why he's trying to kill us," the Kid said.

"He tried to kill you?" Griffin scowled.

"I think he was behind the attack at the Shack, and then he kept me drugged at my own house, lying and saying it was a hospital."

"Sick." Griffin patted his shoulder. "As much as we'd all love to blame you"—laughter trickled through the room—"what we need to figure out is why." Griffin shook his head. "Okay, folks, let's put our heads together and figure out this nightmare."

They went to work plotting the pictures around the missions, talking through possible connections and implications. But the more they searched, the more confusion leaked into the data. Griffin slumped back in the chair he'd taken earlier and ran a hand over his face and mouth. "There's no connection, know what I'm saying?"

The Kid agreed. "It's so. . .random."

"But it's not," the general said. "There's something here, something we're missing." A tweetle jerked him to his phone. He answered it and visibly swayed, then swung around and looked toward the women— no, at one woman.

In the kitchen, Sydney's face went chalky. Then she looked over her shoulder to Danielle, who slowly came to her feet.

"Thank You, God!" The general bobbed his head. "Yes. . .good. . ." He placed a hand on the shoulder of a Mossad agent. "I'll give you to someone who can do that." As he handed off the phone, he let out a long, hard breath. "Midas is alive and safe."

Danielle collapsed into the chair, holding her baby tightly. The women embraced her, crying and laughing. And on the fringe, Griffin saw Kazi watching it all. She seemed disconnected. Or overwhelmed. What was going on in that head of hers? It was like, put her in a room with vipers and murderers, and she came out kicking and screaming. Put her into a domestic situation, and she fell apart.

"He killed my family."

The general looked at the rest of the team of Mossad agents. "We've got two men still missing. I'd like them found—now."

Pulled back into action by the Old Man's words, Griffin straightened. "What's the last known on Frogman?"

"Phone call to Sydney, then he went dark." Lambert eased into a chair beside him. "Same with Dighton. I had sat imaging from the area, and they were both on a motorcycle. Next sweep, they're gone. No communication since."

"We'll assume they're hiding," Griffin said, his homing beacon squarely focused on Kazi, who was drifting closer to the intelligence meeting.

"Leads planted everywhere imaginable. If either of them can get on a connection, secure or not, they'll have bread crumbs to lead them home." It'd been weeks, and the team was still fractured.

"Oorah," Griffin muttered, trying to show his support for their benefactor. "Okay, so what's happening around the globe?"

The Kid hesitated. "Say what?"

"Well, to my way of thinking," Griffin eased forward in the chair, "your old man goes after us—why now?"

"Maybe he just pegged our identities."

Griffin shook his head. "I was put away six months ago for a crime

I didn't commit. This has been a long time coming."

Cowboy came up off the wall he supported. "Reckon he's right. Something triggered this."

"What's he trying to protect?" Griffin asked. "What's he afraid we'll find or interrupt? That is what we want to find."

The Kid turned to an agent beside him. "We need every organization, every benefit, every—"

"We have already winnowed the field." Aladdin pointed to a large-screen TV where a dozen or so names were listed. "These are the most consistent with data and activity—both domestic and global enough to cross paths with Nightshade."

"Have any of those organizations had an imprint on a site where we've interdicted?" Griffin asked.

"Yes, several," Aladdin said. "I've been working on this night and day."

Griffin nodded, his attention snagged for a moment by two men at the far end whose dialogue became animated. They both leaned closer to a screen, then the excitement died down.

"Would you like to join us?"

To the right of the men stood Kazi—now joined by Sydney Jacobs, inviting Kazi into the maelstrom of domestic fellowship.

This won't go well.

Kazi hesitated, then gave a slow, curt nod before she allowed Sydney to lead her to the breakfast area where Cowboy's little girl and Max's boy drew on paper. Sydney laughed and said something to Kazi, but for the noise of the computers, clicking, and constant conversation, he couldn't hear what. Kazi seemed to be holding her own. What a fool thing to say. The woman could bring down entire dynasties.

"I think we got something."

Drawn back to the data, Griffin tried to realign his thinking on the mission. Max. Dighton. Getting them back. Figuring out who did this.

Laughter spiraled out and noosed his mind. Kazi squatted next to Max's Mini-Me, who was chatting a mile a minute. Light flickered through Kazi's soft, pale features as she listened. Piper said something. And as Danielle nodded in apparent agreement, Kazi's light flickered out. She pushed to her feet. The pallor that overtook her pulled Griffin upright.

Sydney moved in, touched her shoulder, and said something— *Argh! Why could he not hear them?*—and Kazi smiled. A fake smile. He could tell by the way it didn't pinch the dimple in her right cheek. Or crease her eyes. But as expected, she held her own.

Relax, G. She's got it.

"Okay, and this." Aladdin slid another data image print toward him.

Griffin looked at it, but his mind ricocheted back to the pallor—pain—in Kazi's expression. Pain. There was pain? Why? What—? He looked back to her to regauge the expression and stilled.

She was gone.

The stampede in her chest seemed to reverberate through the narrow hall. Kazi took the stairs two at a time. Panic pushed her harder. She'd never belong anywhere. She tried. To mingle. To laugh. To act like she could fit in. But those women were—

"Kaz."

A featherlight touch of air scalded her conscience. She hesitated. Then leapt forward.

"Hold up."

On the last step before the landing, she spun toward the gentle giant who'd riveted her heart to a bucket of emotional upheaval.

"What's wrong? What happened?" His voice was thick with emotion. Care. Did he really care? Was Sydney right? She shook her head, aches weaving through her breast as she looked down into the brown eyes that had registered as her center. Breathing hurt. Thinking hurt. Remembering hurt.

"I can't—" She sucked in a hard breath, surprised at the torrent of emotion roiling through her. It was one thing to run. It was another to tell him *why.* Her vision blurred. "It won't work." She gulped. Her eyes stung. Frantic, she shook her head. "I just can't."

In the space of two heartbeats, he scaled the steps and pulled her into his arms.

The firm impact knocked her tenuous hold on her pain from her grasp. A half sob popped from her throat. Kazi hooked an arm around his broad shoulders, and another cupped his head as she buried her face in his neck, holding on tightly as he lifted her from her feet. "Don't—"

"Shh." He swung right, up three steps, then two paces. The glass door to the rooftop patio clicked open. Cool, salty sea air swirled her hair around her face as he carried her into the night, his hold never wavering or crushing. "It's okay, Baby Girl."

She should explain why she was a neurotic mess. "I'm not. . .I can't. . .I just can't. . ."

His biceps and pecs squeezed her into a firmer hold. "It's okay. It's okay."

Her toes caught purchase, and she supported herself, still locked around Griffin's torso. She should let go. Push back. Get a grip. But his arms were strong around her, his breath trickling down the back of her neck.

"I wanted to, Griffin. I wanted to do it."

"Do what, Baby Girl?"

Be your Baby Girl. She squeezed a tear back. Cheek pressed to his, she smoothed a hand down the back of his neck. "I'm not. . .I'm not who you think I am."

"You're not Kazi-smeera Fronky?"

She laughed, knowing his mispronunciation was intentional. "Those women down there, they're strong. They know how to be a wife. How to be a mother. They balance life, they love their husbands, they have children, raise families, and still laugh and play and—"

"Kaz, quiet." He set her on the ledge, which gave her a three-inch advantage to look down into his eyes. See the moon reflected in the pure chocolate irises. She wanted to be what those women were for their men. She wanted to be a beacon of hope, strength, something good to come home to. To be that for him.

The thought choked her as she looked to their future. He'd never want her. Once he knew what she'd done as Boucher's whore, what she'd done for Carrick. "I can't—"

"K—"

"It's not—"

"Kazi, listen—"

"No!" Anguish carved a lonely trail through her heart. "Don't you get it? I can't—"

"Shut up or I'm going to kiss you."

The air knocked into her throat as his breath and words skated over her mouth. Beyond the wall, she heard the crash of the waves and felt their pounding in her chest. She darted a gaze over Griffin's face, mere millimeters from her own. Over strong, angular lines. Smooth complexion. Intensity unlike anything she'd ever seen. Quiet strength that rivaled the moon's pull on the tide. Unwavering. Beautiful. Gentle.

"Are you that afraid of me kissing you?" he said with a smirk, his mouth a whisper from her own.

No, not afraid—desperate. She ran her thumb along the nape of his neck, her senses alive. Curled into the solid mass of a man, she savored his touch—the hands that pressed her hard against him. The arms that bound her to his soul. Melded to one another—but not sensual. It was. . .beautiful. Safe. Secure. Like a fortress against a storm.

I want this forever.

Forever doesn't exist. Kazi reined in her rebellious body and tried to shake off the potion of attraction that muddled her and had her clinging to Griffin.

"I can't figure out what you want," he said, miserably.

She pressed her forehead against his, willing the attraction to be tamed, lessened. *Don't move.* She shouldn't be so obvious. *Don't let go.* Shouldn't be entertaining this.

Why am I so conflicted?

His chest pressed hard against her, the breath he drew in labored. Like a cold wind, he severed the connection when he lifted his head and looked skyward. "You don't even know, do you?"

A different kind of panic furled her hand around his neck and drew his face back to hers. "Please. . . ," was all she could whisper, as she relished the comfort, the warmth of having him close. It spun her mind in a million different directions.

Carrick would kill Griffin just for the psychological effect he had over her. Griffin would never want someone as messed up as her, anyway. He thought he was attracted to her—saw good things in her. Most men were attracted to her because of her ability to kick butt and take names. But nobody wanted to waste time getting to know Kazimiera Faronski.

What would he think of that girl? Silly? Naive? That was a girl who had fantasies of Happily Ever After. Caressing the back of his neck, she wondered if he would. Were they not in the middle of this disaster, would Griffin want to get to know the real her? Even now, in his arms, she found herself angling for a kiss—and that was the seasoned operative side of her.

He lowered his mouth toward hers.

Her pulse skipped a beat. Then two as she moved in to receive his kiss.

Griffin pulled off. Looked away.

Why wouldn't he kiss her? Didn't *he* want it?

Head down, mouth teasing the side of her cheek, he huffed. "What's it mean to you, Kaz?" Husky with attraction, Griffin's voice coiled around her mind.

What did *what* mean? A kiss? Is that what he was asking? Who asked something like that? Would he cast her off for a kiss? He was noble, honorable. He lived for honor and respect. What if she gave the wrong response? Was there even a right one?

"I. . .I don't know." Raw and vulnerable, the answer was the only thing that got past her fog-enshrouded mind. She didn't care anymore what people thought of her. What Griffin thought of her. He'd find out soon enough that she wasn't the angel he'd called her downstairs. She wasn't anything close to that.

Warm hands came to rest on her waist as Griffin pushed back. Though it was only a few inches, the distance felt like a frozen mile. "It's a'right." He swallowed hard. Blew out a breath. Then turned and stalked to the wall.

She felt cold now. Alone. Rejected. "You're mad."

"I'm a lot of things, but mad is not one of them." Griffin hung his head, hands planted on the wall, making him appear gargantuan. Why didn't he feel so big and overbearing when she was in his arms? How had the size difference vanished when they were together? The race difference? How did it all wash away till there was nothing but. . .him?

"I don't understand." Kazi swept the bangs from her face.

"I know." He rolled around to face her and dropped against the wall, his hands tucked under his arms. "When you do—?"

Crack!

"Hey!" The side door flung open, and Marshall skidded to a stop, his gaze hopping between her and Griffin. "Um. . ." He backtracked, as if realizing he'd stepped into the middle of something.

"What's up, Kid?" Griffin asked in a cool, casual tone.

"The Old Man." Again, he checked Kazi before thumbing over his shoulder. "He wants you. Might have a lead on Frogman."

Griffin gave a curt nod.

Which meant he'd rush back to his boys. Leave her jilted. Out in the cold. Kazi turned back to the wall and stared over the Mediterranean blue waters as Griffin and the Kid went back inside. *Just brill, Kaz. Ran off another guy.* How many times would Tina's admonishment rake her soul? But this time, the accusation felt acute. Razor sharp. She closed her eyes and tucked her chin, warding off the tears. *I wanted him. . .*

Like a sun-warmed blanket, something wrapped around her from behind. Realization washed over her—Griffin hadn't left. He stood behind her, his torso melded to her spine and shoulders. A hand around her waist. Another on her hand. He bent close, his scent masculine and taunting.

Heat crept into her cheeks as his face broke into her line of sight. She didn't trust herself to speak, hating the way she responded to him, yet acutely aware of how she found his touch exhilarating.

His soul-rich eyes bored through her last defense. "When you're ready, Baby Girl. . . ." Warm lips pressed against the sensitive spot along her jaw, just below her ear, and lingered for three fabulous seconds. She hauled in a breath as heat blossomed from the epicenter of his kiss.

Then as swift as the mythical creature he'd been named after, Griffin was gone. The embers of his touch lingered on her waist and belly. She placed her hand over the spot where his hand had rested and willed for a happy ending.

But with all the baggage from the past she'd had to pack, one thought plastered itself to her conscience: *I'll never be ready.*

Green World Health Clinic Compound, Uganda

Staring up through a half-missing roof, Scott groaned. Coughed. Rolled onto his side. Had he been run over by a Mack truck? Or a tank? Only as he tried to take in his surroundings did it register that his left eye was swollen.

Scott cringed at the howling the voice created in his head. He peered up through a throbbing brow. And stilled. Men in camo flanked Marie, their faces painted, their stances screaming their readiness to fight. They weren't American. Or British. Geared up for battle, they looked drenched. Not from rain—sweat. The sixty-pound rucksacks that carried foodstuffs, ammunition, first-aid kits, specialty items. . .

Man, I don't miss that.

He dragged himself off the ground, remembering the insanity that unleashed before he was knocked out—by a boot. Heel of his hand to his face, he propped himself against the wall. Marie passed him a towel with ice.

"Sorry about the eye." The words came from the man with an M16 strapped to his chest and holding a water bottle. "You were quick with the gun."

"Better quick than dead." Scott pressed the makeshift ice pack to his face, hissing as the ice deadened the fire and burn in his face. He assessed the soldiers again. "Who are you?"

"Would you like to sit down, have tea and scones, and discuss our history?"

The shorter of the two men who'd spoken patted the other man's stomach with the back of his hand. "It's good." He turned back to them. "We need to know your vulnerable points. The team can get to work strengthening those while we figure out our best course of action."

"Vulnerable points?" Marie laughed. "Try all the holes in the roofs and walls."

The man's lips pressed into a flat line. "How long has the compound been like this?"

Marie pointed at Scott. "Since he showed up."

The shorter man spoke to the other, then commands were issued, sending three men in each direction to assess and secure. Once the room was clear save himself, Marie, and the two commandos, the shorter one spoke again. "Why don't you debrief us?"

"About ten miles north of this compound there is a mine. Originally said to be harvesting diamonds, it's issuing something far more lucrative—and deadly." Scott wondered where Ojore and the others were at the moment. "One of my guys—"

"Scott lives in the village near the mine, teaching the men how to farm and defend themselves." Marie passed out water bottles, but what surprised Scott was the tone in her words. Pride. Was it really pride? His work had severed their relationship years ago. How could she be proud if she'd given him the short stick?

"What's in the mine?" The guy didn't mince words.

"Yellowcake uranium."

He pivoted to the other man, shared a silent conversation, then turned back to Scott. "Proof?"

Scott shook his head as he took a swig of water. "None."

"That doesn't do any good."

"All we have to do is get the UN back to the mine."

"There's a problem with that though." Marie didn't withhold her glare. "They know who he is and have already tried to kill him once. I expect they've doubled or tripled the security, and you can bet they'll shoot on sight."

"Then we stay out of sight." He looked at Scott. "You'll give us detailed maps so we can get in and out."

Scott pulled straight. "I'm going with you."

"Sorry." The man shook his head. "You asked for my help. You don't get to dictate how to help."

"I know the layout. You don't. It's better to have experience on your side."

"You're his brother!" Marie gasped.

"What?" Scott's mind bungeed over the words. "You're—" The man had said he'd asked for help, and Scott just assumed he meant the details he'd provided here. "But. . .I didn't think you'd come. I only sent one e-mail.

The man shrugged. "I only got one."

CHAPTER 29

Green World Health Clinic Compound,
Uganda

Fifteen years ago, he'd told Scott to forget about a relationship, that they were both better off living separate lives. Seeing his half brother, seeing the man he'd become rankled him. He'd missed out. On a lot. And the raging inferno behind those eyes, so like his own, made him wonder what fueled it.

His brother's face riddled with shock. "I can't believe you came." Scott ran his hands through his hair.

Though he hated re-upping with Scott like this, he needed some answers. And fast, because the clock was ticking. Staying off the grid completely wasn't possible. They had trouble coming. He could smell it. "How'd you get my e-mail address—it's ancient."

"Your mom, before she died—she talked with Dad. They both thought we should get to know each other." Scott shrugged, his attention sliding to the bandage holding his shoulder together. "I called your house once. Your wife didn't know who I was."

"Never mentioned you." Not to anyone. Guilt and a strange sense of obligation harangued him as he studied the man before him. Scott had gotten older, taller. Still a wiry scrap of a guy, but the dark eyes and hair left no doubt who fathered him.

Scott snorted. "Not surprised. After our last encounter. . ."

The bitter pill of truth was hard to swallow. God gave him a second chance, so. . ."I was messed up. Angry."

Dark eyes flashed. "You blamed me."

"I blamed everyone. Hated everyone."

"Definitely a family trait," the pretty nurse said as she straightened a tray.

261

Scott guzzled the water, then tossed the empty bottle in a bin. "So what made you come?"

Heat and tension kneaded the dry air. Boots crunched, shifting on the dirt floor as he held the man's gaze. What made him come? Abandon safeguards? Step into the thick of a deadly situation?

The truth. "You've never asked me for anything." He adjusted the weapon strap, which suddenly felt like a hundred-pound weight around his neck. "Figured things must be bad." He shrugged, then smirked. "Besides, my team is. . .indisposed."

Scott blinked and looked at the group of men crowding the room. "Then, who are they?"

The other guy spoke. "My mates from Oz. Had some time to spare. Thought we'd neutralize a little rebellion before getting back to the real work."

He smirked, hoping the lighthearted gesture by his buddy would ratchet down the friction. "Tell us what needs to be done." Motioning to the men got things moving, the focus off the awkward situation.

"Someone's been sniping us," the petite brunette nurse with clear blue eyes said.

"We took him out." It'd been luck—no, not luck, a miracle—they'd seen him on approach.

She paused, then nodded. "Okay, we need to get the villagers out of here before reinforcements come."

Scott sat quietly nursing his wounds, his gaze bouncing back and forth. "Let's get it done."

Yeah, not exactly the family reunion anyone expected, but at least he was here. And so was his brother. He dispatched the men to cover the gates and get sitreps. "I'll head down there with them, check it out."

"Hey." Scott offered his hand to him. "Thanks for coming, Max."

Fingers wrapped around his brother's, Max pulled him into a quick hug. "Sorry." *For everything. Years without talking. That we have the same father. That I never knew you.* "Let's get this place secured!"

Vaughn Residence, Virginia

Vultures. Blood-sucking, meat-eating vultures.

Warren Vaughn stalked down the hall, his Florsheims clicking on the marble floors as he stormed into his study.

"Sir, we need—"

He slammed the door, severing the questions and the assault—on his name, his character, his very identity. His people were haranguing him, insisting he talk to the media. No go. He was through with that for now. He whisked the bar door open and slapped a snifter down onto the mirrored surface. A few clinks and he poured the warm liquid over the ice. Warren tossed the contents into his mouth, held it on his tongue as he closed his eyes, and drew in a breath, then swallowed.

It burned. All the way down.

Just like Marshall's betrayal.

Teeth grinding, he slammed the glass down and poured another drink. "My own son—" He bit back a curse.

The national anthem belted out from his phone, severing his blasphemy. He fumbled with the holster and withdrew his BlackBerry, then glanced at the ID.

SANDS, N.

Warren clenched his teeth as he pressed the phone to his ear. "Sands."

"Senator, how are you?"

Warren growled at the all-too-calm voice. "Where are you? I've been calling all day. We have things to—"

"I'm working on our pet project." Sands's voice slicked through the line like olive oil. "I think you would agree things have gotten out of hand."

"That's putting it mildly."

Shouts and mechanical shrieks bled through the line. "Sorry, Warren. It's hard to hear at the moment, but I've faxed over some documents you need to sign."

Warren's gaze hopped to the three-in-one printer behind his desk, which whirred to life and began spitting out pages. "What documents?" He'd been in government all his life, and the plethora of signatures he'd penned boggled his mind. And why would Nathan need more signatures? He'd said everything was in working order.

"Just a few loose ends we're tying up."

"We?" Warren groused. "Who's 'we'?" Irritation skittered up his spine like a tarantula, tickling his conscience, ready to stab his mood. "I told you these things had to be kept between us, quiet, out of sight."

"Of course. I've done everything you asked."

Then why didn't he feel better. "Where are you?"

More shouts prevailed—from Nathan, it sounded like—then. . . nothing. "Nate?" Warren set down the glass and removed his jacket.

"Nate, you still there?"

With a curse, he tossed aside the phone, shed his suit jacket, grabbed his glass, and plucked the faxes from the machine. The Nkooye Green World Mine logo plastered the head of the page. Requests for more funding. Approval for. . . Warren frowned. "Since when?"

Click.

At the sound of the safety release on a weapon being cleared, Warren froze. Raised his gaze to the framed George Washington print that served well as a reflective surface.

Behind him stood a woman. Long hair. Gun in hand.

He came around slowly, stunned at the way she held the weapon. "Melanie?"

"You're going to take a trip, Daddy."

CHAPTER 30

Golding Residence, Cyprus

Three flat-screen monitors now devoured the wall where a print of Crete once hung. Children slept in the bedrooms, and the women of Nightshade sat talking quietly in the kitchen with the Old Man's wife. Though he expected Kazi to vanish into a room or into thin air, she stood beside him, staring at the images.

"Chile, Africa, Libya—"

"Too radical." The Kid nursed a bottle of water. "My dad likes to keep things low-key."

"Low-key?" Kazi lifted a remote and flicked to a different channel. "Have you seen the news, Marshall?"

Plastered on the news was Marshall's Army picture, complete with flag. The report detailed Marshall's escapade, stealing documents from his father's safe, stealing half a million dollars, and jetting off to some Caribbean island.

"No worries," the Kid said. "Let them think those things—their focus is on the wrong place, and it buys time. In his business dealings, my father kept things clean. He's on the boards of several committees, and he's chaired dozens if not hundreds of charities."

"And you call that low-key?" Griffin chuckled. "I'd hate to see high profile."

The Kid shook his head. "Every senator or congressman has to have organizations and charities behind him or her. My father is no different."

Griffin scowled. "Except that he tried to kill us."

"Gah!" The Kid shook his hands at Griffin. "Would you get off that? We're trying to figure out *why*."

"Why? Because we stepped on his toes—or his pocketbook."

"Yes," the Kid said. "But how? Through what endeavor?"

A soft touch and call of his name drew him to Kazi.

Hand on his arm, she stared at the screen.

A bucket of ice-cold water down his back wouldn't have shocked Griffin as much as seeing his own image on the television. The Kid grabbed a remote and cranked the volume.

". . .terview with the family of former Marine Gunnery Sergeant Griffin Riddell, who is a fugitive, an escaped, convicted felon."

The shot switched to a living room. No. . .not just a living room. *Madyar's*. The blood drained to Griffin's toes.

A young face flashed onto the screen. Beside it, another.

He fisted his hands.

". . .your name is—"

"Phoenix Johnson."

"And you're Mr. Riddell's sister?"

Phee nodded, her wide eyes betraying her comfort level of zero.

The reporter leaned in. "There are a lot of terrible things being said about your brother right now. Of course, the family of Congressman Jones is demanding justice, calling your brother a murderer. If you could send a message to your brother, if he were watching right now, what would you want to say?"

Phee worried a tissue in her hands, then looked directly at the camera, directly at him. "Come home, G. It's not worth it. We all know you're innocent, but this—this makes you look guilty." She looked to the side.

The young man at her side now appeared more eighteen than fifteen.

"And your name is Dante, right?"

Tough, macho attitude oozed through the screen as Dante flashed an ambivalent nod.

"Would you like to say something to your uncle?"

His lips tightened. Smirked up one side. "Nah. He left us, you know? Told me to do the right thing, told me to make my grandparents proud—but then he go off and do this?" He clicked his tongue. "What kind of hero does that?"

"You feel let down."

Dante shrugged.

"You were close to your uncle, weren't you? Your mother said you played sports with him all the time, that he was the one who taught you to play football—and you were scouted, isn't that right?" When Dante didn't play into her hands, she went on. "You used to meet him at the airport when he returned from tours of duty. Is it hard, knowing what people are saying?"

Dante swiped a hand under his nose. Avoided the camera, then stood and walked out.

"I'm sorry," Phoenix said to the interviewer. "It's been real hard on him. He won't talk to us much anymore."

"You're worried about the impact Griffin's actions are having on him?"

Phee's eyes watered. She dropped her gaze, nodding frantically as her lips pulled taut as she struggled to hold back her tears. "We just want Griffin to come back home."

A massive sinkhole sucked in everything he had left. His name. His honor.

Breathing shallowed out. Fists clenched tight.

"Griffin?" Kazi's voice, though soft and pliable, was a torment.

He turned, banged into a chair. Stumbling over it, his fury ignited. He grabbed the chair. Flung it. Demons of hell come to stay. "Guardian of the divine" no more. He was a beast. They believed he'd killed that congressman. They believed he was running like a common criminal. Had to get out of here. Away from people. Before he became like his father.

"Legend." Colton stepped into his path.

Whooshing pounded in his ears. "Step off, man. I don't want to hurt you." Screaming tore at his soul, the sound of his dreams shattering. His hopes exploding.

Though Colton was the same size and could go head to head with him, the man must've seen the volcano building in Griffin, because he lowered his head and eased aside.

Griffin flung back the glass door and winced at the resounding *crack* that snapped through the late night. He paced. Gulped air. "God. . ." Fists raised to the sky, he growled. Howled. Spun and rammed a fist into the wall. Plaster dribbled to the ground. Warmth slipped over his knuckles and fingers.

He punched the wall again.

Again. Right. Left. Right.

Pain spiked up his arms and through his shoulders. Didn't care. Moved beyond the tiled terrace. Sand pushed against him, slowing his movements. Straining against him. He started walking. . .

jogging. . .running. Sprinting. Back. Forth. Willing the cauldron in his gut to simmer.

But each time, Dante's face burned into his mind, so he ran more.

Only as dawn's fingers traced the horizon did he slump against the wall, his ego and heart fractured. *Why, God? Why?* After one mistake, he'd righted his course. Walked the straight and narrow tight enough to hold a quarter between his cheeks.

And now. . .It don't matter.

Tracing the sky, searching for answers, he felt more than saw the presence behind him.

"They ran that interview to draw you out. You know that, right?"

"Don't matter." He let out a long sigh. "It's too late. Damage is done."

"What's this?" Light crunching came to his ears just seconds before he looked to the side and cringed. She stood on the wall. "The mighty Griffin gives up? Unaffected, undaunted Griffin?"

"The things they told him, the things. . .they said about me—"

"Aren't true."

"But he don't know that!"

Kazi peered down at him. "They said you were close. Are you?"

He eyed her, agitated with himself for letting his vault of secrecy open. She had no cause to get up in his business, but what angered him the most was that he had let her.

"Are you?"

"Yes—we *were*. I didn't want him to see me at the trial. Told Phee to keep him at home. She said he got angry, wanted to stand by me through it all, but. . .no way. Won't have him see me like that. Hear those lies. But he talked her into bringing him to the prison. Supermax is not the place for a kid. I made them leave. Killed me to do it, but I didn't want him seeing me like that."

He rubbed his head, feeling a buzz at the back of his brain thinking about Dante, thinking about what must be going through his teenage mind. "He's being raised by good people. My sister and her husband teaching him the right way to live. I worked hard to make sure my grandparents and sister had a good, safe place to be. So they didn't have to deal with the gangs and drugs I grew up around. Dante has good family, but this. . ."

"What about your parents? You didn't mention them."

"They died." Griffin ground his teeth to keep the morbid truth from slipping between his lips. It didn't do no good for this to come drifting up from the grave.

"Died?" Kazi huffed. "Fine, you don't want to tell me—"

"It don't need to be told, K. The past is behind us. I'm looking forward."

"You might be, but you're also looking over your shoulder every two seconds, afraid the past is going to catch up with you. It haunts you, haunts your decisions. Right now, it's infested your mind." Sincerity wove through her words. "Look, God knows I have a history I'd love to remain buried, but it's out there. You helped me face that. You showed me I can be whoever I want to be despite it."

He clicked his tongue and wagged his head, groaning.

"What? Doesn't that apply to you?"

"No, it don't."

"Why?"

"Because."

Her eyes flamed. "What a lame—"

"My father murdered my mother—beat the tar out of her, then shot himself. Not because he was sorry for what he'd done to her, but because he didn't want to get caught or go to jail."

"And my brother sold me into prostitution to pay off the family debt. What they did doesn't define us, Griffin. I get it—you're afraid your nephew will think you're like your father."

He spun, towering over her. "I am that man. I killed a man when he attacked my wife."

Her green eyes widened. "Wife?"

Another brick on the wall he'd built around his past crumbled. Griffin pinched his lips together. Why? Why did she have to dredge all this up? He didn't want to go there. Didn't want to let these memories see the light of day. He'd buried them. Moved on.

"You have a wife?"

"No!" His voice cracked. How could she think he would go after her when he was still married? "She left because she wanted the benefits of being a Marine wife but not the responsibility. I had no business marrying her. I knew she was into me, not like that. I had my club, that's where I spent my nights and weekends. Alone with good music. She went out—with anyone and everyone."

He touched his fingertips to his temples. "After the man died, the attorney got me cleared. There were witnesses. The man was my commanding officer, and there were enough witnesses to prove he was out for my head. That he went after my wife. My record was expunged, but I have *never* forgotten that I took someone's life."

"It's why you won't let yourself feel."

Griffin felt as if his heart stalled out. How did she figure that out? "Treece said she couldn't take it anymore. Neither could I."

"Take what?"

"Me. Who I am. My—" He grunted and huffed. "I don't talk about things, a'right? It don't make sense to. Never did anyone any good to do 'talk' about them."

"Let's talk about this."

"No Reggie. No, please. . ."

"I deal with it in my own way. Bury it. Move on." He patted his chest. "That's my MO."

"But *are* you dealing with the things in your past, or are you ignoring them?"

"What?"

"You don't show your feelings, Griffin. Burying them is just as dangerous as exploding with them." She pointed to the house. "Neeley tried to reason with you, but even he saw the fury in your face and backed off. Is that what you want? People afraid of you, afraid of crossing you?"

"I want respect."

"Then earn it!"

Shoulders hunched, he pushed his neck forward. "Excuse me?" He raised his arms and snapped his hands straight. "I do what I need to so me and mine can survive. Always have. That don't change." He had to do that to survive, to protect Phoenix. Himself. He hadn't been able to save his mom. . . "Look, don't get up in my business, K. You don't know me like that."

Kazi hauled back, her expression stricken. Like he'd hit her. The thought swirled through his gut, slinging him back to the past when his dad had first punched his mom.

His chest swelled at the memory. At seeing that look on Kazi's face.

Shame pushed him to the edge of reason. "K. . .I'm. . .sorry."

"No, fine." She backed toward the house, hurt rimming her beautiful eyes.

Griffin caught her arm gently, pulled her back to himself. He peered down into those green depths. . .then drifted out to the rippling waves. "I don't talk about my business."

"What?" she asked, her voice hard. Her expression harder. "Oh,

I see. It's okay to play hero, but it's not okay to be a victim. Not used to being vulnerable, Griffin?" She tugged her elbow free of his grasp. "Well, don't worry. I'm used to men satisfying their egos through me."

The words were a backhanded smack across his honor. "That's not—"

"Griffin!" Colton's muted shout through the window drew him round. "Max on relay!"

Green World Health Clinic Compound, Uganda

Full engagement in a combat theater had nothing on Max's heart as he hammered on the keyboard, knowing the seconds were counting down. His hands shook, full of adrenaline and images of his wife and sons safe with Lambert. He typed: COPY. INTACT W/ SQUIRT. POSSIBLE NS WIRING. RQST ELECTRICTY.

Hands balled, he blew on his fists, not for warmth but to blow off the adrenaline that had them shaking. He'd given the code requesting a full engagement with the Nightshade team, knowing he had to word the relay as if the entire thing would be blasted on *CougarNews*'s evening report.

"Think they'll agree to help?"

Max bounced a glance to Dighton, who shifted aside from the wall he held up as Scott and Marie entered the room. Promising them a full engagement wasn't possible. Two months ago, he'd have vowed with his life to take down someone who attacked an organization working for the good of the people—assuming they'd fully investigated and were convinced things were out of control. But with the mess everything was in. . .

"Don't know."

A lot would go into consideration. The team's location. Their sitrep. If the Old Man thought they could get to Uganda without getting killed or killing the civilians in the process.

"But we need the help." Max ran a thumb over his lip as he waited for a response.

"At least we have a better chance with you and the Aussies," Marie said. "I don't care about the mine as long as we can get the people to safety."

"The mine may stop them from leaving."

She stared at him.

"If they're earning an income, if their families are safe," Squirt said as he joined Max at the table with the only laptop left in the facility, "they might not leave."

Max had been in similar situations where the families were more afraid of leaving than of staying. Rig a mission to that, and everyone ended up dead.

"Hey." Dighton nodded toward the laptop.

Words fell across the screen.

PARTS MISSING. CONNECTION POSSIBLE. RELAY ORDER NUMBER.

"What's that mean?"

Max glanced to his left at the woman. "Our location." He looked to Squirt for thoughts. "Parts Missing" worried him. That meant someone or someones on the team were missing. Who? He punched out of the seat and stalked back and forth. If they weren't in lockdown, he'd be all over putting the team back together. But every step threatened their existence. Drew attention.

"What do you think?"

"Sending our location over this signal could dig our graves," Max said.

"Or bring us backup, get the people out of here, then you can deal with this threat," Marie interjected.

What, was the woman wearing rose-colored glasses? Didn't she see that reality sucked? Especially in combat.

Max pulled his gaze from her and turned back to the laptop. The facts were simple but incredibly complicated: the compound needed help, something going on in the mine a dozen miles away needed intervention, and bringing Nightshade into the mix could turn the yellowcake situation global.

"Aren't you going to tell them where we are?" Marie's voice bordered on panic. "We need help. You saw that enough to come—and now you're here. Look around you. Do you think you can handle this on your own?"

Anger laced through his system, but he recognized it for the challenge it was. "This isn't just about you."

"*Me?*" Her face paled. "I don't give a rat's behind about me." She flung an arm toward the heart of the compound. "I have more than a hundred people living in tents with disease, famine, and illness, and doing so in mortal fear that whoever is after him"—her hand swung toward Scott—"and what he found might catch up with them." Fury wrested curls from her pulled-back hair, reminding him of Sydney.

272

Not the curls. But the indignation. "Now, are you a soldier who's going to do something or a soldier who's going to whine?"

Her dig at his character didn't faze him. "Tell me, Marie, would you put your villagers on the front page of *CougarNews* in a lineup so whoever is behind this could take them out one by one, then go after their families?"

A hand went to her throat.

Thought so. "That's exactly what you're asking me to do by bringing my team here."

She came forward, her earnestness flaming. "But you *came*. Don't give up now."

"Yes, I came. Now give me room to figure things out." He drew in a steadying breath and locked on the computer. Helping this village, sorting out the mine caper—it's why he was here. Why he'd found Scott's e-mail buried amid hundreds in an account he hadn't checked in years. All because he was searching for contact from Sydney.

He closed his eyes. *Sydney*—his anchor. If he did this, if he sent his coordinates, it'd be a direct bead on his forehead. He could be dead the second he sent it. Then who would take care of Sydney and the boys?

"Max?"

Squirt's quiet call blasted against his indecision. He cleared his throat. "Okay." *God, protect and guide us.* "Let's do this."

Folding the coordinates amid a line of code, he hoped to buy some time against would-be attackers.

"Send it in pieces," Squirt suggested. "Break it up so it's not as easy to track."

Max nodded. Keyed in the latitude.

Hit SEND.

Entered the longitude.

Hit SEN—

BooOOOOooom!

In a surreal encounter, he felt his body lifted from where he stood. Shoved backward by the invisible hand of a bomb's concussion. Walls collapsed. Light exploded through the room, instantly replaced by smoke and dust.

CHAPTER 31

Golding Residence, Cyprus

Connection's gone."

Olin stared at the screen where the first set of coordinates hid among a sentence that, to any bystander, would appear nonsensical. "What do you mean?"

"It's gone."

"Check again."

"I did." Aladdin shrugged as he cast a look in the direction of Max's wife. "Maybe the power went out."

"Right." Olin swallowed hard. The power hadn't gone down. He knew at the core of his being something bad happened. "Run sat images. Get me a scan of that area."

Keys were already clicking as he turned to the others.

At least things were going, generally, in the right direction. Most of the team was together. Midas was on his way. They were almost back together and very close to figuring out the details of what happened. He was certain of it.

"Boss," Colton said, a phone pressed to his ear. "Contact from the bird with Midas."

Olin looked up.

"It's not good. Midas has. . ." The air hung heavy and rancid as Cowboy chose his words carefully, his gaze *not* going to Danielle. His daughter had dealt with enough. "They need a hospital. Now."

Golding snapped a finger. "Evram!" He strode toward the man.

"Get Moshe. Have them prepared." Bent over, Golding wrote on a piece of paper, then handed it to Cowboy. "Divert them to this airstrip. A chopper will meet them and take him to a trusted hospital. They will be discreet."

Cowboy relayed the information.

Had Olin stepped into a massive pit of quicksand that was sucking every tendril of his life into oblivion? The room spun. He dropped into a chair, holding his head as he did. All he'd worked for, the lives of these men. . . And now, on the precipice of the day of reckoning, things—*everything* was falling apart.

"Olin?" Charlotte's worry sang through the room. Seconds later, she crouched at his side, touching the side of his face. "You're cold."

"The world is cold."

"General, you should lie down." Cowboy stood over him, two fingers pressed to his neck. "You're running a bit high."

Olin waved off the attention. "I'm fine. Just. . .not going as I planned."

Cowboy grinned. "All the same, I'd feel better if you got some shut-eye while we work out the rest. You've been up awhile."

"He's right." Griffin, who'd been strangely quiet, spoke up. "Rest up. We got this. We'll find Frogman and get something in play. We'll wake you."

"Come on," Charlotte said as she eased an arm around him.

Numbly, he let her guide him into a bedroom. On the floor, Tala Metcalfe and McKenna Neeley slept soundly. As he stared at the beautiful innocence of his men's children, the only thought he had was: *What if their fathers die at my hand?*

He shook off the morbid thought and stretched out on the bed with Charlotte at his side.

"Give it to the Lord, Olin," she whispered. "You're trying to do this in your own might."

His eyes slid shut. "They're my responsibility."

"They're *God's* responsibility."

"But He entrusted them to my care." He felt his pulse in his temple. "So many hurt. So many. . .mistakes."

"Olin. . . ?"

A weight pressed into his chest. As sleep greedily claimed him, he drifted off wondering if he would ever wake.

RONIE KENDIG

Flight to Cyprus Hospital

"You'll kill yourself."

"Give it to me!" Canyon growled as he swiped for the syringe and wobbled on the edge of the stretcher.

"You don't know—"

When his brother didn't finish, Canyon cocked his head so he could peer at him through the right eye since the left had swollen shut.

Navas held a hand to Range's chest. Two silent sentries.

His mind hooked on the conversation that had pulled him out of the abyss of unconsciousness. He'd been in a near-dead state too many times in the last few years. But he couldn't hang up his beret just yet. There was another battle to fight—an especially large and prickly one.

He eyed the large-bore IV stuck in his arm. The empty syringes on the tray. "How many times have I coded?" His brain felt like one of those Coke-flavored slushes you could buy at the beach on hot days.

"Three."

He flicked the IV, then followed it up to the bag dangling over his head. "What's that?"

"Morphine—"

Gritting his teeth, Canyon yanked it out. Pressed two fingers to the spot that spurted the clear liquid and blood.

"Hey!" the EMT came off the seat beside him. "You need that."

"It's muddling my mind." He gave a quick shake of his head, then looked at Range. With Navas. Now, there was a story he would like to hear. He'd never forget hearing the firefight outside his holding cell. Then the doors opening and his kid brother barging in with all the bravado that was normally associated with the family's silent tormenter—him. Range had looked so shocked. So. . .accosted at what he saw. Canyon was sure he was a sight for sore eyes with all the bruises, broken arm—which was now splinted, thanks to the EMT. Even now, the memory made him smile.

Range snickered. "You were dead two minutes ago."

"Yeah?" Canyon refused the pleading of his body to lie down and give Rip Van Winkle a run for his money. "Well, death is overrated." He had a lot on the side of living worth fighting for. "Roark." His heart rate increased on the bleeping machine.

The edges of his vision blurred. He blinked and shook his head—which only made it worse. Ringing screamed through his ears.

"He's going again," the EMT mumbled.

"Midas, lie back. Relax." Navas's words were surprisingly clear and concerned.

"I need to put the IV back in. He's in no shape to—"

Can't let them do that. *No.* Had to get himself together.

Navas laughed. "I think he disagrees."

"I don't care what he disagrees with."

Hold on. I'll be. . .back.

"Hey!"

The clang of equipment and a scuffle ensued. Navas's gruff tone pulled Canyon from the depths. He rolled his eyes and found the slit where his eyelids were. *Man, didn't think it was that hard.*

Navas had the EMT pinned against the wall. "He said 'no.'"

Wide-eyed, the man held up his hands. "He's dying; we have to do something."

On a tray between them, Canyon eyed a large syringe. Beside it, a vial of epinephrine—empty. Canyon swiped a hand toward it. The needle lodged in his palm. Pain. . .there should be pain. . .but there wasn't. He was desperate. The team was dying. He was dying.

No, I'm not.

Mentally he rammed the syringe toward his chest. He felt nothing.

God, please. . .I need to help them.

He repeated the thoughts, hoping they translated into action this time. In a half-dead state, he wasn't sure what was real or fake. Syringe. . .chest. . .plunge.

A new fire, invigorating and cold, rushed through his veins. His pulse throbbed against his pounding head. *"Auggghhh!"* The sensation pushed his chest off the stretcher.

Shouts erupted.

Canyon's eyes—eye—shot open. He stared up at his brother, a mop of black hair dripping sweat. . .straight into Canyon's face. A strange gurgling met his hearing. *Crap, that's me.* He coughed. Caught his brother's hand dangling next to him—and froze.

Range held the syringe.

He looked up, confused. Pushed himself upright, the room spinning but not near as bad as before. Had his brother injected him?

"The team," Canyon muttered, his tongue feeling like it had three North Face parkas on it. "Status?"

Navas said, "The general got SATINT—compound is flattened. Smoke and debris are all that's left."

So Max was dead or MIA. Which meant. . .they needed a medic at that compound. He snorted. Right. He couldn't even stand up without assistance, and he was toying with heading into a combat zone?

It's my team. . .

Navas nodded. "The Old Man had a stroke. He's alive, stable, and sedated."

"So, sitrep is one big snafu." Fisting his hand, he steadied himself on the stretcher. Everything hurt. *No, "hurt" doesn't come close.* Agony had taken up residence in every cell of his body. His left eye was swollen shut. Left arm in a sling, he couldn't feel the fingers, thanks to the ragged break in the bone, thanks to the VFA jackhammering through it. Literally.

Brown eyes sparked with amusement, Navas eased onto a stretcher across from him. A smile almost tugged back his lips. "We're about twenty minutes from the hospital. They're going to put you under, cut you open, put you back together."

Unless you tell them to do something else. It was as if Canyon could hear the man's thoughts. What was it with this man? He seemed to thrive on this mess.

Canyon smirked. "Take me to my leader."

❋

Golding Residence, Cyprus

Tina had warned her long ago about giving away her heart. Kazi held to the philosophy that men were meant to be loved then left. It'd worked for her steampunk friend, kept her alive and on the edge of every party. Men loved her restless spirit, annoying laughter, and passion for all things dangerous. She'd lived life full and hard, unafraid of being hurt.

Because she never put herself in a position to be hurt.

Kazi monitored the room—the Nightshade team, the Mossad, the women and children—but no one had given a hint that they were aware of her doings. Thankfully. Because they'd probably chop her head off and ask questions later if they figured it out.

"What's the stat on Midas?" Griffin's voice boomed over the din.

Aladdin's blue-green eyes seemed to glow as he answered without looking up or over his monitor. "En route, five klicks." His short-cropped hair, spotted with scabs, seemed to ripple beneath the pulse of his heartbeat.

Ignoring their reports, Kazi adjusted the laptop propped on her knees. She scanned some backchannels, using her own secure site she'd created years ago to surf the net and not expose herself or her locations.

Griffin pored over the data, his hand tracing lines, his eyes creating others, trying to piece together where they were supposed to go, what they were to do. Who they were supposed to stop. His meaty pointer tapped a series of images taped to the board. "What about Frogman or the Ugandan compound? Any word?"

"Negative." Marshall pushed to his feet and snatched pages from a printer that had been whirring nonstop the last twenty-four hours since she and Griffin had been on the rooftop. "But I've accessed a GW satellite and used that to monitor the situation." He snapped the pages straight. "They need help. Yesterday."

As Griffin assessed the images, Kazi assessed the two men. Though Marshall stood almost a head shorter, had black hair and blue-gray eyes, he had a ruggedness about him that was charming. And there was a spark in his gaze that somehow evened up that size difference—the guy was a former Army Ranger for heaven's sake. That alone spoke of the grit and determination that set him apart. Yet mirth and mischief seemed to be the smart aleck's bedmates. Though he'd taken a few head-pops, the taunting had lessened as he slowly pulled the pieces of the nightmare-laden puzzle together. And taking control of a satellite? Did Griffin even realize the feat Marshall accomplished?

No. Griffin wasn't one to get emotional. To show appreciation or let people past that thick skull or barrier of his. He'd been full steam ahead for the last ten hours, which both relieved and irritated her. He'd shoved her out of his life when things got a little too close to home. So much for his pithy comment about when *she* was ready—and to think, it'd actually touched something deep in her. Stirred embers into a molten mixture that she thought might—*might*—be recast into something. . .beautiful.

The ironic thing about his comment was that *Griffin* would never be ready. Which suited her just fine. She had a career. Well, after she re-created herself. That was the key. She'd had to re-create identities in the past. No reason she couldn't overhaul who she was and come out better, stronger. She didn't need Griffin.

When she was ready?

She'd been ready *yesterday*.

He didn't like people getting into his attic, where all his dirty laundry was hidden.

She understood that. She did. Even though she'd spouted the one truth to him that had never crossed anyone else's ears, he'd been so blinded by his own anger and desperation to protect his past and himself that he hadn't even heard her.

And it stung. Like a thousand-pound yellow jacket had rammed his butt into her chest.

Even now, the sting proved acute. *I was ready to give him everything!*

Kazi hauled her mind back to the data. She blinked away the rejection, the hurt, and pushed herself into her new plan, keying in another site. She floated around the hidden portals. . .then stilled. She honed in on a coded phrase on a bakery site. Quick keystrokes carried her to a secure, secretive underground cyberspace.

HELLO, GYMNAST.

Kazi's stomach squeezed. So, word had already gotten out about her identity. She'd have to make this stop brief. She typed: GUESS MY SECRET'S OUT.

YEAH. . .HAPPENS TO THE BEST. WASUP?

LOOKING FOR NOOSE AROUND MY NECK.

Was she too bold?

NEED ANOTHER? LOL YOU'LL BE GROUNDED FOR A WHILE, EH?

Wow, that was fast. She clicked out a reply. YEP. BETTER JET. BYE.

She thrilled over the luck of finding that connection. Kazi logged out and drew in a deep breath, skating her gaze around the room to be sure nobody was wiser to her schemes. Her gaze collided with a pair of blue-green eyes.

Aladdin peered over his monitor. Held fast. Only as the sounds in the room flooded back to her distracted mind did she realize he was talking to the man next to him. So. . .why was he looking at her? Did he trace her?

Cold dread washed over her. He could've had a program on here to monitor keystrokes. It'd make sense—in case someone stumbled upon something, they could backtrack.

Aladdin returned to his search.

Kazi blew out a quick breath. Words emblazoned—particularly, three letters—on the back of her corneas ensnaring her thoughts. She'd have to be an idiot not to figure out what that griefer meant. The trouble was coming up with a plausible explanation Griffin and the others would buy. She studied the data on the giant grease board dividing the kitchen from the command center. She compared them against the possible locations, knowing Carrick would hunt down whoever had tried to take Griffin and Neeley down.

She hit on two words and knew beyond a shadow of doubt where the team was supposed to go. And where Carrick was. She compared the notes with satellite images. She went to Google and did a search of the names. One headline in particular caught her attention.

GREEN WORLD, INC. INITIATIVE IN UGANDA RESTORES HOPE.

She scanned the article, noting names and locations—including one very familiar name: Senator Warren Vaughn. He'd put together the Green World initiative, winning popularity and all but erasing famine and starvation in the area. Recently, efforts were under way to spread the success of this program.

Page after page of results cheered Green World and praised Vaughn. In fact, he'd been named to numerous committees, handed several honorary doctorates.

Pinching her lower lip, she clicked a detractor headline that read: GREEN WORLD RAPES HOPE OF NKYOOE. The document was actually a self-published PDF posted on a "lemon" site. The author, a humanitarian aid doctor named Marie Beck, claimed Green World was in fact promoting sex slave trade, and rather than turning backward the hand of hunger and disease, they were infecting the people with a far more dangerous plague: false hope.

I know where they are.

"I know where they are."

Kazi twitched at the proclamation that mirrored her own thoughts and pulled her focus from the laptop to Aladdin, who now had Griffin hovering over them.

"Let's hear it," Griffin said, expectation on his face—so much so that Kazi dreaded what the assassin would say next.

"This document by Marie Beck mentions Warren Vaughn, his agency Green World, and a small village called Nkyooe in Uganda. She also notes several other similar efforts." Resolution carved into Aladdin's handsome, scarred face.

How did he find the same page I found?

"Out of the eight locations, Nightshade has crossed paths with five of them that I can tell." His gaze hit hers. Seared. Then went back to the information. "The first mission was in a village where a rogue colonel was brutalizing the people."

"Paka," Marshall said with a growl in his voice.

Aladdin had piggybacked her keystrokes. How?

"Give the Kid a brownie. Yusuf just found something that shows Paka was the first military official named in an early report by Warren Vaughn on the success of Green World." Aladdin stood. "I think we have our location."

Griffin held up a hand, staring at the data board. "Wait—let's be sure this is the place. Kid, pull up that satellite you hijacked—"

"Borrowed." The Kid's grin was primal. Obviously in his element with the team and breaking into technology, he went to work.

"A'right." Griffin smiled. "*Borrowed.* Now, see what's happening near that village. We can't go in there blind."

When would the men around Marshall stop referring to him as the kid of the group? He'd taken his place. Silence strangled conversations and movement as they all waited to see what the satellites showed. Humming monitors and whirring cooling fans competed against the quiet.

"Okay," the Kid said. "The place looks like it has a mine." His blue-gray eyes bounced to a wall monitor, which flicked to show a grainy resolution. At the wall, he pointed. "You can see the mine here." He traced a square, then stood staring at the screen. "That. . ." He wagged a finger at a circular machine. "That doesn't make sense."

The Kid rushed back to his computer, scanned, zoomed. "No."

"What're you seeing?" Neely asked, joining Griffin, the two giants considering the data.

"They're intake and exit systems—ventilation fans, essentially." The Kid swept his hand through his hair, which stuck up over his head. "Unbelievable."

"The point?" Irritation seeped into Griffin's voice and stance.

"It's supposed to be a diamond mine." Marshall came up out of his seat. "They don't need ventilation like that. I mean"—he shrugged— "sure, it'd be nice, protect the people working. But the cost for that is astounding." He snorted. "My dad likes his money too much to throw it out on something not mandatory, especially in a third world country."

Griffin looked up at the screen, his brow contorted.

"The only reason to have fans is to remove noxious fumes." Aladdin walked to the monitor. "Those fumes are the product of diesel fumes, blasting explosives, or the ore."

"What ore?" Neeley looked to the Kid. "What's there? What are they mining?"

"Whatever it is," the Kid muttered as he worked on the keyboard, "you can bet my dad's getting rich off it."

A quibble erupted from one end of the table. Golding emerged from a cluster of men, their expressions taut. "Legend, our men believe the perimeter of that mine may be. . .*mined*."

"Mined?" Griffin growled. "Land mines?" He roughed a hand over his face and bald head.

"Okay." The Kid sighed. "There's no telling what's down there—it could be a ton of elements. What we know, what we'll need to plan for, is that it's toxic." He pointed to the wall monitor. "And the mine is a day's walk from the compound where Max was—is." He cringed at his mistake and looked across the room.

"It'll take more than an explosion to kill my husband, Marshall," Sydney said. "He's too bullheaded to die easily."

"Ain't that the truth," the Kid said, laughing.

Griffin smacked the back of the Kid's head. "I'll be sure to tell Frogman that one."

The PDF article was a blazing trail, a homing beacon straight to her. Kazi glanced down at her screen. She clicked out, cleared the history, added a few other security protocols to ensure nobody followed her journey, then logged off.

Regardless of how the assassin stumbled upon the same page—she didn't buy "coincidence"—she had her answer. If she could zoom in on the satellite image on the wall, she'd probably find Carrick's slick smile gleaming in the Ugandan sun. No doubt he'd try to buy out Green World. If he couldn't do that, he'd destroy them. It was just the way he worked. Didn't want some other world power interrupting his trip to godhood.

Which meant if she was going to get out alive, she knew what she had to do. On the chair, she lifted the laptop, logged back in, and dug through the normal channels to a ghosted site. There, she sent an e-mail, her stomach churning.

Don't do this.

There wasn't a choice. Not if she intended to write her own ending. Holding her breath, she hit SEND. *As a dog returns to his vomit. . .* Doing this put her in the hands of Carrick. Posed the greatest risk to her freedom. But if she didn't. . .she'd never know for sure.

"So be it," she whispered.

Bang!

The noise snapped the room into silence as they turned toward the hall. Griffin appeared, a storm raging in his face. Kazi felt as if a javelin had speared her heart as she met his cauldronlike glare for several long, painful seconds. He knows. *He knows!*

CHAPTER 32

Nkooye Green World Mine, Uganda

Buttoning his suit, Carrick stepped over a board and carried himself up three wobbling, creaking steps into the trailer office. He tried to keep the sneer from his face, but in deplorable conditions such as these, he couldn't help it. Honestly, it'd take all of ten minutes to stabilize the rickety makeshift porch that made it possible to enter the dank environment.

Swiping a finger over his nose did little to ease the smell of sweat and body odor inside. A window, partially propped open by a groaning air-conditioning unit, pumped stale but somewhat cooler air into the trailer.

"Welcome," a native said as he stood from behind a desk, perspiration dotting his brow and ringing his brown cotton shirt. The chair behind him creaked, the back slowly tilting to the side until—

Clank! It rammed against the copier stuffed in a corner.

The native jerked upright, then nudged it against the desk. Nervously, he turned back, hands dangling from his almost-emaciated sides. "Welcome." He motioned to a door to his left. "You see senator?"

Carrick nodded. "I do."

The man smiled—yellow, stained, missing teeth peeking out from his almost black-as-night skin. "Come. He wait for you."

Carrick peeked out the filmy window to the Uganda landscape, across the way where his private helicopter had landed. Two armed men stood watch. Not that anyone around here knew how to fly a helicopter, but it was better to be prepared than screwed.

He squeezed past the native and the doorjamb. Inside, cleaner, colder, stronger air accosted him and forced him to take record of the difference—in fact, all the differences. Expensive furniture consumed the office, a large rug spread over tiled floor. Pristinely kept windows. Shiny surfaces—no dust. How often did the native who'd just escorted him into the room have to clean to keep it so pristine?

"They treat me like a god."

Carrick met the brown eyes that he'd studied through photographs and videos en route. The American sought not only riches but power—visceral, tangible power that made his ego as bloated as the starved bellies that surrounded the senator.

"I was told you had an offer for me." Chin raised, he looked down his perfectly straight nose—most likely never broken. Probably not even bruised. The man wasn't the type to get his hands dirty or engage in hard work.

This will be easier than I thought.

"Indeed." Carrick lowered himself into a leather chair and stared up at the man. Some thought that standing over another person gave them power. But Carrick knew that sort of power was illusory and merely psychological. He could cripple this man with a few well-chosen words. Maybe later.

"You have a problem you want to go away."

The senator chuckled. "We all have those kinds of problems—families can be so troubling, work can be demanding, and friends—"

"Play your ignorance as long as it comforts you, Senator, but we both know you've tried to eliminate this problem." He wanted to smirk, but he mustn't show control too quickly. Carrick stood and ambled to the window, looking down at the mine. "But you've failed." Slowly, he turned back to the tailored suit. "And the only reason you're here instead of back home tending the garden of constituents is that"—Carrick slid his hands in his pockets, tilted his head, then shrugged—"quite simply, Senator, you need my help."

"Oh?" Bravado drifted away on the conditioned air. "What help is that, Mr. Burgess?"

"I can take care of this problem, but it will cost you." This time, he allowed the smirk. "Dearly."

"Not interested." Somehow, the air must've recirculated, because the bravado seemed to be making a nasty reappearance. "I'm doing fine on my own."

Carrick arched his eyebrow in a practiced, knowing arc. "Are you?" He smoothed his suit jacket. "Well, then. I'll inform the Ugandan Defense Ministry that the bombing at the Green World Health Compound truly was an accident. But let's hope for your sake, nobody survived to contradict your story."

At the door, he looked back to the man who probably held sway over a lot of American policy. Did the poor sap realize he held no power here? That with one twitch of Carrick's little finger, he could completely alter the man's destiny, fortune, and viability?

"You should know, Senator, that I am intimately acquainted with the woman who took Colton Neeley from you. She is a lethal force." His heart still hiccupped at the thought of the data and the damage she could do to *him*—if she truly had it. If she chose to do something with it. But he'd also employed a little blowback for her. She played her card, they'd all scatter. Wipe out her credibility. But she'd reacted strongly to the news of her family, and that was what he needed. "And I happen to know she's plotting to return here, with the entire team you have been trying to dismantle, and blow your operation completely and utterly out of your hands." He checked his watch and smiled. "Ah, time for tea. Cheers." He turned the knob and drew open the door.

"What do you want?"

Golding Residence, Cyprus

Rumbling outside was slowly followed by the creak and pop of old axles. Griffin snatched a weapon from the table and slipped up next to the door. Behind him, he heard the Kid at the windows. "Beat-up truck. Two—no, three occupants."

"ID?" Griffin nodded to Aladdin who took up position on the other side of the door.

Whoever was coming wasn't invited or expected.

"Negative. Too dark."

Outside, doors creaked, followed by muttering. Then steps. A groan.

Aladdin gave the signal. Three. . .

Griffin placed his right foot slightly back. Brought his weapon to the ready and stared down the sights, past it, to the door.

Two. . .

A whistle sailed through the night.

Griffin lifted his head. Frowned at Aladdin. The Nightshade signal? How was that—?

"Open it, open it!" Marshall growled. "Midas!"

Aladdin ripped open the door.

Griffin, weapon down, met a bludgeoned face. He lunged and caught the man who tumbled across the threshold, one arm hooked over another man's shoulders.

"In the bedroom," Aladdin shouted.

Marshall and the Kid hoisted Midas from the ground. The man groaned and muttered something about not being an invalid.

As they scurried through the room, Griffin heard the gasp from Midas's wife. They set him on the bed, and Midas rolled onto his back. "Man, it's good to be home," he said, his voice almost a whisper.

"Good to have you back, Golden Boy," Aladdin said as he probed injuries, especially a really bad one in his side.

Midas stilled, his gaze locked on something behind them. "Cover me up," he said through gritted teeth.

Aladdin snapped the blanket over him, then straightened.

"Roark." Midas's hand wavered as it stretched toward the door.

Danielle rushed to his side, sans children, and dropped onto the mattress, tears streaming down her face. She kissed him, then buried her face in his shoulder.

Griffin stood back, knowing. . .*knowing* he'd never have that. Never have a woman who loved him no matter what he looked like, no matter what.

"The baby," Midas said, coughing. "Is he okay? Tala?"

A bloodied, scratched, and burned hand cupped her face, and she pressed it between her cheek and shoulder. "They're here. . .good. I love you." She sobbed. "Love you so much. We were so scared. . ."

Aladdin eased into the situation. "We need to get him cleaned up."

Danielle looked at them, then back to her husband. "I'll be right outside."

Canyon pulled her down to him and kissed her.

Once outside, Aladdin drew back the shirt. "Ask Evram for the kit. We need to patch this up."

"We're gearing up to head out in ten," Griffin said. "Someone else will have to take care of him. We got to go."

"No," Midas grunted as he pulled up off the mattress. "I'm going with you."

Griffin would've laughed if he didn't see the dark stain on the mattress. "Why aren't you at the hospital?"

Blue eyes met his. "My team needs me."

"We need you to live. Like this, you ain't—"

Midas turned to Aladdin. "Patch me up—but just enough to get me on the chopper. I can still hold a gun."

"That's about all you can do."

"Then I'm going to do it."

"He's been like that since we got in the bird."

Griffin turned at the new voice.

"Range." Midas waved the man closer. "Stay here—stay with Roark. With my son. My daughter." His face reddened. He swayed. "Don't leave them. *Promise* me."

Unease slithered through Griffin. That sounded too much like a deathbed promise. "Shut up and lie down, Midas." He turned to Midas's brother. "Why did you bring him here?"

"You ever try to stop him?"

"He dies"—Griffin stabbed a finger at him—"I blame you, Little Brother."

"He coded three times in the air."

Midas started mumbling something as he slowly slumped back down and went still. Griffin could only chuckle as he realized the medic was telling them how to treat him.

Griffin hesitated.

"Still with us, Surfer Boy?" Aladdin asked.

". . .uh-huh. . .patch me. . .get me on the chopper."

Griffin laughed. "You heard the man."

Aladdin scowled. "You can't be serious. He can't even hold himself up, let alone a weapon!"

"Then we'll duct tape it to his hands." Griffin left the room, surprised to find Kazi there. She drew up straight, her face blank. Going to betray everyone and act like nothing happened? "Got something to tell me, Baby Girl?"

"He looked bad."

"No, this ain't going to work anymore. Truth." He bumped her toes with his boots. "I want the truth. Why you running things behind my back?"

She swallowed. "I don't know you like that."

Having his words thrown back at him hurt. And revealed the way he'd hurt her. Had he really gone juvie on her like that? "Listen, I was wrong out there. I'm sorry. That whole mess with Dante—"

"Legend!" the general called.

He couldn't leave it like this. She'd be gone. He'd lose her.

"Legend," the general came around the corner. "We need you."

Kazi walked out of the hall, tucking a strand of hair behind her ear.

Griffin's coiled-up tension was ready to pop. Gaze locked on her as she retreated to the kitchen, he followed the general to the team where the Mossad agents worked.

"Okay, the Mossad are going to guard the women and children while you and the team go in."

Griffin nodded, still watching Kazi. What about her? He couldn't leave her here. If he did. . .

"Legend."

He snapped his attention to the general. A man stood across from him conferring with the Old Man. Griffin frowned. "I know you?"

"No," Lambert cut in. "And it's better that you don't."

The Latino had a look that said he meant business. Bad business. "He's going in with you—on his own, with his own agenda. He'll work with the team to secure the compound, then ride into Nkooye, but once down, he's his own man."

Nah, something here wasn't right. Smelled too much like trouble. "What's your game?"

"Killing the man who sold me out."

"And who would that be?"

"The same man who tried to take Midas apart. The same one who hit your team."

Little Brother appeared beside him. "He saved me from the VFA, then helped me get Canyon back."

The man laughed. "Helped *you*?"

Little Brother shifted his weight, holding his thigh. "He let me go in with them."

Smirking, Griffin nodded. "We could use the help. We've got us four, then our two on the ground."

The Latino looked around the room, apparently uncomfortable with the attention. "Don't make the mistake of thinking I'm a part of your team."

"Don't worry," Griffin said. "That won't happen."

Marshall motioned to the Little Brother. "What about him?"

"He's staying—got shot up in Venezuela, and he's going to be working on something here for Midas."

The Kid nodded, and Griffin noticed Range's palpable relief. The man had done well by them, helping get Midas out, but he wasn't a warrior, not like spec ops.

"And the girl?"

Griffin glanced across the room to Kazi. "She's going with us. She can identify one of our targets, so she's valuable but will remain on the chopper till we've secured the compound."

Griffin glared at Kazi so she understood he meant business. He clapped. "Gear up! We're moving out in ten."

Green World Health Clinic Compound, Uganda

Ash and smoke spiraled through the Ugandan sky in a lazy dance. Pockets of fire crackled and hissed, the world tilted sideways as Scott lay on the ground, rocks and dirt poking his cheek. He coughed, cringed at the fire that exploded through his chest, then dragged his hands to either side of his head. Slowly, he pushed up—

Nothing.

The weight pinning him to the ground registered as he searched his memory for what had him in this situation. He remembered being with—Max! The thought pumped vital determination through him. He attempted to free himself, again pushing upward. Dirt and small rocks dribbled down, the sound like a trickle of water to his plugged ears. Stretching his jaw didn't help. Again, he pushed, this time feeling a shift in whatever pinned him.

Pop! Pop!

Thwat.

Tat-a-tat-tat!

The sounds of a gunfight in the distance blazed through him. He strained to see around him. Chunks of the collapsed building barricaded him. Who was firing? And what were they firing at? He wiggled and managed to free his torso. Twisting around gave him a bird's-eye view of the slab that had fallen on him—and a man huddled against what remained of the wall. Max. He shifted, fired, then jerked back.

Scott's hearing had tricked him into thinking the gunfight was far away. He stuffed a finger in his ear to jiggle it free—warm wetness met his touch. Cement blasted up at him.

"Down!"

Realizing a bullet had impacted the slab, Scott flung himself backward, staring down the length of his body, over the cement pinning his legs, at Max.

Blood sliding down his temple, Max fired a few shots, then whipped back. "We need ammo!"

Pulling hard, Scott worked his legs free. His right ankle sat at an awkward angle. Pain and fire licked through his foot, then rushed up his leg. He'd broken it. He ground his teeth as he scrambled to Max's side at the half-blown wall. "No ammo. Marie won't allow it here." And Max had sent the Aussies to the mine for recon, so they were down to. . .nothing.

"Then we're dead!" Max tossed the M16 toward him and snatched a handgun from a belt holster.

Scott spotted the last magazine and clapped it into the M16. "I thought you sent coordinates. . ."

Max shook his head, dust flying from his short, black crop. "Didn't make it."

Scott bit back a curse as he passed the assault weapon back to Max. "Where's Marie? Have you seen her?"

His brother scowled, thinking, *We really do look and act alike*, as he resumed with the M16. "Took the boy and headed toward the hospital."

Boy? "Ojore?"

"Hanged if I know." Max pressed the weapon into his shoulder like the seasoned warrior he was and scanned. "We need backup."

Toes pinched, Scott looked at his booted foot and noted the swelling that stretched the boot laces and crowded his toes. He pulled himself into a crouch. "I'm going to find Marie."

"Round up survivors." Max lowered his face toward the weapon, aimed, and eased back the trigger again. He jerked up. "Crap." In a fluid move, he spun, shoved upward. "Go!"

Scott ran-hobbled as fast as he could, watching as Max rushed ahead. He feared his older brother would once again abandon him. It made sense—the weak got left behind. Is that how Max saw him?

The grating sound of shoes sliding against dirt drew his mind back to the battle. His brother skidded to a stop, glancing back. He scowled, said nothing as he provided cover fire. When Scott caught up, Max hooked an arm under him, supported his weight, and rushed onward.

The simple gesture shed light on the darkest part of Scott's heart. Max couldn't know how much that meant, but at the same time, Scott couldn't let his brother get killed because Scott was weak.

"Go," Scott said through a breath choked with pain. "Get to Marie. Protect her."

"Don't wimp out on me now." Max's arm flexed around him, then hauled upward.

Surprised at the strength in Max, Scott hopped with his right foot. "What'd you see?"

"Twenty, maybe thirty soldiers incoming." Max huffed as they skirted a crumbling building, navigating around chunks and mountains of debris.

Screams and shouts pierced the early morning air.

Scott's heart rammed into his throat. "The hospital!"

Together, they plunged through the rubble. Around tents that sagged like weighted sentries amid a battle-torn village. Scott's mind fastened on the thought of losing Marie. Of all the things he'd done wrong, let get in the way, allowed to separate them. *What an idiot.*

"Ever do something you later regret?" Scott asked before he thought better of it.

"Every day."

Surprise hitched in Scott's chest. He considered the older brother he'd invariably looked up to, wished for a connection with, longed to be *brothers* in heart as well as blood with.

Max shrugged, nearly smiling. "I'm a Jacobs." He hauled Scott over an overturned palm tree.

Though his mother had kept her maiden name, Scott knew the same hot blood that rushed through Max's veins boiled in his own. Their father had been the King of Mistakes and had the illegitimate children like him to prove it.

Behind them, the heavy thud of boots stampeded.

Scott glanced back. Sucked in a hard breath. Went down—his foot tangling on something. He hit the ground hard, the breath knocking out of his lungs. Gray spots sprinkled through his vision. Hearing hollowed, Scott tried to shake it off at the blurry images and sounds assailing his senses. A large shadow loomed over him.

Max lunged, his fist ramming into the face of a soldier. A hard right. A left. The fight seemed to take forever—directly over him—yet happened in less than a minute before the soldier crumpled. As Scott shoved the man to the side, Max yanked up the M16 and shouted, "Get to the hospital." On a knee, he fired.

Adrenaline pounding, Scott glanced at Max's target—and froze. More than a dozen soldiers advanced, weapons trained, firing.

"Go," Max said with a growl.

Scott scrambled around the next collapsed tent, staying low to the ground, ignoring his screaming ankle. Again, he looked back as Max swayed, his right arm flinging out. Blood exploding from his arm.

Then realigning and firing back. One against twenty?

It's no use. We're going to die.

Inexplicably, soldiers dropped. One. Two. Five.

Max must've noticed too because he hesitated, lifting his gaze from his defensive position to gauge what was happening.

More soldiers went down.

His brother reengaged, firing.

A blur of black dove at Max. Tackled him. His brother went down.

CHAPTER 33

arget acquired."

"Nice and easy, gentlemen" Griffin said, sidestepping, weapon to his cheek as he rushed forward, flanked by the Kid and Aladdin.

The compound looked like a day in Fallujah. *Obscene.* Griffin honed his focus on this battle. On finding Max. Following the muzzle of his weapon, he traced a line along the only building that had walls still standing—*half* standing. Window. Door. Roof.

"Clear." He plunged on, aware of his team as they spread out to cover more ground, take down more tangos.

A soldier came around the corner. When he turned and saw them, his eyes bulged.

Griffin coldcocked him. A chopper circled overhead, rounds pelting the ground, forcing the enemy to keep their heads down. Nightshade moved on, unfazed with the shooting, knowing Midas wouldn't hit one of their own. But what whiplashed Griffin's mind was Kazi on that chopper. Leaving her wasn't an option after Aladdin informed him she'd been fishing around websites for Carrick Burgess. Then the coded communiqué.

He shook off the thought as he moved over the unconscious soldier. Advanced.

"Target down," Colton's smooth voice sailed through the coms.

"Cowboy," the Kid said. "Trouble in blue two. Tango on Frogman."

"Tango in blue two, copy." Colton's voice soothed the tension knotted at the base of Griffin's neck as he rounded a corner. The scene before him sped adrenaline through his veins yet stopped him cold.

At first a tangle of bodies. Then it stilled. A soldier knelt over Frogman, who raised his hands as the man pointed a gun at him. Just as the thought crossed Griffin's mind that Cowboy needed to end that fight, the tango pitched forward.

Max's knee snapped up, and he pushed the man over his head. Motionless, Max eyed him, squinted. "Legend?" The hitch in his voice said Max didn't believe his eyes. But then he slumped against the ground, his chest heaving, and gave a hearty half laugh.

"Clear," the Kid said through the coms, announcing the area Griffin and he worked was secure.

As Max peeled himself off the hard earth, Griffin grinned and stalked toward Nightshade's team leader. "Just like a SEAL, lying around while the Marines do all the work."

Body rigid, Max whipped his weapon toward Griffin.

"Hold up."

Max fired. In the fraction of a second it took the bullet to travel between Max's muzzle and the air around Griffin, he smelled the cordite. Saw Max's smirk. And heard the impact behind him. *Thwump.*

Griffin jerked. A man lay on the ground, a machete clattering from his grip. He looked back at Max.

"That's right." Max swiped an arm over his face, smearing blood, sweat, and dirt across his cheek. "A SEAL just saved your sorry, whining butt."

He gripped Max's hand and pulled him into a hug, the relief sweet and powerful that they were back together. "Good to see you're alive and kicking." He gave his face a friendly smack. "We had our doubts." Into his coms, Griffin radioed their situation and called for sitreps from the others.

"So did I." Max gulped the dusty air and looked around. "The team—they're all here?"

"Midas is covering us on the chopper—he got messed up bad in Venezuela, but he's here. We're not sure about Squirt."

"Here." Max stabbed a finger down. "Sent him to recon a mine a day's hike from here."

"Nkooye mine."

Dark eyes appraised him. "How do you know that?" Suddenly Max's face tightened. He spun around, his boots crunching on the debris. "Scott!"

"Blue three secure," Aladdin said.

Again, Griffin spoke into his mic as he trailed Max around the corner. "Regroup in blue two."

"Area secure. Coming in." Cowboy's suppressive fire had been instrumental in taking back the compound. They'd hoofed it a klick to the compound, met with mild engagement, then flooded into the compound right behind the tangos.

As he jogged behind Frogman, Griffin saw a woman appear, sprigs of curls dancing around her face in the hot wind.

"Where's Scott?"

She held back her hair with the crook of her elbow, but what slowed Griffin was her bloodied hands. She bobbed her head toward the tent she held partially open. "In here. Took some lead in the neck."

Griffin hesitated. That kind of wound could drain a man in minutes. And who was Scott?

Max pushed into the tent.

The acrid stench of blood and feces assaulted Griffin as he stepped out of the Ugandan sun. He waited at the edge as Max went to a metal table surrounded by netting. Blood covered the man's upper torso. What looked like a freshly stitched wound in the shoulder caught Griffin's attention. That and the tattoo. Special ops? Who was this man?

"Hey." Max bent over the man. "Action junkie."

The man coughed. "I'm a Jacobs."

Max snickered.

Wait. Hold up. The man was a Jacobs? That meant—

"Oh, for pity's sake," the woman said as she worked on him. "Stop trying to take so many souvenirs home. Besides, I think this may just be a graze."

Griffin didn't miss the look Max and the woman shared. Around them, villagers righted poles, stretched canvas taut between them, laid out new medical utensils, plopped dirtied ones in vats. A lanky—no, bone-thin—woman skirted past Griffin with a bowl of bloody water. He stepped aside, pulling his nose to avoid the strong smell.

"Get well," Max said. "I've got work to do." As Max strolled toward Griffin, he shook his head. "We have a lot to catch up on, but there's no time." He grabbed some sterile bandages and wiped a bloody knot on his temple. "Do you. . . ?" He stared at the soiled cotton. "I should. . ." Outside, Max squinted up at him. "My wife."

Griffin gave a knowing smile. "Safe house. The wives and children are under the protection of Mossad agents."

Visible, tangible relief flooded through Max. He hung his head, let out a gargled laugh, then shook his head. "When her phone went dead. . . Imagined the worse."

"When you went MIA, so did we. Where you been, man?" Together, they stepped into the open. Blinding Ugandan sun beat down on them. Middle of February and home, they'd be suffering through the last cold snap, but here the heat proved merciless. Sweat sped down his spine and temples.

"Anywhere eyes couldn't find me. Mountains, rivers, Australia—"

"Squirt."

Max nodded. "Hid out in the wilds of Australia." He let out a long breath. "Let's clean up and see what we've got to work with. Take care of the people first, then we'll get our game on." He frowned, his gaze locked on something behind Griffin, and drew his weapon around in front of him. "Know him?"

Griffin glanced back. "No, but the Old Man does."

He eased the weapon down, still monitoring the man's movements. "He's got experience."

"Came in with Midas."

"Why's he here?"

"Don't know. Old Man went all cryptic when I asked. The Latino said he has a score to settle."

"With?"

"The man who took us down."

Max's attention snapped to Griffin, a mixture of rage and vengeance enlivening his near-black eyes. "Who is it?"

The Kid appeared beside them. "My father."

Evening snuck in, the sky darkening. A howl in the distance made Kazi pause and gaze at the crimson streaks amid ribbons of clouds. She moved lightly, giving care to her sprained ankle, as she made her way to a secluded part of the compound. Four feet wide and roughly fifteen to twenty feet long, the narrow corridor was perfect. No doors. Darkness. Solitude.

Kazi glided to the end, turned, and swung her leg out. Arms up, wrists bent, she closed her eyes, took two deep, cleansing breaths, then opened her eyes. After a short sprint—ignoring the slight pain in her ankle—she vaulted into the air. She started with an aerial, then a round off into a back-handspring.

Fire spiked through her foot and ankle.

She hissed and hopped on her good foot to alleviate the pain. But she quickly refocused and repeated the move, exhilarated as her body flew through the air. Free. Defying gravity. Breaking laws.

With an audible hum of electricity, light snapped through the compound. A round of huzzahs echoed through the night, no doubt congratulating Marshall, who'd been working the last four hours to restore power. She stilled, searching her surroundings to make sure she hadn't been discovered or exposed.

A dark, round face peered from one alley.

Kazi's heart sped, but she evened out her reaction. Collected herself as a girl of maybe ten or twelve eased into the open. Then, to her surprise, the girl did a cartwheel. A very clumsy, untrained one. But it made Kazi smile. She clapped, bringing a brightness to the girl's face.

She showed her how to keep her legs straight, how to posture before the move.

They practiced a few more, and as the minutes clicked by, a small group of children gathered in the narrow space. On her knees, Kazi helped each child through a turn, guiding, instructing, and laughing.

Then two of the younger children took Kazi by the hand, led her to the mouth of the alley, and pointed to the stretch of sandy space. They wanted her to perform. Glancing around, she made sure only children were watching. Then with a giggle, she nodded. Cheers erupted.

Right leg out and bent, toe touching the ground, she raised her hands. And repeated the routine she'd done earlier, but this time added a double aerial at the end. Though her ankle ached, she determined to land as evenly as possible. She wobbled, caught her balance, then struck her pose. With the children, she laughed, relishing the free-spiritedness that she'd had to harness and suffocate as Carrick's operative.

The realization pressed down on her, pulling the smile from her face.

A child raced into the alley, shouted something in their native tongue, then vanished back down the way he'd come. And with him went every child. Curiosity pulled Kazi out of the alley and in the direction they'd vanished. Shrouded by the low-slung shadows of the buildings and the darkening night, she slowed as the compound opened up before her. Beneath emergency lighting, Griffin, the Kid, Aladdin, and Max engaged in a game of football with several older children.

Griffin, still geared up with his tactical vest—sans weapon—palmed the ball, shouting, "Go!" He waved the young boy of twelve or thirteen farther down. Apparently satisfied with the distance, he threw the ball.

The boy leapt up and snagged the ball from the air. A dozen feet more earned him screams and shouts.

"Oorah," Griffin's voice boomed over the cheers.

Max and the Kid huddled near the makeshift hospital while Griffin congratulated the boy who'd made the touchdown. Arm around him, Griffin spoke as they made their way back toward their side. Something. . .something about him registered with her. What was different? What made Griffin stand out? How was he able to do what he did—fight for freedom, protect women and children with lethal force if necessary—and still be able to laugh and smile? He and the boy drew closer to her.

Afraid to draw his attention, Kazi slipped back into the shadows.

Griffin locked on her. He straightened, then glanced back to Max. "Be right back."

Oh no. Kazi spun and hurried back down the alley.

"Kazi, hold up."

She kept moving.

"We need to talk."

Somehow, his words snapped her spine back into place. She glared over her shoulder at him—which unbalanced her. And her stomach squeezed when she met his eyes.

In his gear, weapon retrieved and dangling down the front of him, Griffin was formidable. And handsome.

No. She had a mission. Made a decision. In a few hours, how she felt wouldn't matter. "We tried that once. You told me to stay out of your business." Her heart hammered. "That I don't know you like that."

"This isn't about us."

Kazi slowed, grief clutching her throat. She hated herself for actually thinking he'd come after her. . .for *her*. Not because of a mission or a plan. But because it was her. But Kazi had learned long ago—*nobody will rescue me.*

"I know what you're planning."

She flashed her eyes at him. "No. You don't. You might wish you did or you might want me to believe that, but I know better."

His jaw muscle rippled.

"You forget, Griffin. I worked with Aladdin once before. He's limited. He's quick on his feet and has an uncanny ability to sniff out trouble, but his problem is accuracy."

"Was."

Kazi frowned.

"His problem *was* accuracy." Hands on his hips, Griffin stared her down. "Not anymore."

Her stomach squirmed. No way they decoded her message already. Impossible.

"What's your game plan, Kazi?"

So he *didn't* know. And he really didn't want the honest truth. He wanted her to do what he needed her to do. "To stay out of your business." Why did those words scald her throat?

He pushed into her personal space, eating up every salvageable cell of oxygen. "Don't get slick with me, Baby Girl." He spread his arms. "A'right. I don't know what your plan is. But I do know—see it in your eyes—that you're planning to jump ship."

Don't swallow. Don't react.

"So, ditch the mind games. Let's play it straight."

He had it all wrong. But she couldn't tell him. "Me? I'm the one using mind games? What are you doing right this instant, cornering me, getting in my face and space?"

Griffin eased back. Drew up his chin. "You're avoiding, turning the discussion back on me. I thought more of you, Kazi."

Sucker punch to the chest. "Yeah? Well, your mistake."

He caught her arm, ferocity in his words and face. "No. I'm right. You don't have to do this—you don't *want* to do this."

How did he know that?

He bent toward her, his face in hers. "You don't have do this. You have a choice—"

"Again, your mistake." She swung her arm up and around, freeing herself. "You'll never get it, so quit trying." She pushed herself away from him, a strange burning in her eyes.

"I told you I'd help you get rid of Carrick. And I believe with all my heart, God is going to help me fulfill that promise. How, I don't know. But it will happen. I promise, Baby Girl. Just don't do this now. Stay with me. I have to see this through with the team, but when we're done"—again he moved into her space—"me and you. We'll work this out."

Kazi shook her head with a sigh.

Sincerity smoothed out his angular lines. "Let me help you."

A harebrained fantasy had her leaping into his arms, kissing him, thanking him for being a hero in her life.

Heroes end up dead. Just like everyone else—only a whole lot quicker. And if she didn't do this thing, if she didn't sever things right now, his "quicker" would be within the next twenty-four hours because Carrick already knew her location.

CHAPTER 34

Green World Health Clinic Compound,
Uganda

Gather up." Max waved to the men, never in his life so glad to have everyone under one roof. The only thing that could make this perfect, give him more assurance, was seeing his family, verifying they were alive and well. Hearing Sydney's voice.

Already at the table, Midas stared blankly at the computer screen in front of him. Sweat beaded on his brow and lip. Was that discoloration in his face on the monitor, or was he really that bad? He shifted—tensed, then let out a labored breath.

"Where's Legend?" the Kid asked.

"Recon. He'll be here." Max adjusted his position so he could see the others as they dropped into chairs around the planks from a picnic table. "Squirt and his team are en route."

Cowboy swung a chair around, straddled it, then folded his arms over the top. "Glad to have you back."

"Ditto." Max nodded. "Catch me up. What do you know?"

"Evidence points to the Kid's father being behind all this."

Max frowned, staring at the youngest member of the team. "Yeah, you said that earlier. Why?"

The mischief and lightheartedness that had normally parked itself in the Kid's bearing was gone. In its place, worry. Shame. Confusion. Anger. "When we were attacked at the Shack, I woke up in what I thought was a hospital. Turned out to be my father's house." The snarl in his words couldn't be missed, giving Max pause for concern. Was the Kid's assessment tainted by the history of bad blood between him and his father? "He was drugging me to keep me there, feeding me lies about all of you."

Max eyed the Kid's fisted hands and saw so much of himself reflected in the demeanor.

"The Old Man figured that out and sent in an angel to rescue me—"

"Squirt's sister," Cowboy interjected.

What would Squirt think of the Kid calling his sister an angel?

"When we escaped, I cleared out my dad's safe."

Max scowled. "Stealing?"

"Dude, I don't need his money." His lip curled. "I was looking for proof. He was lying to me, drugging me—he'd never been so direct in his disapproval of my choices. I wanted to know what was up."

"And?"

"He had copies of the photographs your wife got in the Philippines." The Kid went on to explain how he wasn't in any of the images, then how the team had tracked down his father's Green World charity and realized it had connections in several locations where the team had intervened.

"So, we were stepping on his toes."

The Kid snorted. "You were stepping on his *money*."

"Your father is Senator Vaughn?" Scott asked.

The Kid nodded, clearly not happy.

Scott pursed his lips as he looked up at Max.

"What?" the Kid asked.

"The mine you're all talking about?" Scott rose from his spot. "It's not a diamond mine."

"We figured that much out," the Kid said.

"He's mining yellowcake."

Cowboy whistled. "How has he hidden this from the UN and the Ugandan government?"

"Most likely paid the officials to look the other way. Things were going fine for your father till last week." Scott eyed Max, who nodded. "One of the men I've rehabilitated stumbled into the *wrong* tunnel in the mine. It scared him, so he brought me to the mine to show me. We were seen by the senator."

The Latino poked a finger in the air. "That's why they've been bombing this—trying to kill you?"

"And Marie."

"Who's Marie?"

"My wife."

Max flinched. "You're married?"

"He chose his boys over me," the soft voice from the back drew the team around.

Max tried to see in the darkened area but couldn't till she came closer.

His brother stood beside him. "She's right. I was so convicted by what I saw with the young men forced to serve in the Lord's Resistance Army that I couldn't sleep at night."

"So, he went off to save them, to rehabilitate them. Leaving me here."

"I don't mean to be rude," the Kid said, looking at Scott. "But who are you, dude? Why are we worried about you?"

"I'm nobody," Scott said. "But the people of this country need someone to step in and turn away the hand of greed and power trying to seize it."

Max stood taller, drawing in a breath. Knowing what he had to say. "We care about Scott and this mission because it's what we do— we're Nightshade." He clapped a hand on the guy's shoulder. "And he's my brother."

Shock rippled through the room, and Max felt the weight of his guilt.

Cowboy came up out of his chair. "Wanna explain why you told us you had no family?"

"Because he didn't." Scott sighed. "We have the same father, but we've never been family, never lived in the same house. He hasn't seen me since he graduated from the Naval Academy."

"Look," Max said, trying to pull the conversation back to the mission. To the nightmare. "This mission seems to be pulling all the ghosts from our past. But it's also trying to dismantle us. We need a plan in place."

"The Old Man wants the senator in custody. A confession would help," Cowboy said.

The thought of how they'd get that rankled Max. They interdicted. "We don't do interrogations."

"I do." Though soft, the voice contained a warning.

Max looked at the Latino man. "I don't know you."

A slow, calculating nod.

"No," Max said. "You don't understand. You're not on my team. This is our mission. You won't touch anyone."

He thumbed over his shoulder. "Too late. I killed about a half dozen soldiers."

"I will *not* authorize use of force like that. We don't beat people to get our way."

"It's a fine line."

"No."

The man stood.

Max met him.

"No," Canyon, who hadn't spoken till then, ground out. On trembling arms, he pushed up. Through heavily hooded eyes, he stared at them.

Concern stopped Max when he saw how white Canyon had gone. "Midas—what's wrong?"

Marie was at his side, touching his arm. "How long have you been like this?"

Midas shifted to Max as Marie placed a hand to his forehead. "Vaughn slit his throat. Navas. . ."

"It's okay, Midas. No need for them to know," the man said.

"He's burning up," she said. "How long?"

Pushing her hand away, Midas weaved.

Cowboy lunged toward him.

"No," Midas growled.

Cowboy pulled up short, hovering.

Steadying himself, sweat dripping from his longer-than-usual hair, Canyon breathed—swayed. "I'm staying. With. . .the. . .team."

Max fisted his hand, seeing how every word seemed a complete labor.

"To. . .the end. I'm not—" Midas's face screwed tight. Veins bulged at his temples as he groaned, eyes shut, mouth clenched white. He toppled forward.

Cowboy and the Kid caught him.

Marie started for the side exit. "Get him on my table—*stat*!"

"How's Midas?"

"In surgery." Max dumped water into his mouth as they waited in the tent.

Griffin sighed as he leaned against the table. "What happened?"

"Tear in his kidney. Slow internal bleed."

Griffin stilled, his frustration over Kazi momentarily displaced. "He gonna make it?"

"Don't know." Max shook his head. "He knew—*knew* he needed

a doctor. But he wouldn't go, insisted on fighting. The whole time, he knew he was bleeding and just kept. . .going."

The agony in Max's face both warmed and warned Griffin. Warmed him because of the concern the team leader showed for Midas, but warned Griffin because there was something greater working through Max's intense mind.

"You okay?"

"No." Max paced. "Yeah. I don't have time for this. We need to"—he jerked toward Griffin—"what'd you find out from her?"

"Nothing."

Aladdin joined them. "She denied it?"

"No," Griffin growled. "Fool woman. She knows I know. But she won't budge."

Max's dark eyes darted over the floor as he considered the information. He peered up at Aladdin through dark eyebrows. "What do you know about her?"

"She's one of the best." Aladdin sniggered. "I've never seen anyone so effective. Our paths crossed years ago. I was in an op—apparently, someone sent her in for the same reason. I got caught, thought I was a goner, but she yanked me. Said she'd used my arrest to complete the mission but felt bad for setting me up."

"Setting you up?"

Aladdin shrugged. "She sat there and recounted every piece of data I'd used to put together my mission. She knew because she had planted about 70 percent of it to give herself cover."

Pacing, Max said nothing.

"We have to stop her," Griffin said.

Arms folded and hands tucked under his arms, Max kept walking. "You afraid she'll betray us?"

Rubbing his hand over his head, Griffin struggled for the right words to match what was happening inside him. "I. . .I don't know."

Max raised his eyebrows as he stopped in front of him. "That's new."

Heat crept into his cheeks. "What I *know* is that she looks out for number one, and that's herself."

"Not true."

Griffin spun toward the assassin.

Unfazed by the dirty look Griffin shot him, Aladdin sat on the planks, his feet on a chair. "Her priority is to the mission. Always." He opened his hands and motioned to the others gathered around. "Much like us."

"Don't think you know her like that." What was wrong with his heart? Its rhythm jumped and plummeted. "She has a handler who has a death grip on her neck. She's trying to get free of him. *That* is her priority."

"Not if she thinks you might get hurt."

Griffin whirled on the assassin. Why was it so hard to breathe?

"Whoa!" Max jumped in front of Griffin. "Step off, Legend."

"You don't know nothin', assassin."

"I know she's missed several opportunities to bug out already." Aladdin shook his head. "I sat there wondering why she hadn't. Had she been sent or planted? But that didn't add up, and she wasn't sending information back. Then what was keeping her with us?" Aladdin's blue-green eyes seemed to sparkle. "It's you, Legend. She watches you, gauges your moves, waits for you to execute."

"You're out of your fool mind."

"What happened on the rooftop the other night?"

The Kid hooted at the same time Max repeated his warning for Griffin to stand down.

"I don't know what you're talking about." Griffin turned away, spotted a tray of food, and grabbed a plate.

"Legend."

No way he'd turn around and let them see his red face.

"What just happened?" Max asked.

The Kid laughed. "Yeah, explain why your fist isn't embedded in Aladdin's face right now."

"Why isn't she with Sydney and the others?" Max asked.

"I told you," Griffin said, turning around. "She was going to run back to Carrick. I had to make sure she couldn't."

"So," Aladdin said. "You thought being here with us, a team of six men focused on saving villagers and stopping a crazed senator, would be better and provide more security than seven Mossad agents whose only focus is protecting the women and children?"

Why did it sound so stupid and unreasonable now? He'd been determined not to let her out of his sight.

Light shifted and flickered. Griffin glanced back as Squirt and five men trudged into the tent, dripping with sweat and exhaustion. They smelled of hot sand and body odor.

Max hurried to the Aussies. "Report." Nightshade vacated the chairs, allowing the exhausted men to sit, and grabbed water bottles for them.

"Just like Callaghan said. The mine's there. They're exporting the ore on trucks to an airport, best we can tell. The senator's there with his entourage. They're staying in the nearby city but spending a *lot* of time at the mine." Squirt pulled off his hat, his dark blond hair damp. "We were about to pull out when a chopper arrived."

"Military?"

"Negative. Private." He downed a bottle of water in a breath. "A Brit." He held out a handheld device.

Max glanced at it, then passed it to Cowboy.

"That's him—that's the man who held us in London."

"What you've done, Legend," Max said, "is put her within arm's reach of that man."

As if invisible hands pushed him down, Griffin fell into a chair. What had he done? Tried to control things, tried to save face, not show his hands or his heart. Control his temper. Control his feelings. Control information about his past.

And in doing so, he may have lost the one woman he'd ever loved. *Loved.*

Head in his hands, he propped his elbows on his knees.

"Aladdin, Kid," Max said, "find her. Bring her in."

"Legend, talk to me," Cowboy said from beside him. "To the team."

Stretching his hands, he tried to work through the tension, the building anger. "All my life. . ." The torrent rose, threatening to overcome him. "I've worked—hard—to be in control of myself, know what I'm sayin'? To protect my name, my honor. In the last six months, everything has been ripped from me, but I just shoved aside the feelings, the anger, the emptiness." She was right—she'd asked if he was ignoring it. "I can't lose her. She gets up under my skin something bad, but I need her. I won't let anything happen. Won't let that man hurt her again. Aladdin figured out she was going to run, so I wanted her where I could keep an eye on her."

There was an entire cesspool of ignored feelings, hurts, broken dreams. What would the team think of him when they found out the things he had hidden for months, years, decades?

Flap!

"She's gone!" The Kid panted, gripping his knees.

Griffin shoved to his feet.

Aladdin gulped. "The only working vehicle is gone, too."

CHAPTER 35

If it looks like a potato, smells like a potato. . .

"Then it is a potato," Marshall muttered as he stared down at the lumpy breakfast prepared for the team as they waited for supplies and the go-ahead from the Old Man. But the potato saying from his grandmother wasn't about the foodstuff.

"Eh? What's that?"

Marshall looked up at Squirt, who sat across the table with him and the others, waiting for Max to get final go-ahead and the supply drop the Old Man had ordered, which would come via a parachute drop from a DC10. "Nothing." He scratched the side of his face. "It doesn't add up."

"What?"

"The day of the attack. . ." Marshall looked at Cowboy. "That was the 5th of January, right?"

"Yeah, so?"

"My dad was in Paris meeting with the French foreign minister."

"I repeat, so?"

"Just. . ." Marshall shrugged. Why did he want to believe his father was innocent? The man had screwed with his head, drugged him. Those were facts he couldn't deny. It just seemed over the top for his father. He'd never been so direct, so "in your face." "Why would he keep those pictures?"

"Collateral," Squirt said.

"Blackmail." Cowboy moved to the food station and set down his cup.

"Against who?" Marshall hated the way his voice cracked as if he were just now going through puberty.

Cowboy shrugged. "Whoever he hired to carry out the hit."

Okay, he'd give them that one, even though it just seemed too. . .stupid for his father. The man had tracked down the team. He'd organized multimillion-dollar charities. Served on too many boards.

Cowboy eased onto the bench and leaned in. "Marshall, you having seconds thoughts about going after your dad?"

"No." But what if something went wrong? Or what if *they* were wrong?

"That's a really long answer for a two-letter word."

"Huh?"

"Your hesitation afterward says you aren't sure."

"I'm going crazy with the what-ifs, ya know?"

"He drugged you and held you at your home, concealed your location, and now he's at the mine," Cowboy said. "Aussies confirmed that. Those are facts. Your own research showed he's neck-deep in activities in this area."

"Yeah."

"And we aren't going in to kill him." Kind, compassionate eyes held his. "That's not the plan."

"Not ours." Marshall skated a peek in Navas's direction. "But we aren't the only ones with a beef against him."

"Even though we're taking him down, we'll also protect him to make sure justice is served," Cowboy said, assurance thick and deep in his voice.

"Well. . .who's this Carrick guy? What do we know? I mean, he's there, with my dad. Why? What does he want? That's some coincidence that he is connected to the girl and shows up with my dad, right? Don't you think?"

"No coincidence," Cowboy said. "I think he figured out there was something big happening with Griffin and me, so he hunted down the cash flow and illegal activity like a bloodhound. And he's not someone we can control. He's more a nuisance. It's your dad we're after."

Marshall scrubbed his fingers over his hair. "I know." He pulled himself closer to the makeshift table. "Dude, I don't know why I'm second-guessing. He's made my whole life miserable. He attacked the team."

"Speculation."

"Half spec—the drugging me is fact, and I'm part of the team."

Amusement twinkled in Cowboy's eyes. "You done good work,

Kid. Getting free, getting the women to Cyprus." He nodded. "Well done."

A feather could've knocked Marshall over as he stared at the big guy he'd admired since day one. "Yeah, but try telling that to Frogman."

"Oh, he knows." Cowboy puckered his chin. "He don't miss a thing."

Squirt backhanded his arm. "Oy."

Marshall looked at him.

"What's this I 'ear about you calling my sister an angel?"

Were the tips of his ears red? Marshall could feel the heat creeping through his face. "The Old Man sent her in to play nurse to me."

Squirt's face darkened.

"Oh." His blood chugged through his veins. "Not what I meant, dude. She has nursing skills. She could get me *un*drugged." He groaned, knowing he was messing this up royally. He wanted Squirt's approval for dating Narelle. "Dude, what can I say? I went out with her three or four times and really enjoyed getting to know her—on a *non*physical level. Then we had this incredible journey getting the wives back to the team. She was amazing. Narelle—"

"Narelle?" Squirt growled. "She let you call her that?"

Marshall hesitated.

Squirt cursed under his breath, then stabbed a finger at him. "You hurt her, and I'll wrap your legs around your neck and beat the living daylights out of you."

Marshall couldn't help but laugh. "Dude." He sniggered more. "Am I supposed to be scared?"

Punching to his feet, Squirt shouted. "I'll show you—"

Max appeared in the door. "Supplies incoming! Let's gear up!"

It'd been nearly seven long months since he'd been on a mission with the team. Now, aboard the chopper, heading to the mine where they had authorization to snatch and grab Warren Vaughn and seize anything that enabled the miners to harvest the yellowcake, Griffin stared out the open door of the chopper. Early morning light stretched across the desert landscape, touching the scattered dots of green with an almost ethereal glow as sunlight stroked them. Besides a sparse tree or a random bamboo and thatched-roof hut, brown bathed the landscape in anonymity.

It should feel good getting back into the action. Going after the bad guys. He'd thrived on this once. And while he moved seamlessly with the men aboard, something had changed in him.

Kazi.

Head against the hull of the chopper, Griffin closed his eyes. She'd left, run back to the man who held entirely too much power over her mind and heart. Griffin had longed to believe what Aladdin had said, that Kazi stuck around because of him. *So much for that.*

He hadn't been able to save his mama. Now the same thing would happen to Kazi.

But wasn't that just like her? She saw herself as impervious, able to slip in and out of situations without notice or getting caught. And she was right. She'd done it several times in the short time he knew her. She was like a mouse, scurrying from one hole to another. Man, she was good. He'd underestimated her in that regard. There wasn't anything she couldn't do.

"I just can't do it, Griffin."

Even now he could feel the soft tickle of those words against his ears. Domestic stuff intimidated her, frightened her. That's what it was about. Probably not the type to settle down.

But she wanted to try. He remembered the way she stiffened like cardboard as Sydney tried to ingratiate her to the circle of Nightshade women. She'd looked at Griffin, as if gauging whether he was worth the effort. And he had to admit, it did his heart good to see her with them. To see a piece of the puzzle of his life coming together.

But it wasn't. Kazi told him she couldn't do it, couldn't fit in.

But she wanted to.

More than anything, he wanted her to. How they'd make things work, he didn't know. Couldn't fathom. She was an operative. He was black ops. Always gone.

Maybe they could find a way. Like in the movies, rendezvous in exotic places around the globe. *You reaching with that one, Riddell.*

He swiped a hand over his face, his heart and thoughts tangled around an impossible woman. Regardless of what the future held— more like, didn't hold—for them, one thing was surefire: He'd get her back from Carrick. Alive. Just so she had the freedom to choose the next path for her life.

And maybe he could figure out a way to find out if the man killed her family.

Why was it he realized too late what she meant to him? Didn't make sense. She was white, spunky, and short. Didn't fit his ideal woman at all. But everything about her was. . .perfect.

"*. . .my brother sold me into prostitution to pay off the family debt.*" Those words had haunted him. But when she spoke them, he'd been so hung up on his own problems, his own fear of her getting inside his head and seeing the ugly, that he hadn't even heard her.

No wonder Baby Girl had trust issues. He'd kill that brother if he got close enough. Did that to Kazi, ripped her innocence from her for money.

Her brother, Carrick. . .even if they tried to make things work out between them, would she ever really trust him? Really give herself—her mind and heart—to him? Griffin understood keeping people out to protect the past. He'd done it himself. Hadn't even told the team about his parents or Dante.

Things had to change. Couldn't go on like this. But where did he start? Things were too insane right now.

"*May you never be taller than you are when you're on your knees.*" Madyar's favorite phrase spiraled through his thoughts. Right. Prayer.

Jesus, I've been blinded by my fears. Scared to let her in. Scared she'd think less of me. I want a chance. . .another chance to let her in. Love her and protect her. I believe You put that in me. Help me. Please.

The helo rose and dipped as they traced the landscape, staying under the radar to prevent those at the mine from getting a warning in time to either fire up some antiaircraft weaponry or, worse—escape.

And now she was back with the man he'd promised to protect her from.

But she willingly went back there. The thought stabbed him, his conscience, and made him second-guess everything.

God, I don't know what to do with that. It was her choice.

Trust.

Griffin snorted and lifted his head from the hull. Trust. Right. She went back to the man. By all appearances, she'd gone back to betray the team.

His pulse slipped into a lower gear. What would the guys do if she betrayed them? If she was there, at the mine, with Carrick—she'd be deemed an enemy combatant.

He jerked forward, elbows on his knees. No, he would *not* let that happen.

But what if it came down to her or the team, the mission?

The thought paralyzed him. Aggravated him that he'd even hesitate over whom to be loyal to. Always—*always* his loyalty was to the mission and his boys. But now the thought of Kazi being at the business end of Frogman's muzzle. Or in the crosshairs of Cowboy's scope.

Betray the team?

No. He couldn't. Wouldn't.

Take her down?

He. . . *Jesus, don't let it come to that.*

"ETA in two," Max's voice rang clearly through the coms, signaling the hour of reckoning.

"Remember, we need the senator alive," Scott said.

"Everyone else is a combatant." Max nodded. "Going silent."

CHAPTER 36

Nkooye Green World Mine, Uganda

Senator Vaughn," Carrick said as he shook the man's hand. "I look forward to talking with you more in the future."

Fit and trim with salt-and-pepper hair, Senator Vaughn offered a faint smile. "Of course." He glanced between Carrick and the beauty of a woman beside him. Kazimiera. She'd shown up shortly before dawn in a dilapidated jalopy. "If you'll excuse me. . ." Vaughn strode up the steps into the trailer and opened the door.

The same stale air Carrick detested sailed out as the man entered.

"You have no idea what you're doing," Kazi said with gritted teeth.

He touched two fingers beneath her chin. "Speak clearly, love. Anger doesn't become you."

She slapped away his hand. "Don't touch me."

With the sun bathing her white-blond hair and an attractive sheen of sweat covering her face, she seemed to glow. "Now, love. Have you forgotten *you* came back to me?"

"You can't handle these men, Carrick. I saw them—they eliminated every threat you sent." Defiance glinted too prettily on her small features. "You saw how skilled two of them were—and they escaped from you. Now there are six or seven of them. And they're coming."

"Do you really think I'm not prepared?"

She drew back, her green eyes bouncing over his face.

He chuckled. "That's right, love. I know about these men." He pointed toward the trailer. "I made a few calls. If they try to come, they'll be shot out of the sky."

Her mouth opened. Not for some pithy remark like she was

known for, but that subtle sign of fear.

Carrick memorized the moment. "It's been a few years since I took you by surprise." He traced her face.

She smacked his hand.

He gripped her wrist hard. Pinched her face and yanked her up to himself. "Did you really think a man like him would want you, the scraps from my table?" He squeezed harder. "You forget yourself, Kazimiera. I *own* you."

Rage burned in those beautiful eyes. It could've been so different. If she'd let it.

"I will never let you go. And I will kill anyone who tries to take you from me. *Especially* the big black man you seem to have set your fancy on." He exhaled, amazed at the strength in those words. "He's distracting you. That needs to be remedied." He shoved her back and started for his private chopper.

"He doesn't care about me."

"The pout in your words is disappointing, love. It tells me you'd do something stupid if he showed up." Carrick motioned to the guards flanking him. "Secure her."

Kazi's stance stiffened, her arms drawn up to her sides.

"Fight me, and I promise—you'll watch as I kill him."

Her arms lowered ever so slightly. But enough. He had her. "You'll kill him regardless of what I do."

Carrick smiled.

A shout sailed on the hot air. "Chopper!"

Downwash from the rotors whipped the dry earth into a frenzy. Sand peppered his face, and once again, Griffin was grateful for the sunglasses that shielded his eyes. He hopped from the jump seat of the Black Hawk. On a knee, he scoped the perimeter as the team of ten filed out of the chopper. A pat on his shoulder sent him to his nine, following his team, but even as he moved he continued to sweep his weapon back and forth searching for unfriendlies.

According to the mission briefing, the trailer he was heading toward was an office. The mine he could see to his two o'clock. And to his three and five stood a community of tents. The Aussies were headed that way to contain and protect the villagers. A dozen paces and he noted Frogman, Max's brother, and Aladdin streak toward the mine.

Griffin flanked to the side to come around the south side of the trailer with the Kid. It gave him comfort knowing Cowboy was out there, sitting atop an old safari bus less than a mile out with a sniper rifle so he could take a bead on anyone who got hostile.

"Entering mine," Squirt said as he took point.

"Copy," Griffin said. "Approaching trailer." The methodical recitation was for the benefit of the Old Man, who was monitoring via live-feed satellite.

Griffin's boot hit the first step of the rickety temporary stair and rail platform bumped up against the trailer. He skipped the second and drew himself to the side of the half-glass door. A holey curtain hung over the glass on the inside. Griffin pulled out his baton as the Kid flanked the other side of the door, M4 at the ready. With a firm nod, he indicated his readiness.

Throwing his weight behind the stick, he rammed it into the glass. Griffin tossed in a flash-bang. "Flash out!"

Clink. Clink. Boom!

White flashed through the day.

The Kid took a step back, lifted his leg, and rammed the heel of his boot against the spot just above the knob.

The door flung backward.

The Kid rushed in, tense. Ready. His face to his weapon as he banked left.

"Entering trailer," Griffin said as he rushed into the smoke-filled room. He crisscrossed with the Kid and went right then buttonhooked. With a nod to continue, Griffin moved along the south wall and curved to the left toward another door. This one open. Pulse booming, he bobbed in taking a split-second recon. Bathroom.

"Clear." Swiftly, he traced the wall around until he was exactly opposite the point of entry where yet another door waited. His gaze kicked to the Kid, who kept his back near the wall to cover his six, his weapon trained on the new entry. Ajar.

With a breath, he nudged it open and tucked himself inside. A split-second recon revealed to his three a desk against the east wall with a chair and filing cabinet. He jerked back to the door, the perfect place to hide behind. He sidestepped, his weapon stuffed comfortably into his shoulder. Couldn't help but wonder which door Kazi would hide behind.

Kazi Faron, come on down. You're the next contestant on the Price on Your Head.

He bobbed and found the corner empty. "Clear." He rushed back out, and the Kid moved to a small hall where a plaque marked a closet. They cleared that, which inevitably led them to the last door.

Flanking the door, he and the Kid looked at each other. The Kid blew out a breath. Griffin signaled his readiness. Fingers on the handle, the Kid mouthed, *Three. . .two. . .*

Griffin aligned his sights not on the door but on a spot straight through it. Ready.

The Kid flicked it open.

Griffin hurried in to the left, again crossing over the Kid who went right. Steps softened beneath the thick rug that covered most of the fifteen-by-twenty room. He slipped around the thick leather sofa on the east-facing wall, checked the corner where a lamp hovered, around an ornate glass coffee table, then along the south wall and behind the desk. In the corner, he met the Kid's gaze.

"Clear," Griffin said, the tension sliding out of him. "Not here."

"But he was." The Kid pointed to the coffee table where three glasses with ice and an amber liquid sat, sweating. "That's my dad's." He rushed to a chair and toed a black monogrammed briefcase. The Kid cursed. "He's here." Kicked the chair. "He's *here*."

Lord help the senator, because if one of the team didn't take care of him, the Kid certainly would if the red face and balled fist were any indication.

"Who's he drinking with?" Griffin stared at the glasses. "Your father, Carrick—who's the other? The overseer?"

"Nah, that's beneath my dad. He's good with talk but not with face time." The Kid snorted. "I know."

A flicker of something out the too-clean windows caught Griffin's attention. He bent and looked out across the grounds. The open lot that stretched wide served as an anchor with the trailer on the south side, the mine entrance on the west, and the tent community on the north. Near the mine is where he'd seen something. Had someone gone in there?

Dressed in a dark suit, a man emerged. He glanced over his shoulder back in the direction of the mine. Not running. But definitely in a hurry.

"That's him!" The Kid bolted out of the room, his steps thudding through the trailer.

Griffin took a second to gauge where the good senator was running off to. Beyond the slight bulge the mine created, he saw the long, thin blades of a chopper. Backing up, Griffin leaned to the side, searching for the minefield Scott had mentioned in the briefing. Sure enough, he saw a lopsided sign with a big STAY OUT—MINES! on it.

As he spun around, movement stilled him. And his heart.

Kazi. Hair illuminated in the early morning sunlight, she ran straight into the mine. Dark shadows enfolded her in its greedy embrace.

Griffin turned and rushed from the trailer, chiding himself for not sticking with his fire buddy. He ripped open the door, leapt onto the wobbly landing, then vaulted over the rail that protected the stairs. He landed, skimmed the ground with his fingers, then came up running. He rounded the corner—

"Yimirira!" A muzzle nearly poked his face.

He skidded to a stop, nearly slipping onto his backside. As he drew himself up, instinct registered that the combatant was smaller than him. He could take him. He'd been trained in disarming unskilled warriors. But what froze him—no, *paralyzed* him—was the stunning similarity the boy bore to Dante.

Griffin hauled up straight. Arms raised. "It's okay."

The boy rattled something in his native Lugandan, his face ablaze with fury.

He should take him. He could.

"He left us, you know? . . . What kind of hero does that?" Dante's words riveted Griffin's boots to the Ugandan soil. He couldn't move. Couldn't stop the image of his fifteen-year-old nephew's face from morphing onto the shoulder of the AK-47-wielding boy.

Griffin shook his head. "Dante—" The name tasted acrid. "Don't. It's okay."

More shouting. The boy jerked the weapon straight at Griffin. Curled his finger around the trigger.

CHAPTER 37

"Take the shot! Take the shot!"

At Max's shout and seeing him hurrying, shouldering his weapon, Marshall checked his six. Griffin wasn't there. "Son of a batch of cookies." The Kid swung around, brought his weapon up, and retraced his steps. As he rounded the corner, he chided himself for leaving Legend, who was now staring down the muzzle of an old AK-47.

Marshall couldn't get a bead on the boy, who wasn't wearing a vest, without putting Legend in danger.

Max rushed forward. "Now, Cowboy. Now!"

The telltale *thwat* of a bullet piercing flesh stopped Marshall. Watching a kid get taken down was wrong every day of the year. But necessary to keep Griffin alive. Terrorists put weapons in the hands of children, sacrificing them much the way religious zealots did for centuries.

"Target down," Cowboy's smooth voice carried through the coms and eased Max's tension.

Marshall exhaled and closed the gap between him and the others.

Max turned on him, brows knitted and lips flat. "Where were you! Never leave your buddy, Kid. *Never!*"

"Hold up," Legend said. "It wasn't his fault."

"Explain that."

Legend shrugged, his gaze coming to Marshall's. "My bad. He exited the building. I saw something through the window and hesitated. Cost me time." Legend removed his shades, wiped the sweat from his face, then put them back on.

"Almost cost your life." Max grinned as he took in Legend's face. "I think you're whiter than me right now."

The Kid wanted to laugh, but nearly getting a buddy killed shook him up too much.

Legend grunted. "Not funny."

Guilt harangued Marshall. Seeing his dad through the window told him he had the chance to settle the score. So focused he broke protocol. "Sorry, man," Marshall said to Griffin. "I didn't realize you weren't with me."

"It was my bad." Legend popped the back of Marshall's head. "We all know you a little slow."

Had to admit—with Legend locked up, he actually missed the man's taunting. "Slow?" Marshall laughed, enjoying the camaraderie he'd established with these men, his brothers. "You were the one who couldn't keep up."

"I think you both have your heads in the wrong game." Max glanced around the open area, then at them. "We find Vaughn. That's it. We're not here for anything else."

Legend nodded. "What did you and Squirt find in the mine?"

"Miners," Max said with a snarl. "One-hundred percent perfectly legit miners."

Legend frowned. "Then where's Aladdin?"

"He and Squirt are keeping the miners corralled till we have Vaughn."

Vaughn. *My dad.* And that's exactly what Marshall wanted. To find his father, beat a confession out of him, then leave him for the vultures. Okay, maybe the vultures on the Hill would be more merciless. He didn't care as long as there was little of the Warren Vaughn he knew left at the end of the day.

But everyone here knew Legend was after the girl—the same one who now stood directly behind Legend and Frogman as they talked strategy about their next move. Marshall eased his weapon to the front as two men emerged from the mine right behind her. She whirled on them, words unintelligible but fierce.

"Guys. . ."

Legend turned.

A gun fired. One of the men fell. Kazi screamed—not in a girlie sort of way, but in an "I'm going to kill you" sort of way.

"Kazi!" Griffin rushed away.

Max thudded Marshall's vest. "C'mon."

"Go away, Griffin." Kazi squinted at Carrick. Not trusting him long enough to take her eyes off him.

"Put the gun down, Kazimiera." Carrick's condescension scraped along her spine. "I'd hate to have to carry through on my promise to end the lives of these men."

"Not happening, slick," Griffin said as he eased into her periphery.

On her right, Frogman and the Kid—all with weapons trained on him.

Griffin came closer, his hand resting on the fully automatic dangling across his chest. "Kazi, remember what I said."

Her gaze never left her brother's body. "Roman apologized—right before Carrick put a bullet in his brain." Something dropped on her face. A tear, she supposed, but she was too numb to care. Her brother came here, not to help Carrick, but to try to rescue her. And Carrick figured it out. Killed him. In cold blood. Now, she'd return the favor.

As if in slow motion, the world blurred as Kazi came around, lifting the handgun toward Carrick. Staring down the length of her arm, she aimed.

Carrick sneered. "You haven't got it in you, love."

"Watch me," she bit out through clenched teeth, her heart pounding. "Bit by bit"—the words were the most painful she'd spoken—"you've ripped everyone I love from me. My sisters. Brothers. Roman. Tina." *Me.* He even took who she used to be and killed that naive girl.

"Roman *sold* you to me!"

"Because you convinced him he had no choice." Her teeth chattered from the adrenaline spiraling through her mixing with anger to form a furious cocktail. "You took advantage of that. But that's what you always do, isn't it, Carrick? See a weakness, leap in and cripple the person. That's what you did to the senator." Tears blurred her vision, but she blinked them away. "What you did to me."

"Kazi, no!" Griffin's terse words made her flinch.

Words thickened by saliva and emotion, Kazi tried to swallow. "I thought I'd be happy if you just left me alone—that's why I have all your computer files, recordings of your phone conversations, video surveillance images hidden—but. . .I realized your power is in possession. You would never leave me alone."

"You belong to me."

With a growl, she aligned the sights and brought her other hand up to cradle the weapon properly to ensure an accurate shot.

His hands came up, that slick disgusting smile faltering. "Kazimiera. Love."

"You don't know what that means." *But I do.* "So long, *love.*"

A shadow fell over her, blocking the sun as a dark hand touched her forearm.

"No," she snapped—her voice squawked with piqued emotion. She sidestepped, hands sweaty against the grip of the weapon, hot tears sticking against her cheeks. "Back off, Griffin. Stay out of my business." Throwing his words back in his face hurt her more than she ever could've realized.

"Kaz," Griffin said with a light touch at the small of her back. "Don't do him. Not like this."

"I have to. *Have* to." Throat raw, she ground out, "He took everything from me."

Air near her ear swirled. "If you do this, he takes the last thing you have—your soul." Dirt scrunched as Griffin's chest pressed against her shoulder. "I'm not going to lose you to him." The pressure on her arm increased. "Let go, K." His hand on her back curled around her waist.

Like a tumble off a cliff, the fury within collapsed. In the second she lessened the tension in her arm, Griffin plucked the gun from her. Hauled her into the strength and safety of his hold.

Kazi pressed her nose to the tactical vest that hid the heart of a man so amazing he'd talked her down from the singular goal she had in returning: killing Carrick. Tears streamed down her face, remembering Roman's face, his words. His apology. Now he was dead. She'd get no resolution, no way to hold him accountable for what he'd done to her. No justice.

"Legend!" A shout made her tense.

Griffin's chest expanded. His grip on her tightened. He lifted. Turned.

Crack!

Kazi felt herself swirling around. Each thump of her heart beat like a cannon blast.

Back arched, Griffin brought both hands around her.

Thump!

Griffin's chest rammed into her face. Pushed her backward. *"Oomph!"*

CHAPTER 38

The blow to his back slammed him forward. His legs buckled. Hand on the ground, he braced himself on one knee. Fire wove through his spine and muscles. He couldn't breathe. Saw stars. Eyes bulged at the deprivation. Instinctually, he reached for Kazi as she stumbled backward.

Arms flailing, she yelped and hit the ground. But her face was locked on his, a mixture of shock and panic.

He blinked, waiting for oxygen to seep through his chest.

She scrambled forward. "Griffin?" Cool hands gripped his face. "Griffin, tell me you're okay. Please."

Painful breaths expanded his lungs. Around him he heard shouts, gunshots, angry epithets as he waited for the blood to trickle between his shirt and the Interceptor vest. And waited. . . Maybe the bullet hadn't pierced his vest.

Kazi tugged on his face, drawing his attention back to hers. Tears streaked her face with dirt. But she was the single most beautiful thing he'd ever seen. "Are you okay?"

"Yeah." He hauled in a breath—filled with molten lava. "I'm good." He felt around the back of his vest. And fingered the hot case of the bullet lodged there. It hadn't penetrated. No blood.

"Legend, you with us?" Frogman called as he trotted over.

"Yeah." Drawing up his courage, he shoved aside the prickling sensation—he'd have a trophy of a bruise to take home—and started to rise.

"The snake shot you in the back!" Max's words held a snarl

he hadn't heard in a long while. But he turned to the Kid. "Good shooting."

Griffin winced and arched his back, gaze hitting where Kazi's brother lay—with Carrick. Lifeless. "I feel like A-Rod took a bat to my back."

"Aww," the Kid said with a snicker as he slapped Griffin's shoulder. "Did the poor baby get shot?"

Griffin widened his eyes. "I know you didn't. . ."

Blue-gray eyes sparkled with the taunt. "Oh, I see. It's okay to call *me* a baby when I'm bleeding out on a mission, but you get a bump on the back and you're whining."

He lunged toward the Kid. "C'mere. I'll show you a bump!" Wait. Kazi. He circled round and reached for her.

Unmoving, frozen in time, Kazi stared at the body on the ground. "He's dead." Her shoulders sagged in relief. "I never thought I'd be free of him."

Griffin wrapped an arm around her small shoulders, and she fell into his arms as naturally as if she'd always been there. "I told you God would help get him off your back."

"By taking a bullet to yours?" She peered up at him. "Is that how God handled it?"

"Baby Girl, do you see me hurt? I'd take that bullet every day if it meant you were free. That's what God did for you—He sent me." A wide grin filled his sweaty face.

He saw her chewing on that hunk of meaty information, but he had to know one thing. "Why'd you leave me?"

A facade slipped into place. "I knew I had a better chance of being effective, of helping your team, if I was on the inside." But then vulnerability skated into her face. "And after the way you yelled at me, I wasn't sure. . .if you even wanted me around. Where I stood."

His heart tugged on those words. "Where you stand?" He nodded, then shook his head, grinning as his heart thumped crazy as a fool's. He traced her face, loving the silky whiteness that was Kazi Faron. "Baby Girl, you standing in my arms."

"Dude, kiss her already!"

Griffin swung around. "I am going to hurt you."

Max laughed—until the Kid's eyes widened. His face went hard.

"Dad!" The Kid took off running.

Looking in that direction, Max spotted two men heading around the back of the mine. *Choppers.* They were going to escape.

"Move, people!" Max hopped into a jog and headed along the trailer. "Cowboy, you got eyes on the Kid?" His boots thudded as he hurried across the exposed space that sat at a right angle to the mine. Around the back of the loading bay.

"Negative. No eyes."

Max wanted to curse. The Kid—and just about every other Nightshade member—wanted blood. From Warren Vaughn. But the Kid didn't need that burden, the one he'd have to live with for the rest of his life over killing his own father.

Slowed, Max moved with precision, with expertise, scanning up, down, under the deuce and a half parked in the bay.

"Tents secure," an Aussie voice announced through the earpiece. "Holding."

"Copy," Max said as he eased around the front of the two-and-a-half-ton truck. Careful. Scan right. Left. Up, down. He walked backward, checking the cab.

Shouts pulled him up straight. He hustled forward, weapon ready.

The road rose and dumped them onto the loading platform. Around the back of the packed-up earth that formed a roof with the aid of the pier and beams he'd seen inside.

He eased around the corner, down the barrel of his weapon—

The Kid threw a hard right.

Older but still fit, Warren Vaughn stumbled backward.

"You tried to kill us!" The Kid's shout echoed through the narrow gorge.

"No, no!"

The Kid threw another punch.

Max let the weapon dangle from the harness and raced forward. Hauled the Kid backward. "Easy, easy."

The Kid wrangled free. "Get off me, man." He shuffled to the side. "He's getting what he deserves."

"No." Legend stepped between the father and son. "That's not going to happen. Not on my watch." Hand on the senator's chest, Legend guided him back against a wall.

It almost looked comical. The senator in his slick suit and now-bloody shirt from the busted nose his son gave him, and about a head shorter than Legend, who pinned him with a single hand.

Legend pointed a finger in the senator's face. "You *deserve* to die a long, painful death for what you did to me and my boys. Know what I'm sayin'?"

"We have the senator," Max spoke into the coms.

"But we're not like you." The storm in Griffin's face brought Max a step closer. Then another. "The respect and honor we have—your son has—it's real. Not trumped up and built on the lives of innocent people and terrorism."

"No," the senator said with a frantic shake of his head.

Legend drew back a fist.

The senator clamped his mouth shut.

"Now, see? You're learning. What I'm extending you is called mercy." A sinister gleam shot through Legend's expression.

"He doesn't deserve mercy!" The Kid lunged forward, shoving his forearm into his father's throat.

Legend pulled the Kid into a full nelson.

"Legend, get off me, man!"

"Not till you calm down." Legend nodded to the senator. "See? I'm doing you another favor."

"Listen to me," the senator said.

"Not yet." Max motioned to him. "Assume the position." He held the senator's right wrist and turned him around, face against the wall. With a zip cord, he secured the man's hands behind his back. "Bring in the chopper," Max said into his coms. "West side of mine."

Senator Vaughn looked over his shoulder. "It's not me. I didn't do this." Released but cuffed, he flopped around. "I swear I didn't try to kill you men."

"Bull! This is all your fault."

Warren hunched his shoulders. "It's my fault—yes."

"Augh! I'll kill you." The Kid's feet lifted off the ground, but he remained locked in Legend's thick arms.

The senator blanched at the fury emanating off his son. "It's my fault because I should've paid more attention to the details. Saw between the lines rather than hearing what I wanted to hear."

"What details?" Max asked.

"It's true that I sponsored this mine—but I was under the belief it was a *diamond* mine. That the operation was entirely legal. Everything looked clean."

"Plausible deniability." The Kid used the full nelson hold to his advantage, throwing his weight into Legend and driving a kick straight into his father's chest.

The strike nailed the senator in the ribs. A crack resounded. Senator Vaughn doubled.

"Get him back!" Max pointed to the Kid. "Get it under control."

Grunting, Vaughn came up—but not all the way. Pain etched into his face.

"If you aren't behind this, then why are you here? At the exact moment we'd be here."

"Melanie."

"No way. No way, Dad! Don't bring her into this. Don't dirty her name." Something shifted in Marshall's face.

Vaughn coughed and shook his head. "All this time. . .she'd been faking the mental instability, said it was the only way to get Nathan to leave her alone." He groaned.

"Nathan?" Max looked between the Kid and his father.

"Nathan Sands," the Kid said. "My father's protégé—he forced my sister to marry him."

"No." Vaughn groaned again. "Not true. Melanie admitted she was smitten with Nate at first, but he turned on her." His brow knotted.

"Frogman!"

Max glanced back toward the loading bay and found his brother jogging toward them. He met him halfway. "Report."

"I have Squirt and a couple of men who are loyal to me guarding the mine to make sure it's not destroyed."

"Good."

Legend spun toward the senator. "What did you promise Carrick?"

"Nothing!"

"Carrick said he met with the senator," Max said. "We need to know what to stop."

"It wasn't me. I got here, and Sands was already well ingratiated into the man's graces. Whatever they planned, I don't know. But it's not my deal."

"Enough," Max said. "Chopper's en route. Round up what we can. The Old Man is sending in high profiles onsite to investigate and shut this place down. Let's ghost ourselves. Legend, get the senator."

The Kid jogged up to Max. "Listen," he said, intensity weighting that word. "We take him back there, he'll just talk his way out of all this. He's done it for fifteen years—actually, all my life."

"You want him to pay."

"I want justice," the Kid said earnestly. "Do you see what he's caused? Every villager who's worked that mine will need to be tested for radiation poisoning. He may have wiped out an entire village. Then he attacked us—went after your wife and kids."

Max felt the anger rising. "I don't need a history lesson."

"It wasn't me. Why won't you—?" Vaughn groaned. "I know where he is, where he's going. You can stop him."

Max turned to the senator. "Who?"

Vaughn seemed to waver. "Nathan."

"I knew you were a loose cannon."

Max turned toward the new voice.

A man in a suit with sandy-blond hair stood with a weapon. Despite the twenty feet that separated them, the muzzle seemed but a breath away. Even the wisp of smoke and the miniature explosion when he fired seemed close.

The Kid dove into Max with a primal shout, *"Nooo!"*

CHAPTER 39

Marshall flew through the air, his pulse ricocheting through his chest. He'd seen Nathan Sands emerge from the side just as his father mentioned him. Disbelief had spread through him as the weapon registered—aimed at Max.

The sensation of free-falling startled him.

Because it didn't end. Still. . .falllllinnng. . .

Fireworks crackled in the air.

Why are there fireworks?

He heard his head hit the boulders that lined the outer tunnel of the mine that led to the loading bay. Heard himself hit the ground. Heard shouts.

But felt nothing.

Staring up, he saw the gray sky streaked with storm clouds. Sun blocked out.

Max's face burst into his field of vision.

Marshall blinked and smiled. "Ma—" The word gurgled in his throat. He coughed. "Dude. . ." He choked.

Max's hand clamped on his throat. "Shut up, Kid."

Why did Max look worried? "S. . .kay. . ." What was that noise?

"Medic!"

CHAPTER 40

White. Like a ghost. The Kid's lips had no color. White in the folds of his nose. Even his tongue was gray. Griffin's chest knotted and tightened as the Kid's eyes rolled into the back of his head.

To the side, he saw Sands sprint out toward the chopper.

Navas sprinted after him.

An explosion rocked the ground. Griffin spun, glancing back. Navas lowered his weapon as dirt and body parts rained from the sky. Fool Sands had run straight into the minefield. Served him right.

Max's curses and panicked noises pulled Griffin back around. He knelt beside Marshall.

"Kid, don't chicken out on us." He pressed his hand over Max's. *"Medic!"*

"Let me help." Warren Vaughn shoved Max back. "Get back. Let me help."

Max came up swinging. He punched the senator. "Get off me, you piece of—" Max pushed him against the wall. "You don't deserve a son like him!"

"Say what you want," Warren shouted, his lower lip quavering. "But he's *my* son. Get out of my way." He lumbered back to where Griffin held both hands over Marshall's neck.

The Kid coughed. His eyes refocused.

Warren dropped next to him. "Marshall? Marshall, can you hear me?"

Blood pooled beneath Marshall's head, forming a sick, wicked halo. It grew. . .spreading closer and closer to Griffin's knee.

The Kid gurgled, "Wa. . .hap. . . ?"

A stream of curses flew as Max pressed his hands back over Griffin's. "Kid, shut up. Don't talk." Max shouted. "Where's the medic?"

Nothing they could do. The bleeding had slowed—a lot. That wasn't good. Griffin fisted a hand, pushing back the tide of emotion as Max took over.

The Kid's dazed eyes rocked to Max. Then to Griffin.

Blood dribbled from his mouth. He coughed as he gripped Max's vest. "So. . .rr. . .y."

"Shut up!" Max cursed again, his face screwed tight. "You fight. Do what you do best! Hear me, soldier?"

". . .make. . .proud."

Oh Lord God—stop this!

A wheeze issued the breath from the Kid's lungs.

Griffin stumbled back, crouched against the earthen wall, hands fisted as he watched the nightmare unfold. *It's no good. No good. He's dying.*

"Kid?" Max sounded frantic. "Marshall! No, don't you die—fight!" Max glanced over his shoulder. "Medic!" He turned back. "Kid! Kid, come on. Don't do this." A half growl, half whimper sprung from Max's chest.

Griffin hung his head, hands on his helmet.

Footsteps pounded behind them.

He looked up. An Aussie rushed toward them, slung a pack from his back. As he dropped on the other side of the Kid, his movements slowed. Though he went to work, Griffin saw it. Saw he'd already given up. Strapped a high-oxygen mask over the Kid's face. Jabbed two fingers on the other side of the Kid's neck. "I. . .I can't find a pulse."

Griffin lifted his head. Buried his head. Gripped his helmet. Unsnapped it. Yanked it off. Threw it aside. Paced. Shaking his head. Shaking off the fear. The tears. The pain.

"I'm. . .sorry, mate."

Hands bloodied, Max grabbed the medic. "Do something!"

"I. . .can't. His carotid is severed." The medic swallowed. "I'm sorry. There's nothing I can do."

With the back of his fist over his mouth, Griffin stared at the Kid's face, splattered with blood. Bold, blue-gray eyes. The laughter. The smart aleck. The stupid remarks. The intelligence. The wit.

The hero.

Gone.

CHAPTER 41

Golding Residence, Cyprus

The opening door pulled Sydney to her feet. Silently, she thanked God the men were returning in the middle of the night when the children were asleep. Hands on the chair behind her, Sydney willed herself to be strong. The general hadn't allowed them to watch the video feed, but he'd reported the ominous news that hovered over her, Dani, Piper, and Rel. . .especially Rel, as they waited for the men to arrive.

First through the door was Max—with a fistful of an older man's collar in his hand. He practically threw the man into the couches. "Don't move." With a breath, he shifted. Met her gaze.

Three large steps carried her to him. He snapped his arms around her and crushed her to his chest. Face buried in her neck, Max breathed—hard. Each breath harder, more shuddering.

"I'm sorry." She kissed his ear. "I'm so sorry."

Max didn't let go. And she wondered if he would ever let go of Marshall Vaughn.

Quiet sobbing pried her attention to the corner. John Dighton held his little sister, stroking her hair. Rel collapsed against the wall, her cries gaining momentum. Only then did Sydney notice the long pine box placed on the table. She clenched her eyes tightly.

Was it over? Was the battle they'd fought so hard over?

Was Nightshade over?

RONIE KENDIG

Arlington National Cemetery, Arlington, Virginia
Three Weeks Later

The somber notes of Taps drifted across the field of green dressed in white solitary crosses. Early morning sunlight glinted off the dew, making the grass seem encrusted with diamonds. Fitting, since that's where Marshall died.

Warren Vaughn sat on the padded seat and stared ahead stoically, his sobbing daughter clinging to his arm.

In full dress, Griffin stood to the side. Fisted hands at his side. His mandarin collar stiff against his neck. Though the uniform was meant to instill respect, there was none of that today. They'd failed their teammate. Marshall had died saving Max from the bullet of an obsessed man—who'd gotten justice when he ran for the chopper. . . straight through the minefield. God had his own sense of justice. And this time, Griffin was glad for it.

The honor guard removed the flag, folded it with crisp, haunting precision in perfect silence—save the sniffling of Melanie Vaughn Sands, grieving the loss of her brother as well as the father of her children. She was free mentally but would always have the scars.

An Army chaplain marched to Warren, pivoted, then almost robotically lowered the flag to Warren. The senator stared at it, and the chaplain did not remove his hands till Warren's closed around the flag. "On behalf of a grateful nation. . ."

Griffin turned his attention back to the coffin. The grateful nation didn't know the half of what the Kid had done for them. To protect shores from enemies foreign and *domestic*. And Warren Vaughn didn't deserve that flag. But maybe, maybe it would haunt him. Maybe it would remind him of how his prejudicial beliefs alienated his son from him and even *killed* his son in the end.

An almost imperceptible nod from General Lambert caught Griffin's attention. He signaled the team as the crack of rifles signaled the end of the ceremony. As Griffin made a complete U-turn, not for ceremonial drama, but to honor the man who'd sacrificed everything, he marched up to the foot of the coffin.

Paused as he held a token in his hand. Felt the poke of the pin's nail, then placed it on the center of the coffin. He raised his fist and slammed it down on the coffin. "IN!" Griffin saluted, then stepped back.

Max followed. Planted his Nightshade pin in the wood. "ALL!" He offered a final salute.

Canyon next. *Bam!* The pin glinted in the sun. "THINGS!" He snapped his hand to his forehead, then down, and retreated.

Squirt next. He seemed to struggle. But then he pounded his pin down the line of Nightshade pins into the oak. "PREPARED!"

In a crisp black suit, Aladdin stepped up. With a guttural growl, he hammered his pin. "FOREVER!"

CHAPTER 42

Riddell Residence
One Month Later

Sitting on the back porch where Madyar spent the years rocking away the evening hours, Griffin stared out across the pristine lawn. The annoying *snap-pop* the rocker made wasn't annoying this time. In fact, it comforted him as images of his grandmother filled his mind. Her sitting here, sipping her sweet tea—and when he said *sweet*, he meant *sweet*!

This home that he'd provided for his grandparents, who were more like parents, had given them great joy. Buying the property and home had been the best investment he'd ever made—not because of the value of the property, but because of the fulfillment and happiness he saw in their eyes each evening. His grandfather took to gardening, taking meticulous care of the yard. Once Madyar passed, he planted a row of roses along the back. *"So her fragrance never leaves our lives."*

"You need to talk to him, Griffin."

Staring at his dress shoes, he nodded to his grandfather sitting on the porch swing. "Yes, sir. I do." Pushing back in the chair, he sighed. "I've asked Phee to bring him over."

"It's the right thing."

Again, Griffin nodded. "Yes, sir."

Creak. Creak. Snap-pop. Creak. Creak. Snap-pop.

Songbirds serenaded them as the early morning awakened the small neighborhood. Warmth draped the day with a humidity that made his silk shirt cling to him. He'd lost fifteen years of Dante's life to a misguided belief. He'd missed special occasions and important events while deployed with the Marines or on missions with Nightshade.

That time could not be made up. But it was time for a new beginning.

Would he do a good job? What if his anger got loose, got away from him?

"You are not your father. He had serious problems he never dealt with."

The words forced Griffin to look at the aged patriarch. It'd been taboo to talk about his father, about the man who'd robbed his mother—his grandfather's only child—of her life. Was Pop-Pop about to change that unwritten rule?

Jaw set, dentures clenched, Pop-Pop fastened his gaze on the green grass, his handiwork. Years of hard work carved unkind lines into the eightysomething face. White hair sat atop his head like a swab of cotton on aged, dried-out leather. "What about that woman you talked about? Thought you said she was something special. Why ain't she here with you?"

Griffin dropped his attention back to the hardwood deck. He hadn't heard from Kazi since the team shipped back—and of course, she couldn't just enter the country and assume an identity without drawing suspicion. Lambert convinced her to come in later, secretly.

When exactly is later, K?

"It's not in my hands, Pop-Pop."

"But you want that girl, don't you? I see you lost in thought—you never been a loud, outspoken boy, but that internal struggle has been greater since you returned. And I know it's about that girl."

"Yes, sir. I want her. But. . ." Who knew if she still wanted him? He'd tried to give her room, space to figure herself out, what she wanted, but what if she misread that? Thought *he* didn't want her? He blew out a breath and sat back. He'd done the right thing. Knew he did. "She's smart. She knows where I stay, I'm sure." He hoped. Prayed. Every night.

"What if she showed up? You gonna get all up in her face about being late?"

Griffin snickered. "No, sir." Not a day went by that he hadn't worked through what he'd done wrong, what kept her from coming to him. Or what he'd do if she showed up. Romance her. Give her time to take things as she wanted.

Inside, a clatter of noise drew him from the chair. "That should be Dante."

"Do it right."

"Yes, sir." Griffin opened the screen door and let himself in through the light panel door. He crossed through the kitchen and into the living room. Quick, quiet words met him at the threshold. Dante looked up, his face softening.

And in that instant, Griffin knew two things. One, that the Dante on the television interview was a facade, a boy who didn't want the world in his business. *Just like his father.* And two, secrets had their own way of finding the light of day. Dante knew.

Phoenix, shorter by a head, turned to Griffin. "I'm sorry, G." Tears ran down her face, marring her face with black streaks. "I don't know how he found out. He wouldn't—"

"It's a'right." Griffin kept his gaze on the boy. "Pop-Pop is outside. Why don't you go see if he needs something, Phee."

Sniffling, Phoenix hurried past him, her hand trailing along his arm as she did.

"Go on," Griffin said to the boy.

Dante stared.

"Say what's on your mind."

Dante's gaze fell. He wrestled with a piece of paper in his hands. His shoulders lowered. Whatever was on that crumpled ball held the key to the boy's confusion.

Griffin closed the six-foot gap between them and took the paper. Glanced at it. Felt his heart squeeze, making it hard to draw a breath.

"I got a friend who stays up with his cousin. He knows how to. . .do things. Find things. Documents."

"You mean hack computers and databases?" He tried to make the comment light, help Dante through what seemed a painful dialogue.

Disquiet hung rank and thick in the clean living room. Griffin thought of asking the boy to sit and talk, but the tension wadded up in his shoulders was probably close to what Dante had in his own. Unlike Griffin who had been raised with a violent father, Dante had the benefit of being raised in a Southern Christian family, where he was taught to respect his elders. He would no more talk out against Griffin than he would Pop-Pop.

"Say what's on your mind, Dante."

"Why?" Eyebrows knotted, Dante's wounded gaze shot to his. "Why'd you give me to your sister? I was your *son*." Dark orbs glistening with tears, the boy bore a grievous wound. And there were no words or magic potions to make this go away.

"I thought I was doing what was best." Griffin sighed. "My father wasn't a man I was proud to call Dad. He was violent." So Griffin would break the self-imposed family rule and talk about this. "We don't talk about this; it was too painful for Madyar—my father killed my mother. Then killed himself. Right in front of me and Phee." The bitter pill of truth from the past was laced with heartache and proved hard to swallow. "I saw him in me. That made me angry and pushed me in the wrong direction." He let out a long, ragged breath. Hating confessions. Hating the truth of what he once was. "I wasn't always a man of honor. The man the Marine Corps Creed demands, the man I became."

Attention swung center mass.

"When I was seventeen, I got messed up in a gang. Thought I owned it all. Know what I'm saying? I was big, took care of my body, the girls liked me, and I liked them. I was drunk on power, on thinking I had it all."

Dante smirked.

"But I didn't know nothin' about respect. Treating them with respect or treating myself with respect. There was one girl I would've done anything for." Griffin swiped a hand over his bald head, noticing the sweat. He went on before he lost his nerve. "She and I had a baby."

Full attention now.

"One day I pulled up to where she stayed. I hadn't even gotten out of the car, and she was already coming down the walk." He shook his head. "Most beautiful sight, her with my baby. But a car screeched to a stop. And they shot her. Shot her right there. A drive-by. They targeted her and my baby because of me." He patted his chest. "They killed her to show me I didn't have no power. That I wasn't all that. And it scared me. Scared me *bad*."

"What'd you do?"

"I got in control. Asked Phee to raise the baby, give you a family, a home, something I couldn't do." Man, this was harder than he thought. "Joined up with the Marines. Didn't look back." He shook his head. "That decision has chased me for the last sixteen years."

Dante didn't move.

"Dante, you're my son." Forcing himself forward, Griffin owned up. "I've missed a lot, and this last mission—it burned into my memory that life is precious but so very short. I wanted to get back here, see that you were still alive, that you didn't hate me."

"I did. I did hate you." Dante shrugged again. "Least I thought I did. But Pop-Pop just told me I was hurt." He straightened the paper and sighed. "He was right. When they cleared you of all charges last month, I wasn't surprised. I *knew* you didn't do those things they put you in jail for. That's why it didn't bother me to see you up in there at Wallens. But when you escaped. . .I didn't know what to do with that. Know what I'm saying? It hurt me that you escaped and vanished. Pop-pop was right."

"The man always is. There's a lot of wisdom beneath those burdened shoulders." Griffin raised his hands in surrender. "I didn't want to escape, to break the law doing that, but I knew something had to be really bad. So I went. But not without a struggle in here"—he thumped his fist over his heart—"knowing what you might think. It does my heart proud to know you believed in me even when they said those things."

A crooked smile spilled through Dante's face. "I tried to sort it out, you being my dad, being there for me as an uncle. And you were. You were there whenever you could be."

"It wasn't enough."

"Yeah." Dante stuffed the paper in his pocket. "Maybe. You were gone. A lot." He met Griffin's gaze for a second, then sniffed and drew his hand across his face. A nervous gesture. "Missed my birthday, ya know? Missed a lot of them."

Without another thought, Griffin pulled his son into his arms. "I thought I was doing the right thing, thought you would have a good life. I'm sorry. Very sorry, Dante. I was wrong."

The boy held him tight. "I can see why you did it. And it's not like you *abandoned* me—you've always been there, mostly." Dante eased out of the hug. "Wish you hadn't given me up. Know what I'm saying?"

Griffin tugged the back of Dante's head closer. "I know. I hated it." He rubbed his knuckles. "Every mission, my only thought was that I had to get back home—to you. Thoughts of you kept me alive."

"Missions?" Dante wrinkled his nose. "But you got out of the Marines."

The boy needed to know. "Will you take a ride with me?"

Dante hesitated.

"There's a memorial dedication in honor of a man I knew. He was one of the bravest, truest heroes. My friends—*brothers*—will be there. I want you to meet the men I call family."

Bad idea.

She should just get back in the cab, hop back on the plane, and vanish back into the anonymity she'd thrived in for the last twenty years. No. Not thrived. Survived. Barely. And the last month had been scraping by, her every thought of the man who'd made her believe. In life. In him. In God. *In myself.* As she took in the supposed tranquility of domestic bliss, she heard the wheels of the cab rolling away. Okay, so no going back now. Tranquility. Domestic bliss. *More like blister.*

"You no more belong in a house with kids and a husband than rain belongs inside." She and Tina had laughed long and hard over that. But. . .was it true? Could she do this? It all seemed too. . .tame. Confining.

Kazi fisted her hands. She wanted this. Wanted to be where Griffin was. Wanted to fit in and stop feeling like an outsider, like she didn't belong anywhere. *Do I belong anywhere?*

"God. . .sent me." Those words had clung to her like this oppressive air since Griffin spoke them. The dichotomy of that moment carved a permanent line through her heart—seeing the body of the man who oppressed her laid out flat by the man who'd freed her. God had done that for her? It still was a lot to take in. To believe. But. . .maybe Griffin was right.

The sun beat down on her as she stood on the sidewalk staring at the charming home with bricked columns, a front porch, and four rocking chairs. Her chest hurt.

Do I belong here?

No. None of this was familiar. Quaint homes. Children laughing. A woman ambled past her with a baby in a stroller.

No, this is wrong. Very wrong.

Only because it scares you.

She swallowed. True enough. She could disarm security guards. Sneak into a Taliban camp. Evade assassins. But. . .family. . . committing. . . to Griffin.

Chewing her bottom lip, Kazi stood frozen. He was in there. Griffin was in that house. She saw him an hour ago. Saw his son and sister enter. His family. That's who belonged here. Not her. Not some woman from a mission that left him heartbroken over a friend. She'd seen the difference in him as they waited for the jumbo jet to whisk them back here.

The front door opened.

Heat streaked through her stomach as a familiar shape filled the entry. She spun away. What if he didn't want her here? She ground her teeth. *But I want him!*

"Kazi?"

She closed her eyes. Took a step back.

341

"Kazi!"

She stopped. She couldn't leave him. Not like this. Not without knowing what he thought, what he felt. Slowly, she brought herself around. The smile faltering on her lips made her insides quake. "Hi, Griffin."

" 'Hi, Griffin?' " He stood on the bottom step, a teenager behind him. "That's all I get after you leaving me high and dry?"

Dante went back into the house.

Heat rose through her cheeks. *Not quite how I thought this would go.* Or maybe it was exactly what she feared—he didn't want her. Which is why her eyes were burning and her lip quivering.

Biting the inside of her lip to keep it still, she made herself face him. At least she could be strong about saying good-bye. "I'm sorry. I'll le—"

Griffin stepped off the porch. Strode forward.

Hope rose like a swell on the ocean.

His speed increased. Faster. Till he was all-out running.

Surprise jolted Kazi as he bore down on her. Tears sprung like a leak in a oil line. She rushed forward. Or at least she wanted to. But his reaction pinned her to the sidewalk.

Griffin jerked her into his arms and pulled her against his chest. "You scared me," he breathed against her neck. "I thought you weren't coming."

Pressing her face against his, she held on tight. Loved that he lifted her from her feet, from her problems, from the past. Off her toes, she eased back in his arms.

He looked at her.

"I know what it means, Griffin."

His expression had a rapid-fire change. Went from happy relief to an intensity that made the snakes of fear and rejection slither through her belly. Gently, he set her down. "What's it mean to you, Baby Girl?"

She traced his face, smiling through the bevy of emotion. "Everything."

Griffin cupped her face with his hands and smirked. "You mess me up good, Kazi-smeera."

Holding on to his thick arms, she laughed.

"But I love you." He captured her mouth with his.

She curled her arms around his large shoulders, her hand on the base of his neck. A sigh sifted out the earlier turmoil and with a deep, contented peace draped over her life like the warm sun. His kiss deepened, filled with passion. Demanding yet gentle. Loving yet urgent.

Whoops and hollers erupted amid applause.

Griffin swung her around, and there, on the steps stood Griffin's family.

" 'Bout time you caught a live one," the older gentleman said. "But you might want to bring her out of the sun. She's turning pink."

EPILOGUE

Tatra Mountains, Poland
A Month Later

Kazi stuffed her hands in the wool coat. A bitter wind swirled up and rustled loose strands from her face. She cast a furtive glance to Griffin, who stood on the other side of the Land Rover.

"You can do it, Baby Girl." His smooth skin rippled under the confident smile.

She licked her lips and returned her attention to the small gate that protected a rustic home and barn from the country road that wound through the mountains. A brilliant blue sky tossed clouds around. With a slow exhale, she crossed the road. Dirt and pebbles crunched beneath her boots. She swallowed.

At the gate, she paused with her hand on the sodden wood. The snow had melted but only recently. She lifted the iron catch and pushed against the barrier. It gave with a slow creak.

As she trod down the left rut gouged into the earth, she wondered why it didn't feel familiar. Right. Shouldn't she feel some connection to this place? According to city records, the family had owned the land for more than a hundred years. She rounded a small bend. Trees embraced her into the small fold of forestation.

Kazi checked on Griffin—but now she couldn't see him.

She stopped, feeling as much cut off from an oxygen source as from the line of sight on the man who'd changed her life. Convinced her to make this trek. No, she couldn't do this without Griffin. She shouldn't have insisted on trying. She should go back. Before anyone saw her.

She pivoted.

"Nie wierzę w to!"

Jerked around by the rough voice that cut through her panic, she found herself staring at a pair of familiar green eyes and blond hair.

No. . .not familiar. Her own.

Their gazes locked, neither moved.

He stared and slowly lowered his hands—the bundle of wood slid from his grasp. "*Przepraszam!* Sorry." He bent toward the wood but then stopped, his gaze flipping back to hers. "You are the image of her. I. . .can't believe it."

"My name. . ." A lump swelled in her throat.

"Kazimiera." He smiled, as if relieved.

Something warm and intimate passed between them, but she wasn't sure what.

"H–how do you know my name?"

The man placed a large hand on his chest, his features softening. "I'm Kazpar."

Her heart thudded. Raced. She tried to take a breath not weighted by the anchor of revelation. "My twin," she whispered. He'd changed so very much. Grown up. Become a man.

He took a step forward, and she saw in his face the decade of loneliness and emptiness that had plagued her. Kazi rushed into his opening arms. His embrace held the scent of family, of acceptance, and. . .love. Hot tears streaked down her cheeks.

He stepped back and cupped her face. "*Jesteś tak piękna.* So beautiful, like our mother."

"Kaz?" A feminine voice called through the wintry day. "Where is that wood?"

His eyes brightened. "Come. She will not believe this!"

"Wait," Kazi said. "I need to get someone." She jogged back to the car.

Leaning against the car, arms folded and blowing on his hands, Griffin looked up. He scowled as he came off the small compact—fists tight, shoulders hunched—all fight. "What's wrong?"

"Nothing." She smiled through her tears—she'd cried more tears since meeting Griffin Riddell than she had in the last ten years. Kazi threw her arms around him and held on tight. "I can't believe you found them. Thank you!" That he'd done the research, tracked them down, then brought her here. . . "I love you!"

"That's all I want, Baby Girl. Your love." He kissed her head. "I can face anything if I have that."

Location of Former Shack, Virginia

Max strolled across the landscaped lawn toward the large building, a sense of awe infusing him as he took in the structure. Built on the same plot where the Shack once stood, a multistoried building now stared out over the Hudson. A cluster of about a hundred chairs gathered around a fountain—laid out in the shape of the Nightshade symbol—just outside the front doors.

At the front of the gathering huddled the Nightshade team. With Dakota in his arms and Dillon holding on to his first two fingers, Max guided his family that way. The men stood in a semicircle, children running and playing around the fountain, which danced and sang.

Colton and Canyon stood in suits, their wives monitoring the children. Max handed Dakota off to Sydney, who joined the women.

"Max." Colton hugged him tight.

So did Canyon.

Gone was the machismo that once held their heads high. Days like this changed lives forever. A raw moment to remember a fallen hero. To make sure nobody forgot his name or what he did. To honor his sacrifice. Max still struggled with nightmares, with survivor's guilt—as the team shrink called it—that Marshall had given his life to save Max's. A debt he could never repay. But maybe he could say thanks in a different way.

The Old Man approached, the signs of the stroke gone. He shook each of their hands, then moved to a chair with his elegant wife. Now there. . .there was a couple he could admire. Thick and thin, through good and bad, they were together.

In black pants and light-blue button-down, Squirt nodded behind Max. "There he is."

When Max turned, it took every ounce of strength not to unload on the man walking down the center aisle with his wife and daughter.

"Mr. Jacobs."

Max bit his tongue. The guy just didn't get it. Didn't understand—

"I don't expect you to like me," Warren Vaughn said.

"Good. We don't have to waste time pretending."

The words dug deep, Max could tell when Warren looked up at the building, then slowly brought his focus back to Max. "You told me six months ago I didn't deserve a son like Marshall."

Don't respond.

"You were right." Vaughn's voice cracked. "I've had the chance to review the records, the feats of what my son did with your team."

"*Our* team."

Vaughn swallowed and looked at his wife. "I was a fool. And

now. . ." He knuckled away a tear. "Now I get to live the rest of my life never being able to tell him how *very* proud I am of him."

The candor, the complete 180, silenced Max.

"I prided myself for years on being an activist, a humanitarian." He snorted. "I see what men like you have done and are doing. . .and realize you're the biggest humanitarians out there, helping people. Fighting for those who can't fight for themselves."

Was he hearing the guy right?

"I've deposited the whole of Marshall's inheritance, all his bank accounts—every last penny he'd earned and invested—into the Marshall Vaughn Memorial Fund."

Max felt his eyes widen.

"Marshall would've wanted soldiers like him to get help."

"How much exactly are we talking?" Squirt asked from behind.

Max glanced at his SEAL buddy, his mind hustling to catch up.

"Let's just say, you men won't have trouble funding your endeavor." Vaughn tucked his wife's hand in the crook of his elbow. "For a very long time."

A microphone creaked beside the podium. And the early morning sun illuminated an enormous poster bearing the likeness of Marshall "the Kid" Vaughn as a Nightshade member, in full tactical gear, with a cocky grin and bold eyes, outside the Marshall Vaughn Center for Discarded Heroes.

Metcalfe Residence, Virginia

Two hours later on the back forty of the Metcalfe property, the Nightshade families gathered for lunch. Griffin could not help but watch as the men struggled to shift from a somber memorial in honor of a very good friend and warrior to a happy time with family. Children, laughter, and good food.

Some might say it was disingenuous, dishonoring to the Kid. But Griffin knew better. He'd been the hardest on the Kid—well, besides Max's fist—but Marshall would not have wanted the team moping around. In fact, if the Kid were here right now, he'd be shouting and rounding up teams for a rugby match.

"Hey," a soft, beautiful voice blanketed his mind the same time a hand slid around his arm. "You okay?"

Griffin lifted his arm and wrapped it around Kazi. "I am now."

She rolled her eyes. "It's a good thing I like you."

"You told me you *loved* me."

"Yeah," she said lazily, "I did."

His heart had swelled when she attended an early weekend service with him at church last night. She'd gone up to the bishop during an altar call. Baby Girl, it seemed, was making her way back to God.

Lord, thank You. You turned it all around. Despite the peace that had taken up residence in his life, what would happen to the team, nobody knew. The general told them to take a sabbatical. Get some rest. Get reacquainted with their families. In Griffin's case, he'd ordered him to start one. There wasn't no hurry. And rushing Kazi Faron was about like trying to wade the Mississippi during flood season.

"Hey, Squirt. Get your hand off my sister!" Midas shouted as he tossed the Aussie a football.

Bold and unfazed, John Dighton didn't move from his position next to the long-legged woman, Willow Metcalfe. He caught the ball and spiraled it to Aladdin.

"She's got a boyfriend—a military lawyer. Don't want to mess with that." Midas snickered and hefted his son from a picnic blanket.

"Back off, Midas. We're just having a chat," Dighton said from where he leaned on the fence next to Willow, who laughed and shook her head.

"Did you see that?" Kazi nodded toward the back patio.

Glancing back, Griffin raised eyebrows. "Now that's interesting."

Range Metcalfe, the pouting brother whom Griffin had to give credit to—he did, after all, brave a guerilla facility to rescue Canyon—sat talking with the Aussie's sister. The one Marshall had taken a liking to.

"Not sure if I approve." Seemed wrong for someone to go after the Kid's girl. But then. . .she couldn't exactly stay single forever, not being that pretty and sweet.

Okay, enough thinking. Time for some action. Griffin pushed to his feet, clapped his hands to Dante, who was already out on the back forty. "A'right. Who's up for some football?"

His son threw the ball in a perfect arc.

Heading into the yard, much like heading into the field, Griffin knew that you might knock them sideways a bit. You might take down Nightshade. But the team, the men, the heart, would always beat on.

Dear readers,

Thank you for journeying with the Nightshade team, for opening your minds and hearts to the great toll war/combat takes on our men and women in the U.S. Armed Forces. Though I am incredibly sad this series has ended, please remember that we have heroes out there still fighting for your rights and freedom.

It's one thing for me to write about our military heroes and for you to read about them. It's one thing to say I/we support them, but it's another to put that talk into action. I'd like to challenge you to take that knowledge and compassion one step further—adopt a soldier!

Rapid-Fire Fiction is partnering with Soldiers' Angels, a volunteer nonprofit organization that provides comfort and aid to our troops and their families. You can adopt a soldier and positively impact his/her life simply by following the link below and signing up to send cards, letters, and care packages to a soldier today. They're sacrificing their lives every day for you. Won't you please sacrifice time and a few dollars for them? Regardless of whether you partner and become a Soldier's Angel, please commit to pray for our soldiers, both those abroad and those at home, those who are active duty and those who are veterans. They need your thoughts, prayers, and support!

Blessings in Christ,
Ronie

http://www.soldiersangels.org Soldiers' Angels is a volunteer-led 501(c)(3) nonprofit providing aid and comfort to the men and women of the United States Army, Marines, Navy, Air Force, Coast Guard, and their families. Founded in 2003 by the mother of two American soldiers, its hundreds of thousands of Angel volunteers assist veterans and wounded and deployed personnel and their families in a variety of unique and effective ways.

Discussion Questions

1. Each of the Discarded Heroes books tackles post-traumatic stress disorder (PTSD) in a different way with the hope that readers will become more aware that trauma endured by those in combat and those who face terrifying situations comes in many forms. Have you experienced a traumatic event?

2. Firethorn addresses the issue of denial. Griffin rarely deals with his issues, instead believing that once he is "past" them, there is no need to look back. He thinks it isn't worth his energy or focus, yet the pain and the repercussions of not adequately dealing with those issues leave him unable to relate to others well. Is there something in your life that you have pushed aside and not really dealt with?

3. Unhealed hurts and unforgiveness can lead to bitterness, which is detrimental to mental health. In fact, Katherine Piderman, PhD, staff chaplain at Mayo Clinic, Rochester, Minnesota, offers this list of the benefits of forgiveness:

   Letting go of grudges and bitterness makes way for compassion, kindness, and peace. Forgiveness can lead to:

   - healthier relationships
   - greater spiritual and psychological well-being
   - less stress and hostility
   - lower blood pressure
   - fewer symptoms of depression, anxiety, and chronic pain
   - lower risk of alcohol and substance abuse*

   Jesus said, "If you forgive other people when they sin against you, your heavenly Father will also forgive you. But if you do not forgive others their sins, your Father will not forgive your sins" (Matthew 6:14–15).

   Is there someone you need to forgive, perhaps even yourself, and move on to a healthier mind, body, and spirit?

4. If you have read the other books in the Discarded Heroes series, you have seen a recurring element of the Nightshade men making sacrifices for one another and for loved ones. In John 15:13, Jesus says, "Greater love has no one than this: to lay down one's life for one's friends." It is impossible to know with 100 percent certainty what we would do in situations like these, but do you feel one life is worth trading for another? In light of your answer, how would you respond to Christ's sacrifice for you?

5. As a military brat, I grew up around a large diversity of races and cultures. My father was in the military and was exposed to these same experiences, yet he held tightly to many prejudices. Jesus says in John 13:34, "A new command I give you: Love one another. As I have loved you, so you must love one another." And Acts 10:34–35 says, "Peter began to speak: 'I now realize how true it is that God does not show favoritism but accepts from every nation the one who fears him and does what is right.'"

It's clear that God shows no partiality regarding skin color but rather regarding the condition of the heart. Have you encountered discrimination or prejudice? If so, how have you handled it? Also, how can we as Christians show the love of Christ and do as we are commanded: "Go and make disciples of all nations" (Matthew 28:19)?

6. One very important character trait for Griffin is respect, which directly ties into honor (as with the Marines). After a tragedy diverts his life from his prideful ways, Griffin does his best to live a life of honor. In *Firethorn*, events happen that systematically disassemble the reputation he has built over the last dozen or so years. Such is life. It does not take into consideration our careful planning and future goals. Have you had experiences like this? Have you seen all your diligence undone in one unexpected or tragic incident? How have you handled it?

7. *Firethorn* sees the return of characters from throughout the series (this was so much fun for me—I hope you enjoyed it as well!). In bringing them back, I sought to show reconciliation of family relationships. Families are extremely instrumental in the development of who we become, but they are not the determining factor. In *Firethorn* you meet Scott Callaghan. An illegitimate son, he has worked to overcome his father's legacy. We have a choice and—thankfully—through Christ, the power, to break devastating family cycles. What legacy are you creating?

8. Kacie/Kazi survived a brutal experience in her teen years, and now she has an inclination to maintain control in every situation. This is a common coping mechanism, one that even I struggle with (silly me, thought I could control my characters—ha!). Unfortunately, control is an illusion. We, in fact, can only control one thing—ourselves (how we react, respond, etc.). Do you struggle with control?

9. The members of Nightshade travel the globe and have the opportunity to experience various cultures and diversity. In Kazi's line of work, she does the same thing. Do you enjoy traveling and meeting others from different cultures? What is the most unique culture you have encountered?

10-9-12

10. At first Kazi is angered that Griffin calls her Baby Girl. What significance does this have to her? Do you have a pet name that is special to you, either yours or one you've given to someone else? (Hint: In chapter 21, what does "dziewczyna" mean?)

11. In chapter 28, Griffin and Kazi have a heart-to-heart conversation, which draws out their attraction to each other. Griffin shows great restraint during the rooftop scene. Why does he do this? Do you think it is the right decision? What impact does it have on Kazi?

12. The cemetery featured in *Firethorn*, Shanganagh Cemetery outside of Dublin, is where I buried my mom in 1995. Just as Kazi said good-bye to her best friend, we are—at least for now—saying good-bye to the members of Nightshade. So let's give them a bit of honor: Which character was your favorite? Why? If you'll e-mail me your response, I'll post your "In Memorial" on my blog!

*http://www.mayoclinic.com/health/forgiveness/MH00131

ABOUT THE AUTHOR

An Army brat, Ronie Kendig married an Army veteran. They have four children and two dogs. She has a BS in Psychology, speaks to various groups, is active with the American Christian Fiction Writers (ACFW), and mentors new writers. Ronie can be found at www.roniekendig.com or www.discardedheroes.com.